Psychic Surveys: Book Two

Rise To Me

ALSO BY SHANI STRUTHERS

EVE: A CHRISTMAS GHOST
STORY
(PSYCHIC SURVEYS
PREQUEL)

PSYCHIC SURVEYS
BOOK ONE:
THE HAUNTING OF
HIGHDOWN HALL

PSYCHIC SURVEYS
BOOK TWO:
RISE TO ME

PSYCHIC SURVEYS
BOOK THREE:
44 GILMORE STREET

PSYCHIC SURVEYS
BOOK FOUR:
OLD CROSS COTTAGE

PSYCHIC SURVEYS
BOOK FIVE:
DESCENSION

PSYCHIC SURVEYS
BOOK SIX:
LEGION

BLAKEMORT
(A PSYCHIC SURVEYS
COMPANION NOVEL
BOOK ONE)

THIRTEEN
(A PSYCHIC SURVEYS
COMPANION NOVEL
BOOK TWO)

ROSAMUND
(A PSYCHIC SURVEYS
COMPANION NOVEL
BOOK THREE)

THIS HAUNTED WORLD
BOOK ONE:
THE VENETIAN

THIS HAUNTED WORLD
BOOK TWO:
THE ELEVENTH FLOOR

THIS HAUNTED WORLD
BOOK THREE:
HIGHGATE

THE JESSAMINE SERIES
BOOK ONE
JESSAMINE

THE JESSAMINE SERIES
BOOK TWO
COMRAICH

REACH FOR THE DEAD
BOOK ONE:
MANDY

REACH FOR THE DEAD
BOOK TWO:
CADES HOME FARM

CARFAX HOUSE:
A CHRISTMAS GHOST
STORY

Psychic Surveys: Book Two

Rise To Me

"I see you, Ruby…"

SHANI STRUTHERS

For Patrice Brown,
who taught me everything I know.

Acknowledgements

Once again thanks to my trusty band of beta readers, Patrice Brown, Lesley Hughes, Louisa Taylor, Alicen Haire and the long-suffering Rob Struthers who has to put up with me endlessly asking 'but do you really like it?' Also thanks to my children, Isabella, Jack and Misty for yet again enduring burnt dinners during the writing of this latest Psychic Surveys adventure.

Thanks also to all at Authors Reach for their continuous support and help, particularly Gina Dickerson, for her formatting and cover skills and her incredible patience too!

Finally, thanks to the Psychic Surveys team, Ruby, Cash, Theo, Ness, Corinna and Jed, you're all great characters who are so easy to work with.

Shani Struthers
April 2015

Prologue

THE noise, the commotion, pulled Ruby from sleep. Where was it coming from? Dreams quickly fading, she realised where she was: in her bedroom, in the home she shared with her mother and grandmother. The shouting, the cries, were coming from downstairs.

"Jessica, calm down!"

"Mum, I can't. You don't understand."

"I do understand, darling, I do, but you *have* to remain calm."

"He's here; he'll always be here. He's seen me now; he won't give up."

"*He* doesn't exist."

"You don't know how wrong you are. He does exist. He does, he does, HE DOES!"

Wide awake now, Ruby sat up in bed. What were they talking about? *Who* were they talking about? In her stomach, she felt a cold, crawling sensation, as though it were filled with hundreds of tiny spiders, clamouring over each other, desperate for escape. She looked down at herself almost in wonder. Was it fear she was experiencing? Aged seven, she'd never felt such a curious emotion before, despite her 'gift'. She could see the dead – those who'd *passed*, as her grandmother said – and they were not to be feared. If anything, they were sad, not scary like the ghosts on TV or in books.

"That's just make-believe," Gran insisted. "The living can be really quite strange sometimes. Quite a few of them love nothing more than to scare themselves silly. I see those who've passed, your mother can too, and, because we can, it's our duty to listen, to help them if they need it."

This confused Ruby.

"Help them? How?"

"To move on, to let go of their earthly lives, to go home."

Which confused Ruby further. To her, home was Hastings, a sweet little cottage in the old town – the only home she'd ever known.

"Home is where we come from," Gran had explained patiently. "Where we truly come from, I mean." Her green eyes glistening, she'd added, "It's the light."

"The light," Ruby repeated, not really knowing what she meant but somehow *knowing*. The thought – the light – gave her comfort.

If she should wake to find someone sitting on her bed – it had happened several times before with hunched figures, so forlorn – the last thing she'd be is afraid. She'd talk to them, tell them to go to the light, that they'd be happy there. Sometimes these 'people', if people she could still call them, would talk back; would tell her why they were sad. *'I thought I had more time,'* or *'I love my girlfriend, I'd only just told her. We were so happy.'* Climbing out of bed, she'd sit beside them. After a while, the person – *'call it a spirit'* her gran advised – would rise and walk towards the door, which she always left slightly ajar, as an exit of sorts, and disappear through it. Sometimes they looked back;

mostly they didn't. Ruby would stare after them, hoping she had indeed been some help.

"You have," Gran would assure her. "Sometimes they just need to know they're not alone, that someone can see them, can understand their predicament. If, however, you feel a spirit is unhappy, too unhappy for you to cope with, call for me. I'm never far away."

And Gran did keep close, but her mother not so much. Jessica dazzled Ruby. She was… Ruby always struggled for the right word to describe her… so *'alive'*. She had many friends – a wide circle of them. She was rarely at home, but when she was, Ruby loved it – her presence completing the trio. As exciting as Ruby found her mother, she knew Gran worried about her. Not that she'd say so. Gran never said anything against anyone, least of all her daughter. But Ruby would catch the way she looked at Mum sometimes, her brow furrowed, her eyes not as bright. She'd hear the things she said. *'I wish you wouldn't go out so much. Stay at home. Ruby needs you.'* And, *'That crowd you knock around with, I don't care for them.'*

Mum would laugh and go out anyway.

Ruby wished Gran would confide in her more, tell her why she didn't like Mum's friends. But she was a child. No one confided in children. Except, of course, the spirits.

A loud crash – as though plates and cups had been swept off the kitchen table – brought Ruby back to the present. She clutched at her duvet as voices grew louder.

"Stop it!" Gran shouted. "Remember Ruby's upstairs."

As if she'd been forgotten.

Taking a deep breath, Ruby threw back the duvet, swung her legs onto the carpeted floor, and hurried forwards. At the door, she hesitated, as if she were a spirit herself, unsure about where walking through such a portal would lead. She waited, and then she grasped the handle, pulled it towards her, and stepped onto the landing.

There was sobbing now. Loud, choking sobs – the kind that rose up from deep within a person. Ruby shook to hear it – the nightdress she had on clinging to her thin frame. With one hand she reached up and pulled at the neck of it, as though it were strangling her when really it was loose. Why was Mum crying like that? Had one of her friends hurt her? Had he hurt her, whoever *he* was?

Ruby had a father. To be born, you needed a mother *and* a father. But who he was, she had no idea. 'You don't need to know him; your Gran and I are enough,' Mum had said once, irritably, when Ruby had asked. And, in many ways, her mother was right; they *were* enough. But still, she couldn't help her curiosity. So many children at school had dads; so many asked why she didn't. They looked at her as though she were different – and she was, but how different they didn't know. Not even her best friend. That was Gran's idea. 'Keep it to yourself for now, Ruby. Your ability to see those who've passed, it… well, it unsettles people.' A good girl, eager to please, Ruby had done as she was told, despite being unsure why her 'gift' would unsettle anyone – it seemed perfectly natural to her. But she didn't ask too many questions – certainly not the questions that span round and round in her head. She wished she'd asked more about her father, especially if he'd caused her mother's distress.

"Ruby!" It was her grandmother's voice. "Go back to your room."

Having descended the narrow stairs – thirteen of them – she was in the hallway below. From the living room, her grandmother saw her.

"I…' Ruby began, but could say no more. Her gaze fell on her mum instead.

Her dark hair – not black, but the darkest shade of brown – was normally flat and shiny, but now it was wild, like a wig worn at Halloween. Ruby didn't expect her to be smiling – not from what she'd heard upstairs. But she didn't expect her to look the way she did either – her features twisted, barely recognisable. But it was her eyes that startled Ruby the most. She had laughing eyes normally – eyes Ruby delighted in, so similar to her own. Now they were filled with fear. No, not fear. They were *terror*-filled, round and protruding as if desperate to burst from their sockets.

Gran came hurrying towards her.

"Ruby, please, go upstairs." It was as though she were pleading with her.

"What's wrong with Mum?"

"She's… unwell. But she'll be fine by morning."

The fact her grandmother faltered in her reply frightened Ruby even more. Her grandmother was strong, confident. She *never* faltered.

"Mum," Ruby called, a part of her amazed she was defying instruction.

Jessica remained mute, not looking at her anymore, but staring straight ahead – her body juddering in an almost rhythmic fashion.

"Ruby, I'll explain in the morning."

But would she? Or, like the identity of her father, would the truth always remain hidden?

"Ruby!" Gran's voice was torn between anger and desperation. As young as she was, Ruby could sense that.

Slowly, reluctantly, she turned around.

Back in her room, Ruby closed the door and padded over to her bed, sitting down heavily on top of it. She listened carefully. There was silence. Perhaps it was all over – Gran had managed to calm Mum down and everything was going to be all right. Ruby started to relax. Her shoulders, so tense before, fell to a more natural position. Yawning, she realised how tired she was. She had school in the morning – a spelling test. If she had any hope of doing well, she'd need some sleep. Lying down, making herself comfortable, she heard another cry – a wail this time – even more piercing than before. Whatever was happening downstairs, it was far from over. She had to go back, find out more, risk upsetting Gran further. This was something that affected them all.

As she'd done a few minutes before, she bolted forwards, but this time she didn't get very far – not even halfway across the room. Stopping abruptly, as if she'd slammed into an invisible wall, all she could do was stand and stare.

Spirits. She saw them everywhere. Even in school – a child wandering the corridors, not searching for their classroom, but in search of something. She was used to them, liked them even, but this one she didn't like. This one caused the hair on her arms to stand upright, her stomach to churn, and the fear she'd felt earlier to turn to ice.

"Who are you?"

Although it took on human form – a man, his age indeterminate – it was not human. Instinctively, she knew that. It was masquerading as such. Undefined, ragged even, he stepped out of the shadows and became more visible. As he did, Ruby's breath caught in her throat and threatened to lodge there.

Surprised she could even move, she took a step backwards, and then another. He mimicked her – the two of them engaged in a macabre dance.

"Who are you?" she demanded again.

The man, the creature, stared at her in amusement, his features blurred, except for his eyes, which were as black as pitch – the yellow around them neon. He continued to stare, and it was as though he were devouring her. Not with his mouth, as a lion might devour an antelope, but with his very being – the core of which, she suspected, was blacker than the surrounding night. Should she turn? Switch her bedside lamp on? The light might chase him away. But she couldn't take her eyes off him. If she did, she feared he might cross the divide between them. Sink his teeth into her. Rip her apart.

She tried to be brave, tried to be Lucy from *The Lion, the Witch and the Wardrobe* – a story she loved. "Get out of my way. I need to go downstairs."

There were still sounds coming from below, but somehow they seemed much further away, muffled even. All that was real was in her room – she and this 'something' she couldn't put a name to. This 'something' with the malevolent eyes that barred her way.

"Please…"

A part of her hated herself for pleading. Determined, she started to move forward and then stopped. If there had been amusement on his face, it vanished at such daring. Instead, fury marked him, but not of the wild kind. It was deliberate, focused, and all the more frightening because of it. Lifting his hand, one finger – long and bony – was put to where his lips should be. Slowly, measuredly, he moved his head from side to side.

Despite this, Ruby still considered rushing past him. It was what Lucy would have done, and she encountered magical creatures every day in Narnia. But this creature was not magical, and there was no way she could cross it or even call for help. Gran was busy.

As the being continued to warn her, Ruby did the only thing a child could do. She ran back to bed, dived under the covers, and brought down the shutters in her mind.

Chapter One

Present Day

"AND *that*, Cash Wilkins, is what's wrong with the living!"

As he looked up from his laptop, Ruby noticed an amused smile on his face.

"So, come on, Ruby Davis, enlighten me. What have the living done now?"

Despite feeling irked, Ruby couldn't help but smile too at his use of her full name. It was something they did – one of their quirks.

"Don't laugh," she said, trying to remain serious. "It's not funny."

"I'm sure it isn't," he said, his grin widening. "Tea?"

"Tea would be good. And I'll have sugar this time – two spoons."

"Two spoons? Woah! Things must be bad."

As Cash walked over to the kettle – all of a few paces in her tiny attic office, the headquarters for Psychic Surveys, specialists in domestic spiritual clearance – she plonked herself down at her desk with a sigh. It had pissed her off what had happened this morning.

In a few moments, he was back by her side, placing two

full mugs down on coasters before pulling his chair over so he could sit too. Reaching one hand across to tuck some rogue strands of hair behind her ear, he asked her again what the matter was.

"Do you know Emily's Bridge?" she said.

"Never heard of it."

"Me neither, until today. It's the nickname the locals have given to an old disused railway bridge a few miles from Uckfield. That's where I've just come from."

Cash took a sip of tea – the colour of the liquid the same colour as his skin, Ruby noticed. A gorgeous shade of caramel – an inheritance from his Jamaican-born mother.

"And?" he prompted.

"It's haunted."

"By who?"

Ruby stared at him in disbelief.

"Oh, by Emily, you mean?"

"Hence the name…"

Cash shrugged. "So, what you going to do? Work your magic? Go back and move her on?"

"It's not magic, Cash!"

"Hey, come on." Again, he reached out a hand, this time to stroke her cheek. "I'm just playing with you, you know that."

Ruby's shoulders slumped. "Yeah, I do. Sorry, I'm feeling a bit tetchy, I suppose."

Instead of agreeing, he asked her what she was doing at Emily's Bridge. "I thought you were going to that house in Crowborough to do a survey."

"I did. I went there first."

"Anything of interest?"

"No, it's pipes again, I reckon. There's no spiritual

presence that I could detect. As usual, though, the owner's disappointed; she doesn't believe me. I'll type up a full report for her later. The thing is, her daughter was at the house too. She's in her teens – sixteen or so, I think. She's the one who mentioned the bridge." Cash looked at her intently as she started to explain. She loved the way he did that, the way he was so interested, soaking up every word. "When I said all was clear, the daughter piped up. *'If you wanna see a ghost, Mum,'* she said, *'get yourself along to Emily's Bridge – that's haunted.'* Well, naturally, I asked her what she meant."

"Naturally," Cash said, smiling again.

"It's where she and her friends hang out at night. A lot of the local kids do, apparently, with bottles of cheap cider and beer too, no doubt. They go there to contact the ghost, and when I say contact, I don't mean in a good way. The daughter was very scathing about Emily; said they like to wind her up and call her names. She said it's the ghost that's frightened of them – not the other way round."

"Ah, so it's a taunting, not a haunting."

"It is," Ruby agreed. "A taunting of poor Emily."

"And she's real, is she? This Emily?" Cash asked, turning from Ruby back to his laptop and typing the words 'Emily's Bridge, near Uckfield' into the search bar.

"I got directions and stopped off on the way home, and she's real enough," Ruby confirmed. "I couldn't 'see' her, but I could sense her, and she seems to be in great distress. And I'm not surprised, if teenagers are making fun of her night after night."

"What else do you know about her?" asked Cash, his eyes scanning the list of pages that had appeared on screen.

"Not much really. I thought I'd come back to the office

– see what I can find out."

Cash was on the case already. "There's nothing about an Emily's Bridge near Uckfield on the 'net. In fact, there's nothing about any haunted bridges in Sussex. There's plenty about Clayton Tunnel, though, which is just outside of Brighton." His attention captured, he sat back in his chair and crossed his arms. "Actually, Clayton's pretty spooky, isn't it?"

Ruby leaned across to peer at the picture he was examining. A grainy shot – the entrance to the tunnel was shrouded in mist.

"Now you see, that pisses me off too. If they'd posted a colour picture on that website instead of a black and white one, it wouldn't look half as dramatic. It's all done for effect."

"Even so, it says Clayton is haunted by the ghosts of those killed in a horrific pile up in the tunnel running underneath the signalman's house. It happened in 1861 and was the result of a misunderstanding between the signalman at the north end and the signalman at the south end. One train was in the tunnel, a second was trying to back out, and a third crashed into it." Cash paused. "Nasty," he said, shuddering. "Twenty-three people died, and their bodies were laid out in the house above, their spirits continuing to linger there."

"The haunting – it's an urban myth." Ruby was dismissive.

"How do you know? Have you been there?"

"Not me, but Theo has," she replied, referring to another member of the Psychic Surveys team. In her late sixties, she was the eldest amongst them, and very often the wisest. "She went there, not because she was asked to, but to satisfy her own curiosity. Years and years ago, it was, before I'd even met her, but I remember her talking about it once. The signalman's house was empty by that time, and by empty, Theo wanted to ensure it was exactly that. It may even have been derelict, but whether it is now I don't know. It's probably been reincarnated as a cosy family home. Anyway, she levered the door open and went in, cleansed it with oils and herbs, just in case."

"She broke in, you mean?"

"But for a good reason."

"To try and minimise the chances that something *would* attach itself to the building – something attracted by the loneliness of the place, thinking it's a good place to 'hide'."

Ruby was impressed. "You're becoming really quite expert in spirit behaviour, aren't you?"

If Cash was the type who blushed, Ruby was sure he'd be doing so right now. He seemed genuinely pleased she'd said that. Cash had 'joined' her team, which comprised of Ruby, Theo, Ness, and Corinna, several months ago, albeit in an unofficial and, more to the point, unpaid capacity. Unlike the rest of the team, he was not a psychic – he was a freelance website developer and he had work enough of his own to occupy him. When he could, he helped out, as he'd done to great effect on their most challenging case to date – the removal of 1950s movie star diva, Cynthia Hart, from her somewhat baronial home in East Sussex: Highdown Hall. Not only had he helped out, he'd stepped into the role of boyfriend too – hers. Although he usually worked from his flat in Lewes – a technical den, stuffed with Macs, PCs and printers; all the stuff he needed to test his websites on – he sometimes worked alongside her at the cramped office she rented in the High Street. 'Any excuse to be with you,' he'd said once. And today was such an occasion. The three of them, including Jed – a black Labrador, long since passed – rubbing along very nicely together. Cash couldn't 'see' Jed, but from time to time he could sense him, and he seemed to be as fond of him as Ruby was – or as fond of the 'idea' of him, at least.

As Cash continued to peruse the Internet, Ruby finished her tea.

"Ah, here we go," he said, "I've found something – not under haunted bridges, under 'Sussex Local Legends'. Emily Harvey, aged eighteen, threw herself off the bridge in question when she was jilted at the altar. Suffering from a broken heart, apparently." He sighed. "It's the 'same old, same old'."

"Cash!" Ruby admonished. "There's no same old, same old about it. I'm sure Emily *was* heartbroken at being jilted by her lover. Anyone would be."

"But perhaps there was a reason she was jilted. Perhaps she was a pain in the arse."

"Read on," Ruby commanded imperiously.

Cash started to read verbatim. "Distraught and humiliated, Emily, the daughter of a local landowner, rushed from the empty church and across the fields to the bridge. Despite her father running after her, pleading with her, begging her to wait, she threw herself off the bridge, her body crashing onto the rail lines below. The fall proved fatal."

"Ouch," Ruby winced. "Poor her and her poor father. What a thing to witness."

"You should also feel sorry for the groom," Cash said sombrely. "According to the article on this website, he hadn't jilted her but had been severely delayed. En route to the church, his carriage wheel got stuck in the mud. He ended up heartbroken too."

"Ah, a twist in the tale," Ruby commented. "When did this take place?"

"1898," Cash replied, before sighing again. "I mean, don't get me wrong when I say this, but Emily seems a bit highly strung to me, you know – jumping to conclusions and all that." Straightaway, he realised what he'd said. "Ha! Jumping to conclusions. D'ya see what I did there?"

She did, but it was Emily's story that was occupying her mind – not Cash's joke.

"Does the article mention any sightings of her?"

"I should imagine so – that's the whole point of it, isn't it?" He scrolled further down the page. "People have reported a sensation of being touched or scratched as they walked under the bridge. There's been wailing. Never during the day – it's always at night, of course. Some have even seen a white apparition hovering around the area and, incredibly, one bright spark's managed to capture it on camera, thanks to a bit of jiggery-pokery on Photoshop, I reckon, because it looks like someone dressed up in a white sheet to me." Pointing, he said, "Yep, you can see his or her shoes sticking out – they forgot to Photoshop them. It's the usual stuff they put on these 'death' sites."

"Except in this case it could be true, if what I sensed is anything to go by."

"But you've never heard of Emily's Bridge before?" he double-checked.

"Cash, I'm not a walking encyclopedia of haunted places, you know!"

"I suppose…" Cash said, grudgingly conceding.

Contemplating for a moment, Ruby stood up and

grabbed her bag.

"Where you going?" he asked.

"Back to Emily's Bridge. Want to come with me?"

* * *

The bridge – set within the countryside near Isfield, close to the Lavender Line – was actually quite beautiful. Typically Victorian, it was built in red brick, with a gently curving arch disappearing into bushes either side of it. The rail line that had run beneath it had long since been tarmacked over, providing a route for walkers and cyclists instead. It was the beginning of summer and the trees were in full bloom, contrasting shades of green interspersing with the tiny white flowers of cow parsley, which grew in abundance. Looking at the bridge straight on, Ruby sighed.

"What can you feel?" she asked Cash.

Although he claimed no psychic ability, sometimes he could be intuitive. Corinna, the youngest team member at twenty-two, was not a psychic either: only Ruby, Ness and Theo were. But Corinna was 'sensitive' – someone who could tune into the spirit world, who could sense grounded spirits, even if she couldn't see them. Cash was the same, Ruby suspected, but his ability was very much in its infant stages.

"It's not a particularly happy place to be," he said, after a while. "It's bloody depressing if I'm honest – there's something bleak about it. How about you? See anything?"

"Not yet. I need to tune in."

Drawn to the right-hand side of the bridge, Ruby went and stood closer. Cash kept a respectful distance, holding in his hand the black bag in which Ruby kept Psychic

16

Survey's 'cleansing' paraphernalia: herb wands, known as smudge sticks, which they used to cleanse the air; an assortment of protective crystals such as obsidian, citrine and – the queen of them all – tourmaline; and oils too, amongst them eucalyptus, geranium and cinnamon bark, all created from pure ingredients. For added protection, Ruby had dabbed fennel oil onto her neck and wrists, as well as Cash's, before climbing out of the car. Besides smelling nice, the scent was useful in warding off psychic attack. After all, they had no idea how pissed off Emily might still be. Around her neck was her great grandmother's tourmaline necklace – a treasured family heirloom. And around Cash's was the obsidian necklace she'd given to him soon after they'd met – he rarely took it off. Tooled up, as she thought of it, Ruby closed her eyes and surrounded them both in white light – more protection. The path was empty, and she was grateful for it. Being called in to tend to a problem with Psychic Surveys was one thing – she was acting in a professional capacity, on demand as it were. Out here, she was still acting in a professional capacity, but she might have a hard time convincing a passer-by of that!

"Emily, can you hear me?" she began, saying the words out loud but only for Cash's benefit. She was perfectly able to communicate with spirits by thought alone.

It took a bit of prompting, but finally Ruby got a reply.

My name's not Emily!

The tone of voice was distinctly waspish and Ruby sighed. Bloody Internet story! That was one detail wrong of God knew how many.

After apologising, Ruby asked what her name was.

Susan, the spirit said, but the information was given

reluctantly.

"Susan. That's a nice name. How long have you been here?"

I don't know! How should I know?

Again, that angry tone. Undaunted, Ruby introduced herself.

"Please understand, I'm not here to upset or provoke you. I'm here to help."

There was silence at this, but Ruby detected a slight lessening of anger. She wished she could actually see Susan, but at this stage all she could do was sense her.

You're different, the spirit said at last.

If she meant she wasn't a teenager, Ruby could only agree. She'd just turned twenty-five – her teenage years long gone.

"Susan, how old are you?"

Old enough.

She sounded defensive, and Ruby wondered why. She tried asking another question.

"Do you know what year it is?"

Of course I do! It's 1966.

1966 as opposed to 1898 – another detail that blew the Internet story right out of the water. Had Emily even existed, or was she just another urban myth? If she *had* existed, she was haunting the bridge no more; Susan was, and she was clearly having a hard time coming to terms with her physical death. Ruby's job, of course, was to help her understand. Once she understood – or rather, *accepted* – her fate, she'd be able to move on, go home. That was the theory anyway. Realising Susan was speaking again, Ruby inclined her head to listen.

Why is everything hazy? I can't see properly.

"Everything's hazy because you're in spirit form. You've passed. From what you've told me, it was in the year 1966, which was nearly fifty years ago. For some reason, you remain grounded on this plane, but I can help you move on, move towards the light. It's where we come from, and where we all return. There's no need to be afraid. The light is safe, Susan. The light is home."

Initially, spirits of the grounded variety didn't tend to take the news they'd 'died' too well, and Susan, it seemed, was no exception. Ruby could sense a build-up of energy around her and she wished for Jed. She'd 'met' him at roughly the same time she'd met Cash. His spirit had been guarding a house long after his owners had departed. The new owners, who could sometimes 'hear' him, didn't appreciate his presence at all, no matter how benign or well intentioned. Although Ruby had tried to send Jed to the light, he'd attached himself to her instead, his protective instincts still needing an outlet. And she couldn't deny it, she felt safer when he was by her side, more confident. Well, him *and* Cash. As the atmosphere grew tenser still, Jed did indeed appear, and Ruby found herself smiling. What was he? A genie of sorts? That thought had crossed her mind many times.

Before Susan could get too het up, Ruby spoke again.

"I know you're upset. If a death is sudden or traumatic, it can take time for us to come to terms with. But, Susan, you've been here for a long time now – too long. The local kids, they upset you too, but they don't mean what they say, not really. They don't understand your plight. It's a miserable existence for you here, but if you go to the light you won't be miserable anymore. There's love and joy in the light – you'll be going home, and you'll be welcomed."

They call me Emily!

Clearly this enraged her.

They say I was jilted, that I jumped to my death. I didn't!

"What did happen?"

I was pushed!

Ruby's eyes widened. Perhaps because the story of Emily was fresh in her mind, she'd presumed Susan was another jumper.

They call me Jilted Emily, Stupid Emily. They laugh at me! People always laugh at me!

Ruby cursed the teenagers, as well as the Internet, for feeding them such rubbish.

"Susan, tell me what happened. Who pushed you?"

The air around Ruby rippled – Susan trying to gather enough energy to materialise. Jed stepped forward, sniffing tentatively. Cash looked from side to side, aware too of the change in atmosphere. Even the trees started to sway, despite there being very little breeze. Like it or not, they were heading towards crux point – often a dangerous time – the moment a spirit either denies or accepts what has happened to them. At this moment, Ruby couldn't call it either way.

He pushed me. He said he loved me, but he pushed me!

Susan's voice had become scathing.

Patiently, Ruby repeated her question from earlier. "Who pushed you?"

He did. He was nervous. He's not like that normally.

Losing that scathing quality, she sounded dreamy almost.

Normally he's nice. He said I'm pretty. No one's ever said that before.

Ruby calculated the years once again. This 'nice man' –

was he ever convicted for his crime? She tried to prise his name from the spirit – he could still be alive. But Susan refused to play ball. Changing tack, Ruby asked why she thought the man had pushed her.

Because I said I'd tell his wife about us if he didn't.

Ah, she'd had an affair with a married man. The same old, same old, after all, as Cash had said.

"Tell me his name, Susan, please."

Why should I?

As frustrated as she felt, Ruby had to remind herself the only thing that mattered was sending Susan to the light. Later, perhaps, she'd investigate her case. She couldn't deny it – her curiosity was piqued.

He pushed me!

That was the only thing Susan was concerned with.

He pushed me and then he walked away, smiling.

Squinting, Ruby could just about see the misty outline of a shape starting to materialise. A female form: short, but not thin and waiflike as she'd been half-expecting. Instead, she had a sturdy frame. She focused, tried to see more clearly. Something was different about her, and it took a few moments to realise what. When she did, her mouth fell open. Susan had Down's syndrome! Not only that, she was young, really young – a teenager. The reason she'd been defensive when asked about her age? Not the same old, same old, after all – far from it. Ruby was appalled. The girl had been taken advantage of in the most heinous of ways. Her determination to investigate Susan's case increased tenfold. She wanted to check justice had been done on her behalf and, if not, rectify the situation.

"Susan, what's your surname?"

Perhaps she'd be more forthcoming with that

21

information. Susan, however, wasn't listening.

"Susan…" she said again, but the shape turned from her, towards where Cash was standing. Before Jed could dive in between them, before Ruby had time to reinforce his protective shield, Susan had lashed out, raked her nails down his face. Immediately, three thin lines of blood appeared on his cheek, and his hand shot up to where he'd 'experienced' the attack. This scratching business – the article on the Internet had got that right at least.

"Ruby, what the…"

Instead of answering Cash, Ruby darted forward. "Susan, stop it! Get away from him!"

I hate men. ALL of them!

"Not all men were like your lover. Now get away. Leave him alone."

Susan span round. She was clearer now – her eyes twin orbs of fury. Jed, who'd started barking, ran towards Ruby, aware that she, not Cash, was now the focus. Cash looked on – still bemused by the blood on his fingers – unable to see what was playing out in front of him, but certainly able to feel something was wrong.

Ruby spoke hurriedly. "I am so sorry at the injustice of your situation. What happened to you was awful, Susan. It was horrendous. But your anger, your hatred, they're weighing you down. They're anchoring you. You have to let those emotions go."

He said he loved me!

As Susan uttered these words, she flew at Ruby, but Jed was quick this time and knocked her back.

"Jed, leave it," Ruby commanded, but the dog was having none of it. Usually mild-mannered, he looked ferocious as he bared his teeth.

Despite him, Susan rushed forward again, her face contorted, her hands held out in front; fingers like claws, and ready to strike again. As much as Ruby feared for Jed – in case the spirit should hurt him too – he was buying her time at least.

"Ruby, I think we'd better get out of here – come back with the rest of the team." Cash had to shout to get her attention – the agitation in his voice plain.

"No, wait, please," Ruby answered. "Susan, listen to me." Aware she had to do something more than just plead, she held out her hands too, but in a placating manner.

Some of Susan's fury evaporated. Clearly, she was surprised at Ruby's gesture.

"Take my hands," Ruby said. When Susan hesitated, she repeated the request.

Slowly, Susan relaxed, her hands becoming less like weapons of violence.

"That's it, that's right. Come on."

The distance between them remained.

"Don't be afraid. I'm not going to hurt you."

In her, Ruby sensed such a need to believe.

"Honestly, Susan. You can trust me."

At last, she came forward, slowly, laboured; her gait more of a shuffle than a glide. All the while, Ruby was careful to maintain eye contact, barely even blinking. Their hands touched – such a cold sensation – and Ruby started speaking again.

"I'm sorry for what happened. But it *did* happen, and there's nothing you or I can do to change that. What we *can* do is change what we do about it now. I can help you to let go of your pain and suffering, move towards the light. But you have to help me. The light – point to where it is and I'll walk there with you. You're not alone."

He said he loved me.

Utter sadness characterised Susan as she repeated this, and Ruby suspected it was not just because of her lover. Living with Down's syndrome could not have been easy. If you were different, you were a target. And some differences you couldn't hide.

"We don't know he didn't love you. Maybe he did in his own way."

It pained Ruby to say such words, but appeasing Susan was of the utmost importance. As Ruby had guessed, the spirit cleaved to her words.

Do you really think so?

No, she didn't think so – not for one minute. But on rare occasions, the truth could hinder, not help. Nonetheless, she hated having to lie.

"Yes," she answered.

Susan nodded, but there was no triumph in it. It was more sombre than that, as if, somehow, deep down, she realised the predicament Ruby was in. As she continued nodding, she grew in clarity. Her eyes were blue – a pure shade – and her hair the colour of fresh straw. After a moment, the spirit did point.

Is that where I'm supposed to go?

"I'm sure it is. Why don't you lead the way?"

To Ruby's relief, she did, only one hand holding onto hers now, but that hand - she sensed rather than felt – holding on tightly. Jed quietened as he watched them go, Cash was contemplative too, his brow furrowed; the blood on his cheek already congealing. As they drew closer, Ruby felt a sudden rush of warmth – a glow that intensified, flooded right through her. Briefly, she wondered if someone might come forward to assist Susan – a spirit guide. Sometimes they did; sometimes they didn't. She didn't know why, on either count. Despite being able to see through the veil that separated both worlds, she didn't have all the answers. In fact, she barely had any – just her beliefs: that the light was good, the light was love, and the light was where the departed should go when they shed their bodies. But they were strong beliefs – her grandmother's beliefs; her great grandmother's. Beliefs that had been instilled in her; had stood her in good stead.

"Go on," she urged Susan, who looked hesitant again. "Those teenagers will be coming back soon – tonight probably."

Susan almost smiled at this.

They'll be disappointed.

"Unfortunately not. They don't need to see or feel anything. They'll make it up anyway."

Susan was quiet for a moment, as if contemplating, and then she spoke again.

I'm sorry about him.

"Cash? Don't worry. He'll understand."

Is he a good man?

"Oh yeah. He's one of the best."

Susan did smile, then – a big, beaming smile that transformed her entirely. She wasn't just pretty; she was beautiful. Without another word, she turned away and disappeared.

Feeling another presence by her side, Ruby realised Cash had joined her.

"You okay?" he asked, his concern all for her even though he was the one who'd been hurt.

"I'm fine," she said, touching the marks on his face

lightly. "Sorry about that."

"Not your fault," he replied, "and probably not hers either. Like you've said to me countless times, fear makes people do things they wouldn't do otherwise."

"Fear? In some cases." But in the case of Susan's murderer, what had motivated him? The fact he'd walked away smiling didn't suggest fear. It suggested a terrible callousness instead. When Ruby formed a connection with someone, she sometimes gained an insight into the lives they'd led – images in her mind held up like a series of flash cards – but not with Susan. Susan had been on guard. Like Jed, she'd been protective – but of the enemy. Why hadn't she relinquished his name? Demoralised despite her success, she added, "Come on, let's get back to the office. I'll explain about Susan on the way home."

"Susan? I heard you call her that. So, it's not Emily's Bridge then?"

"It's not anyone's anymore."

Chapter Two

BACK at the office, after tending to Cash's face – despite drawing blood, the cuts had been largely superficial – Cash got on with his work, whilst Ruby got on with hers. She was typing up her report for the house in Uckfield she'd visited that morning. Although words flowed steadily onto the page in front of her, her mind wasn't on what she was typing. Susan had moved on; that much she was satisfied with. But what she wasn't satisfied with was whether her perpetrator had been caught and punished. If he had, wouldn't the teen that had told her about Emily have known about Susan too? Wouldn't she be another local legend? But the teen hadn't mentioned her. Ruby tried to guess Susan's age – fourteen, fifteen or thereabouts: a child. How could someone do that to her? Take advantage of someone so vulnerable? She would definitely make an effort to try and find out his identity – the smiling man – but right now she needed to finish her report, listen to answer-phone messages and check her emails. At Psychic Surveys, it was another busy day.

Cash had developed a website for her when they'd first met. Fresh, clean and modern, it highlighted the various services they offered: distance healing; space clearing; and, of course, the ultimate – spiritual removal, largely of the domestic kind. Although Ruby and her services were in demand locally – mainly fuelled by word of mouth – she was keen to cast the net further. Hence the need to get technically savvy. Her office was the only one of its kind in the United Kingdom, as far as she was aware. What she wanted were more psychics banding together up and down the country; more Psychic Surveys offices to open and their profession regarded as valid as any other. So many spirits seemed to be caught between this world and the next, and both the living and dead suffered because of it. Charging was a moot point. Some people felt money shouldn't be exchanged for such services, that there was an ethic involved. But psychics had to make a living, just like everyone else; they had to eat, drink, and clothe themselves. But certainly, the people her company had helped seemed only too happy to pay, and Ruby always ensured her rates were reasonable. She was, as Cash sometimes said, 'cheap at twice the price'.

Since the launch of the website, interest in her business *had* increased further afield. Just last month, she'd driven to Wiltshire to investigate strange activity in a terraced house on an ordinary suburban street.

Phoning Psychic Surveys after reading all about them on the 'net, the terrified occupants had complained of mugs flying off tables, rapping on walls, and doors slamming in the night. But, as Ruby had explained, such activity needn't be linked with ghosts.

"It feels like a bloody ghost to me!" Mrs Ledbetter protested.

Agreeing to an initial survey, Ruby had taken Theo and Ness with her; both were curious about the case when she'd described it to them. Once all three of them were seated on the sofa in front of the Ledbetter's and their teenage daughter, Tegan — all of whom were standing — Theo asked if they'd ever heard of the word 'poltergeist'?

"Poltergeist?" Mrs Ledbetter repeated. "Well, yeah, we've seen the film." Her eyes widening, she continued, "Oh God, it's not going to be like that is it? You know, hands coming out of the telly and trees coming alive in the back garden, that sort of stuff?"

Imagining Theo silently cursing the film's director, Steven Spielberg, Ruby had to strive to remain straight-faced.

"I can't account for what happens in your garden, but the only thing we need to fear from the telly is the usual rubbish BBC and ITV see fit to plague us with." Theo cleared her throat before continuing. "Poltergeist is a German word. It translates as 'noisy ghost or spirit'."

Tegan spoke next. "That's exactly what it is — a noisy ghost! It's bloody noisy at times. It keeps me awake."

"As I said, it's a rough translation, and often a misleading one."

"Misleading?" Mr Ledbetter asked, pushing the somewhat owlish glasses he wore further up the bridge of his nose. "How?"

"Because usually there's no ghost at all."

Mr and Mrs Ledbetter looked confused at this, but carried on puffing their way through their respective cigarettes.

"Have you actually 'seen' anything?" Theo probed. "A figure — no matter how hazy?"

Mr Ledbetter shrugged, but Mrs Ledbetter confirmed they hadn't.

"Have you, Tegan?" Ness asked.

"No. I'd crap myself if I did."

Theo coughed again at this. Addressing her parents solely, she asked, "Does much happen when Tegan isn't in the house?"

Mrs Ledbetter had taken a moment to think. "Do you know, it doesn't. It's usually quiet when she's not here. It's lovely."

"Thanks, Mum!" Tegan had been distinctly put out. "Thanks a lot."

"Just saying," Mrs Ledbetter mumbled, taking another drag of her cigarette.

"I thought as much," Theo said, sighing. Looking at Tegan, she asked, "Are you going through a particularly hard time at the moment, sweetheart?"

Instantly Tegan's eyes filled with tears. "I'm doing my mock GCSE's. Bloody hate them. They're so hard. Oh, and my boyfriend dumped me."

"'Cos he was shagging your best friend," Mr Ledbetter interjected.

"Dad!" Immediately Tegan turned on him. "Why do you have to remind me?"

"I told you in the first place not to trust him, didn't I? I never liked him. He had shifty eyes. But would you listen? Do you ever bloody listen to a word I say?"

"I'll listen when you've got something worth saying!"

As more angry words between parent and child were hurled, Ruby could feel the energy around them build.

Theo leaned across and whispered in her ear, "Wait for it."

No sooner had she said it than the lights above them flickered on and off.

"See?" Tegan immediately stopped screaming at her dad and screamed at them instead. "The ghost – it's at it again!"

Ness had taken over then, asking all three Ledbetters to calm down and to sit down too, vacating her space on the sofa so they could do just that, and indicating for Ruby and Theo to do the same. They were the ones standing now – a decidedly more advantageous position. Firmly, Ness told them that there was no ghost 'at it' in the house. She explained teenage angst was an extremely powerful thing. Tegan was clearly going through a hard time, and emotions such as anger and frustration were building up within her – so much so, they were beginning to manifest physically.

"Manifest?" Mrs Ledbetter repeated the word, frowning as she did so.

"Yes," Ness said. "Another word for it would be venting. Her emotions are *venting* – seeking expression as emotions are sometimes wont to do. Hence the slamming of doors, the rapping against walls, the lights flickering, the TV going kaput." Although younger than Theo – in her early fifties, as opposed to late sixties – Ness also had an authoritative air about her. When she talked, people tended to listen – even the sceptics. "In its most basic form, it's energy affecting energy. There is no spiritual presence here."

Mr and Mrs Ledbetter were visibly relieved to hear this, but Tegan got even angrier. Consequently, the light bulb shattered.

"Tegan!" Mrs Ledbetter shouted. "If you're responsible for this, I want it to stop. Those energy saving light bulbs are not cheap, and nor are my bloody mugs."

Tegan looked angry still, but confused and remorseful too.

After the situation had calmed a second time, Theo and Ruby took Mrs Ledbetter aside, although Theo did most of the talking. She suggested that shouting at Tegan was perhaps not the best way forward.

"How am I supposed to deal with her, then?" Mrs Ledbetter asked, pouting as her daughter had pouted earlier. "She's a bloody liability with her temper, she is."

"By supporting her – by trying to understand what she's going through. Life for teenagers is never easy. Perhaps you could draw on your own teenage years, and remember it wasn't all plain sailing for you either. In a nutshell, Mrs Ledbetter, instead of shouting at Tegan, give her love, a ton of it. Smother her in it if you like, because right now she needs as much as she can get. If you do, her temper – and, more importantly, the fallout from it – will cease."

"But what if it doesn't?" Without a cigarette in her hand, Mrs Ledbetter had started chewing at her nails.

"It will, I promise. There's no spirit in your house. What there is, is a huge build-up of negative energy. Psychic Surveys can help with that. What we can do is perform a house cleansing using herbs and oils. As you read on our website, we are not affiliated with the church in any way. We use only holistic methods to deal with spiritual problems."

"Yeah, I saw that. That's what made me call you. I'm not into that religious stuff. It's all a load of tosh, if you ask me."

Theo didn't ask her. "We'll also leave crystals behind for you to place in rooms – in Tegan's bedroom, primarily, your own bedroom, and the living room. Rose quartz would be a good choice. It's the love stone – and a really pretty colour too."

"It's pink," Mrs Ledbetter said knowledgeably, "like the colour of your hair."

"Like the colour of my hair," Theo agreed, reaching up a hand to pat at it. "We'll leave you several, as well as some amethyst, which promotes peace. But do go out and buy some more; they're relatively inexpensive. Invest in plenty; dot them around, in plant pots, on windowsills, and the mantelpiece. With crystals, it really is a case of the more the merrier. Like sponges, they soak up bad vibes and keep the air clean."

Mrs Ledbetter said she'd do that, paid them their fee, and bid them goodbye.

At the door, Ruby noticed Tegan still had an angry aura about her, but Theo just shrugged her shoulders when later she expressed concern.

"We've done what we can. We can do no more. We're not a bunch of counsellors."

Although all three enjoyed their trip to Wiltshire – veering off the motorway on the way back to stop at a pub with a mock-Tudor façade and a thatched roof for an early evening meal – travelling far and wide was an issue of concern for Ruby. Their budget simply didn't allow for it – not unless clients wanted to pay their travel expenses, which, to be fair, the Ledbetter's had been more than happy to do. Hence, making contact with other psychics up and down the country and hiring them on a freelance basis whenever cases further afield needed investigating, was also part of Ruby's weekly workload. She never worried whether the people she contacted were genuine or not. A charlatan couldn't fool a psychic. So far, she'd spoken with more than a dozen interested in participating under the Psychic Surveys umbrella, who were as keen as she was to bring their business out into the big wide open – ironically, out of the darkness and into the light – to 'legitimise' it.

Cash ended her reverie, brought her back to the moment.

"It's after five. We said we'd meet Presley in The Rights of Man at six – we'd better start winding down for the day."

Presley was Cash's brother; older by almost two years. Ruby had met him on several occasions. She liked him, but not nearly as much as Corinna did, who'd also met him previously and was coming along to meet them at the pub tonight too. Presley had just split from his girlfriend, and Corinna – her sassy, Goth-attired but very bright-natured colleague – thought if the coast was clear she'd test the waters. Cash was twenty-eight, nearly twenty-nine, and his brother was thirty. Corinna was only twenty-two, but the eight-year age gap between her and her intended didn't seem to bother her.

"I've always gone for older men," she'd confided in Ruby. "Although, to be honest, Presley's the oldest I've ever gone for."

Ruby hoped Presley would go for Corinna too. She was a sweet girl, and for Presley she really did seem to have it bad.

Putting her Mac into 'sleep' mode, Ruby turned to Cash.

"Presley does know Corinna's joining us, doesn't he?"

"He does," Cash confirmed.

"And he's happy about it?"

"Seems to be."

"He doesn't think he's being set up at all?"

"I don't think so."

Ruby grew frustrated with his casual responses. "Because you do know he is?"

"He's what?"

"Being set up!" She all but screamed the words at him.

Cash graced her with a dazzling smile. "He hasn't got a clue."

Still, Ruby was agitated. "But do you think he'll like her? Corinna, I mean."

Having shut down his laptop, Cash pulled Ruby to her feet.

"I know who you mean, and we'll have to wait and see, won't we?" His arms encircling her, he murmured, "I'm proud of you, you know."

His close proximity, the smell of him – clean, like soap and water – made her wish they were going straight back to the flat she rented in De Montfort Road, a ten-minute walk from her office.

"Why's that?' Any frustration she'd felt earlier with him melted.

"Because you're cool, unflappable. When you decide to do something, you do it. You don't let anyone, or anything, put you off."

She pulled back slightly. "Are we talking about Susan here?"

"Yeah. After she scratched my cheek, I was ready to bail out. But you, you didn't give up."

"I don't blame you for wanting to bail out. She hurt you."

"No, she didn't, not really."

"Cash, I'm psychic, I can see what's going on, but with you it's all guesswork. I can't imagine what that's like, or rather, I think I'd imagine too much."

Cash laughed. "It's not a problem, I take my cue from you."

Ruby started laughing too. "Oh, you do, do you? So, if I shout 'run', you're not going to argue?"

"I'm not going to argue."

"What *are* you going to do?"

"Get the hell out of Dodge," he replied, pulling her very close this time.

* * *

The pub was busy for a Tuesday night; several tables had been set up outside to take advantage of the warm weather. As all those tables were occupied, they had no choice but to head inside – Ruby pleased to see her favourite window seat was empty at least.

Gracie Lawless, who managed the pub, greeted them with a smile. "Ruby, Cash, how you doing?"

Assuring her they were fine, Cash ordered a rum and coke for Ruby and a pint of Tom Paine Ale for himself, a seasonal special, brewed to commemorate the bicentenary of Thomas Paine's *Rights of Man* – a hallowed book that helped shape the American nation no less, and which was also the name of the pub.

"Viva la Revolution," Cash said, clinking his glass against Ruby's and making her giggle. As he did, Presley walked in.

When Ruby had first met Cash, he'd told her his mother was a big fan of the music of Johnny Cash and Elvis Presley – hence her children's names. Ruby liked their music too, but she liked their namesakes even more. Cash was a good-looking man and so was Presley. Tall in stature with close-cropped hair and chiselled features, they made a striking pair. Presley was a guitarist in a band: *Thousand Island Park*. Ruby had been to see them a while back and had been impressed – their music a blend of folk, country and rock. Cash had been in a band too, a few years back. He was a drummer. He missed it, he told Ruby, but was considering joining Presley's band. Their drummer, Danny, wasn't in the best of health at the moment, apparently, although Ruby didn't know exact details. It was an ongoing issue, and one that Cash reckoned was going to come to a head sooner rather than later. It was also the 'other' reason the brothers were meeting tonight, to talk about Cash standing in for future gigs. Walking towards them, Presley looked slightly downcast, but if Cash noticed he didn't show it.

"Hey, Presley!" His greeting was enthusiastic. "Fancy a pint of Tom Paine?"

Without waiting for an answer, Cash turned to the bar and ordered. Meanwhile, Presley plastered a smile on his face and leant in to kiss Ruby on both cheeks. After Gracie had done the honours, commenting on how alike the brothers were, they took their drinks and followed Ruby to the window seat.

"Corinna's joining us soon. I hope that's okay," she ventured.

"Oh, really? Yeah, that's great," replied Presley, but in a vague manner.

Ruby felt unsettled by his attitude. He was present, but he wasn't present; to her, it was glaring. She looked at Cash to see if he'd caught on yet, but Cash just carried on talking, telling Presley about his day, including the visit to the newly christened Susan's Bridge.

Pretty early on in their relationship, Cash had told his mother and brother what his girlfriend did for a living. Neither of them had seemed fazed. That was the beauty of the modern world. In olden days, she'd have been dragged through the streets half-naked before being burnt at the stake for her supposed 'powers', but now people simply shrugged their shoulders, said okay and carried on chatting about other things. Her vision of injecting the normal into the paranormal, making Psychic Surveys a high street business, seemed like a viable goal. Although she had to remind herself it was not *all* people who were so relaxed about what she did. Before Cash, she'd had a hard time keeping a boyfriend. They soon tired of her dealings with otherworldly matters. There was no father figure in her life either; no grandfather. Sarah, her grandmother, and Jessica, her mother, had experienced the same difficulty. The Wilkins brothers were clearly exceptional. She was lucky to have found Cash, lucky he wanted to get involved in her work, lucky he adored her as much as she adored him. But as lucky as she felt, Presley's current detachment was nagging at her. What was wrong with him? Concern for Danny, or something else? She'd just decided to ask when Corinna appeared.

"Hi, everyone! Sorry I'm late. It was really busy at the pub. Must be all the sunshine – it draws the punters from far and wide. I thought they were going to make me work a double shift!"

Corinna had a new job at a pub in Ringmer, the next village along from Lewes. Her freelance work with Ruby wasn't enough to pay all her bills but it was certainly a welcome extra. Attired in her 'uniform' – a black sleeveless top and a long, hippy-style skirt, black, of course – she had the loveliest hair Ruby had ever seen. Whilst her own was pretty enough – brown with natural highlights, hanging just below her shoulders – Corinna boasted a magnificent head of auburn curls. They were reminiscent of Lizzie Siddal, the model the Pre-Raphaelite Brotherhood tended to favour in their paintings. Ruby often pointed this out to her, but Corinna, in her usual self-deprecating way, would brush it off.

"My hair's a pain," she'd complain. "It's got a mind of its own."

Corinna also had gorgeous green eyes and the widest smile ever. How could Presley *not* fall at her feet?

"Anyone need a refill?" Corinna asked.

"I think we're all right," Cash said, glancing around. "You sit down. I'll get yours. What you having?"

"A glass of wine, please. Chardonnay, if they've got it."

"A large one?"

"Is there any other kind?"

As did Cash, Presley smiled at her somewhat risqué reply, but his eyes still held that faraway look. The 'meeting' had got off to a dubious start.

An hour passed and then a second, Corinna and Cash mainly doing the talking whilst Presley and Ruby listened. By the time they were on their third round, however, and despite Presley not drinking – after his first pint of ale he'd gone on to coke – he'd relaxed a little, and even talking directly to Corinna. Cash and Ruby glanced at each other. Perhaps the evening would be a success after all.

"Ruby tells me you're in a band," Ruby heard Corinna say, "that you're pretty good. Is it possible to download some tracks to listen to?"

"You can find us on Soundcloud right now, but we've

got a commercial release due out soon that'll be on iTunes."

"Cool," Corinna said, leaning into him further, which Presley didn't appear to mind.

Cash, meanwhile, had moved to sit beside Ruby in the window seat, one arm slung casually around her shoulders, his fingers every now and again lightly tracing patterns on her skin. Every time he did that, she shivered, wondering when they'd become superfluous to requirements and could leave Presley and Corinna to it. Soon, she hoped.

"So, you're the guitarist. That's right, isn't it?" Ruby heard Corinna say.

"Yep, lead guitar."

"Do you sing as well?"

"Often."

Corinna sighed. "I bet you've got a nice voice."

"You'll find out if you download me."

The gleam in his eye matched hers at last.

Pleased that things were finally going according to plan, Ruby smiled to herself. She was actually feeling quite lightheaded from several rums when Presley's phone rang. The gleam disappeared and his troubled look resurfaced – immediately.

"Excuse me," he said, snatching the phone off the table, "I have to take this."

As he hurried off, Ruby, Cash and Corinna exchanged glances.

"Do you think he's okay?" Finally, Ruby gave voice to her concern.

"Presley?" Cash replied. "He's fine. Why?"

"It just seems as though he's got things on his mind, that's all."

"Hopefully me," Corinna said, giggling.

For a 'sensitive', Ruby thought, Corinna could sometimes be anything but. But could she blame her for that? She was young, she was playful, and, where Presley was concerned, she was determined. Still, didn't she sense something was wrong with him either? Presley was being polite, certainly. But enthusiastic? She wouldn't go that far.

Within minutes, Presley was back. "I'm sorry to do this, ladies, really I am. There's a problem. I've got to go."

"Got to go? But, Presley," Cash inclined his head in a not very subtle manner towards an obviously disappointed Corinna, "surely whatever it is, it can wait?"

"Actually, it can't, and here's the worst part, Cash. You need to come with me."

"Me?" Cash seemed horrified at the prospect. "Ruby and I – we've got things to do tonight. We've—"

Ruby interrupted. "It's okay. Go with your brother. It's clearly important. I'll see you later."

"But what about food? We haven't eaten yet!"

Cash's preoccupation with his stomach was legendary. She'd never known anyone who could eat so much yet remain so slim. "Go," she repeated, fixing him with a steely glare.

Cash finally got the message. Neither food nor she was on the menu right now.

"Call me later," Ruby said, leaning across to give him a conciliatory peck on the cheek.

"Yeah, yeah, later," he agreed, his tone nothing less than begrudging.

Just as they were about to go, Presley turned to Corinna.

"It was nice meeting you. Perhaps we can meet again soon?"

Corinna's face flamed as red as her hair. "Anytime," was her slightly breathless response.

As the two men left the pub, Ruby and Corinna stared after them.

"But I wonder how soon is soon," Corinna mumbled, somewhat forlornly.

The unease of earlier returning, Ruby wondered the same thing.

Chapter Three

RUBY heard Jed growl before she heard the phone ring.

Pushing herself up onto one elbow, she ran a hand through her hair. What time was it? Removing her eye mask, she checked the clock on her bedside table. It was two in the morning.

"Settle down," she called across to the dog. "It's just the phone."

Reaching for her mobile, she checked the caller ID before answering. It was Cash.

"Ruby, sorry, were you asleep?"

"It's two a.m. Of course I'm asleep! I know I said call me later, but this might be taking things too far. What's the matter?"

"A friend of Presley's is in trouble."

"In trouble?"

"Yeah."

"And what's that got to do with me?"

"I think you can help."

"Cash," she said, sighing heavily. "Can't it wait 'til morning?"

There was a brief pause before Cash replied. "Ruby, he's seen something."

Again, Jed growled, and Ruby held up a hand to hush him.

"Seen something?" she questioned. "Seen what exactly?"

"Well, that's where you come in. To be honest, he's not

making much sense."

"*You're* not making much sense."

"I need you, Ruby." The way he said it stirred something in her.

"Okay," she conceded. "This friend of Presley's? You mean Danny, don't you?"

"I do, yeah."

"Where does he live?"

"In Brighton."

"And where are you?"

"In Brighton too, but don't worry, I don't expect you to drive. I'll come and get you. I can be with you in about twenty minutes. Actually, make it fifteen; there'll be nothing on the road at this time of night."

"Okay, see you in fifteen. But, Cash, drive carefully, okay?"

"Always," he said, ending the call.

* * *

It was actually just shy of fifteen minutes later that Cash's car pulled up outside her flat. He hadn't driven carefully at all. As soon as she spotted him, Ruby closed the door behind her and hurried down the path, Jed following at her heel. Just as she opened the car door, he started barking. Thankful he was a 'ghost dog' – that the neighbours wouldn't be able to hear the din he was making – she told him again to pipe down before climbing into the passenger seat.

"Something up with Jed?" Cash asked.

Ruby glanced towards the back of the car where Jed was sitting, glaring at Cash.

"Yeah, ever since you phoned. Well, before you phoned,

actually – he started growling. And right now, he's not looking at you like you're his favourite person in the world either."

"Me?" Cash pulled away from the kerb. "What have I done?"

"Woken us up at an ungodly hour?"

"Ah, yeah, there is that."

Driving past Lewes Prison on the road back to Brighton, Cash turned serious. "Thanks for this. Danny could really use your help. Remember me saying he was having a bit of a tough time?"

"I do, although you didn't say why."

"No, well, it's not really my place, is it?"

"That would depend," said Ruby, turning to look at him, "on what it is."

Cash sighed, but kept his eyes on the road. Ruby noticed the speedometer was nearing ninety. On the surface he might seem calm, but underneath it was a different story.

"Cash," she said finally, "enough mystery. Just tell me."

"Danny's an alcoholic. Sorry, that's the wrong thing to say. He's a recovering alcoholic."

"Okay…"

"But it's the recovery he's having a hard time with. He's trying to do it on his own, without help. Presley's tried to persuade him otherwise, but Danny's having none of it."

"He hasn't joined Alcoholics Anonymous?"

"No, he's dead against it – don't ask me why. But, the thing is, he's suffering from terrible withdrawal symptoms – the DT's I think they call it, don't they?"

"I think so." Ruby was no expert on alcoholism.

"Yeah, the DTs," confirmed Cash, more to himself than

Ruby. "He's seeing stuff. You know, the usual – clawed hands coming out of the wardrobe, phantoms rising up from the floor."

Ruby baulked. "The usual? It doesn't sound very usual to me!"

"Apparently, it's standard stuff for someone in withdrawal. But that's not the worst of it. He keeps seeing one thing in particular. Or, more to the point, one thing in particular keeps seeing him. He describes it as a demon, something chucked up from the bowels of hell. He's terrified, Ruby. He says he can't stand it anymore; he's threatening to kill himself."

Ruby inhaled. "Cash, this sounds pretty serious. I'm not sure I'm equipped to help him. He needs to see a doctor or a psychiatrist – probably both."

"Don't you think I've thought of that? That Presley hasn't? We have. Danny's a lovely bloke but he's a bit off the wall; he won't agree to it. It's his way or the highway. But he did say he'd see you; you're not one of them, one of the institutionalised. He hates anything that smacks of institutions. That's probably why he won't join AA. But the couple of times he met you, he liked you."

One of those couple of times had been about two months ago. Ruby and Cash had gone to see Thousand Island Park play at Brighton's Concorde club. She was only surprised Danny could remember her at all – he'd been so drunk. But, drunk or not, he could still hammer out a beat. There was no denying it, the man was talented, his passion for the instrument he played evident. Ruby suspected he never started off a gig drunk, but sipped steadily at something throughout. Afterwards – well, afterwards, it was game on.

As they drew into the city of Brighton, heading down Ditchling Road and turning left by the traffic lights at Fiveways, Ruby pondered the case.

"The D in DTs stands for delirium, doesn't it?" she asked Cash, before taking her mobile phone out of her pocket and Googling it. "Yep, it does – Delirium Tremens to be exact. Common in those who drink four to five pints of wine or seven to eight pints of beer over a sustained period of time. Crikey, four to five pints of wine – can you imagine?"

Entering the estate at Hollingdean, Cash said, "I don't think wine's his tipple. It's the hard stuff he likes – vodka, whiskey, rum. You get the picture?"

"I do. His liver must be shot."

"His liver *and* his mind."

"When was the last time he had a drink?"

Stopping outside a block of flats right at the top of a hill, Cash shrugged. "I'm not sure. Why?"

"Because it says here symptoms often occur within 48-96 hours after the last drink. However, they may occur up to ten days after the last drink. It also says it commonly affects people who have had an alcohol habit for more than ten years. Cash, how long has he been drinking?"

"Heavily? For about two or three years."

"Does he do drugs as well?"

Cash turned to Ruby, his face marked with concern. "Drugs have been involved, yeah. I don't know about currently, but in the past – cannabis, cocaine, that sort of thing."

"That might explain why he's suffering so badly then," she answered. And then another thought occurred to her. "Does Presley do drugs as well?"

"Presley? No, no, he doesn't. He's trying to help Danny, not join him on the rocky road to ruin."

Immediately contrite, Ruby apologised.

"It's okay. It's a fair question. Look, all I really know is that the poor bloke is suffering. Maybe we can help him, maybe we can't. But if there's a chance, we have to try."

He was right.

"How well do you know him?"

"I know him well enough but he's Presley's friend really. They're not just in a band together; they've known each other since their first day at school. They're close."

"And before he started drinking heavily, did he drink at all?"

"Oh yeah, he's always been a drinker, has Danny."

Taking on board all Cash was saying, Ruby came to a decision. "Okay, I'll see if I can tune into what he's seeing; try and assure him it's nothing more than a hallucination, however horrid it is, and that it'll pass in time. If he stays off the drink, that is – something I still think only the professionals can help him with."

Clearly relieved, Cash leant across to kiss her. Not a quick kiss despite the apparent urgency of the situation. Pulling away, he said, "What would I do without you?"

She remembered saying the exact same words to him not long after they'd met – so quickly had he become her anchor. Remembering his reply, she echoed that too.

"You've got me. You needn't worry on that score."

The smile on his face was immediate... and intense.

"Come on, let's get going," she said, reaching for the door.

* * *

Danny's flat was tiny, a glorified bedsit, although Ruby noticed a separate bedroom en route to the living room. The double bed in it was not even made up, the naked duvet grey instead of white, and the pillow scrunched up as if it had been wrung in anguish. The air reeked of tobacco.

The door had been left ajar, so Cash walked straight in, reaching behind him to take Ruby's hand, either to guide her in or pull her through – she wasn't sure which. From the car to the flat, Jed had stuck to her like chewing gum to a pavement, but at the door he hung back, refusing even to step over the threshold. Unable to worry about him right now, Ruby focussed on Danny instead. He was on the sofa, his body – painfully thin, with no trace of the muscled arms she remembered – hunched over, a cigarette burning between his fingers. Presley was in the chair opposite, just staring at him.

On seeing them, Presley was the first to react.

"Cash… Ruby… thanks for coming."

"Not a problem," Ruby replied.

Cash grabbed another chair – one of a set of four scattered haphazardly around a small dining table – and placed it opposite Danny too. He indicated for Ruby to sit down on it. Grateful she didn't have to sit on the sofa – it looked as sticky as the carpet felt beneath her feet – Ruby obliged. Casting a quick glance at the doorway, Jed's eyes were fixed not on Cash but Danny. *Jed, come in.* Ruby projected her thoughts towards him. *There's nothing to be afraid of.* But Jed could not be persuaded.

"Danny, hi, it's Ruby," she said, keeping her voice low.

When Danny didn't respond, Presley interjected. "Danny, Ruby's here. Remember what I was saying. She might be able to help you."

Danny looked up at this – first at Presley, then at Ruby. In his eyes, Ruby could read his thoughts all too well. *No one can help me.*

She leaned forward. "Danny, tell me what you've seen."

At her words, Jed started growling again. She couldn't fathom what was wrong with him.

Danny had what she would call interesting looks. His features were in no way refined; his nose was just that bit too wide and his skin pockmarked from teenage acne. His teeth were crooked and stained with tobacco. But there was something about him. Something feral almost. Dangerous but attractive – to some. Cash had already told her he'd been at school with Presley, but, if so, he seemed older. Today, especially, he could have had years on him. His grey/green eyes were sunken, and around them black circles seemed to have been drawn on with a marker pen. If they and the scrunched-up pillow were anything to go by, sleep – restful sleep, at least – hadn't been in plentiful supply. His skin was grey too, a pallor common to those being 'haunted' – the spirit draining their life force, depleting them. But Ruby could sense no spirit in the flat, although the atmosphere was certainly oppressive. Stubble around his chin indicated he hadn't shaved for days. He was grubby, unwashed. Stale sweat vied with cigarette smoke for precedence. He'd been cheerful at that gig she and Cash had attended at the Concorde. He'd been a laugh – joking with her, with everyone. The audience had loved his vivaciousness. But there was nothing cheerful about him tonight.

Her heart constricted to see him like this – to see *anyone* like this.

Because Danny still refused to speak, Presley stepped

into the breach. Meanwhile, Cash had pulled up the third of the four chairs, and had sat down beside her.

"Danny's an alcoholic," Presley endeavoured to explain. "He's acknowledged that and is doing his best to sober up. The trouble is, every time he tries, he sees stuff, bad stuff. One thing in particular."

"You get the DTs?" Ruby addressed the question to Danny. "You hallucinate?"

"This is no fucking hallucination!" Danny spat the words at her.

"Hey!" It was Cash, starting to rise from his chair, anger on his face also.

Ruby laid a hand on his arm to stay him. "It's okay," she said. "It's fine."

But Cash still looked uneasy; so did Presley. As for Jed – just as he had bared his teeth at Susan, he was now doing so again.

"I'm sorry if I upset you, Danny. I'm not pretending to know what you're going through. That's why I need you to tell me."

Danny did indeed look remorseful, but only for a few seconds. Then it was fear back on his face – causing his eyes to blink rapidly.

"Come on, mate," Presley cajoled. "Tell her what you told me."

Presley's voice was so gentle, so concerned, it moved her. He really did think a lot of his friend – proof enough for Ruby that Danny was a good guy.

"It's hard to talk about," Danny muttered. "If I do, it makes it even more real."

"I can understand that."

"Can you?" Danny's eyes finally locked onto hers. "Can

you really?"

Ruby nodded. "It's as though you're giving whatever it is that's frightening you energy by thinking about it, feeding it, if you like, making it grow bigger."

"That's it. That's exactly it. I'm… feeding it."

"But if you share it with me, perhaps I can explain it at least. When you understand something, it can often make you less fearful."

Danny seemed to ponder this. As he did, Ruby noted the silence. It was heavy; uncomfortable. Not even the sound of breathing punctuated it. It was almost preternatural.

"I don't *know* what it is," he said at last.

"But maybe I will," Ruby countered.

Again, that silence – all eyes on Danny, awaiting his consent.

"It's… it's dark," Danny said, his shaking becoming more obvious. "It's evil. It's filthy. It's cruel. It's like nothing I've ever seen before, not even in books."

Immediately Ruby was curious. "What books?"

"Just books!" Danny was defensive again. "Occult books."

It was as though a light had switched on over Ruby's head. Danny had an interest in the occult. He'd seen pictures on pages that had stuck in his mind, got lodged there – images which, at low moments, came back to haunt him. She relaxed a little.

"How deep into the occult are you?'

"It's nothing. It's just an interest."

"You… haven't practiced anything? Performed any rituals of any sort?"

"Of course not!" His denial was emphatic, perhaps a

little *too* emphatic.

"Ouija boards?" she pressed further. "Have you ever used one?"

"I've done nothing wrong!"

Cash was again itching to get involved – she could sense it – indignant on her behalf. She couldn't afford to interrogate Danny anymore. To carry on would lead to tension overload.

"Look, I'm no expert on alcoholism; you need to seek professional help on that. But if you want my theory, this is it: there's stuff in your mind already – controversial stuff. Thoughts, in other words, which have taken a bit of a negative turn." She paused briefly to check his reaction before continuing. "When you use mind altering substances, these thoughts can take on a life of their own and become more potent. Thoughts are energy. They're transmitters; they attract one another. You've heard of the saying 'like attracts like'?"

"Of course I have."

"Well, negative thoughts attract other negative thoughts. Like magnetised iron filings, they clump together. Scientifically, we know that energy doesn't dissipate. It has to go somewhere. My great grandmother, Rosamund, did some research into this. She called the place where negative thoughts gather a dumping ground. With the barriers in your mind lowered, you might have caught a glimpse into this dumping ground; seen something that's really nothing more than an image you've seen in a book. An image that frightened you subconsciously, but which frightens you now in a more conscious way. It's a thought form, in other words. Something your mind has created, or, if not created, *embellished* – blown up out of all proportion. It seems real, but it isn't."

"I didn't create this. And it *is* real."

"Does it look familiar at all?"

"What do you mean?"

"Those occult books you mentioned—"

"It's not in there."

"Think, Danny," Ruby persisted. "It could even be an amalgamation of images."

She detected the first glimmer of uncertainty. "No... I don't know... Maybe."

"Shall we try and find out?"

Danny hesitated.

"Please, Danny." It was Presley again. "I'm here. *We're* here. Let her try."

Still Danny was uncertain, but Ruby waited patiently, appreciating how much courage he needed to summon up. It took a few minutes, maybe longer, but eventually he agreed.

Ruby leaned forward. "What I need to do first is surround us in white light. I do that because light is powerful. As humans, it's something we gravitate towards. We find it preferable to the dark; we feel safer in it, less vulnerable. I want you to imagine a ball of pure white light hovering six inches above your head. As you concentrate on this light, notice it gets bigger and bigger. Can you do that, Danny?"

Danny, who had closed his eyes, nodded.

"Okay, good. Slowly bring this ball of beautiful white light down so it covers your head, neck and shoulders. Let it move further down your body; let it wrap itself around you, encasing you completely. Feel how warm it is – the perfect temperature – how comforting."

Seeing him start to relax, she held out her hands. "The last thing I need you to do is put both your hands in mine, and I'll try and see what you can see."

Danny did as Ruby instructed.

To Cash and Presley, she said, "If you want to wait outside, that's fine."

Cash merely raised an eyebrow at her whilst Presley replied, "I'm staying."

"Okay, but I need you to visualise white light around yourself too, just in case."

As they closed their eyes, so did Ruby, ignoring more growls from Jed. Danny's hands, she noticed, were like blocks of ice, despite the warmth of the summer night.

Making sure her grip was firm, she tried to look inside Danny's mind, to see what he could see – to *feel* it. It was like wading through mud at first – layers and layers of it – not easily negotiated. Danny had put up quite a barrier to block out whatever was frightening him, but not enough of one it seemed – the creature able to break through regardless.

Nonetheless, she persisted. *What's in here? What's frightened you so much it's turned you into a shell of your former self?*

Visions flew at her – she likened them to 'flashcards' – Danny as a small boy, one in particular making her smile, him, aged around seven, in shorts with a scuffed knee and a wide grin. The boy standing beside him, she guessed, was Presley – a sidekick of sorts throughout the years. It was as a teenager Danny had got into music and learnt to play the drums. He and Presley formed a band – a successful band, although they, like the other band members, still had day jobs. Presley was a motorcycle courier. Danny worked in a record shop. Oh, hang on – Danny had been fired from his job at the record shop on account of turning up late repeatedly. How recently was that? She couldn't tell. And then alcohol, like a demon itself, had caught him in its grip, intent on crushing the life out of him – insidious at first and then more blatant. Danny was hedonistic, reckless in nature. He liked being in a band, and the attention it got him – especially from the girls. He liked girls; he'd had plenty of them. He didn't like commitment. Danny was wild – too wild. Becoming unbalanced.

Minutes passed, and Ruby worried that Danny might be getting impatient. Often people expected her to 'see' things straightway, but it didn't always work like that. Sometimes, it took time to connect – to the living as well as the dead. She probed further, continued to walk through shadowed corridors. Yes, a liking for the occult, for arcane matters – she could see he had an interest in it. What images had he seen in dusty tomes that dealt with this vast subject? She saw plenty, but none coated in fear necessarily. Growing tired, her concentration began to falter. If she weren't careful, she'd lose their connection. *Focus, Ruby. Focus.*

She tried but it was no use. Her grasp was becoming tenuous and images started to fade – like watercolours left too long in sunlight. She would come away clueless and she silently cursed. Danny didn't need clueless. He needed something a whole lot more substantial than that. You didn't have to be psychic to sense his desperation. The man was on the edge.

"Danny, I'm sorry…" she started to say, when Jed started barking again, furiously this time. He had edged his way into the room – a few steps only – his eyes trained on her, and on Danny. No, not on them, she realised. He was staring just slightly beyond.

For goodness sake, Ruby thought, starting to get annoyed with the canine. She was about to admonish him further, convinced the way he was acting was partly responsible for putting her off her stride, when she caught sight of something strange, something misshapen, out of the corner of her eye. Something that wasn't in Danny's mind, but in the room… actually *in* it. Something familiar; that found her familiar too – ravenously so.

As she flew to her feet, the chair fell backwards and crashed to the ground.

Turning to Cash, she screamed, "Get me out of here. Get me out. NOW!"

Chapter Four

RUBY cursed the fact she didn't smoke. She needed something – *anything* – to calm her down.

"What is it?" Cash asked. "What did you see?"

"I... I don't know," stuttered Ruby, inhaling big gulps of air.

"You could have fooled me; you were terrified. You still are terrified. Christ, Ruby, look at you. You're shaking!"

Cash tried to enfold her in his arms, and a part of Ruby yearned for his touch, his strength, but another part recoiled. The air wasn't doing a good job of cleansing her lungs; she felt contaminated still. The last thing she wanted was to contaminate him.

Using her hand as a barrier, she pleaded with him to give her just a few more moments. During this time, she looked over to where Jed was standing, between the pathway and the entrance to the flats. She knew what he was doing – he was trying to prevent her from going back in. But she had to. Danny was in a bad way. Her reaction just now was hardly going to reassure him.

"Ruby, talk to me. Tell me what you saw."

"I saw... nothing." It was only partly a lie.

"Ruby..." Cash's voice grew stern. He was not going to be palmed off.

"I don't know what I saw, okay? There was something

in the room, but I only caught a glimpse of it. No more than that."

"A bloody frightening glimpse!" Cash declared.

"Yeah, yeah, it was. I don't know, it... it seemed familiar somehow."

"It?"

"You don't miss a trick, do you?"

"I try not to. Familiar? In what way?"

"That's just it. I don't know!" Exasperation building, she all but shouted her next words at him. "Will you stop asking me questions I can't bloody answer?"

This time, he wouldn't be resisted. Almost roughly, he pulled her to him. As his arms encircled her, she was immediately grateful for his warmth; she felt so cold. And gradually her body calmed – even if her mind took a while to follow suit. Her head sideways on his shoulder, she stared again at Jed. *You knew, didn't you? You knew something was in that flat, even before we left for Danny's. Even before the phone rang.*

He had known and he had tried to warn her.

"I'm sorry," Cash was murmuring into her hair. "I should never have got you involved."

Perhaps not, but if he hadn't, where would that have left poor Danny?

Pulling away, she tried to explain. "I *did* see something, Cash, but the strange thing is, I couldn't describe it to you if I tried. It didn't have a face or a body, and yet... it did. If I had to think of a description, the only word I'd be able to come up with is rancid."

"Rancid? As in smell?"

"As in everything about it."

"Do you think it's the same thing Danny is seeing?"

She looked into his eyes – concern for her had made them even darker. "Undoubtedly."

"Something dredged up from the depths of his mind – something he manifested?"

"It's the likeliest explanation."

As she spoke, her gaze flew upwards, straight to the window of Danny's flat. She half expected what she'd seen to be looking back at her, marking her in some way. Its hunger far from satiated.

"Or maybe… I don't know. I let my imagination get the better of me too."

"Only you know that, Ruby. I saw nothing."

"But what did you *feel*, Cash?"

If she'd wanted validation from him, she was disappointed.

"I didn't feel much either. Not on this occasion. Sorry."

"I've got to go back in."

Cash was adamant. "No, no way. I'll go back in."

She was tempted to let him. She never wanted to set foot in that flat again. What was in Danny's mind was now in hers. Although, as Cash had asked, what was it exactly? Not human – not a grounded spirit in need of help. If it were, she'd be able to relate to it.

Ruby couldn't help but think of her mother, Jessica. She'd had a breakdown when Ruby was a child. She had seen something: *'the face of evil'* she'd called it. *'It's real, Ruby.'* As recently as last year, Jessica had said those words to her: *'Evil is real.'* Ruby had disagreed vehemently. She'd taken her grandmother – Sarah's – stance. *'Love is what's real. Up against it, evil is obliterated.'* According to Sarah, Jessica had allowed what she'd seen – nothing more than what was in her own head: a thought form – to harm her.

And it had continued to harm her for years afterwards, causing her to hide away, fearful that the shadows would consume her. '*You have a choice*,' Sarah had said. '*If you walk in the light, the light will protect you – never doubt it.*' And that's what she'd done – ever since she could remember. But despite that, upstairs in Danny's flat, she had seen something as far from the light as it was possible to get. Poor Danny. How long had that thing plagued him?

Her mind was made up. "I'm going in, Cash. It'd be great if you came with me, but I need to do this." *I am not my mother and I will not hide.*

"But how are you going to explain your reaction? What are you going to say to him?"

Ruby contemplated his words. He had a point; a very good one.

"I'm going to lie," she said eventually. "I'm going to say my reaction was not because of something I saw, but because of the effort involved in tuning in."

Cash didn't look convinced.

"I'm also going to say that what's happening to him is nothing that the Psychic Surveys team can't deal with."

"And is that a lie too?"

"Of course not," she said, aggrieved he had to ask.

* * *

Back in the flat, Danny eyed Ruby suspiciously as she tried to explain.

"When you tune in so intently to something…" She stopped to correct herself. "*Someone*, you can experience a kind of burning sensation – a searing. It hurts." Although untrue, her words sounded believable enough; logical even. "But don't worry, it hasn't put me off. I'm coming back. Actually, *we're* coming back – my team and I – to perform a cleansing."

That did seem to worry Danny. "I… I don't have much money—"

"There's no charge," she assured him.

Presley offered to stay with Danny until work the next morning.

"I won't leave you, mate," he said. "And if need be, work can wait."

Ruby admired his loyalty, his eagerness to help his friend.

She was also glad to note that whatever had been standing behind Danny when he was seated on the sofa – that she had glimpsed, albeit briefly – had gone. For now, anyway.

Driving back to her flat, Cash asked about the rest of the team.

"So, you think they'll be up for it, all of them? Coming back to help Danny?"

"Yes, of course they'll be up for it. The lack of money's not an issue here."

"No, I know that. I was thinking, if it scared you—"

"If it scared me, that's exactly why we have to come back en masse; collectively we're stronger. We can smash that thought form to pieces, hopefully, or at least send it back to where it came from – to fester alongside other thoughts of an unsavoury nature."

"What a place to tune into, though. No wonder you were scared."

"I was alarmed more than anything," Ruby insisted.

"My fault really. Danny's mind is tortured. It makes sense it's going to throw up all sorts of tortured beings."

"And that's what you saw – a tortured being?"

"A tortured being that tortures too."

Back at her flat, Ruby turned to Cash. She didn't want him to go and he sensed it.

"Shall I come in?" he said.

"Do you mind?"

"Of course I don't bloody mind."

Ruby couldn't help but laugh. She felt lighter suddenly, as though the darkness she'd experienced earlier was already in retreat. To banish it entirely, she knew what to do. Love and the making of it would do the trick. Luckily, on that score, Cash was happy to oblige.

* * *

After a series of phone calls, the team agreed to meet at Ruby's attic office at five the next day. Corinna would have finished her shift at the pub by then and, regarding time restrictions, Theo and Ness were pretty easy going – both were officially retired from work, although whether a psychic ever truly retired was cause for debate. As well as freelancing for Psychic Surveys, Theo and Ness kept pretty busy; not just with family (in Theo's case, she had three sons, and grandchildren galore) but with their own cases too.

Ruby had only explained the bare bones of what had happened the previous night to Theo and Ness on the phone. To Corinna, she'd explain when she arrived.

Due to not falling asleep until dawn, both she and Cash had woken late. It was nearly midday before Ruby made it into the office. Jed, who had conveniently made himself scarce once she and Cash had hit the bedroom, was waiting for her.

Spotting him curled up under her desk, she said, "Jed, I owe you an apology – for telling you to pipe down when you were clearly trying to protect me." She wished she could stroke his fur. "You knew that... *thing* was going to be there, didn't you?"

Jed wagged his tail slightly. An answer she'd have to be content with.

Although she fielded calls, replied to emails and typed reports, Ruby found it hard to concentrate. After a while, she decided to see if she could find any connection on the Internet to Susan's death. She scoured the online archives, but without a surname the job was an arduous one. Frustrated, Ruby could have kicked herself for not trying harder to extract that information from the spirit before walking with her to the light.

The National Archives guidelines suggested you arm yourself with the person's full name, the approximate date of their death, and the district where the event was likely to have taken place. She knew the year had been 1966, but she hadn't pushed Susan for the day, or the month either. *Note to self: it's all in the detail. Never forget that.* She idly wondered, and not for the first time, whether she should rename the company Psychic Investigations, but then she reminded herself of the ethos behind her company. Their principal aim was to free grounded spirits, not to avenge them. She would, however, like to think the girl's assailant had been properly dealt with. What he'd done to her, he might have done to another. Even if his crime had gone unpunished, Ruby consoled herself he wouldn't get away with it, not entirely. On the other side, she was certain there was rehabilitation. Not punishment for wrongdoing as such, but a spirit would have to realise the pain he'd inflicted on others – be on the receiving end of every emotion he'd been the cause of. A horrendous experience for some, depending on what earthly misdeeds they'd committed, but necessary in order to learn, to develop, to progress through the stages. That was her belief, but on this occasion – the first time ever, she was surprised to note – her beliefs afforded her little consolation. She might not be in the business of avenging, but the thought of that man walking away smiling whilst Susan lay broken on the ground, well... if he was still alive, justice should be meted out in this world too.

Ruby spent well over an hour searching; typing in *Susan*, the year, and the district – all the things she did know – and getting nowhere fast. Glancing at the clock, it was after four; the team, ever prompt, would start arriving soon. Deciding to call it a day regarding Susan – she could always return to her case later – she left the office and went in search of biscuits to accompany the tea Ness would invariably start making on arrival.

On the way to the Flint Owl Bakery on the lower part of Lewes' High Street, she stopped off at Sussex Stationers. She'd ordered a copy of *Season of Gene* by American author, Dallas Hudgens, and wanted to see if it had come in yet. When she'd met Cash, they'd both been reading the author's debut book, *Drive Like Hell,* in The Rights of Man pub. Gracie had been the one to spot they were doing so, and had pointed it out – kick-starting conversation between them. That had been last year, in early December. She'd liked the book, but Cash had loved it, declaring

Hudgens his new favourite author. He had another of his books, but not *Season of Gene*. It'd be a nice surprise to get it for him.

"Hiya," Toby said as soon as she walked in.

It might be the County Town of Sussex, but Lewes was also small. Everyone pretty much knew each other, or at least those who lived and worked on the High Street did. Cash lived further down the High Street in a flat in Fullers Passage – the opposite end of town to her – and she hadn't met him or even seen him until that time in the pub. Still, that little hiccup had been quickly rectified. They knew each other now – intimately.

"'Fraid your book's not in yet. Another day or so and it should be," Toby continued, a wide smile on his slightly goofy face; his blonde hair sticking up in random tufts.

"Not a problem," Ruby replied. "Whilst I'm here, I may as well have a quick browse."

Ruby had somewhat eclectic taste in books. She read across a wide variety of genres, including romance, thrillers and crime. The paranormal was another favourite, but you could have too much of a good thing. On the shelves, she perused the latest bestsellers, taking down a Michael Connelly book to read the blurb. Deciding it was not for her, she was about to replace it when she heard someone calling her name.

Presuming it was Toby, she turned to answer him, only to realise he was deep in conversation with another customer, and couldn't possibly have been responsible. Slightly confused, she turned the other way to see who it was, but the only two other people in the shop were staring at bookshelves, just as she was. Shaking her head slightly, she continued with her original intention of putting the

Connelly book back where it had come from, when it was whacked out of her hand, landing on the floor with a thud.

"What the…" she began.

Toby looked up. "Butterfingers," he said, still grinning.

"No, it wasn't me…" she said and then stopped. It would take too long to explain that an unknown force had done the honours.

Having never experienced a spiritual presence at Sussex Stationers before, Ruby tuned in. *Is someone there?*

Often it took a few minutes to form a connection. Whilst she was doing so, she picked up the book, replaced it successfully this time, and pretended to keep browsing.

Hello, this is Ruby. Who are you?

Whoever it was had gone quiet.

There was a limit to how long Ruby could loiter in Sussex Stationers before she started to look suspicious. Moving further into the shop, to the part where the greeting cards were, she picked up a few and pretended to be interested in them instead. All the while, she tried to see who it was that had knocked the book from her, who'd called her by name. She also tried to remember if Toby had addressed her as 'Ruby' – hence the spirit *knowing* her name. But she couldn't remember, and asking him to confirm it would look plain odd. Most people hereabouts knew what she did and were cool with it, but that's because she was normal, or so Ruby liked to think – a regular girl, with nothing particularly outstanding about her. Often, people called her pretty. They commented on her eyes – hazel in colour; the exact same shade as her mother's. But most girls were pretty. She was not beautiful; she wouldn't stop traffic. She was ordinary, average, and intentionally so. The last thing she wanted to do was to act abnormally. It would impact on her as well as her profession.

Getting nowhere fast with the connection, Ruby could spare no more time. It was ten to five. She'd have to hurry back to the office, sans biscuits.

A little disgruntled she made her way to the exit, said goodbye to Toby, and was just about to leave the shop when she heard her name again.

Ruby, it said, the voice deep and rasping. *I see you.*

Ruby swung round. Who the heck was that? Like before, she could see nothing, or no one.

"Are you okay, Ruby?" Toby asked, frowning slightly.

"I'm fine," she lied – something of a regular occurrence in the last two days. She didn't feel fine at all. She felt... how did she feel? *Unsettled.*

"I can call you when the book is in," he offered.

Wishing he could deliver it as well, so she needn't return to Sussex Stationers, she smiled her thanks and hurried back up the High Street to the sanctuary of her office.

* * *

Ness was already in situ. She, like all the regular members of Ruby's team, had a key to her office, so did Cash. As Ruby entered, she turned to her.

"Cup of tea?"

"Oh God, yeah. Strong."

Ness – her pale heart-shaped face such a contrast to her black bobbed hair – stared at Ruby for a moment, her dark eyes searching. After a moment, and with a slight frown on her face, Ness turned back, and got on with the task at hand.

Up the narrow, rickety stairs, Ruby could hear Theo and Corinna approaching – Theo huffing and puffing, cursing how steep they were, and Corinna laughing at the fuss she was making. They burst into the room and immediately filled it. Jed came out from under the desk to greet everyone. Like Ness, he stared at Ruby too before settling himself at Theo's feet. As Cash was already up to speed on what had happened – well, everything that had anything to do with Danny – he wasn't in attendance. He had a lot of work to catch up on, she knew. An image of him surrounded by nearly half a dozen computers came to mind – testing pages he'd written on various operating systems; making sure they worked on other platforms. What he did for a living – the complexity of it – baffled her.

Helping Ness to hand round the teas, Ruby apologised for having no biscuits.

"Not a problem," Theo replied. "I need to lose a few pounds apparently."

"Apparently?" Ruby enquired.

"According to my doctor," Theo explained. "I went to see him a few days ago; he said I was obese. Obese, I tell you. The cheek of it."

"I thought he said you were morbidly obese?" Corinna piped up, and Ruby shot her a look. There was a real bond between Corinna and Theo – almost like mother and daughter. Even so, would she get away with such a cheeky remark? She did.

Theo was in hysterics. "Morbidly obese," she spluttered. "I'm the least morbid person there is!"

Ness watched the exchange with ill-disguised impatience. Theo and Corinna were outgoing people, often outrageous. Ness was far more subdued. Despite her unsmiling face, Ruby knew Ness cared about them all very deeply. Able to read minds on occasion, as could Theo, or 'catch thoughts', as Ness described it, she'd been involved in psychic matters all her life – had even worked for Sussex Police and Brighton Council respectively in a psychic capacity. Ruby had been surprised to find out the council consulted psychics.

"Oh yes," Ness had told her. "There was so much paranormal activity reported by council tenants at one time, they thought they'd better do something about it."

"And what was going on?" Ruby remembered asking. "Actual hauntings?"

"Sometimes," Ness had imparted. "But mostly it was people's imaginations at work. Oh, and dodgy plumbing, which of course the council are liable for too."

Right now, watching the team settle themselves in – each and every one of them complaining about the heat, almost as much as they complained about the cold during wintertime – Ruby started to relax, her earlier encounter in Sussex Stationers pushed to the back of her mind. Danny was at the forefront – and the 'something' that haunted him.

As she explained, Theo and Corinna matched Ness in seriousness.

"Poor Danny," Corinna said, after a while. "Sounds like he's really suffering."

"He is," Ruby agreed.

"Thank God he's got a friend like Presley," Corinna continued, sighing at the mention of his name.

Theo's eyes widened. "Do I detect a liking for yet another Wilkins brother?"

How smug Corinna looked. "Wow! I've managed to keep something from you at last."

Before their banter could develop further, Ness butted in. "You said Danny's into the occult?"

"He has an *interest* in the occult," Ruby replied. "I'm not sure he was actually into it as such. That's something we'll have to find out."

"Let's hope it was nothing more than a passing interest," Theo commented. "That stuff and nonsense can mess with your mind terribly. Combine it with an illness such as alcoholism or drug addiction, and it can blow up in your face, as Danny proves."

Ness leaned forward, pushing her empty mug aside. "And you saw what it is that he sees?"

Ruby faltered. "I... I don't know to be honest. I think I saw it, but if you ask me to describe it, I can't."

"Really?" Ness wasn't convinced. "Try."

It was the last thing she wanted, but she knew she had no choice. "It was black – but then the room was black. There was only a standard lamp switched on; not much light at all. It was formless... no, that's not right. It was *half-formed*. Like a man, but it wasn't a man. A man would have had a soul, and this thing, well, I couldn't detect one."

"How did it make you feel?" It was Theo asking now, a look on her face that Ruby had never seen before. All trace of joviality had gone.

"Scared," she admitted.

Both Theo and Ness seemed to contemplate this.

"And from what you say about Jed, he didn't like it either." Corinna broke the silence.

"No. Jed had a real problem going to Danny's flat. He

was even different towards Cash."

"Different? How?" Ness asked.

"Kept growling at him. Staring. That sort of thing."

"As if he blamed him for involving you?" Theo asked.

"Maybe," Ruby replied. It was definitely a possibility. "He's okay with Cash now, though. It was just, you know, as we were going to Danny's flat."

Deciding she had to mention the incident at Sussex Stationers too – the bizarreness of it – Ruby opened her mouth to speak again, when the phone rang.

"Excuse me," she said, reaching across to answer it. Before she could extend the usual Psychic Surveys greeting, the caller started speaking.

"Ruby, it's me, Presley. I'm at Danny's flat. Well, I'm outside it. I just popped out to get us something to eat. He won't let me back in. There's noises coming from inside – banging, crashing, like he's smashing the flat up. Bloody hell, Ruby… he's screaming now."

Ruby sat up straight. "Presley, listen to me. Have you shouted to him? Can he hear you?"

"I've shouted. I've banged on the door. I've made as much of a racket as him. But he won't open it. He's just… I don't know. He's ignoring me!"

"Have you tried breaking the door down?"

"It's one of those fire doors; it's heavy. I can't break it down. Not on my own."

"Have you called the police?"

Presley faltered. "I… I can't call the police. There are drugs in there. Class A."

So, he wasn't an historic drug user after all. He was very much a current one.

Ruby thought for a moment. "If he's making such a

72

racket, perhaps the neighbours will do the honours?"

"No, they won't. Not on this estate. The police aren't popular."

Ruby heard a crash in the background. At the same time, Presley shouted, "Christ!"

"Hang on, we're coming. We'll be there as quick as we can."

"Thanks, Ruby."

"Have you phoned Cash?"

"He's on his way."

"See you soon."

Placing the phone back in its cradle, Ruby didn't need to say a word.

Theo, Ness, and Corinna were already out the door.

Chapter Five

THE journey to Danny's flat wasn't as quick as it had been in the early hours. Rush hour traffic was bad on the A27 – both going into Brighton and towards Lewes. Ruby cursed at how slow going it was, and only hoped Cash was making better time. When traffic did start to move, Ruby floored it, going as fast as her battered old Ford would allow.

"Steady," said Theo, who was sitting beside her in the front. "Better to get there eventually than not get there at all."

"Or get there in spirit," Corinna offered from the back – a joke even she didn't laugh at.

Turning onto the Hollingdean estate, Ruby cursed further.

"It's like a bloody rabbit warren, this estate. I can't remember where the flat is."

"You *can* remember," Theo said calmly. "You were here only hours ago."

"But I came at night," Ruby protested. "It was dark. Cash drove."

"Nonetheless, you've travelled this road before; it's mapped in your mind. Now, concentrate. It's a flat he lives in, isn't it?"

"Yes," Ruby said, wondering whether to turn left into

Hartfield Road.

"We appear to be in a dip," Theo continued. "Is it down here or on a hill?"

"Definitely on a hill."

"Head upwards then."

At the top of the hill, Theo asked whether she remembered turning left or right.

"Erm… er… left, I think. But I don't know, it could have been right."

"Go with your first instinct – turn left."

Following the road round – it appeared to be crescent shaped – several blocks of low-rise flats came into view.

Removing one hand from the wheel for a second, Ruby pointed. "That's it. That's them!"

"Well done – you did it," said Theo.

"Thanks to you," Ruby replied, relieved also.

As they drew up outside the flats, Ruby recognised Danny's block. It was the middle one of a row of three. She hadn't noticed last night, but the building was named: *Seren.* A word she recognised; it was Welsh for star. Such a beautiful name did not suit it.

Her feet had barely touched the pavement when Cash came squealing round the corner. Jed, too, materialised. Rather than ride on someone's lap, he had chosen his own method of transport.

On seeing her, Cash abandoned his car and ran towards her. "Ruby! Presley phoned you as well? I told him not to."

"Well he did, so let's not argue about it – we haven't got time. We need to get ourselves up there. Find out what's wrong."

With Jed leading the way, all five climbed the concrete stairs to the second floor – Theo, despite her age and girth, having no trouble keeping apace on this occasion. Presley was above them, hanging over the banister and calling to his brother.

"Cash, come on. We need to break down the door."

On the floor above, Ruby noticed an elderly couple staring.

"Bloody Danny," the old man cursed. "What's he causing such a rumpus for?"

Ruby offered the old man a smile, but was duly ignored.

As Cash and Presley both pitted their weight against Danny's front door, the noise inside died down. Ruby's skin prickled. Somehow, the silence was worse.

Hurry up, she kept repeating, but only in her head. Cash and Presley, she knew, were doing their best.

Glancing at her friends beside her, they were all staring ahead – their eyes trained on the door. Ruby knew they'd be doing what she was doing: visualising white light. Not only around themselves, but around all three men too. Used to doing it; it was never a problem. But right now, Ruby was having trouble imagining a shield protective enough.

"Concentrate," Theo hissed at her, despite Ruby not having said a word.

I am, she shot back. But silently so.

The door eventually gave way – Cash and Presley stumbling forward together; the rest of them not far behind. Jed was barking again. Not only that – he was rearing back; getting ready to pounce. But pounce on whom?

"Danny!" Presley shouted. "What the fuck's going on, mate?"

Rushing down the narrow hallway, Presley was the first

to reach Danny, but Danny was in no fit state to reply.

As the others did, Ruby stood aghast. The room was a mess: furniture broken or upturned; posters clawed down from walls; records – of which there were huge numbers – smashed into myriad pieces. It was totalled. And so, it seemed, was Danny – an empty vodka bottle by his side. The only thing that wasn't broken. There was smoking paraphernalia too – of the suspicious kind.

The elderly couple from upstairs had ventured in.

"Bloody alcoholics," the old man swore again.

Theo whirled round. "Will you please leave. This is private property, and you're trespassing."

Theo was not to be messed with, and they knew it. Instead of arguing further, they beat a hasty retreat.

"We need an ambulance," Ness said, digging out her mobile phone.

Theo nodded her agreement.

Presley was cradling a now-unconscious Danny in his arms. "What have you done?" he kept asking. To Cash, he said, "I only left him for a few minutes, to go down to the shop. He said he was hungry."

"It's not your fault," Cash tried to console him. But there was no consolation to be had.

"Is he… is he dead?" Corinna asked, wincing.

Having finished placing the phone call, Ness knelt down too. Taking Danny's hand in hers, she said, "There's a pulse, but it's faint. I think we can safely assume it's a breakdown he's suffered."

As Presley continued to rock Danny, Theo turned to Ruby. "Can you sense anything?"

"No," Ruby whispered back. "Can you?"

Theo didn't reply straightaway.

"Theo…" Ruby prompted.

"There's nothing here at the moment, but that doesn't mean to say there wasn't. There's a… a residue, and it's leaving a bad taste in my mouth."

Using the word she had used last night, Ruby said, "It's rancid, isn't it?"

"Rancid?" Theo considered. "That's exactly what it is."

"So something has been here?"

"I'd say so."

"Something real, or something conjured from Danny's mind."

Theo's answer surprised her. "Define real, Ruby."

Right now, she found she couldn't.

* * *

Danny was taken immediately to the Royal Sussex County Hospital, and Presley went with him. The others stayed behind in his flat, attempting to make it at least habitable again. Jed, meanwhile, sat in one corner – the opposite corner from where Ruby had glimpsed the creature the night before. On red alert, she guessed.

"I hope he'll be okay – Danny, I mean," Corinna said, as she up-righted chairs, dragged them over to the dining table and pushed them underneath.

"He's in the best place," Ness replied, sweeping up the shattered vinyl. "He'll not only get medical help but also psychiatric help."

"Whilst we continue with the spiritual," Ruby said, eyeing Cash.

"All angles covered," he agreed.

Theo had gone into the bedroom to tidy up; that was a

mess too.

"We need to perform a cleansing," Ruby said to Ness. "A lot of negative feeling has built up."

"Definitely," she answered. "Did you bring the bag with you?"

"Damn, I forgot. We left in such a hurry…"

Ness shrugged. "We can always come back. Open the windows, though – all of them. The air needs changing."

While they did that, Theo returned to the living room.

"Well, well, well," she said, not looking at anyone in particular. Rather, she was looking at what she held in her hand: a leather-bound book.

"What is it?" Ness said, rising, her expression not only interested but concerned.

Theo held the book up for all to see.

"*The Book of the Law*," Ness said grimly.

"Never heard of it," Corinna shrugged. "Who's it by?"

"Aleister Crowley," Theo replied.

"Crowley?" Cash gasped. "I've heard of him!"

"I think most people have," Theo answered. "The Great Beast, The Wickedest Man in the World – his reputation went before him."

Ruby came forward, her eyes wide. "So it's Crowley Danny was interested in?"

"I'd say so," Theo continued. "There are several books either by him or concerning him in his bedroom. Lots of sketches too, of demons – creatures that Crowley in his infinite wisdom was always trying to invoke. It seems Danny had quite the fascination."

"Not good," Ruby heard Ness mutter behind her. "Not good at all."

Ruby reached out to take the book from Theo, but Jed

started snarling. She drew back.

"Do you know what the book's about, Theo?"

Theo sneered. "I haven't wasted precious time reading it, but I know something of it, yes. It's the book he believed his guardian angel, Aiwass, dictated to him. It underlines the ethos he lived by – 'Do what thou wilt shall be the whole of the Law.'"

Ness stepped forward. "Love is the law, Love under will," she said.

Theo looked at her. "Ah, yes, the completion of the quote."

"Love is the law… guardian angel…" Cash repeated the words he'd heard. "It all sounds okay to me. Was Crowley really the wickedest man in the world? Or misunderstood?"

"Depends on your perspective," Theo said. "To some, he had a forward thinking, truly progressive mind. But the proof's in the pudding. So many who involved themselves with him ended up either insane, alcoholics or drug addicts. There's a difference between self-will and true will in my opinion. True will does not conflict with another will; it doesn't harm anyone, or cause suffering, discord or pain. It isn't negative. When self-will runs riot – well, that can be extremely harmful."

Ness nodded in agreement whilst the younger members of the team tried to digest Theo's words.

Theo laughed suddenly. "Don't look so confused," she said, addressing Ruby, Corinna, and Cash. "This stuff takes a lifetime to understand – several lifetimes. Believe me, I don't know much about it either – barely the tip of the iceberg." She grew serious again. "But what I do know is that, in the course of my life, those I've encountered who've held a fascination with Crowley couldn't be considered stable, well-adjusted people. More often than not, they've been damaged people seeking answers. Unfortunately, through him they tend to find nothing but continuing despair."

In the room, silence fell once again.

"Did you know," Theo asked Ruby after a few moments, "that Crowley lived for a while in Hastings – your hometown? That he died there?"

"I was aware of that, yes."

"I thought you might be. He died an old man; a lonely man. Heroin was involved."

"Is he buried in Hastings?" Cash asked.

"No," Theo replied. "His body was cremated in Brighton."

"Ashes to ashes," Cash muttered.

"Indeed," Theo said, casting her eyes once more over the book. "Some people say there are passages in here that read like poetry; they're so beautiful. 'Every man and every woman is a star' – it says that, which is very poetic indeed. What they talk about less is how it implies women are meant solely as objects of lust; that compassion is weakness, and the impoverished are filth. There is *nothing* beautiful about this book."

Ruby tended to agree. She hadn't read it and nor would she. In her line of work, it was essential to stay in the light, not be drawn towards murkier depths. Still, there was one thing she was curious about – something Theo had said earlier.

"This guardian angel of his…" she began.

"Aiwass."

"Yes, Aiwass. What was he really, do you think?"

Theo knitted both brows together. "Crowley argued he

was an object separate from himself – someone with incredible knowledge who used a familiar form to connect with mankind. The most familiar form of all in fact – a man."

Ness joined in at this point. "It's more likely that Aiwass was an unconscious manifestation of Crowley's personality. Something imagined – no more."

Ruby glanced at Cash, who looked rapt by all he was hearing, and then back at Ness and Theo. "Are there any illustrations of him in that book?"

"I'm not sure," Theo admitted. "But if there aren't, there'd be descriptions aplenty. Enough for each mind reading it to form a picture of him in glorious or – perhaps it would be more apt to say – not-so-glorious detail."

Listening to this, Ruby's mind was working overtime.

"Ruby, tell us the direction your thoughts are heading," Ness said.

"You mean you don't know?" Ruby asked, only part jokingly.

"I mean for Corinna and Cash's benefit," she replied.

Ruby hesitated before speaking, but only briefly. "I'm thinking Danny saw Aiwass – or at least his interpretation of it."

Theo shrugged. "He could well have done."

"And if he saw Aiwass," she finished, "perhaps I did too."

Chapter Six

LATER that night, Presley called Cash to tell him Danny was stable, and his parents had been informed.

"They'll be here soon. They live in Exeter now, so it's a bit of a drive."

"You go home then," said Cash. "Get some rest."

"Yeah, and a shower. I stink."

"Thanks for that, bro. There's such a thing as TMI."

"TMI?" Presley queried.

"Too much information," Cash informed him.

Presley laughed. As Cash had his mobile on loudspeaker, Ruby could hear it too, and was glad. They needed an injection of laughter today.

Saying goodbye to Presley, Cash walked over to where Ruby was microwaving lasagna.

"Danny's going to be okay," he said, wrapping his arms around her.

"Thank goodness," she said, leaning into him.

"Shall I pour us some wine?" he asked.

"That'd be good. A large glass of red, please."

"And I'll make up a side salad?"

Ruby nodded. "I've got some tomatoes and lettuce in the fridge."

"Leave it to me."

Later, as they sat chomping their way through their

hastily prepared meal – Cash lamenting the fact they had no French bread to accompany it – Ruby brought up the subject of Susan again. She told Cash she'd tried to find out more about her death, but as she didn't have a surname and her first name was a common one, there wasn't much to go on.

He seemed surprised she'd gone to such effort. "You've done your part; you've released her. Why are you so concerned?"

"I don't know. I just feel bad for her, that's all," she replied, wiping at her mouth.

"But she's at rest now. She's happy. Everybody's happy in the light, aren't they?"

"Yes."

"Funny – you don't sound convinced."

"Of course I'm convinced," she shot back.

"Okay, okay. But right now, we've got bigger fish to fry."

His use of the word 'we' was not lost on her.

"This Danny case – I don't think you should get involved."

About to take a sip of wine, Cash paused. "Excuse me? I think I'm the one who got you involved."

"Yeah, but I can take over from here."

"So, what? I'm being dismissed, am I?"

"Whatever affected Danny, I don't want it to affect you."

"But I'm supposed to sit back and let it affect you?"

"It's a hazard of the job!"

"I know it is, and I can't make you undo what you do, but what I *can* do is help." He stopped speaking and frowned instead. "Does that actually make sense, what I've just said?"

Ruby couldn't help but smile. "It was a bit garbled but, yeah, I get the gist." Quickly, her insecurities kicked in again. "Cash? My profession – are you getting fed up of it?"

"No, Ruby Davis," he said, smiling at her too. "I am *not* getting fed up with it. What I am getting fed up with, though, is you trying to protect me all the time. I know my job is mine and yours is yours, but your job is likely to need a bit more extra-curricular attention and, when it does, I'm on call. Don't you realise?" he continued. "I'm the one who wants to protect you."

"You and Jed," she replied, softly.

"The three of us, we're a team – watertight."

Speaking of Jed, where was he? She hadn't seen him since they'd left Danny's flat. Maybe he was frolicking in some sun-dappled grassy meadow somewhere. When he wasn't with her, that's what she liked to think.

Finishing their dinner, Cash made them both a cup of tea and they took it through to the living room to sit down. Switching on the TV, they settled in front of a BBC drama – *The Lonely Boys* – based around a group of boys growing up in the urban jungle that doubles as London's inner city. Running in packs, but isolated from society as a whole. It was a good drama, by turns fascinating and disturbing. A bit like Crowley himself, thought Ruby, resting her head on Cash's shoulder.

As though her eyes had lead weights attached, she struggled to stay awake. She still hadn't told Cash about the strange incident at Sussex Stationers earlier. What would he make of it? But it was too late to find out – sleep had claimed her.

Images, murky at first, as they so often are in dreams, gradually became more vivid. She was a child again. How old she was, she didn't know – six or seven? She had on a pink, short-sleeved t-shirt with a picture of a grey kitten on it, and a grey pleated skirt that stopped just above her knees – neither item she recognised. A plaster was on her right knee – a sizeable one – and she bent down to peel it off, curious to see what lay beneath.

"Ruby, don't do that." It was her grandmother's voice – Sarah. "You'll make it bleed again."

"How did I do it, Gran?" she asked, confused.

"Don't you remember?" Sarah said, coming closer.

As she looked into her grandmother's face, Ruby noted she was younger too. The lines around her mouth were not so deeply etched, and her hair still had traces of brown in it.

"I'm surprised you don't; you cried hard enough," Sarah continued. "You were playing on the beach and you fell over. Someone had left a bottle behind them, the careless souls – a broken bottle. You fell on that. It's a miracle you didn't need stitches."

A broken bottle. Was she sure about that? She remembered seeing a bottle recently, but it hadn't been broken. Where was that? It was in a room somewhere. Trying to recall, she found she couldn't. How strange. But then, dreams were strange. They twisted and turned in all sorts of weird, wonderful, and not-so-wonderful ways. If they had been at the beach earlier, they weren't now. They were at home – just the two of them.

"Where's Mum?" Ruby asked, as the kitchen materialised around them – the smell of home baking redolent. Gran loved to cook, and Ruby loved to help her.

"She's gone out. She'll be back soon."

Ruby shrugged. It was nothing new. Mum was always out.

"Can we make cookies?"

"We can do anything you like, Ruby Davis."

Ruby Davis. Someone else called her by her full name. But again, it was a detail that eluded her.

Dragging a chair over to the sink, she stood on it to wash her hands. Whilst she did that, Gran got the flour, butter, sugar, and eggs out. Soon, she was sinking tiny fingers into soft goo and squeezing it together. Ruby loved this bit – the 'ickiness' of it. When the mixture was ready, Gran added a generous quantity of chocolate chips before dividing it into several rounds. Ruby helped her to do this, and Gran was laughing because the rounds she was making were so much bigger.

"I can see which cookies you've got your eye on," she declared.

As the timer went off fifteen minutes later, the front door opened. Ruby heard the high-pitched sound of laughter – her mother returning.

"Hi, Mum, we're home! Where's Ruby? Where's my baby?"

Ruby felt excitement surge within her at the prospect of seeing her mother again, but also something else – something she didn't understand. Concern, perhaps? She didn't pay too much heed to it, though, because there was a lot she didn't understand. Like why she could see the living *and* the dead. Gran had explained on plenty of occasions, and mostly she made sense, but not always. The biggest thing that didn't make sense was why she couldn't tell anyone. Like it was some kind of secret – a bad one. If she told Lisa – her best friend at school – what would happen? Wouldn't she like her anymore?

As Jessica bustled into the kitchen, Ruby saw she wasn't alone. She had a 'friend' with her. A friend Ruby instinctively knew Gran didn't like; her back stiffened on sight of him and the smile slid from her face. Being picked up by her mother, Ruby smelt something sour on her breath – perhaps the wine her mother loved to drink. Her nose wrinkled at it.

"Cookies!" Jessica declared. "You're making cookies! Can I have one?"

In contrast, Gran's voice was solemn. "We're having dinner soon."

"Oh, okay. I hope there's plenty for my friend?"

It wasn't really a question. Ruby knew that because her mother didn't bother to wait for an answer. Instead, she turned round to face her friend and started giggling about something. He seemed amused too, but whatever the joke was, they didn't share it.

The man did stay for dinner, and all the while they ate, Ruby could feel his eyes on her. She began to shift in her seat – the food stuck in her throat.

"What's the matter, darling?" Jessica leant across. "Do you need to go to the toilet?"

Ruby flushed bright red. Why had she asked that in front of a stranger!

"Mum!" Ruby shot back, but again Jessica laughed. That's all she did – laugh. And usually Ruby loved to hear it, but not now. Now, there was a strange quality to it. Gran was uncomfortable with her daughter's behaviour too. She was frowning again; staring at Jessica as if trying to communicate silently with her – trying to get her to stop. But Jessica wouldn't stop. She continued to laugh – the man joining in. They laughed and they laughed until Ruby felt sure her eardrums would burst.

"Stop it!" she said. If Gran wasn't going to say something, she was. But they carried on – ignored her as they would have ignored Gran.

"Stop it!" she repeated, her voice rising.

She wished Jed would come bounding in; growl at the man; help her. Jed? The name seemed familiar, but how come? She'd never had a dog as a child.

As the laughing continued, the room began to swim in and out of focus.

"Mum. Gran. What's happening?"

They too were swimming backwards and forwards. Backwards again. Further and further. Out of reach. Only the man remained static, with his long face, his cold eyes, and his ice-white hair. He did, and Ruby did – the pair of them sitting across the table. Staring at each other. The meal Gran had set down before him, he'd picked at earlier, but he hadn't looked particularly hungry. Now he did, but not for food.

As she continued to stare at him, he grinned. Another smiling man. But who was the first? And there was someone else. Someone who hadn't smiled: a ragged man. Who was he?

The man at the table recaptured her attention.

"Ruby," he said, and his voice, rasping, set her teeth on edge. "I see you."

* * *

"Ruby, wake up. You're screaming!"

"What... I... What's going on?"

"You tell me!" said Cash, staring at her.

Although they were still on the sofa, she was no longer leaning against him, she suspected, because he had had to sit her up to wake her.

Wiping at her mouth, which felt slightly damp with spittle, she turned her head away from him. "Don't," she said.

"Don't what?"

"You're staring at me. Don't do it."

"I'm not staring at you," he protested, before softening. "Ruby, what's the matter?"

Although the dream she'd had was vivid, it was already fading. She'd been a child again, at her grandmother's house in Hastings. Quickly she tried to recall details, but the more she tried the harder it became.

Leaning forward on the sofa, she let her head fall into her hands. "I had a nightmare," she said, after a while.

"I gathered that." Cash also leaned forward and put an arm around her, but tentatively, as if he was scared she'd tell him off for that too. "It's been a long day and a confusing one."

"No, Cash, you don't understand – I *never* have nightmares."

"Never?" He seemed impressed.

"Well… hardly ever," she corrected.

Cash ran his hand over his head. "Look, that Crowley shit – it's enough to give anyone nightmares. Don't worry about it."

She couldn't help but agree. "I know. It's seriously creepy, isn't it? To wilfully align yourself with the dark side – to become a disciple of it."

"It reminds me a bit of Geoffrey Rawlings. Do you

remember?"

Rawlings was the man that Cynthia Hart – the spirit reluctant to leave Highdown Hall – thought had sold her soul to the devil. But Rawlings was not the real deal; he'd faked it to make it, or, rather, to bed the beauties. Yes, he'd started a coven back in the nineteen sixties, but when his followers had turned out to be genuinely into all things Satan, he'd turned tail and run – sought asylum with the police. Rawlings' soul might have been black, but there were plenty of souls – Crowley's included – that were blacker by far.

Thinking about him, Ruby had to remind herself that no one was beyond redemption – not even someone who went around calling himself *The Beast 666*. Besides which, it was not Crowley she was afraid of. He was just a man, and he was entitled to his metaphysical views. It was something else entirely – something *beyond* human.

"Cash, I need to go to bed – work in the morning and all that."

She tried to sound casual, but there was no fooling him.

"Do you want me to stay?"

"Would you?" She hadn't wanted to ask – had worried about being seen as needy.

"Of course."

"But just… just hold me, okay."

"Just holding is fine."

Later, cuddled up together, she wondered why she hadn't told him about the voice in the bookshop. Why she hadn't told Theo, Ness, or Corinna either. She wondered, but the only answer she could come up with was that she didn't want to feed it energy. What had happened might be related to Danny; it might be entirely separate. But worrying about it would only make it grow. She had to go back to Sussex Stationers soon, when Cash's book came in. She'd use that opportunity to scope the joint again. Until then, she didn't want to think about it – about Danny or Susan either.

She just wanted sleep to treat her kindly.

Chapter Seven

FROM the comfort of her bed, Ruby was busy eyeing Cash the next morning. He'd just stepped out of the shower, and beads of water clung tantalisingly to his toned frame. More to the point, he was eyeing her back, when his phone rang.

"Damn," he muttered, clearly frustrated at any imaginings he might have had cut short.

Rifling through his jacket – slung over the back of a chair the previous evening – he eventually managed to retrieve the item that had caused offence. Noticing the caller ID, his face grew serious.

"It's Presley," he mouthed to Ruby.

Immediately attentive too, Ruby studied his face as he talked to his brother. From his calm expression, however, it was clear nothing more dramatic had happened whilst they'd been sleeping. As soon as he ended the call, Cash confirmed it.

"Presley just wanted to give me a further update on Danny."

"And?"

"They've flushed his system through, and he's recovering – albeit slowly."

"Has he come round yet?"

"He has but he's groggy."

"Can we go and see him?"

Cash shook his head. "His parents are letting Presley in, but they don't want anyone else there. They think it'd be too much for Danny to cope with right now."

Although she was disappointed, she could understand their decision. They'd be feeling incredibly protective. "Does Danny have any brothers and sisters?"

"An older sister, but she lives in Canada."

"So he's the baby of the family."

"Yeah," Cash said, sighing.

He'd started to pull his jeans on.

"Where do you think you're going?" she asked him, her voice deliberately sultry.

"Work," he said, stopping short of stepping into them. "Why'd you ask?"

"Why'd you think?" she replied, patting the bed beside her.

* * *

Grabbing a sandwich and a drink en route to the office, Ruby felt hot and sticky by the time she got there, despite lingering in the shower with Cash an inordinate amount of time. The day was a scorcher but, as beautiful as it was, she couldn't help but groan. In her office, perched on high, she froze in winter but tended to boil in summer. What she wouldn't give for an air-conditioned ground-floor office, but those days were a long way off yet. Psychic Surveys was doing well – this was their best year yet – but money was still tight, and a part of her feared it always would be, unless she got a stint with the council, that is, or Sussex Police, following in Ness's footsteps. Working with them, as well as on her own cases, could prove interesting.

As she feared, walking into her office was like walking into an oven. Even Jed had eschewed it this morning. Sitting at her desk, she fired the computer up before leaning over to check the answer machine – its red light flashing furiously.

As she listened to enquiries, Ruby necked the orange juice she'd bought earlier, wincing slightly because it was lukewarm. Space cleansing was one of their most popular services and, sure enough, two messages related to just that – new house owners worried about negative vibes left behind by the previous owners. They wanted the atmosphere, if not purified, neutralised at least. And rightly so; negative residue could lead to headaches, fatigue and mood swings. Very often there was no accompanying spirit – but energy was energy and the bad stuff brought you down. One call excited her particularly – a large office in Burgess Hill wanted several floors cleansed. Mrs Woods, who had placed the call, was sure it was the atmosphere in the building they'd recently taken over that was affecting staff morale. And not just morale either, but the efficiency of output.

"It's dark and gloomy," the recorded voice informed her. "Oppressive. We're going to have the whole place repainted. But I'd like a psychic survey too – to see what you think."

Ruby was excited because a large cleansing meant a decent pay cheque; she'd be able to buy herself that new pair of jeans she had her eye on in the Levi's store in Brighton. The last message was from a woman called Gwyneth who lived in Cardiff. Her young daughter was complaining of an old woman appearing in her bedroom at night.

"She keeps telling Mai to come with her – bloody cheek! Go where, I ask you?"

Where indeed?

Ruby had recently made contact with a psychic who lived on the Hereford border – a woman of a similar age to Ness and similar in manner too, subdued but nonetheless passionate about helping grounded spirits. She decided she would give her a call to see if she'd go to the client's house and perform the survey for Mai and her mother on behalf of Psychic Surveys. List making was something Ruby did a lot of, and she was listing all the day's tasks when the phone rang. It was Theo.

"Busy, darling?" she asked Ruby.

"Erm… just a bit," Ruby replied, scanning the list. She also wanted to fit in a visit to the East Sussex Record Office, The Keep, at some stage – to sort through local and national newspapers to see if she could find reference to Susan's death. But today might not be that day.

"You're about to get busier."

"Hit me with it. What's happened?"

"I've been asked by a neighbour's friend to come and survey their house. They keep hearing a baby cry at night, but they don't have children."

"Do their neighbours have children?" Ruby knew she didn't really have to ask this question. Theo was nothing less than thorough.

Proving her point, Theo replied, "One neighbour is child-free. The other has teenagers: two of them – both boys. I could go and check it out under my own steam, but I think we should do this in a professional capacity, under the Psychic Surveys banner."

Ruby agreed. "Just you and me, I take it?"

"Just you and me," Theo confirmed.

Asking for details, she continued adding to her list.

* * *

Less than a couple of hours later, Ruby was parked outside a house in Horam, waiting for Theo to rock up in her pearlised white Fiat 500 with go-faster Italian side stripes. On the way to this East Sussex village, she'd passed the Brookbridge Estate – a housing development built on the grounds of a former psychiatric hospital, the Cromer Asylum. Ruby and her team had cleansed a lot of houses there – old walls torn down and fresh new walls put in their place not enough to deter the original inmates – but she hadn't been called there lately. *All quiet on the western front,* she mused as she passed it… *for now.*

A couple of minutes after she'd parked, Theo arrived. Ruby couldn't help but smile. For such a large lady, she'd chosen one of the smallest cars on the market.

Reaching for the door handle, Ruby alighted. Theo was already on the pavement, slightly breathless from the exertion of exiting her car.

"Hello, sweetie," she said to Ruby. "Thanks for responding so quickly."

"Of course. Got to carry on the crusade."

"Haven't we just." Theo rolled her eyes as she said it. A slight frown developing, she asked Ruby if she was okay.

Ruby shrugged and said she was.

"Good, good. You're just a bit… pale, that's all. Despite the sunshine."

"I'm tired, I suppose."

"Of course you are. It's been a busy few days." Looking

around, she said, "No Jed?"

"You know what he's like. He comes and goes."

"Always around when you need him though, huh?"

"Yeah, I… suppose he is."

Theo averted her eyes and looked over Ruby's shoulder instead – lingering for quite a while before Ruby plucked up the courage to ask her if *she* was okay.

Immediately, Theo adjusted her gaze. "I'm fine. Let's get this underway," she said, stepping aside so Ruby could lead the way.

The door opened after a couple of knocks. A woman around her mid-fifties stood before them, neatly dressed in beige slacks and a similarly coloured blouse.

"Good afternoon," said Ruby, extending a hand. "Psychic Surveys."

"Ah, yes." The woman took Ruby's hand and shook it firmly. "And your name is?"

"Ruby Davis."

"Hello, Ruby, I'm Jane Clark." Turning to Theo, she added, "Thank you so much for coming, and so promptly too. I really do appreciate it."

Inviting them to take a seat round the kitchen table, a cup of tea was served whilst Jane told them what was being experienced in the house – the baby crying, basically. Usually heard to full effect in the dead of night, disturbing not just their sleep but also their peace of mind.

"We thought it might be cats or foxes at first," Jane continued. "Everyone knows what a racket they can make. And barn owls – have you ever heard them? Gosh, they can screech. But it's not. When we first started to hear it, my husband used to sit for hours at night, peering out of the window, just in case. But it's a baby – there's no doubt about it. And a newborn, by the sounds of it. She mewls, you know, like tiny babies do? Poor mite."

"How do you know it's a she?" Theo asked.

Jane frowned. "Oh, I don't. I haven't a clue if it's a he, she or an it, to be honest."

Her mention of the word 'it' was an innocent one, but it still sent shivers coursing down Ruby's spine. Silently she berated herself for being so jittery.

Usually, Ruby explained what they would do next – a walk-through in every room to see what they could detect – but Theo did the honours today, and she was grateful. Despite no more nightmares – no more dreaming at all – the sleep she'd had hadn't left her refreshed. She felt drained, as though someone had unplugged her.

Jane listened carefully to Theo before commenting. "All sounds good to me. I thought about contacting my local priest, you know – for an exorcism or whatever it is they do. But my husband and I, we're not churchgoers. It seemed hypocritical somehow. So I asked around and was told about you. Theo and I share a mutual friend. Can you believe it? What are the chances?" She paused slightly before adding, "Novel idea, by the way – creating a place we can come to with our 'ghostly' concerns. I love it."

Although she bristled slightly at her business being described as 'novel', Ruby smiled politely in reply before declaring they'd best crack on. Surveying each room, neither she nor Theo could detect any spiritual presence. Jane met this verdict with abject disbelief.

"I'm *not* lying," she said. "And I'm not imagining it either. There is crying; it happens night after night. It's getting us down."

After assuring her they weren't in any way insinuating

she was telling them untruths, Ruby looked at Theo, imparting a silent question to her.

Where's the sound coming from?

Theo had heard her, she was sure – her ability to catch thoughts came in very handy sometimes. The older woman's subsequent question to Jane confirmed that.

"Your neighbours? Could we have a word?"

Jane was apprehensive. "I don't know. I mean, I'm quite enlightened, but I can't vouch for them."

"We'll be discreet," Ruby promised.

"And, above all, professional," Theo added. "You have a problem, and talking to your neighbours might help us to fix it."

"I don't see how," Jane replied, before relenting. "Give me a moment; let me go round first and explain."

"Of course," said Theo. "Shall we wait here? In the kitchen?"

"If you wouldn't mind."

Within minutes, Jane was back.

"Mrs Maxwell is fine with it. If you go now, I'll pop to Su and Pete's and ask them too."

"Mrs Maxwell is on which side?" Theo asked.

"Go out of the front door and turn right."

Mrs Maxwell was indeed fine with Psychic Surveys' impromptu visit.

"You're real-life psychics?" she asked, as soon as they set foot over the threshold.

"Real-life ones," Theo confirmed, able to sound good-natured rather than sarcastic.

"I mean, you're not faking it?" Mrs Maxwell continued – a slight woman with clearly dyed blonde hair and wide blue eyes. At least they were wide now.

"Psychic Surveys wouldn't still be in business if we were faking it," Ruby assured her.

The woman unfortunately insisted on following them into every room – her two teenagers' bedrooms included – asking countless questions. Trying to be polite, Ruby answered as briefly as she could get away with. She was trying to tune in, but it wasn't easy when under constant interrogation. Theo, however, seemed to be more successful at zoning Mrs Maxwell out – perhaps she'd be able to pick up something.

Back in the woman's kitchen – an exact replica of Jane's except for the colour – Theo gave her house the all clear.

"Oh, really?" Mrs Maxwell looked downcast. "That's a shame."

Jane was waiting for them on the garden path when they returned.

"Well?" she said, her arms lightly folded across her chest.

Ruby shook her head. "There's nothing there."

Jane looked perplexed. "Su and Pete are both in and they're fine with you going round. Well, they're a bit bemused to be honest, but they've given you the go ahead. Is that okay?"

"Of course," said Ruby, retracing her footsteps and turning left this time, Theo by her side.

A young couple, almost self-consciously trendy, Su and her partner Pete blatantly studied Ruby and Theo as they stood aside to let them enter their house. Although not as vociferous as Mrs Maxwell, Ruby didn't have to be a mind reader to tell they were thinking along charlatan lines also. Explaining for the third time that day their procedure, the couple agreed – suspicion leaking from every pore. Thankfully, unlike Mrs Maxwell, they didn't insist on shadowing their every move.

"There's no need," Pete said, when Ruby asked if they wanted to. "I'll know if anything goes missing."

Ruby bridled at the intimation they were thieves and so did Theo, but they said nothing. Instead, they cut them some slack; a pair of psychics had, after all, been thrust upon them from out of the blue. Upstairs, in the couple's bedroom, a baby started to cry.

"Can you hear it?" Theo asked Ruby, stopping her in her tracks.

Ruby nodded. "It's very faint."

"It'll get stronger, don't worry."

In the bedroom itself, the baby was making quite a racket.

"There, there," soothed Theo. "What's all this noise for?"

The baby carried on regardless.

"And Su and Pete can't hear this, whilst their next door neighbours can?" Ruby queried.

"A lot of people live with spirits and don't realise. You know that well enough."

Ruby shrugged. "Yeah, yeah, I suppose. But this presence – it's strong as well as noisy. They must be completely closed off." A 'gift' too, Ruby mused, in its own way.

Like Theo, she began to tune in – both of them careful to surround themselves in white light beforehand. It might be a baby they were dealing with, but procedure was procedure.

"Something happened to the mother," Theo said eventually. "Something unexpected."

"Yes, but not here, not in this room; this house even.

The baby was left alone."

Theo concurred. "I wonder why."

There could be so many reasons – a whole catalogue of them.

"Darling," soothed Theo again, "there's no need to cry. We're here now. You're no longer alone."

Su appeared in the doorway.

"Who you talking to?" she said – an accusation rather than a question in her voice.

Theo pulled herself up to her full height. Even though she was a short woman, she always looked magnificent when she did that – as though she was vastly taller. As though she was six foot tall. 'It's a psychic trick,' she'd explained to Ruby once. 'An age-old one. It's called *the glamour*. There's a simple ethos behind it really – it's just a matter of confidence.' Ruby had never heard of it before, but glamorous (and confident) it certainly was. Formidable too. That's exactly what she looked.

Turning towards Su, Theo answered her. "We're trying to soothe the cries of the baby. The noises Jane hears, they're coming from this room."

Su looked around her. "Rubbish! You people are bonkers."

Ruby tried to remonstrate, but felt unable to do so all of a sudden, as weariness descended with a vengeance. To her horror, she couldn't stop herself yawning.

Both Theo and Su were aghast.

"Sorry," she muttered.

Once again, Theo took control.

"I understand your scepticism, Su, but we are professionals in the field of psychic investigation, with the track record to prove it. There is a spiritual presence in your bedroom – that of a baby. Our job is to try and connect with the spirit, and to send it home."

Pete had come up behind her. He and Sue were almost the image of each other. Both had dark hair, dark eyes, and flat features – a narcissistic attraction.

"Home?" He repeated. "Where the bloody hell is home?"

Ruby cringed, not only at his words, but also at his attitude. Su and Pete were closed off to the spirit world because they were closed-minded. Explaining where 'home' was would fall on deaf ears. Nonetheless, Theo attempted to do so, but, met with blank stares, she stopped – aware she was getting nowhere fast.

"I think you need to talk to Jane," she said instead. "Perhaps between the three of you, you can come to some sort of decision as to what you want done here."

Without another word, Theo walked to the door, swept past the couple, and went downstairs. A few moments later, Ruby followed.

On the path outside, Jane was still waiting.

"You were gone ages," she said. "Did you find something?"

"You'd better speak to your neighbours about that," Theo replied frostily. She'd not taken kindly to being called a thief as well as a charlatan.

Jane hurried towards her. "Wait. Don't go anywhere. Please. I'll speak to them."

Conceding, Ruby and Theo took up position beside Theo's car.

"How long shall we give it?" Ruby asked.

"Ten minutes," Theo said decisively.

"But what if they say we can't go back in? What about

the baby?"

"Ruby, I'd love to send the little one home as much as you, believe me. But what can we do if they won't let us? Tie them up whilst we carry on regardless? We can't."

"No, I know that." Such were the frustrations of the job.

"Ruby," Theo said again, more sympathetically this time. "Are you sure you're okay? You seem distracted today, as well as tired."

"Really, I'm fine," she answered.

"What you saw at Danny's – has it affected you more than you're letting on?"

Ruby hesitated. Had it? She was trying *not* to let it – that she did know.

"Nothing's happened since, has it?" Theo probed further.

"Just a nightmare," Ruby said. "It was about my mum."

Theo looked suitably sombre. She knew Ruby's mother had suffered a breakdown when she was a child – her disrespect for her gift, the reason behind it. And the subsequent chasm between mother and daughter – she knew about that too.

"Anything else?"

Ruby was about to tell her about the Sussex Stationers incident, when Jane reappeared.

"They've said yes, you can go ahead – you can remove the ghost."

Theo smiled. "Good news. Good news indeed."

As Jane came to a halt in front of them, Su and Pete appeared as well.

"But we're not paying," Pete said. "Jane, the bill's yours."

Immediately Jane rounded on them. "But it's your

house that's haunted – not mine!"

Su joined in the altercation. "We've only got your word for that. We don't hear a thing."

"Oh, come on. You know money's tight since Graham lost his job," Jane pleaded. "Meet me halfway at least."

Pete was adamant. "We're not contributing a penny."

Ruby stepped forward. She just wanted to get the cleansing underway so she could return home and rest. "I'll halve the bill. How's that, Jane? Call it… a good will gesture."

Jane brightened considerably. "If you're sure?"

"I'm sure." Now more than ever, she hoped that office cleansing in Burgess Hill would come off.

Before returning to the house, Ruby asked Su and Pete if they knew who the previous occupants of their house were.

Pete shrugged. "The house was a repossession. We got it on the cheap at auction."

"Jane, do you know anything?" Ruby asked.

"No, I don't, sorry. Su and Pete were already living there when we arrived."

Oh great… nothing to go on as usual. She was surprised at how irritated she felt by this.

Back in the bedroom, the baby hadn't ceased its crying.

"I think the cot was over here," Theo said, walking to the far side of the room.

Joining hands, they tuned back in, Ruby speaking after a few moments.

"My name's Ruby and this is Theo. We can hear you crying and we've come to help you. We're with you now."

The wailing grew louder.

"What are we going to do, Theo?" Ruby asked. "How

do we communicate with a baby?"

"It's a soul, Ruby – presenting itself in baby form, admittedly, but a soul nonetheless. On some level we'll be understood."

Ruby carried on trying to quiet the child. *Jed, where are you? We could use some help.*

Children loved animals, usually – spirit children included. And Jed had proved very useful when dealing with them in the past – calming them instantly. Jed, however, was a no-show.

After repeated attempts, both Theo and Ruby had to admit defeat.

"Any idea of timeframe?" Ruby asked.

"None at all. This could be from way back."

"The house is Victorian, isn't it?"

"Yes, but we don't know what stood here before. Another house probably. And before that, a dwelling place of some description."

As both contemplated this prospect, Theo said, "Time for a new tactic, I think."

"Which is?"

"We need to call on those in the light to come forward. It's time this mite got happy."

Ruby agreed. "Can you see where the light is?"

"Can you?" Theo batted back, surprising her again.

"Erm… no, not right now." Normally she had an idea at least.

Theo frowned. "Really? It's to the left of you."

Both of them turned and Ruby began to call on someone to come forward to claim the spirit baby. By now, her head was aching from the noise it was making.

Oh, for pity's sake, she thought after a while, *will you give it a rest!*

Immediately Theo rounded on her. "Ruby, that's not the attitude!"

"I know... I..." Damn! At times, Theo's other psychic gift wasn't handy. It was a pain.

"If you're too tired to carry on, leave the room."

Ruby bit down on a retort. Theo was right. Her attitude stank today.

"No, I'd like to continue," she said meekly.

"Then do so with respect."

Theo this time addressed the light, continuing their plea for help. Ruby, meanwhile, concentrated on sending love towards the traumatised being. As she did, the cries became whimpers, became more intermittent, became hiccups and occasional sniffs.

"Someone's coming," said Theo.

At her words, Ruby stiffened.

Who is it? Who's coming?

With relief she saw two female figures emerge – a part of the light but momentarily separate from it. A sigh escaped her. She couldn't believe how tense she was lately.

The figures glided past them to where the cries where coming from – the cot, presumably – although Ruby could see neither that nor the baby. She suspected her tiredness was blocking her. One bent down and picked the baby up, making a gentle rocking motion with her arms. Immediately the baby hushed. Still silent, all three glided back towards the light, to become absorbed by it. After they'd gone, Ruby and Theo stood in silent awe. A question niggled at Ruby, however.

"How come we have to call them, Theo? The spirit guides, I mean. How come they don't just *know* when someone's in need?"

"I may be an old lady, sweetheart," Theo replied, her eyes still dancing with wonder, "but I don't know everything. I haven't got a clue either. But you know what they say about the best-laid plans – sometimes they don't work out. And when they don't, we pull together. You, me, the spirit guides, the spirits themselves – we get there in the end."

"Through team effort?"

"Exactly."

A part of Ruby was still dissatisfied. "I thought it would be perfect on the other side."

"Perhaps perfection is a myth too – nothing more than a human longing."

"Clearly."

"Why clearly, Ruby?" Theo probed.

"Because so many souls slip through the net – more than we can possibly help. They're left to linger, and for so long sometimes. The process – it's not just imperfect, it's shambolic."

At her words, some of Theo's dazzle lessened and immediately Ruby felt guilty. Her mood had infected her, brought her friend down, when really they should be celebrating another success – a success, Ruby had to admit, which felt hollow. Just as Susan's had felt hollow. Just as everything felt hollow lately. Deciding it was best not to say any more, not to even *think* any more, she left the room, Theo following behind her.

Chapter Eight

RETURNING to the office to type up the report for Jane Clark, Ruby finally called it a day just after six. Cash was coming round again tonight. They spent most evenings together nowadays – except when there was a girls' do going on, or a boys' night only – and, thankfully, he'd offered to cook. If he hadn't, Ruby doubted she'd have bothered. Even the sandwich she'd bought earlier, she'd only nibbled at – her appetite not up to much in the last day or so, ever since… ever since Danny really.

As she started walking up the High Street, Jed fell into step beside her.

Hello, boy, where have you been?

Jed merely glanced at her in response.

Towards them came a group of young adults, all brightly clothed and chattering loudly to one another. Foreign students, Ruby guessed. To avoid them, she had to step into the road, but Jed, she noticed with amusement, walked right through them. Checking their reaction, not one of them so much as flinched. They walked on – completely unaware of what had just happened.

As Jed re-joined her, she smiled. His 'party trick' had just brightened what had been a strange day. Not only concerning how irritable she'd become with the incessantly crying baby, and how deflated she'd felt after her release, but also the fact that it was another case unsolved. Why had the baby been abandoned? What had happened to the mother, that she would leave her child to die? Rationally, Ruby knew she'd never find the answers to everything, but still it irked her. Susan's case irked her. It seemed everything irked her at the moment – except Jed.

Entering her flat, she decided to take a quick shower – the day had been a humid one. She had another twenty minutes or so before Cash was due. The thought of him cheered her some more, chased away the tiredness she'd felt earlier in the day. In fact, she felt a stirring in the pit of her stomach. Stopping short, she realised the stirring was lower than that, and growing in intensity.

To Jed, she said, "Better make yourself scarce later. I think I'm going to be busy."

Jed looked unimpressed and sloped off to the bedroom almost in defiance.

The shower was deliciously cool, and Ruby made the most of it, sliding soapy fingers gently over her body. At the top of her thighs, she stopped. *Should I?* The desire in her really was becoming all encompassing. With great effort, she decided not to – she'd let Cash do all the work. Quite why she was so horny was beyond her. The tiredness of earlier had dissipated entirely.

Stepping out of the shower, she dried herself, slowly, sensuously. Her sex drive was as healthy as the next person's, and certainly with Cash she was always eager. But this eager? She could barely wait for him to walk through the door! To occupy the minutes that remained – each one lasting an eternity – she imagined him instead. How toned his slim, tall build was. His beautiful hands – the fingers strong and sturdy. His eyes – the depth of them. Her breathing became short. At this rate, she was going to need another shower – an icy cold one.

The doorbell rang.

"Thank God," she breathed.

Cash barely had time to say hello before she pulled him over the threshold and kissed him – hard.

Coming up for air, Cash looked astonished. "Blimey, you've missed me, have you?"

"Like you wouldn't believe," she whispered, literally dragging him down the hallway to what she suddenly thought of as her lair.

Entering the bedroom, Jed sat up straight and growled. Not at Cash, she noticed, but at her. For a moment, she was stunned. He'd *never* growled at her before.

"Jed, make yourself scarce," she ordered.

When he refused to budge, she said it again, her voice harsher.

"Hey, go easy on him," said Cash, surprised, she could see, by her change of tone.

Ruby immediately retaliated. "Well, do you want to do it with him in here?"

"No, but…"

"There you are then. Jed, out!"

Jed did as he was told, but he edged away slowly, sulkily, before vanishing.

"Now, where was I?" she said, starting to tug impatiently at Cash's tee shirt.

"It's all right. I can do that." Lifting it up and over his head before discarding it, he stood in front of her, bare-chested. "Ruby, are you okay?"

"Of course I'm okay," she replied, letting her towel

drop, cursing she hadn't thought to do that at the front door. Now that would have been some welcome! "Why'd you ask?"

Cash shrugged, "I don't know. You seem… different."

"Different?" Ruby rolled her eyes. "For God's sake, Cash – I'm standing here naked in front of you and all you can say is I seem different. Don't you want to fuck me?"

"Ruby!"

Cash was no prude, Ruby knew that. He was experimental in bed, highly imaginative – but her crudeness had clearly shocked him. *Ruby, cool it,* a voice inside her head warned, but she was unable to heed it. She was beyond cooling anything.

"Cash…" Her voice held a whiney quality instead.

"Okay, okay. Give me a minute… get on the bed or something, wait for me there."

She did as she was told, watching him remove the rest of his clothes. His body was divine – better than her recent imaginings – young, hard, and firm. At the sight of him, her fingers became claws, reminding her, in a way, of Susan's hands.

This is no time to think of Susan.

No sooner had he settled himself beside her than she grabbed the back of his head, brought his mouth once again to hers, her lips immediately opening, her tongue searching. She wanted to *consume* him. He responded in kind, his hands travelling over the swell of her breasts, reaching down between her legs. *That's it, that's it. Don't stop.*

One finger slid inside her, but it wasn't enough. Reaching down, she made what she wanted perfectly clear. Cash obliged, pushing a second finger in, a third, but still it wasn't enough. It was *him* she wanted inside her. Nothing else would have the same impact. Pulling him roughly on top, she positioned his hips above her.

Before entering her, he pulled away again, a quizzical look on his face.

"Don't stop," she begged. "Please, I need you!"

How could he deny her? What man could? She was a goddess, or at least she felt like one. As they joined, she felt whole again, powerful. He may have been on top, but she was the one in command, bucking her hips, pushing them against his. *Slamming* them. She felt as though she was riding a wave – a wave building higher and higher that would drown them both when eventually it came crashing down. As Cash continued to pound her, her hands moved up from his hips, to his back, and stroked the smooth skin there. She *loved* his skin – the colour of it – how even it was, unblemished. She wished he had longer hair, something she could grab onto besides his hips. Instead, her hands became claws again, which she started to drag down his back, sinking them deeper and deeper into his flesh. She wanted to be inside him as he was inside her – meld with him, truly become one. In her mind, she imagined bone, blood, and sinew – the *rawness* of it.

"Ruby, what the hell are you doing?"

Cash pulled away from her. Worse than that, he pulled *out* of her.

She gasped. "Cash! What are *you* doing?"

Manoeuvring himself into a seated position, he reached one hand behind him. When he brought it back, she saw blood on his fingertips.

Her mouth fell open. "Did I do that?" she said.

"Yes, you bloody did!" He looked furious, his dark eyes

nothing less than stormy. "Christ, Ruby, I don't mind a little bit of passion here and there, but you know what? I draw the line at being attacked." Bewildered, he continued, "First Susan, and now you."

Attacked? "I didn't mean to do it," she protested. "I got a bit carried away, that's all."

"If I thought you were getting carried away by me, I wouldn't mind. But, Ruby, I didn't."

"What did you feel then?" Still she was defensive.

"I felt… as if you were *using* me."

Whatever she'd expected him to say, it wasn't that.

"Using you? Don't be so ridiculous!"

Wanting nothing but space between them now, she leapt off the bed, kicking furiously at the towel she'd discarded earlier and reaching for her dressing gown instead.

"I need a drink," she said, heading for the kitchen.

A few moments later, Cash was beside her, his jeans back on, but his chest still bare.

"Ruby," he said, his voice much softer now. "I didn't mean to upset you."

Pouring from a bottle of wine into a mug – she couldn't be bothered to look for a glass – she started to neck its contents.

"Ruby," he said again, but she carried on drinking, ignoring him, savouring the alcohol instead. Wanting it to affect her, to blur things – the memory of what had just happened.

"RUBY!"

His raised voice made her jump. He'd never shouted at her before.

"What?" she said, placing her mug back down on the

counter before turning to face him. Tears started to fall. She'd never felt so humiliated, so... rejected.

"You don't want me..." she started to say, but couldn't continue.

Immediately his arms went round her.

"Of course I want you. I've never wanted anyone as much as I want you. I love you. I have done since I first met you in the pub back in December. Why'd you think I pushed to help out on Highdown Hall? I wanted to be with you. What you do is fascinating, I'll admit, but it's *you* that fascinates me first and foremost, and you always will."

Ruby blinked hard. "Why, then? Why did you stop?"

He pulled away slightly. "Because you were hurting me, Ruby. It's not like you to hurt anyone."

His words shamed her.

"Let me see," she said.

Cash looked unsure. "It's probably nothing."

"Let me see," she repeated.

"Honestly, it's fine."

"Now!"

Sighing slightly, he turned.

It was *not* fine. The track marks she'd made on his body – two clusters of four – were either bleeding, or raised and angry looking. She could hardly believe her eyes. Had to blink again, twice. He was right: there was a difference between passion and an attack, and she'd just crossed the line.

"I'm so sorry," she whispered.

He'd turned back round again and was holding her. Her tears became sobs, burst out of her – the wave she'd ridden earlier crashing, but in the most unexpected of ways.

Although he tried to soothe her, even started to make light of it, she could not be consoled. What she'd done was wrong, twisted even.

"It's been a strange week," he said, releasing her again. "Susan, Danny…"

"The baby, today," Ruby added, wiping at her eyes.

"The baby?"

"Yeah, I haven't told you about it yet."

"Pour me some wine too, and let's go back to bed. You can tell me about it there."

* * *

The night had been resurrected. After telling him all about the case she and Theo had dealt with earlier that day, detailing how frustrated she felt sometimes at not being able to find out the whole story behind why a spirit was grounded, he'd taken her glass from her, laid her back and made love to her – keeping the tempo slow and gentle, deliberately so, as an antidote to what had happened before. Desire still consumed her – there was no denying it – but in a completely different way. It had a softer edge to it. If she'd had to describe it further, she would have said it was *healthier*.

The next morning, after a long lie in, Ruby mentioned to Cash she might just spend half an hour checking her emails to see what work had come in overnight.

"Oh no you don't. The spirit world is just going to have to do without you for a day or two. I'm going to phone Presley. You phone Corinna. Let's go somewhere – the four of us. Have some fun."

Although she hesitated, it was only briefly. She could do

with spending her day like every other twenty-five year old in the land – in 'live' company, as opposed to dead. And she was damned sure Cash could do with some normalcy as well.

"What have you got in mind?" she said, lying back down again.

"Lunch somewhere. The beach? It's another hot day, after all. We could go for a swim."

"I hate swimming." She made a face as she said it.

"Do you?" He was clearly surprised. "Well, I love it. And I guarantee, you'll love what we can get up to under water."

"Wow, you're the one who's full of surprises now."

Looking down between his legs, Cash grinned. "The biggest surprise – to me at least – is that this needs attention again. We're not going anywhere for a bit."

Ruby burst out laughing as he lay back down beside her.

Chapter Nine

RUBY had to laugh. Corinna was *very* keen to meet up –
so much so she was practically hyperventilating on the
phone.

"And Presley's coming too? You're sure?"

Ruby looked over to where Cash was on the phone also,
but to his brother.

Is he coming? she mouthed.

Cash gave her the thumbs up.

"Yep, he most definitely is."

The scream Corinna emitted practically deafened her.

After confirming when and where to meet, Ruby ended
the call. To Cash, she said, "I'd say Corinna's up for it!"
Worrying slightly, she asked, "But how keen is Presley?"

"Keen enough."

What that meant was anyone's guess, but Ruby didn't
press the matter.

"How's Danny? Did he say?"

"He's come round fully – he's calm and he's coherent
apparently," Cash replied, nodding his head for emphasis
as he said it. "His parents are still standing guard over
him."

"Didn't Presley say his parents live in Exeter?"

"That's right."

"They'll insist he goes back home with them, I should

think."

"Danny's thirty. He's a grown man. They can't insist on anything."

"But it'd be for the best, though. Don't you think?"

"Yeah, but what I want to know is why *you* think so."

Ruby exhaled heavily. "That… that thing I saw. The flat feels sullied by it."

"And you still don't remember what it is you saw? It's still vague?"

"It's still vague," answered Ruby.

"It wasn't a spirit?"

"No, I wouldn't say so."

"But a thought form – it could be that?"

Like yesterday, irritation was quick to rise in her.

"Look, can we please stop talking about it? Like you said, today we forget about the paranormal and concentrate on having fun. Or have you forgotten already?"

"No, I haven't forgotten." His tone was also waspish. Brightening, whether naturally or forcibly she couldn't tell, he clapped his hands together and said, "That skimpy bikini you bought last week – the red one – are you are going to wear it today?"

Ruby felt herself brighten too. "So what if I am?"

The smile on Cash's face was genuine now. "Because if you are, I'm going to have to keep you close. Especially under water, if you know what I mean?"

She did – exactly.

* * *

Cash and Ruby arranged to meet Corinna and Presley just after one, at Blue: a Brighton restaurant situated right on the beach. The place was crowded but, after waiting patiently, Ruby managed to bag a table – the debris from the last customers hastily cleared by a harassed-looking waiter as they sat down.

Set between the city's two piers, their view was spectacular – if the bare bones of a ruined pier could be considered spectacular. Which Ruby decided they could. The West Pier had been hit by fire and several storms since its birth in 1866. Now, only an outline of the once-grand concert hall remained, its shape supported on spider-like legs of iron. Because the council had chosen to leave the structure, rather than remove it completely – for reasons unknown to Ruby and half of Brighton, she suspected – it had become something of an iconic city scene. Perhaps even its most famous. It was beautiful; hauntingly so – home to swarms of starlings in the autumn. In contrast, the Palace Pier – a mile distant from the West Pier – boasted amusements galore, fun rides and fortune-tellers. Cash had suggested a visit there after lunch, to go on the ghost train – at which Ruby had shot him a look.

"You're a cheeky bastard," she said, elbowing him in the ribs.

"What? You don't like the ghost train?"

"Oh, it doesn't faze me. You'll be the one who ends up screaming, I guarantee."

"Rubbish," he retorted. "I've got you to protect me. What's there to be scared of?"

Corinna joined them.

"What a beautiful day," she enthused, taking a seat opposite them. Leaning forward, she whispered to Ruby, "Thanks for inviting me, little Miss Matchmaker."

Ruby laughed. "It was Cash's idea."

Corinna looked even more pleased. "Mr and Mrs Matchmaker. I like it."

Presley turned up a few minutes after Corinna, completing the foursome.

Also taking a seat, he said, "I do love a set-up," before turning to Corinna and winking.

In response, Corinna blushed, and Ruby was pretty sure she was doing the same. Cash, in turn, chuckled.

As they were by the seaside, everyone decided on fish and chips – everyone but Corinna. She didn't eat meat and, as she informed the others, she was trying to give up fish too. Perusing the menu, she decided on grilled halloumi with a side salad.

"Halloumi," Presley said. "So you're not vegan then?"

"Oh no, no," Corinna replied. "I just don't eat meat or fish, that's all."

"Anything with a face, you mean?"

"Well, yeah, I suppose so."

Presley sighed. "Tricky," he muttered.

Corinna looked stricken. "It really isn't," she rushed to explain. "I don't impose my views on others, honestly I don't. People can eat what they like as far as I'm concerned."

"I mean, when I invite you round for dinner. Everything I know how to cook revolves around meat and fish. Still, I like a challenge," he added, raising an eyebrow suggestively.

Interrupting Presley's teasing of Corinna, Ruby took drink orders and went to the bar. By the time she came back, all three were chatting – the 'set-up' working beautifully. Unlike the last time all four had met, Presley seemed relaxed, happy even, and she was glad – the jovial atmosphere rubbing off on her. The waitress came to take food orders and the light-heartedness continued. Presley had the same smile as Cash; a few of his mannerisms too – the way his head tilted to the left side when he was listening to what someone was saying, for instance. But Cash was Cash. He was unique – to Ruby at least. And she was grateful for him. Especially considering what had happened yesterday – how she'd hurt him. Something she still felt shamed by – not to mention confused. He, however, appeared to have forgotten all about it in that way that men did. They don't brood; they moved on, lived in the moment. And really, what had happened, it was probably best forgotten about anyway.

When the food came, Cash dived in, declaring he was 'starving'. Ruby rolled her eyes. He was *always* starving. Presley matched him in appetite, and Corinna was polishing off hers at a rapid rate too. Ruby's appetite was still not what it was; she ate most of the fish but less than a handful of chips. It was an improvement on no appetite at all, though, which had been the case lately.

Presley and Cash insisted on paying the bill. Corinna protested slightly but was told by Presley she could pay next time – a prospect that clearly delighted her.

They literally had to push their way through the marauding crowds to reach the pier, but Ruby didn't mind. The atmosphere was good-natured enough – everyone pleased that the sun was shining. The winter that had just passed had been a long one.

Cash took her hand as they walked. Corinna and Presley were slightly ahead.

"I thought we were going swimming," Ruby whispered to Cash.

"We are – after the ghost train."

"You and that bloody ghost train!"

"I love it," he said, his enthusiasm endearingly child-like.

The ghost train wasn't the only ride they went on, but it was the most fun. All four of them crammed into one car, Presley and Corinna in the front, she and Cash in the back. Corinna screamed all the way through. Not because she was scared – Ruby knew that. It was a feminine ploy to get Presley to comfort her, which he did, his arm around her, pulling her close. *Their first physical contact*, thought Ruby. *Clever Cash*. Cash had put his arm around her too, a grin on his face all the while. He knew damned well how clever he was.

Cash and Presley also managed to stuff down a stick of candy floss each – eaten as they exited the Pier.

As Ruby looked askance at him, Cash simply shrugged. "When in Rome," he said.

"Not sure they had candy floss in ancient Rome, Cash," Presley pointed out.

"They had to ply the punters at the Coliseum with something."

"Yeah, but it was probably wild boar heads on sticks, as opposed to this."

"Boar heads, boar eyes," Cash mused. "Or perhaps even boar testi—"

Before he could finish, Corinna dreamily declared she'd love to go to Rome.

Presley put his arm around her. "Me too. What you doing next weekend?"

"Going to Rome by the sounds of it," she replied, smiling up at him.

Down by the sea it was also crowded – locals and tourists vying for space. Nonetheless, the group managed to secure themselves a space, Ruby taking the towel out of the bag she'd brought with her and laying it on the pebbles before sitting down. She'd thought to put her bikini on before leaving her flat, and Corinna had done the same. As her friend climbed out of her skirt and tee shirt, Ruby saw she had on an emerald two-piece.

"Corinna, your bikini – it's not black!" She'd never seen her in anything so bright.

"I know. Do you think it's okay?"

"Okay? It's gorgeous. That colour's fantastic against your skin."

Clearly, the boys thought so too. Presley's eyes were on stalks and even Cash looked impressed. Jealousy flared up inside Ruby, taking her completely by surprise. She was *not* a jealous person. Quickly she extinguished it, refusing to be at the mercy of such a dire emotion. Even so, she suddenly felt shy about disrobing. Corinna had a curvaceous figure; her own was boyish. But so what? Such things never bothered her… normally.

Fed up with her thoughts, she slipped off her clothes. Cash and Presley did the same. Before heading onto the actual beach, both the boys had nipped into the toilets to change into swim shorts. As Cash turned towards the sea, Presley noticed his back.

"Bloody hell, bro," he said. "What happened to you?"

For a moment, Cash looked confused, but quickly he realised what Presley meant. Ruby froze. How was he going to answer?

Cash was obviously wondering too. "Erm… gardening," he said, after a few tense moments.

125

"Gardening?" Presley asked. "Where?"

"At Mum's. I was cutting down brambles, with my shirt off, stupidly."

Presley's eyes flickered for just the briefest of moments towards Ruby. There was no accusation in them, but it was obvious he was questioning Cash's explanation. She felt ashamed all over again. What had she been thinking? Raking his back like that? The good mood she'd been in all day dissolved, but she plastered on a smile. The last thing she wanted was to spoil things – for Corinna especially. That would be so unfair.

"Wear a shirt next time," Presley advised, before pointing out that all four couldn't go swimming at the same time; someone had to stay behind to look after clothes and bags. "Shall we do the honours, Corinna?"

Corinna agreed without hesitation. "Definitely." To Ruby and Cash, she said, "You guys go ahead. Have fun!" *Don't hurry back,* the clear intimation.

As Ruby had told Cash, she was not a fan of swimming – never had been, and never would be. She was a terra firma kind of girl, but Cash had taken her by the hand and was pulling her forwards towards the less-than-blue sea. It was more green in colour; not a beautiful shade, but murky, like a swamp. Not welcoming at all. On the contrary, it was distinctly *unwelcoming.*

She started to hesitate. "Cash… I…"

"Come on," he cajoled, clearly determined. "I'll look after you."

Again, she had that sense she'd spoil everyone's fun if she didn't comply. She should lighten up. Go with the flow.

The day might have been hot, but the sea was cold,

bitter even, causing her breath to catch. Not that it deterred those around her. People were swimming, splashing and shouting at each other; so much so, the noise was deafening, making her head ache. Someone splashed her – cold droplets like sharp pin pricks against her skin – and she felt a flash of rage. Felt like shouting too, like cursing, screaming and lashing out.

Ruby! This is supposed to be fun!

But she couldn't deny it – she'd had more fun at the dentist.

Cash had briefly left her at the shore's edge and swum several strokes, but now he'd returned.

"The water's lovely," he called.

"It's not. It's horrid. I'm going back."

Rising out of the water, he grabbed hold of her wrists. "Come out a bit further."

"Don't," she said, being pulled forwards.

The water wasn't just cold; it had a slimy quality to it, as though it were filthy. It *was* filthy. Why hadn't he noticed? Why hadn't anyone noticed? Mothers, fathers, children, and teenagers – how could they possibly want to splash about in this… cesspit?

"Let me go," she pleaded, but he wasn't listening to her – he was too caught up in the moment. Worse than that – he was laughing.

"Cash, I'm not joking."

"Oh, babe, come on."

Babe? His use of the word infuriated her more. She wasn't anyone's *babe*.

"Cash!"

As she yelled his name, the ground beneath her shifted and gave way. She plunged downwards, into the sea, her whole body immersed; her head too. Salt water rushed into her mouth and the taste was acrid. She started coughing, gagging – a reflex action – but it only made things worse. She took in even more water. It was filling her lungs, drowning her. Where was Cash? Where the bloody hell was he? And how could she be falling so deep? She'd only walked out a few feet, but she was definitely sinking – as though she were an anchor, able to penetrate the sands below.

Cash! Please!

Despite her eyes stinging so badly, she forced them open; saw what she thought was a patch of sunlight. Relief cutting through the horror, she started swimming towards it. She'd break the surface soon. And when she did, she'd get away from here – far, far away. Just as she was making headway, hands grabbed at her ankles and started pulling her down again. *Cash, what the fuck…?* Surely he hadn't meant this when he'd talked about their underwater antics – that he wanted to kill her? Hands reached up further. They were large hands; cold, much colder than the water. And their grip: it was like being caught in a vice – impossible to shake off. It had to be Cash. Who else could it be? He was trying to drown her! But why? Why? Why? Why? With all the strength she could muster, she continued thrashing – with her arms, at least – screaming, unable to stop. Swallowing more and more water; choking on it. Her mind became dark around the edges… hazy. It seemed ludicrous you could die surrounded by so many people; that not one person amongst so many would notice, that they wouldn't respond. But no one did. Above her, where the light seemed to hover, so near and yet so far, everyone continued having fun – oblivious to her plight and confusion, her sheer desperation. She was going to be killed. Her *boyfriend* was going to kill her. And still, laughter rang out. Incessant laughter. *Mocking* laughter. The crowds weren't oblivious at all; they were *glad* she was suffering so much. Cash was playing to the gallery, delighting them with his vile antics – a gladiator at the Coliseum mentioned earlier, and she the sport. He'd duped her. He'd lured her in. Whispered words of love he hadn't meant. Hatred... she was burning with it.

"Ruby! Ruby! Calm down! What are you doing?"

She was above water again, but how, she didn't know. As water spluttered from her mouth, she shielded her eyes from the sunlight.

"Ruby, stop panicking! I've got you! You lost your footing, that's all."

Lost her footing? What was he talking about? She hadn't *just* lost her footing.

"You... bastard!" She forced the words from her mouth.

"What?"

"You fucking bastard! Why did you do that?"

Cash looked shocked. Those around her who heard did too. Immediately, they stopped what they were doing to stand and stare.

Not giving a damn about them, Ruby screamed again. "How fucking could you?"

Tears burst from her eyes – hot tears that seemed to scald her cheeks.

"Ruby, I don't know what you're talking about—"

"You tried to kill me!"

"You fell. I reached down to help you up, that's all."

"Oi, mate, what's going on?" A large man with tattoos came up behind them.

Cash turned towards him. "Nothing. She's my girlfriend. It's a misunderstanding."

"I've misunderstood nothing." Almost falling again as she span round, Ruby waded out of the hateful water, back towards the shore and safety. "And I'm not your girlfriend, not anymore."

Cash hurried after her. "Ruby," he hissed. "We need to get away from here."

"Why? So you can try and kill me again?"

"I did *not* try and kill you! How can you even think that?'

On the shore, Presley and Corinna were waiting. They'd heard the commotion and both looked concerned. The tattooed man was still following, but Cash turned round to glare at him and he backed off; not so chivalrous after all. Beside Corinna stood Jed. Would he bark at Cash? Would he bare his teeth again? If he did, that would confirm she was right – Cash was the enemy.

Corinna stepped forward. "What was all that about?"

"Why don't you ask *him*?" Ruby sneered, motioning towards Cash.

Jed, meanwhile, was not baring his teeth or barking at all. He was still staring out to sea – his head tilted to one side.

Presley spoke next. "Are you okay, Cash?"

His misplaced concern sent Ruby over the edge. "You're asking *him* if he's okay? What about me? He pulled me under the water, Presley. He tried to drown me! I was under for ages. Why didn't you come and help me? Why didn't *anyone* come and help?"

Presley looked as confused as Cash, as Corinna even.

Laying her hand tentatively on Ruby's arm, she said,

"You weren't down there for ages. You were down for a couple of seconds or so. You slipped, that's all, and Cash helped you up."

"I was down there for a lot longer than that!"

"No, Ruby." Corinna's voice was calm, reminding her of Theo. "You weren't."

Ruby was too stunned to speak. Were they in cahoots, the three of them? Plotting together, planning her demise. They had to be! Didn't they? Confusion – always so close by nowadays – enveloped her, just as the water had done, and she staggered slightly.

"Cash… Cash. Where are you?"

"I'm here, babe. I'm here." The term of endearment – instead of infuriating her as it had done earlier – comforted her. He was here, despite the fact she'd accused him so outrageously.

She reached out blindly for him. As she did, his arms came around her, held her close once again. Burying her face in his chest, she wanted to blot out the circle of people that were still staring – the looks of concern, the pointing, the whispering, and the laughing.

'Keep it to yourself for now, Ruby. Your ability to see those who've passed, it… well, it unsettles people.' The words Gran had said to her when she was a child came back to her as she hid. Another memory too – *Spooky Ruby*. That's what she'd been called when she dared to tell someone at last: her best friend, Lisa, who thought it was hilarious, who thought she was lying. Lisa wasn't her best friend for long after that, and Ruby managed to turn the tables on her, at least. Whenever another child had asked her about her ability, Ruby had denied it, calling Lisa the weird one for dreaming up such a thing. She'd tried so hard to live a

normal life, despite her ability. She'd tried to fit in. Now she'd shown herself up, in front of everyone – her friends, her boyfriend, the whole damned world. Lisa was right – she *was* Spooky Ruby. She'd spooked everyone. But, most of all, she'd spooked herself.

"Cash, I don't know what's happening to me."

"Me neither," Cash whispered back, "but we'll find out, don't worry. We'll find out."

Chapter Ten

"YOU are *not* possessed, Ruby." Theo grimaced as she mentioned the 'p' word. "Believe me, darling, we're not dealing with a re-enactment from *The Exorcist* here."

"But it *feels* like I'm possessed," Ruby retaliated. "The way I'm acting – it's not me. I don't even recognise myself right now. Anger, irritation, jealousy. I mean, I'm no saint – of course I feel those things – but it's *all* the time at the moment. And something else – in the water, there were hands on my legs, pulling me down, dragging me. The water itself – it seemed so much deeper than it was. It was dirty, too, and yet Cash assures me it wasn't. But I didn't imagine it. It was real." To Cash, she said, "Tell them what I told you."

Cash obliged, going into further detail. Corinna, who was sitting quietly, already knew.

"And in the bedroom, Cash. Tell them what I did to you there."

"Really?" His reluctance was plain.

"It's important. Tell them everything, from the minute you stepped through the door."

The others were also bemused by her insistence.

As he continued talking, she was grateful his voice was low and calm – he was downplaying events, if anything. She also appreciated how swiftly he'd removed her from the beach; being stared at by all and sundry was not something she'd enjoyed. Back on the promenade, Cash had immediately phoned Theo and Ness, insisting they make their way to Ruby's flat as soon as possible. She and Cash had caught the train into Brighton from Lewes because parking in the city was a nightmare, but there was no way she could deal with public transport on the way back. Instead, Cash had summoned a cab from the road running parallel to the beach, and paid for them all to get home. Corinna had accompanied them, but to Presley, Cash had said he'd call him later; let him know how she was getting on. In the cab, she'd sat between Cash and Corinna – Cash holding one of her hands, Corinna the other. Unbeknown to the taxi driver, Jed had ridden up front, looking back at her every now and again as if making sure she was still there. The taxi driver had kept glancing at her in his wing mirror too, but little wonder. She hadn't stopped crying all the way home – the words *Spooky Ruby* going round and round in her head like a renewed taunt. As much as she wanted to be normal, she had to accept she wasn't. She only hoped the lunacy that had affected her lately wouldn't put Cash off for good. She had to get help. She *was* getting help – from the best.

After Cash had finished speaking, there was silence.

"See? I'm possessed," Ruby said after a while. She'd also told them about what had happened in Sussex Stationers – finally. The book being knocked out of her hand. The voice that said it could see her, that knew her by name.

They listened carefully, but still denied possession.

"Theo's right. You're not possessed," said Ness. "You are still very much you. I think what's happened is something has attached itself to you."

"Attached?" Ruby repeated the word. "But how? I always protect myself before a psychic cleansing. Always."

"And usually that's sufficient," Ness replied. "But sometimes, and this is rare, it isn't."

Ruby looked at Cash for reassurance, but he was just as grave as Ness. "Okay, so the attachment, what is it?" she asked.

"Negative energy. A spirit, an entity, or, as mentioned before… a thought form."

"A thought form," Ruby repeated before realisation hit her. "Aiwass?"

"If it is, it's your interpretation, Ruby. Not entirely what Crowley saw, or Danny either. Each person is unique; they'd put their own spin on it."

"Danny?" queried Cash. "This is happening because of Danny?"

"Yes… no… in a way," Ruby began, but Cash wasn't listening to her.

"What made him go berserk – it's now attached to you?"

Ruby chewed at the inside of her mouth. "It's the only thing that makes sense. All this has been happening since I went to see Danny."

Cash looked stricken. "This is my fault, then. I'm the one who got you involved."

"No, Cash, it's not your fault…" Ruby insisted, but Theo interrupted.

"Please let's not waste time trying to assign fault – it's a wearing pastime at best. All we need to know is, it's happened; shit tends to at times. Our task now is to address it."

"How?" Ruby asked, baffled.

"A psychic cleansing, of course," Theo replied. "We

need to cleanse you."

* * *

Before they got started, Ness explained more about psychic attacks.

"Dark energies or entities that find their way into physical bodies are often sent without awareness, even though they're sent by humans. Others are sent intentionally to create harm and damage – their purpose to control and manipulate, or even punish, the individual. If you seriously think the same thing that affected Danny is now affecting you, we can safely assume it's the former; it's been sent to you unintentionally."

"Danny was into Crowley – that book he had, those drawings he did," Corinna pointed out. "Clearly he was fascinated by thought forms, demons, and the like."

"He may well have been into Crowley, but that doesn't make him a bad person – just an interested one," Ness replied. To Ruby, she said, "What was your impression of Danny?"

"Erm, I've met him a couple of times. He's nice. A bit of a livewire. But apart from that, okay. Cash, what about you? You know him better."

"He's a good bloke. He's Presley's best friend, and, yes, he's a bit wild at times. And lately, drink's been a problem, but that doesn't make him bad either."

"Nobody's saying that," said Theo. "Despite having died in the 1940s, Crowley still has many devoted disciples, and a lot of them genuinely believe him to be an enlightened soul. And perhaps he is – it's all a matter of opinion. Personally, however, and as you all know, I'm not a fan. The man was prone to exaggeration, *dangerous* exaggeration. The thing is, if you don't fully understand what you're getting involved with – if you don't have direction or another perspective to balance things out – it's easy to run into trouble. Which Danny clearly did. Trouble exacerbated by the use of mind-altering substances." She paused for a moment. "Trouble that's rubbed off on us."

"On me," Ruby corrected. "It's only rubbed off on me. You needn't get involved."

"Dear girl," Theo said, a gentle smile on her face, "you're not just our colleague, you're our friend, and we're going to help you. On that subject, you'll find us immoveable."

Despite the warmth of Theo's words, Ruby still felt cold inside.

Ness resumed explaining. "Psychic attacks can be debilitating to say the least – severely affecting body and mind. I've dealt with one or two cases in my time, and, Theo, I know you have too. The thing is, even if a cleansing is successful, it can still take a long time for the person affected to recover. Like any attack, I suppose, it can leave scars."

Immediately, Ruby thought of her mother and what she'd suffered. It was still such a mystery to her. Another damned mystery.

Spurred on perhaps by the stricken look on Ruby's face, Ness quickly added, "Which is why it's imperative to deal with it sooner rather than later – perform damage limitation, if you like. Ruby, you're used to dealing with the psychic world. You understand the gravitas of the situation; the necessity of banishing such a destructive energy. But more importantly, *most* importantly, you understand that light is the greatest force of all."

Again, Ruby thought of her mother, of words she'd exchanged with Jessica the previous December – a rare moment of interaction between them.

Ruby, she'd said, *there is more between heaven and earth than you can possibly know.*

More good things, Ruby had replied. She'd been so sure of it.

"Ruby," Ness interrupted her reverie. "Are you ready? If so, we should begin."

"Yes, yes, I'm ready."

Ness looked at Theo. Ruby caught their exchange. There was worry in it – definitely.

"Your tourmaline necklace," Ness said. "Where is it?"

"I took it off before I went to the beach. It's in the bedroom."

To Cash, Ness said, "Can you please go and get it?"

Cash hurried off, returning only a couple of minutes later and handing it to Ruby.

"Corinna," Ness continued, "could you dig out the smudge sticks from Ruby's bag and start cleansing corners. Cash, perhaps you could help her to do that."

As the sage began to burn, Ruby inhaled deeply. Many times she'd used this herb when cleansing houses for clients, but never had she used it in her own flat. She'd had no need to... until now.

"Cash, hand me one of the smudge sticks too," Theo said.

Meanwhile, Ness had taken a dining chair and placed it in the middle of the room. She motioned for Ruby to sit down on it. "Ruby, you're a good person. The dark cannot find a home within you."

The way she said it – her certainty – was encouraging.

The smudge stick in her hand, Theo passed the smoke around her head a number of times. When moving a spirit on, it was normal practice to leave a window or a door open, representing to them a physical exit. On this occasion, however, Ness had instructed that all windows and doors remain shut – her aim to dissolve the negative energy that had built up around Ruby. Smudging alone, however, was not enough to deal with the problem. Ness also took several obsidian stones from Ruby's bag and placed them round the room.

"That should keep negative influences at bay," Ness said. "Just remember to rinse the stones every morning with water, to wash away any nastiness absorbed."

"The other important thing to do, Ruby," Theo added, "is to stay in the present. At present all is well. *You* are well."

"And be positive," Ness continued. "Replace any negative thoughts or feelings with something positive; keep on doing that until you *feel* positive too. Anything that worries you, discuss it with me, with Theo, with Cash and Corinna – talking about it will help to dispel it."

"What about Ruby's chakras? Do they need restoring?" Theo asked Ness.

She nodded. "To be on the safe side."

Restoring people's chakras – centres of vital energy located at strategic points throughout the body – was part of Ness's repertoire. Blocked chakras could lead to illness and therefore ill-being. It was important to keep energy flowing freely, to close any holes that appeared – especially in someone under attack. The Crown Chakra – located at the very top of the head – represented a person's ability to be fully connected spiritually. It was this one Ness seemed to concentrate on – this and the Solar Plexus Chakra, which represented the ability to be confident and in-control of our lives.

"How severe is it?" Ruby's voice was barely above a whisper.

"Not too bad," Ness replied, her eyes closed as she concentrated. But whether she was saying that just to appease her, Ruby didn't know. The words *not too bad* offering a kind of placebo effect – intended to make you think the opposite of what was true.

As the two older women worked on her, Corinna and Cash, who had both finished smudging, stood side by side in the far corner of the room, their faces solemn.

For a brief moment, Ruby wondered if either of them had expected dramatics from her: for her body to go into spasm, her head to jerk back, and vomit to spew from her mouth. She realised a part of her had expected the same. Instead, the process was peaceful, levelling.

Ness and Theo also surrounded her in white light of the most intense kind. She could feel the heat of it, finally warming her.

When both women were satisfied the process was complete, Theo asked Ruby how she felt.

"Better."

"Honestly?" Ness probed.

"Honestly," Ruby insisted.

Rising from the chair, Ruby stretched her arms wide. "I'm tired, actually, but in a good way. It's different to the tiredness I've been feeling lately."

Ness looked satisfied. "A friend of mine makes an energy spray from black tourmaline. I'll get you some. Again, it will help to repel any negative influences surrounding you."

"Thanks, Ness," Ruby said. "But what next? What about Danny?"

"Cash tells me Danny's being cared for by his parents," Theo said. "If he needs our help, obviously we're here for him. But if not, we won't involve ourselves anymore."

Ness agreed. "We'll basically cross that bridge if and when we come to it. Right now, you don't need to be worrying about Danny or anyone. Just relax for what's left of the day."

Cash stepped forward. "She won't be alone. I'll stay with her."

"Good lad," Theo said, smiling at him.

As they waved goodbye to their friends, Cash put his arm around her. Leaning into him, she relished their closeness.

"Are you really feeling better?" he asked.

"Yeah, I am, especially now you're with me."

Closing the door, she turned to face him, intent once again on apologising for her behaviour at the beach. Before she could say another word, he kissed her.

When they parted, Cash mentioned bed – the suggestion like music to her ears.

Discarding her clothes, Ruby climbed in, pulling the duvet right up to her chin, despite the warmth of the night. Cash did the same, spooning his body against hers. In front of her, Jed materialised – the pair of them, she thought, like soldiers on guard.

Despite the fact it wasn't particularly late, she felt drowsy. It wouldn't be long before sleep encroached.

"You're not scared of me, are you?" she asked Cash,

exhaustion causing her voice to slur.

"I'm not scared," he answered. "But I warn you, if your head starts spinning, I'm gone."

She laughed – all the way into oblivion.

Chapter Eleven

INITIALLY, sleep had been deep and dreamless. Now, Ruby had resurfaced, but not fully. Her mind kept going off on tangents, meandering down hazy lanes, zipping off here, shooting off there – random, yet determined. Although her arm felt heavy, she reached out. Cash was still there – of course he was – and Jed too. She relaxed. She'd drift off again soon, surely? Her mind and body needed rest.

Deciding not to fight her thoughts, too *tired* to fight them, she followed them instead, hoping they'd eventually end in silence. One thought in particular held her captive – centring around her childhood, again. Would it be pleasant this time or lead to another nightmare? There was no reason it should. Aside from her mother's breakdown, her childhood *had* been pleasant; Gran had made sure of it. They were close at least – very close. There was no need for her subconscious to take ordinary events – her mother bringing a friend home for dinner, for example – and subvert them.

In this curious half-dream, she was at home again, in Hastings, the curtains drawn against a cold and wintry night. She was sitting by the fire, aged six, or seven – the age her dream-self tended to favour lately. In her hands was a book, a ghost story, the ghost isn't human, though, it's an animal.

She felt like she was spying on this scene, as if she was standing behind a gossamer screen, looking on. That book in her hands, had she actually read it during childhood? Possibly. She'd loved reading then as much as she did now – weekend trips to the library with Gran always such a treat.

The book is about a shuck. The pictures in the book make it clear what a shuck is: a dog, big, black and hairy. Some people in the story – *most* people – think it's a demon, but there was one who didn't, a little boy. He regarded the shuck as his friend. The little boy – Tom – is nice. The young Ruby liked him. She liked the fact that he could see stuff, just like she could see stuff. She didn't like his father, though. He told Tom the shuck was an omen of death, something evil, that if you saw it, trouble followed. But Tom had seen it, several times, and so far, trouble had kept away.

"What's a demon?" Ruby addressed the question to her grandmother, who was also sitting in front of the fire, knitting; a hobby she'd only recently taken up.

Gran looked up. "A demon, my dear, is a human imagining – nothing more."

"An imagining?"

"That's right. People imagine all sorts of things to frighten themselves. I've told you before – people like being scared. It excites them. But demons aren't real. They don't exist."

Ruby returned her attention to the book. In one illustration the dog is baring his teeth and his ears are alert, as if he's about to pounce. His eyes are black and yellow surrounds them.

She pointed to the illustration. "He looks scary. I thought he was a good dog, but he doesn't look good in this picture."

Placing her knitting on the table, Gran asked to see the picture. "He does look scary, I'll admit."

"But Tom likes him. How can he like something bad?"

"People just do sometimes." There was such sadness in her voice – both the Ruby observing and the young Ruby thought that. "But Tom could still be right. Read me the rest of the story, and let's see."

Delighted to show off her reading skills, Ruby did as Gran asked, stumbling over a few of the longer words only. Tom had gone wandering one dark and stormy night, down to the beach. He hadn't seen the dog for a few days and was worried about him, that he might be lonely. But the beach was treacherous in such weather, the tide racing in, and slamming against the rocks, the wind whipping the foam into peaks. Despite this, Tom walked on, his head bowed against the elements and his shoulders hunched. By the time he realised he'd walked too far, it was too late. The rocks and the sea had conspired to form a barrier that held him captive, barring his route back.

As the waves grew higher and higher Tom began to quake with fear.

"Dad!" he cried, but no one could hear him – no one except the dog.

On the landing of Tom's house, the black shuck barked and barked, finally managing to rouse the boy's father from sleep. Spying what was before him, fear clutched at the man's heart. In his eyes, the shuck was hideous: a snarling, growling hellhound.

"Get away, get away," he shouted, overcome with terror.

145

But the dog persisted.

Tom's mother woke too. "Perhaps he's trying to tell us something," she whispered, trying to be brave, but stricken too.

"Tell us what? That death is coming?"

"Death?" the mother replied in horror. "Where's Tom? Is he in his bed?"

Without waiting for an answer, she shot from her room and into Tom's bedroom. Seeing it was empty, she let out a piercing scream. Immediately, Tom's father was by her side.

Instantly he blamed the dog. "He's taken Tom!" Turning to glare at the dog, he bellowed, "What have you done with him? Where is he?"

The dog turned, and Tom's father followed, stopping only to grab at the fire poker, wielding it above his head in a threatening manner. Keeping a wary distance, the shuck led him all the way to the beach, to where Tom was hunkered down, his arms wrapped tight around his body in a desperate attempt to shield himself against the ferocity of the night. Hearing his son's cries, Tom's father dropped the poker and threw himself into the surf. Losing his footing once or twice, thankfully he managed to regain it. Reaching Tom at last, he clasped the boy to him before hoisting him upwards and struggling back to safety.

On the shore, the dog waited. No longer barking at them, he was silent and watchful.

Tom's father placed Tom on the sand and warned him not to move. Returning to where he'd left the poker, he picked it up and ran at the dog.

"Get away. Don't ever come back, do you hear? Ever!"

Initially the dog stood its ground, but then it lowered its

head and started to retreat.

"Dad," cried Tom, "don't tell him to go. He led you to me. He saved me!"

"Stay back!" his father commanded his young son. "You don't know what you're dealing with here. I do. We need to destroy this... this demon."

After casting one last glance at Tom, the dog disappeared. He seemed so forlorn, as sad as Gran had been a few minutes before. As he faded from sight, the little boy cried, reached out for him, but it was no use. In that moment, Tom knew he'd never see it again, but even so, he called for it, in dreams, and whilst walking along the shore. Even in manhood, he did that, tracing the water's edge, whispering his thanks – the wind carrying his words to a place he couldn't follow.

The dog *had* saved him, and he'd never forget it.

The young Ruby was elated. "It *was* a good doggie!"

"It was," Gran said, smiling lovingly at her.

"But Tom's father didn't think so."

"No, he didn't, and sometimes there's nothing you can do to change a person's mind. Once it's made up, it's made up. We have to accept that about some people. It's called conditioning, Ruby. They can't see beyond what society has taught them. They've become indoctrinated, afraid to think for themselves, to question, to go against what's considered normal. But I've taught you differently. Despite what people have done, what they look like, search for the good in them. It might be hard to see at times, it might be deeply hidden, but it's there, at the core of them – always."

"Even in demons?"

"You'll never encounter demons. I've told you, they don't exist."

Sighing, Ruby closed the book. "I wish I had a dog like the one in the book, Gran."

"Someone to watch over you?"

"Someone to keep me safe."

Gran frowned. "Don't I keep you safe enough?"

Putting down the book, Ruby climbed onto her grandmother's lap – a favourite resting place. "Of course you do," she said, snuggling into her. It was a lovely moment, one to be treasured.

Don't I keep you safe enough?

Gran's words presented themselves again, not just once, but twice, a third time too. They bounced off the walls of the cottage, and grew louder and louder.

Don't I keep you safe enough?

What was going on? Why was this moment being spoilt?

Wake up, Ruby. Wake up.

I am awake!

Wasn't she?

The young Ruby's attention seemed to be on something else in the room, her eyes growing ever wider. In a dark corner, something darker stirred. Although her grandmother was oblivious, the child stiffened. Whatever it was, it was familiar.

This is a dream. This is definitely a dream.

It had to be. This hadn't happened. This had *never* happened.

Beside her, Cash muttered something then turned over on to his other side.

No, don't do that, Cash. Come back!

Gran continued to rock her – such a gentle movement, a movement meant to soothe. The older woman seemed content. But why was she? Couldn't she see what moved

148

towards them? No. She was like Tom's father – she couldn't see or perhaps she *wouldn't* see. But Ruby had no choice – her vision was crystal clear. Whatever it was that approached them, it wasn't like the dog in the book they'd just been reading – something beautiful in ugly clothing. It was ugly all the way through. Terrified, the young Ruby, the Ruby that she'd once been, started to bounce up and down on her gran's lap, one finger jabbing furiously at the air, trying to get the older woman to take notice.

"Gran, you're wrong, there *are* demons. Look, please look, I can see it. Oh, Gran, it's coming. Please look, before it's too late. Before it gets us both."

But Gran stared blindly ahead, not keeping her – keeping *them* – safe at all.

Chapter Twelve

RUBY'S eyes snapped open, her breath coming in short, sharp gasps, her chest heaving with the effort. Turning her head, Cash was still asleep, and she was thankful. She didn't want him to witness yet more madness on her part. Jed, however, was sitting up.

There was a dog, she told him silently. *A good dog*.

And something else, something that wasn't so good.

Reaching her hand to check her necklace was still in place – it was – Ruby glanced at the time. It was after nine a.m. Twelve hours they'd been in bed; sleeping, dreaming, maybe not dreaming. Sitting up, she let her head fall into her hands, almost overwhelmed with despair. What Theo and Ness had done, the cleansing, it hadn't worked. Something was still attached to her – something indefinable, something bad.

Cash's phone rang.

He'd miss the call if she didn't answer it. She couldn't afford for that to happen – what if it was about Danny? Danny was the key. They needed to speak to him, get past his parents somehow. Find out exactly what he'd seen – Aiwass or a demon of his own devising. Knowing *exactly* what they were dealing with would help in some way – surely?

Throwing back the covers, she hurled herself out of bed,

almost slipping as she rushed forward. Cash's mobile was in his jeans' pocket. She grabbed at them and shook them furiously. The phone crashed to the floor – the carpet preventing the screen from smashing. Snatching it up, she pressed the receive button.

"Presley, is that you?"

"Ruby, yes, it's me." His voice was thick with emotion, barely even recognisable. "Is Cash with you?"

"Cash is asleep," replied Ruby, although, glancing over at him, she noticed he was beginning to stir, a bewildered look on his face as to the commotion occurring in the room.

"Are you on my phone, babe?" she heard him call from the bed.

"Presley, what is it?" Ruby asked, indicating for Cash to keep quiet.

"It's erm… I… shit… It's bad news. The worst…"

Ruby's hand started to shake, the phone banging against her ear.

"Danny…" It was all she could think to say.

"Danny's dead," Presley said at last, his voice cracking. "He'd gone home with his parents to Exeter. They found him last night, in his bedroom. He'd slit his wrists."

"Suicide?" Ruby breathed.

"Yes," Presley confirmed. "Danny's committed suicide."

* * *

As Ruby sat in the passenger seat of Cash's car, she was still shaking.

"I can't believe it," she kept saying, over and over again.

"Me neither." That had been Cash's stock reply too.

They were on their way to Presley's flat in the centre of Brighton to find out what they could. Cash had also rung Theo and Ness, who had received the news as gravely as they had.

Staring almost blindly out of the window as they drove, Ruby started talking again.

"Do you think it's because…"

"Ruby, this isn't the time to speculate. We need facts."

Cash was right. Cold, hard facts – nothing less would do.

Parking in the centre of town was nigh on impossible, so they bagged a spot in the Waitrose car park – they'd buy something from there on their return to make up for utilising customer space. Sillwood Road, where Presley lived, was just a short walk away. They climbed the stairs to the Victorian building. Once a grand house – complete with veranda – it was now divided into several living quarters. Locating Presley's bell, Cash pressed it.

A few moments later, Presley buzzed them in. Entering the communal hallway, they climbed three flights of stairs to his flat, where he was waiting for them on the landing. He seemed smaller somehow, nowhere near as tall – his eyes red and sore.

"Come in," he said, before turning.

A studio rather than a flat, it was neat and tidy, and the location was good – a short walk to numerous shops, bars, and restaurants. She knew from Cash he was in the process of looking for something larger – something with one or two bedrooms – but right now he seemed firmly entrenched. To the left of the TV were several guitars. Other than his motorbike, they were the tools of his trade.

Cash sat down on the sofa. "What happened?" he asked.

152

Presley pulled up a chair and sat down too, indicating for Ruby to do the same.

"I don't know much more than what I've told you to be honest," he said. "I knew they'd taken Danny back with them. I went to see him just before he left; he told me that was the plan."

"How was he when you saw him?" Ruby asked.

Presley started speaking, but his voice caught in his throat. Coughing slightly, he tried again. "He was okay. He said he thought it was a good idea he went to stay with his parents for a while. Said he couldn't face going back to the flat, and I agreed."

"Was he calm or was he agitated?" Cash looked at Ruby as she asked.

"Calm, I suppose," Presley replied. "Resigned even."

"What about his colour? Was it good?"

"Ruby…" Cash started, but Ruby ignored him.

"What I mean is, was his complexion grey?"

Presley frowned. "Yeah, I suppose, but then everyone looks grey in hospital, don't they?"

Not necessarily, thought Ruby.

"Did he… did he mention anything about what he'd seen at the flat?"

"All that demon stuff, you mean? No, he didn't. Look…" Presley seemed to go on the offensive. "I know he had a bit of an interest in the occult. That Crowley shit – I told him to leave it well alone. But he's always been a bit like that, has Danny – a bit mystical. It's just an interest, that's all, nothing more than that. The real demon he fought was alcohol. The last couple of years, he was just knocking it back." Presley hung his head then. "I should have realised it was more serious than it was. I should have made him get help sooner."

Cash leaned closer to him. "You were a good friend to Danny. Don't doubt that."

Presley disagreed. "Not good enough."

Silence hung between them.

"Was it one of his parents who told you what happened?"

"Yeah." His head still low, it was clear Presley was crying again. "It was his father. I rang this morning to see how he was. I was hopeful, you know, that the worst was over, that from here on in the only way was up. When his dad told me, I... I still can't take it in."

Ruby paused. Hope may have deserted Presley, but she was still hanging on to it – praying Danny's spirit had passed into the light where nothing could torment him further.

"Did he leave a note or anything?" she asked gently.

"He did," Presley replied.

"Do you have any idea what it said?"

Cash was looking at her again and Ruby knew why. He thought she was pushing Presley too hard, but she had to know. If things were serious before, they were more so now.

"Presley," she prompted, risking Cash's wrath.

"He apologised for what he was about to do, but he said it was the only way – he couldn't take it anymore. His dad was so confused. He asked me what he couldn't take, exactly. I don't think they had a clue about his interests." Presley's head came up. "When you were at the flat, those books of his, those drawings, what did you do with them?'

"We left them there," Cash replied.

"His parents must have been to the flat," Presley

154

continued, becoming agitated. "They must have seen them. They'll know, start asking questions."

"Presley." Cash's voice was firm. "Danny was troubled, more troubled than you, me or anyone realised. We don't know exactly what was troubling him, though, so let's not get carried away with this occult stuff. We've got to keep calm. Did they mention they'd seen anything?"

Presley shook his head. "No, they didn't."

"For some people," Cash continued, "that sort of stuff doesn't register. It's not even on their radar. If they didn't mention it, there's a good chance they didn't see it."

His choice of words struck Ruby particularly. *They didn't see it.* It was the theme of her 'dream' – seeing and not seeing. Once again, she reached up to touch her necklace.

The doorbell rang, startling them all. Even Cash, Ruby noticed. He was clearly more spooked than he was letting on.

"That'll be Jem and Daz," Presley explained. "The rest of his band mates."

As he buzzed them in, Ruby noted how bereft they looked. Part of their family – their gang of four – was gone.

Cash stood up next and said that he and Ruby would go. "But if you need me, call. It doesn't matter what time of day or night it is."

Presley assured him he would, and walked to the door with them. Fishing around in his pocket, he pulled out a key.

"I've still got the key to his flat. Do you think I should go back there and remove the stuff? You might be right about his parents. If they'd seen something, they would have mentioned it. I don't think it's right they know about his interests. It might... I don't know, taint his memory."

Tainted, thought Ruby, was not a strong enough word.

Cash took the key from him. "I don't know how quick off the mark Brighton police are, but, as this is a suicide case, they might have gone to Danny's flat already and cordoned it off. If not, I'll get in there, find anything incriminating and dispose of it."

"Are you sure?" Presley looked relieved.

"I'm sure," Cash replied. "I think in this case, ignorance really is bliss."

Enfolding Presley in a bear hug, the two brothers clung to each other for quite a while. Upon release, Presley hugged Ruby too.

"Take care, Presley," Ruby said. "We'll call you soon – later on today, perhaps."

"Take care, bro," echoed Cash, before returning to the street outside.

In daylight, Ruby felt brave. "What you said about the police and Danny's flat – you're right, we need to act quickly."

Cash shook his head. "You're not going back there, Ruby – only I am."

"On your own?"

"Yeah."

"No way, absolutely no way."

"Ruby." His voice was as firm as hers. "You are not setting foot in Danny's flat again."

Anger rose in her. "For God's sake, Cash. What I saw, it's not confined to Danny's flat, you know. If it was, this would all be a lot simpler. It's like the Eye of Sauron in Lord of the Rings – it's all seeing. It follows me bloody everywhere. It makes no difference if I go back to the flat or not."

"If it makes you feel better, I'll take Theo or Ness with me, but you're going to stay away."

"Give me the key!"

"No!"

"Damn!" She swore under her breath.

"Ruby." Cash looked at her, his brown eyes so intent. "Please, let me protect you."

The intensity of his words, the love in them, quenched her ire.

Realising he'd got his way, Cash chanced a smile. "What I'm going to do is call Theo first, ask her to accompany me, and then I'll drive you back to your flat. If we're able to, Theo and I will do the dirty deed, whilst you, I don't know, take a bath or something. Then I'll come back and we'll spend the rest of the day together. I don't want to set foot in Danny's flat either, to be honest, but I'm not scared. Despite the cleansing, I think that you still are. No, don't argue. Listen to me. I might not know as much as you do about the paranormal, but I do know that fear makes a person vulnerable. And my instinct is you don't go into Danny's flat feeling vulnerable."

As frustrated as she felt, he *was* right. Vulnerable is exactly what she was right now.

"Okay, go and do what you have to do. I'll wait for you at home."

"And keep Jed with you," Cash said, taking his mobile out of his pocket. "At all times."

Chapter Thirteen

RUBY stood on the pavement outside her flat, waving Cash off before turning to go in. The sight of Jed waiting for her by the door was a happy one. She scrutinised his actions – he seemed glad to see her, was wagging his tail. She relaxed. He wouldn't be doing that if harm was close by.

Kicking off her shoes, she sank onto the sofa in the living room.

Danny was dead! He'd killed himself, unable to take it anymore. But, as his father had questioned, take *what* exactly? The weight of his addiction? Or something else entirely, something that weighed far heavier? She cursed herself for not having gone to the hospital whilst he was still alive, for not insisting to his parents that she needed to see him, for not having tried harder. But she hadn't. She, like Cash, like Presley, thought they'd had all the time in the world. She'd failed Susan, and now she'd failed Danny too.

I'm so, so sorry, I hope you're at rest.

But what if he wasn't? What if his spirit wasn't able to move on because he was still too troubled? Perhaps he'd returned to his flat, been drawn back to it. If so, Theo would be able to pick up on his presence. She was an expert; she'd know what to do.

Lying back on the sofa, she closed her eyes, wondering if sleep might come. The threat of nightmares, of memories becoming strangely distorted, sent that idea packing. Cash had suggested she take a bath – it might help her to unwind – but the thought of being submerged in water didn't appeal either. Frustrated, she sat up again and looked around. Where was Jed? Panic flared. He'd gone! Chased off, perhaps? Too frightened to stay. No sooner had she thought it than he came sloping in to lie at her feet.

Stop spooking yourself, she ordered. Immediately, the *Spooky Ruby* mantra started in her mind. She put her hands to her ears. *Stop it! Stop it! Stop it!*

From the kitchen came a loud bang.

Abruptly she stood up, and so did Jed. He was no longer relaxed; his body was as rigid as hers. She tried to control the crawling feeling in her stomach, but it wouldn't subside. It didn't restrict itself to her stomach either: her skin suddenly felt as though tiny creatures were crawling all over it – hundreds and hundreds of spiders, thousands, their touch maddening. She started to scratch at her arms, her legs too, but that just made the itching worse. If she didn't stop, she'd draw blood – again.

Jed started barking.

Oh shit!

Her flat: so often she thought of it as her sanctuary, but now it felt like anything but. Sprinting for the door, the dog disappeared into the hallway.

Jed, come back!

She hurried after him, catching sight of his tail as he rushed into the kitchen. Abruptly, she stopped. She didn't want to follow him, but she had to. If there was something in there, something bad, it would be unfair to let him face it alone. Even so, she found herself unable to hurry. Her legs felt heavy, as though she were wading through treacle. With every inch she progressed, the itching became more intense – she felt as if she was on fire.

After what seemed like an age, but could only have been moments, she reached the kitchen door. It was open, but only slightly – not enough to reveal the interior. Before moving further, she listened, trying to calm her breath. Jed wasn't barking. All was quiet. But it wasn't a comforting quiet – far from it. It felt like the calm before the storm.

Oh, Jed, don't make me do this!

But he wasn't making her do anything – he had simply gone to investigate, and so must she. Reminding herself to be brave, that she *was* brave, she forced her hand back and pushed – the movement hard, sharp, and fast. The door creaked as it swung open – a sound she never normally minded, but which now set her nerves on edge, the way that nails being dragged down a chalkboard might.

As the room came into view, her eyes darted furiously about – side to side, up and down – expecting to see... what exactly? There was no one, *nothing*. Everything was as it should be, except for a heavy wooden chopping board, previously propped up against the tiles on the kitchen counter, but now lying flat on its side. Is that what had made that loud bang? It was entirely feasible.

Moving further in, she looked for Jed, but he was nowhere to be found. He could come and go at will – she knew that. But she had *seen* him come in here.

In her mind, she called out to him – too afraid to say his name aloud. The last thing she wanted was to draw attention to him or her. She wanted to remain silent, hidden.

Don't be ridiculous. This is your home – you do what you want. Don't be bullied.

Is that what was happening? She was allowing herself to be bullied, and by an attachment, of all things? The thought angering her, she almost stomped over to the chopping board. This was her house – her sanctuary – and she would not be driven out. Taking the board, she propped it up again – that was how she liked to store it and how it would stay. Looking around again, she was satisfied all was in order – *her* order. Her eyes resting on the kettle, she wondered if she should make a cup of tea. Something herbal perhaps – chamomile would be nice. The effort involved, however, seemed vast. All she wanted was to return to the living room, to lie down again and rest.

Intending to do precisely that, she retraced her footsteps. Perhaps Jed would be in the living room waiting for her. She hoped so. She needed him. A moment or so before re-entering the hallway, a loud bang once again rang out from behind her. Ruby span round. The chopping board had fallen again; not onto the kitchen counter this time – it had been flung to the floor.

Flung?

The spiders started their march again, on myriad legs – heading upwards into her hairline. The pressure on her scalp immediate, as though they were trying to force their way inside her head. Bone, tissue and sinew – nowhere near strong enough to withstand them – giving way so easily; caving in. Not only swarming, they were *consuming* her.

Get out! Just get out!

Worried her head might explode – like something volcanic – she obeyed her own command. As she started to turn again, back towards the front door, she caught sight of Jed. He'd materialised, his front legs outstretched, as though he were jumping off a ledge or something, eventually touching the ground and racing past her, urging her as he flew by to do the same. Where he had gone to investigate, she didn't know, but wherever it was it had frightened him, as she was frightened; the hair on his back was decidedly raised. Ruby suddenly had a vision of a very dark place – somewhere desolate, without hope, without any glimmer of kindness at all. And the spiders – they were driving her mad. As she ran too, something else was gnawing away at her. Not a vision this time, or a sensation, but another memory – buried deep but on the rise, almost within reach. Almost…

* * *

If anyone had happened to be following Ruby in the car, they would have thought she'd lost the plot; she kept driving round and round the town of Lewes in a loop, not knowing what else to do. Every time she did, she passed Sussex Stationers, barely able to cast a glance towards it. Nowhere was safe. Not her flat; not a crowded beach. Not even a bloody bookshop!

She had to find answers. Was the thing that had attached itself to her the same thing that had attached itself to Danny? The thing that had pushed him over the edge? Had caused him to take his own life? They were answers that wouldn't be easy to find, not now he was dead. Her only hope was if his spirit was grounded, but that was a terrible thing to wish for. The man deserved to rest in peace – not hang around for her benefit.

"I NEED ANSWERS!" she screamed aloud, frustration boiling over.

The only positive she could cling to – as Theo had told her to do at all times – was that the insane itching she'd experienced earlier in her flat had finally eased. It was something to be grateful for, but all she felt was horror and revulsion – they consumed her as much as the spiders had.

Every time Ruby drove past a stretch of road that would take her out of the town of Lewes, Jed barked furiously. Otherwise, he remained mute in his seat as she continued in her mindless loop. Several times he did this, jumping up and down the last couple of times – his behaviour at that exact point nothing less than frantic.

"What?" she said. "What are you trying to tell me?"

How she wished dogs could speak. It would make her life so much easier.

The eighth time she did it, or it could have been the ninth or tenth – she'd lost count – realisation began to dawn.

"Are you trying to tell me to get out of Lewes?"

Jed wagged his tail.

"To go where?"

He stared at her – his eyes almost pleading with her.

"Home. You want me to go home."

Jed's expression changed immediately. If dogs could grin, that's what he was doing.

"Clever dog," she said, realising that in his own way he *was* trying to speak to her.

Quickly changing route, she drove out of Lewes towards the Cuilfail Tunnel and the road that would lead to Hastings. The jury was out as to whether Danny could give her answers, but maybe there was someone else who could – someone who was haunted too, and had been since Ruby was a child: her mother, Jessica. She and her grandmother both knew something she didn't. Something they'd kept from her all her life. *For your own good,* Gran always said. *You don't need to know – it wouldn't help you if you did.* But Ruby thought it might help her.

Right now, it might be the *only* thing that would.

Chapter Fourteen

PARKING as close as possible to Lazuli Cottage in the Old Town of Hastings, Ruby abandoned her car and walked swiftly along several streets, relishing the familiarity of her hometown. En route, she phoned Cash. If he went to her flat and found her missing, he might panic. She also wanted to speak to Theo, who she knew was with him.

Cash answered the phone on just the second ring. "Ruby, are you okay?"

"I'm fine," she answered. "Now."

"Now? What do you mean *now*? Where are you? At the flat?"

"I'm in Hastings."

"Hastings! What are you doing there?"

Ruby explained as succinctly as possible what she'd experienced in her flat – or at least what she thought she'd experienced. She glossed over the bit about the chopping board being flung – it didn't sound so impressive in retrospect. Instead, she mentioned the itching.

"You're sure it's not just heat rash?" Cash asked.

It was an innocent enough question, even a logical one, considering the weather. Nonetheless, if he had been standing in front of her saying it, she would have swiped him.

"It is not a bloody heat rash!" she replied.

Accompanying that remark with a frustrated sigh, she asked to speak to Theo next. Within seconds, she was on the phone.

"Ruby." Her voice was firm but calm. "Tell me exactly what you told Cash."

Ruby did as she was asked. Blessedly, Theo didn't mention heat rash at all.

"And right now, how do you feel?"

"I'm fine. I just… I want to know what it's like at Danny's flat. He's not hanging around by any chance, is he?"

"Danny's not here. I'm rather hoping he's in the light."

"I am too. I just…"

"Want answers. I know. We all do."

"Did you find anything else amongst his personal possessions, besides the book?"

"No, nothing else. Look, Ruby, I don't think we should set too much store by his interest in Crowley. It's one book, at the end of the day – one book and a few drawings."

"I know, Theo, but what I saw—"

"Was unfortunate. I think it's affected you dreadfully – fear's getting the better of you."

"Like it got the better of my mother for years and years. That's some fear, Theo."

"Darling, once it takes hold it can last a lifetime, and beyond. You know that as much as I do."

"But the itching…"

"Could be your mind playing tricks on you."

"Fear induced?"

"Exactly. Are you at your mother's now?"

"Almost."

"Surround yourself with white light before going in, just to be on the safe side, and stay put. We're coming over. Cash can lead the way."

Before Ruby could reply, Theo cut the call. She considered ringing back. Did she want them here? Would it be appropriate? She didn't know.

At the front door to the cottage, Ruby stood for a moment, before ringing the bell. It opened in less than a minute.

"Ruby!" Gran's face was a picture of delight. "Come in, darling, come in."

Ruby hesitated. Should she set foot over the threshold and risk bringing what had attached itself to her into the house as well? That might only compound what had happened to her mother; make it worse. But what choice did she have? Where could she go if home was barred to her? And not just her own home; the family home too?

Kissing her grandmother on both cheeks, Ruby followed her down the narrow hallway and into the kitchen. "Where's Mum?" she said, before pulling up a chair.

"Your mother decided to take a stroll to the beach. She's been doing that a lot lately."

Ruby was surprised. "You never said."

"I'm sure I have, darling. You probably don't remember. You've been busy lately, what with your business expanding and a new young man. I suppose I haven't really seen you much to talk to."

Although there was no rebuke in Sarah's voice, Ruby was taken aback. She hadn't been over much lately, she knew that, but she'd kept in touch by phone. Gran could have said something then. Why hadn't she? Mum going out on her own, it was unusual. It was... She struggled to think of the right word, settling after a while on 'momentous'.

Selecting two cups from the cupboard – her gran's favourite floral-patterned china – Sarah placed them on the table, before filling a teapot and bringing that over too.

Swirling the pot to mix its contents, Sarah poured. "There's something on your mind, Ruby. What is it?"

Clutching at the cup Sarah had given her, relishing its warmth between her hands – they felt so cold, lifeless almost – Ruby swallowed hard. "Gran, something has happened. Something…terrible."

Sarah didn't say a word. She just looked at Ruby, her gaze penetrating.

Taking a quick sip of tea, Ruby started from the beginning: her visit to Danny; what she'd seen; what she'd experienced afterwards; the feelings that had risen up in her – alien feelings; the attack on Cash; and the attack on her in the water. Finally, what had happened in her own flat, *after* it had been cleansed. "I don't care what Theo and Ness say. I'm possessed, Gran. I'm possessed."

Uttering these words, Ruby expected her gran to reassure her, just like she always did. Instead, she sat there, staring at Ruby – her eyes wide as the colour in her face drained.

"Gran, are you all right?"

Immediately, Ruby berated herself. Gran didn't look all right – not at all.

"Gran!" she said again.

As though jolted by Ruby crying out her name, she seemed to quickly recover. Her expression changed completely, however, became harder. Ruby had never seen it so.

Placing her cup on the table, Sarah leaned forward. "You can't be here when your mother gets home."

"What? Why not?"

"Why do you think?" Gran's normally serene voice was almost a bark. "Your mother. She's been better lately. I can't have her brought down again by this... this nonsense!"

"Nonsense? Gran, what I'm experiencing isn't nonsense!"

Abruptly Sarah stood up, pushed her chair back, and started pacing the floor. "All these years, Ruby, all these years. Haven't you listened to a thing I've said?"

Ruby could barely speak, she was so surprised. "Y... yes, of course I have."

Sarah stopped and glared at her. "Then you'll know that nothing can harm you unless you let it – *nothing.*"

"I'm not letting it..." Ruby started to protest.

"You are. Your fear is feeding it. Just like Jessica's fear fed the demon inside of her."

"Demon?" Ruby gasped.

"It's just a word, Ruby, like cancer. That word also terrifies people. So many live in a bleak state of anticipation. They wait for bad things to happen – convinced the good times can't possibly last. Fear is what truly kills people; it wears you down, it weakens you."

Ruby listened to what Sarah was saying before daring to reply. "But you look scared, Gran. You have done from the moment I walked in here."

"Not scared, Ruby – tired." Sarah almost threw the words at her. "I've been dealing with people's fear all my life – your mother's, in particular. I know you were young when your mother had her breakdown, but surely you remember that before she was hardly ever at home. She was wild, reckless. She wanted to explore the bad as well as the good. I couldn't stop her. I tried, but she was a force of nature, a whirlwind. But the bad broke her, as it breaks so many. This life we get to live, that we're so *privileged* to have – the bad ruined it. But it did that because she let it. She allowed it to take hold. It sounds as though Danny did too. But you, Ruby, you can't do that. You're not possessed, you're fearful. But you're also powerful. When will you realise just how powerful you are? If something negative has attached itself to you, banish it. You are not power*less*."

Ruby pushed her own cup aside before leaning forwards. "Tell me how I can do it, Gran, please."

"By doing what I've been telling you to do all your life – by believing. It's your beliefs that define your world. They *are* your world. Believe in the good within you, and *align* with it. If you do that, nothing bad can touch you. When people hit rock bottom, they think the way back up is hard, but it's not. Once you've decided you're going to rise, all the forces in the universe conspire to lift you too. Do you know what? What so many people don't get? It's harder to *stay* at rock bottom."

"I'm not at rock bottom…"

"Not yet, but you will be if you continue to believe you're possessed."

Ruby sat back.

Her gran's words made so much sense. They *always* made sense. And yet, her mother had refused to listen, had always disagreed. She'd claimed that Gran was naive. But truly, where was the harm in naivety? Perhaps it was protection too.

Ruby noticed Sarah glance at the wall clock. Her mother would be home soon.

She stood up. Theo and Cash were on their way. She had to intercept them.

"Gran, you're right. I doubted, and this is the result." It wasn't for the first time either. She'd had doubts when fighting the darkness at Highdown Hall, and needed her morale boosting then. Biting at her cheek, she added, "I'm sorry to bring this to your door… again."

Sarah stepped forward and took Ruby by the shoulders. "We can talk more about this if you need to – just not here."

"No, of course not. I… I don't know what I was thinking. Cash and Theo are on their way. I need to call them, tell them to meet me back in Lewes instead. I'll be fine, Gran. I *am* fine. You always make me feel better."

Sarah hugged her, the fierceness of it belying her age and increasingly fragile frame. But then Gran had always been strong – the rock on which she and Jessica leant. What would she do without her? It was another negative thought that left a trail in her heart – a trail she covered with sand.

Eventually parting, Sarah looked at her. "I love you, Ruby, and I'm here for you. It's just…"

"I know," Ruby reassured her. "And it's great Mum's started to become more independent. I'm really pleased. You know I'll be okay."

"I do," Sarah said, looking away as she said it.

Chapter Fifteen

HAVING stopped Cash and Theo from reaching Hastings, Ruby agreed to meet them both at Cash's flat instead. Part of her knew she should meet them at hers, but she couldn't do it. She was trying to eliminate the fear inside her – the emotion that made her so susceptible – but she was only human, and it wasn't as easy as she wanted it to be. Jed had kept her company on the ride back, but had disappeared once they arrived at Cash's – Ruby wondering if such high-tech surrounds offended his otherworldly sensibilities.

Inside, Theo had managed to liberate an armchair from various leads, plugs and keyboards, perching herself tentatively on it. Her expression, usually jovial, was anything but. On seeing Ruby, she rose and hurried towards her; hugged her as Sarah had.

"Do we need to know anything more about what happened?" she checked.

Ruby shook her head.

"Fair play," Theo responded. "Then put it out of your mind."

Cash broke in. "What about that spray Ness mentioned – the black tourmaline? I mean, put it out of your mind, sure, I'm all for that, but the spray's not going to harm, is it?"

"On the contrary," Theo informed him, "it'll assist in keeping harm away. I'll phone Ness in a minute and see if the spray's available to pick up."

"This friend that makes it – does she sell it in bulk?" Ruby joked.

Theo smiled approvingly. "That's it, that's the way. You can't be frightened when you're laughing." Serious again, she asked, "But tell me, why did we have to meet at Cash's flat? Why couldn't we meet at yours?" To Cash, she said, "No offence of course."

"None taken," Cash assured her.

"I…" Ruby tried to explain, but failed.

Theo looked at her. "When you fall off a horse, the best thing to do is get straight back on."

"I will. I'll go back home, just as soon as the spray's ready."

Keen to change the subject, Ruby asked again about Danny's flat.

"It's clean as a whistle," Theo replied. "No remaining residue, no nasty books or drawings, and no untoward substances, eh, Cash?"

"Not anymore. I flushed them down the loo."

"Oh, that's good." Ruby breathed a sigh of relief. "I think his parents have suffered enough."

"I think poor Danny suffered enough too." Theo was solemn as she said it. "But I pray he's at rest now. The funeral will be soon, won't it?"

"Probably."

"We need to attend, pay our respects and… make sure that he *is* at rest."

"Definitely," Cash agreed. "I'll talk to Presley about it."

Theo clapped her hands together – a thunderous action

that signalled her involvement in today's events had come to an end. Wriggling out of the chair, she said, "Right, I'm off home for a bite to eat and an episode or two of *The Walking Dead*."

"*The Walking Dead*?" Cash repeated in a slightly stunned manner.

"I love a zombie," Theo declared. "Don't you?"

Cash shrugged. "I'm not mad keen, to be honest."

She rolled her eyes at this reply, before turning to Ruby. "Get back on the horse – soon."

"I will."

"Continue the crusade, eh?"

"Yeah." Ruby laughed at this.

"I'll wait to hear regarding any cases to help out on."

"Oh, there'll be plenty," Ruby warned. "I'll go to the office tomorrow and check."

Waving Theo off, Ruby and Cash returned to the living room.

"Sorry about the mess," said Cash, starting to herd even more wires and plugs into a corner.

Ruby stopped him. "I love the mess," she said, putting her arms around his neck. "This glorious world of technology you live in – it's *exactly* what I need right now."

* * *

Ness dropped the spray round to Ruby's office the next morning – two bottles of it. After replying to email and phone messages and booking in several appointments, Ruby decided to make her way back home – alone. En route was St Anne's, and she stopped off there for a few moments.

Cemeteries – so often portrayed as grisly in books and on film – tended to have a calming effect on Ruby. Far from frightening, she found them peaceful places to be – imagining those who'd walked the earth previously now enjoying adventures elsewhere. Graves belonging to young people and children did sadden her slightly. As her Gran said, life was a privilege, and she wished everyone could enjoy it to the full. To be fair, it was those left behind that Ruby felt most sorry for, relatives, partners and friends – their grief often depthless.

Walking idly amongst the headstones, knowing full well what she was doing – delaying the inevitable return home – she stopped at a marker with the name David Ryan on it. She'd known his namesake at school; he'd been a bit of a tearaway – all swagger and cheeky quips. But underneath, there'd been a good enough heart. David had noticed the gravestone on a trip to Lewes with his parents and taken morbid delight in it. So much so, he'd dragged several friends over from Hastings the week after to show it to them – Ruby included – insisting they took pictures of him lying on top of the grave with his hands crossed over his chest. Much hilarity had ensued as they'd snapped him in situ; even Ruby had been able to see the funny side. David and her school friends hadn't meant anything nasty by their actions; they weren't being disrespectful as such. They'd just been having fun – a strange kind of fun, admittedly, but it was harmless enough.

Looking at David Ryan's marker now, Ruby wondered how the 'live' David was? Despite his relaxed persona, he'd actually done very well at school, leaving Hastings at eighteen and going to university in Manchester. As far as she knew, he was still living there. He'd wanted to be a lawyer. Had he fulfilled his quiet ambition? She hoped so. He was probably a very different person now; all business suits and brisk efficiency. Someone she probably wouldn't recognise; someone reinvented. They'd all reinvented themselves, she supposed; morphed into different people entirely. Lost in memories, it took a moment to register slight movement to her left, but when she did, all thoughts of her former school friend fled. Instead, her mind went black, as though a curtain had been pulled across it – her body as stiff as the stone statues that surrounded her.

Oh no, not again!

Beads of sweat broke out on her forehead, which had nothing to do with the heat of the day.

Knowing she had to look – that she had no choice – she moved her head slowly to the side. At the sight of a young woman sitting on the step that intercepted the path, the breath left her body in a whoosh. There was no demon boldly staking sacred surrounds in pursuit of her. Yet again she'd allowed her imagination to rule.

The woman – not of the living and breathing variety – was staring straight ahead, her expression dejected. Since moving to Lewes a few years ago, Ruby had been a regular visitor to the cemetery, but this spirit she hadn't seen before. In fact, the last time she'd seen a spirit in these surrounds was that time she'd visited with David. It had been an old man who'd been leaning against one of the graves. He'd noticed Ruby staring at him and had smiled genially at her. She'd wanted to go over and talk to him, but there was no way she could have done that in front of David and co. They had no idea about her gift.

Instead, whilst they wandered further into town, Ruby hung back. There was a big crowd of them, at least ten.

Nobody would notice her absence if she kept it brief.

As she approached, the old man pointed to the marker.

My son, he said, pride evident not just in his voice but in his expression too. Reading the stone, Ruby noticed his son – Paul Anthony – had died aged nine months in June 1957. Looking again at the old man, she suspected he'd died only recently and the suit he was wearing had been his burial clothes.

"How old were you when your son died?" she asked.

Young.

Often the dead didn't elaborate. Still, it was information enough.

"And now you're going to join him?"

The old man seemed bewildered at such a prospect.

I come here to see him. Every week I come here, sometimes more.

"But this isn't where he is. He's in the light."

The light? Where's that?

"It's where we come from and where we return. It's source – or home, if you like."

And my boy, he'll be there?

"He will. He'll be waiting for you. There's no separation anymore."

The old man looked again at his son's gravestone, at the altar he'd worshipped at for so many years.

My son, he said again, but wistfully this time, before turning and walking away, Ruby watching him as he retreated, as he dissolved like stardust, glittering brightly before fading entirely. Just a few words – that's all some spirits needed to encourage them to cross the divide. No drama, no fireworks, not much resistance at all – just a few simple words.

Feeling wistful herself and with her own 'quiet ambition' brewing in her head – to somehow make a living from her 'gift', to bring it into the big wide open, to offer it as a service rather than keep it as a secret – she'd rejoined her friends. A few of them had asked where she'd been, but believed whatever excuses she'd made – the time had not yet come to stand out. Instead, they'd carried on enjoying their day, weaving in and out of shops, visiting the park, playing on the swings, the slides, the roundabout, flirting with each other, but in an oh-so-innocent way, before heading back to Hastings on the train. And here she was again, years later – not only a Lewes resident, but also a Lewes businesswoman – in the same graveyard, but with someone different.

Walking towards the woman, Ruby sat down beside her. "Hello. My name's Ruby."

The woman continued staring ahead, not acknowledging her at all.

"Why haven't you gone to the light?"

Again, the woman ignored her.

"Are you waiting for someone?"

Ruby detected slight interest and paused because of it. She'd asked enough questions for now. It was the spirit's turn to answer.

Life isn't what I thought it would be.

It was a common enough complaint amongst the recently deceased.

So disappointing.

"I'm sorry to hear that," Ruby replied.

Life is hard.

"It *was* hard, but it's over now. It's time for something different."

I know.

Still staring ahead, the woman spoke again. *I don't need your help.*

"You're happy to move on?"

When I'm ready.

Ruby looked at her watch and sighed. She had to go home. There was no point in putting it off any longer. As the woman had said, she wasn't needed.

Standing up, Ruby spoke again. "I'll come by in a day or two; if you're still here, perhaps we can talk again. If not... well, I'll be glad. The other side – I don't think it'll disappoint you at all."

Pointing herself in the direction of home, one hand clutching at the black tourmaline spray in her pocket, Ruby steeled herself to address more pressing matters.

Chapter Sixteen

A fortnight later, Ruby found herself in another cemetery in another town. One of a huge group of mourners who'd gathered to pay their last respects to Danny Eldridge – dead by his own hand, at the tender age of thirty. Standing alongside her were Cash, Theo, Ness and Corinna. Presley was with his band mates – their faces ashen despite the August sunshine. His parents, Ruby noted, looked only to be in their early sixties. How they were feeling, she couldn't imagine. Her heart went out to them.

As Danny's body was being lowered into the ground, Ruby, as she knew her other team members would be doing, tried to connect with Danny – something that should be possible if his spirit had chosen to linger here instead of at his flat in Brighton. Drawing a blank, she surreptitiously looked at their faces. An almost imperceptible shake of the head from both Theo and Ness told me they weren't able to connect either. Which, of course, was a good thing.

The wake was held at Danny's parents' house – a typical retirement bungalow only a couple of miles from the town centre. A buffet had been prepared, but people only picked at it – the death of someone so young and in such tragic circumstances an effective appetite suppressant.

Again, Ruby and the team staked the joint.

Danny, are you here? Ruby silently asked – wandering into as many rooms as she could without causing suspicion.

Theo sidled up to her. "I'm getting nothing. What about you?"

"Nothing," replied Ruby.

Ness joined them. "He's not here. He's gone to the light."

"Good." Relief flooded through Ruby. No demon – conjured or imagined – had blocked his path.

Since returning to her flat two weeks ago, to find nothing waiting for her, Ruby had felt lighter, more *recognisable*. Despite the flat being 'empty', she'd sprayed it liberally; opened all windows and ramped up the white light surrounding not just her but the entire property. Jed had followed her faithfully from room to room as she'd done it. Facing up to her fears had been cathartic somehow. She was ready to fight negativity with genuinely felt positivity – to be the victor not the victim.

The possibility of Danny's lingering spirit had been a real concern, but today – as sad as it was – had heartened her too. Danny was where he should be. He was home.

Whilst Theo, Ness and she had put out the feelers, Cash and Corinna had gone to join Presley. He was distraught at the loss of his best friend. Ruby resolved to talk to him later, to tell him Danny was at rest, that they'd tried to connect with him but failed – a good failure this time. She hoped in some small way it would console him. She'd like to do the same with Danny's parents and sibling, but she didn't know their spiritual beliefs; it might not console them at all.

After the funeral, the team drove back to Lewes, and life

returned to normal, or as normal as it could be when your day job revolved around the spirit world. Her grandmother's words, harsh though they were, had knocked some sense into her, and for that she was grateful. They'd provided the short, sharp kick she'd needed.

One thing that still played on her mind, however, was Susan. She may have gone to the light, but how tormented she'd been beforehand vexed Ruby. Cash had been surprised when she'd explained how she felt.

"Ruby, you've done what was necessary. You've released her."

She had, but somehow it wasn't enough. Susan's case had touched her deeply. It was like she'd got under her skin – her as well as... Before that particular thought could develop, Ruby headed it off at the pass. To starve such thoughts was the best protection of all. But Susan, she *could* think of her. That was safe at least.

She'd finally found time to visit The Keep – poring through old newspapers in search of Susan-related reports. 1966 was the year she'd died. Scouring both the locals and the nationals, it was clearly a death that hadn't made headlines. If it had been identified as a murder, it might have done, but there was nothing, not even in papers a year or two on from that date. From this complete lack of documentation, she wondered if Susan's death had indeed been regarded as suicide; either that or an unfortunate accident. Whatever, it didn't warrant column space. Had Danny's death made the papers? She hadn't checked. If his band had been more mainstream it most certainly would have, but they weren't.

The girl who'd been taken advantage of in life and taunted in death began to preoccupy Ruby's mind. As she'd done so many times before, she berated herself for not asking the girl's surname. If she had, it would have made her search so much easier. How old were Susan's mother and father? Statistically, she knew older parents were more likely to have a child with Down's syndrome. Had that been the case? Had they been too old to look after her properly, and to have noticed her being taken advantage of? Too tired? Indifferent, even? Or was she doing them a huge disservice thinking that? Surely they'd have been devastated by her death, as Danny's parents had been. If so, why hadn't they pushed for answers, as she was pushing? Why hadn't they brought her case to national attention? So many questions made her head hurt but, equally, they filled it, stopping her mind from wandering down other avenues.

Summer days turned colder, and skirts, tee shirts and sandals were gradually replaced with jeans, jumpers and boots – Ruby's preferred attire. She was, as she told Cash, more autumnal in nature. In reply, he'd pointed out it was almost their one-year anniversary.

As it was September, and they'd met in December, it was actually only nine months, but Ruby wasn't one to split hairs.

Corinna and Presley had finally got together too – Corinna something of a rock to him after Danny's death. She might be several years younger than him, she might be relentlessly cheerful, but she was also what he needed: a breath of fresh air. They'd got very close, very quickly – Cash and Ruby surprised at just how quickly.

"You psychics," Cash said one evening, his tongue very firmly in cheek. "It seems me and my bro can't get enough of you."

"Corinna's a sensitive not a psychic," Ruby reminded him.

"Same difference to the uninitiated," he replied, pulling her close.

Although there'd been plenty of sex between them – Ruby's desire for Cash as keen as ever – there'd been no repeat of that nail-raking episode. She was back on track; where she'd been before she met Danny – her love life and business thriving. Even her home life – her original home life, that is, with her grandmother and mother – had improved. Ruby made a point of visiting regularly; she also made a point of keeping all chat between the three of them lighthearted. Although Sarah had said Jessica was much improved, Ruby hadn't noticed a big change – she was still not overly responsive. But the visits were enjoyable enough. Cash had accompanied her on a few occasions, Gran adoring his enthusiasm concerning her cooking.

Another cold, crisp morning dawned, and Ruby was walking from her flat to her office when her mobile rang.

"Sweetie, how are you?" It was Theo.

Ruby glanced over at St Anne's as she answered. She always did that, nowadays, checking the coast was clear. The woman she'd seen sitting on the step, staring balefully ahead, was long gone, and no one else had taken her place. Walking further down the road, past The Pelham Arms, cars driving steadily past her, Ruby focussed her attention on what Theo was saying.

"We've got someone to see. Derek's his name – Derek Lytle. He insists he sees spirits everywhere. In his bedroom, his living room, the bathroom – on the street outside. He sees them, and sometimes they see him, but not always, apparently. Sometimes they're oblivious. He's another friend of a friend. I said we'd help."

"Of course," Ruby replied, checking her watch. "Where does Derek live?"

"In Shoreham, in the Ropetackle building. Do you know it?"

Ruby did. It was a relatively new block of flats overlooking the harbour.

"To be fair, he was a bit dubious at first about meeting us, but when my friend explained we're a high street business, he was far more receptive."

That was good news – her vision of normalising the paranormal in action.

Glancing at her watch, she said, "I'm halfway to the office right now, but I can easily turn back and jump in the car, meet you there."

"That'd be perfect. See you in about forty-five minutes?"

"Thirty if I hurry," said Ruby, turning round and retracing her footsteps.

* * *

Parking on Shoreham's High Street, just a few metres from the Ropetackle, Ruby found Theo doing the same.

"Bit of a nip in the air," said Theo on spying her.

"Another harsh winter on its way," agreed Ruby.

They walked side by side to the building, Theo announcing which bell to press as they neared the door.

Over the intercom came a suspicious-sounding voice. "Who is it, please?"

"It's Psychic Surveys, Mr Lytle. Theo and Ruby."

There was a slight pause before they were allowed in, during which Ruby looked a little despairingly at Theo. "Maybe he's too sceptical for his own good?"

"We'll soon find out."

Mr Lytle's flat was on the third floor, Ruby went to take the stairs but Theo stopped her.

"My dear girl, there's a lift here."

"Yeah, I know, but…"

"Ruby, you're not worried about taking the lift, are you?"

"Of course not," Ruby countered. As she waited for the grey metal doors to open, however, she surrounded herself in white light. Just to be on the safe side.

The trip to the third floor passed uneventfully. Nonetheless, Ruby was glad to be free of such a confined space. Mr Lytle was waiting in the hallway to greet them.

"Wow!" he exclaimed. "You're not spooky at all."

Spooky… why did he have to use that word? She rushed to shut down the mantra before it could begin.

In his mid-fifties, perhaps a little younger, Derek Lytle was well-built, with a good head of hair – dark in colour, still – and good dress sense. He had on navy trousers and a blue pinstripe shirt. He ushered them in, doing what so many clients did: surreptitiously checking from side to side that no one had spotted the strangers at his door. Apart from Theo's pink hair and colourful scarves – which actually managed to look tasteful rather than weird – they wouldn't give the neighbours too much to gossip about.

Offered the obligatory tea, they took their cups and went to sit down on the sofa, whilst Mr Lytle – *'call me Derek'* – explained what had been happening to him.

"Just last night, I woke to find two people standing at the end of my bed. I'm getting quite used to ghosts popping up everywhere now. I wasn't even that scared. I sat up and said hello."

Theo looked impressed. "And did they reply?"

"No, they just stared straight ahead. They weren't sinister or anything. Quite the opposite, they seemed benign."

"And then what happened?" Ruby asked.

Derek shrugged. "I don't know what happened to them, but I lay back down and went off to sleep. They were gone by morning."

"These people you see," Theo probed further. "Have you always seen them?"

"No, that's the strange thing – it's only been in the last six months or so."

"Nothing before that?"

Derek shook his head.

"I see," Theo replied, before turning to Ruby. "Shall we?"

Ruby explained the procedure to Derek, asking for permission to do a walk-through in every room. Derek agreed. As they stood up, he shook his head again.

"I don't know what I expected," he said, staring at them both. "Flowing capes and dreadlocks; the awful smell of patchouli. But you two – you could be anyone."

"We *are* anyone." Theo smiled tightly as she said it. "Just like you."

"Well, yeah, I can see spirits too!"

That wasn't what she'd meant, but Theo didn't bother to correct him. Instead, they got on with the job at hand. Returning to the living room after only a short while – it was a small flat, one-bedroomed – Ruby announced to Derek they could detect no spiritual presence or presences.

Derek looked downcast. "But these people – they're real. And not only that – they're everywhere!"

"May I?" asked Theo, indicating she'd like to sit down again.

"Of course," Derek replied, his hangdog expression firmly in place.

As they'd assured Jane Clark, they assured him. "It's not that we don't believe you. We do. But we don't think these people are grounded spirits. We think they're hallucinations."

"Hallucinations? Whatever do you mean?"

"In your bedroom, Ruby and I noticed tablets. You're on medication, aren't you, Derek?"

Rather than hangdog, Derek seemed embarrassed. "I suffer from depression."

"Which is nothing to be ashamed of," Theo continued. "Many people suffer – myself included, in the past."

Ruby looked at her. That was something she didn't know.

"I hope you don't mind," Theo said, holding out a piece of paper in her hand: the leaflet that had been stuffed inside the box of tablets, listing, amongst other things, the side-effects. It made for alarming reading. Besides hallucinations, there was insomnia, dizziness and palpitations – a whole smorgasbord of reported symptoms. When she'd finished reeling them off, she asked Derek how long he'd been on this particular tablet.

"About six months," he said. As realisation dawned, his mouth fell open. "The same time I started to see things!"

"Have you ever read this leaflet?" Ruby enquired.

"No," he admitted.

Theo took up the reins once more. "It's your medication that's the problem. Go back to your doctor and explain what's happening. He or she will be able to prescribe an alternative."

Derek's shoulders slumped. "Oh, that's such a relief. I thought I was going mad. I don't know how you cope, seeing what you do."

"It's not all the time," Theo assured him. "And think about it, the more you saw, the less scared you became. I wouldn't quite say you were blasé, but you might have been if it had continued for much longer. Well, it sort of works along those lines for us too."

As Theo and Ruby got up to go, Derek hurried over to a small desk beside his window, on top of which sat a laptop and random piles of papers. Theo had already discussed rates with him on the phone, but he insisted paying double the amount they charged.

"You need to up those rates of yours," he commented, handing the cheque over. "How can you make a living charging such paltry sums?"

"Volume, that's how," Ruby said, thanking him for his generosity.

Outside on the pavement, Ruby turned to Theo. "Hallucinations? Interesting."

"It is. They can seem as real as the real thing on occasion."

Ruby was very careful to cloak her thoughts lest Theo pick up on them. But she didn't agree with that last sentiment. There was no mistaking the real thing. She knew that now.

Chapter Seventeen

RUBY'S prediction of a harsh winter was proving correct. Not just cold, it was stormy – the coast of Britain battered into submission as low front after low front blew in across the ocean. The weather affected everyone. Wherever Ruby went – into shops, to meet clients, the pub even – people grumbled about how unrelenting it was. Ruby tried not to grumble too, but even she couldn't help it at times – she was fed up of looking like she'd been dragged through a hedge backwards every time she spent more than ten minutes in the great outdoors.

The Calor gas heater in her office had been pressed into service, with Jed often snoozing in front of it. Cash as well, on occasion. Ruby rarely had time to snooze; the phone rang almost constantly and enquiry after enquiry flew into her online mailbox. As much as Ruby wanted to spend more time researching Susan, time for personal pursuits was limited, although on one occasion she visited villages within a ten-mile radius of the bridge – some of them home to no more than a handful of houses – to enquire if anyone remembered Susan or her family living there. No one did.

As well as trying to build up a UK-wide network of psychics to investigate cases further afield, Ruby's local area seemed to be drowning in domestic spiritual problems.

Activity at the Brookbridge housing estate had started up again. They'd been called to several houses there in the last month, all of them genuine cases – the former residents of Cromer Asylum stirred up by the weather too, perhaps.

"There's definitely something in the air," Ness had said one morning – all four of them and Jed packed into Ruby's Ford for a second visit to one troubled spirit in particular.

Theo had simply shrugged, her usual joie de vivre dampened.

The spirit had been a hard one to shift. A man prone to violence in life, the team suspected he'd suffered from a wide range of mental dispositions, including schizophrenia.

The voices, he kept repeating. *They won't leave me alone.*

Something Ruby could empathise with.

Cash had wanted to accompany them on their second visit to deal with the man – his name they couldn't extract, although they'd tried their damnedest – and Ruby was fine with that; Cash knew how to protect himself. But he was called away by a client of his own at the last minute.

"Send Jed in first," Cash advised. "Use him as armour."

Ruby had, of course, done no such thing. She led the way, ensuring she and everyone else involved were surrounded in white light – the only armour needed.

The man railed at them, shouted an assortment of profanities, materialising in front of Ruby – his face contorted – but she and her team had stood firm.

"We understand how much you suffered in life," reiterated Ruby. "That possibly you were ill-treated rather than helped, your condition misunderstood."

There was no 'possibly' about it; he *had* been ill-treated. Abused, as so many of the vulnerable in society were. The images she'd been able to pick up on concerning his incarceration had been blurred at best, but what did come across clearly was the amount of beating this man had sustained. And not just beating, either, but starvation and long periods of isolation. Guidelines concerning client care blatantly ignored.

The cleansing had taken hours. There had been periods of inactivity – the man as exhausted as they were – each and every one of them needing to replenish energy levels. Equally, there'd been many moments of screaming and wailing – the man tearing at his hair and gouging at his eyes. A horrific sight to some, but not to them.

The house the man inhabited was modest in size and belonged to Mr and Mrs Cragg, who lived there with their two young daughters. Although the man hadn't manifested, he could be sensed keenly: the two daughters – Ellie, aged eight and Scarlett, aged five – tearful since they'd moved in three months before. Everyone who bought into the estate knew its former history. Favourable house prices, however, were too big a temptation to resist. What the Cragg's perhaps weren't aware of was that their house and the few either side of it occupied the former site of the high-security wing, home to Cromer's most troubled patients – information that had been glossed over by the estate agent.

"But the previous owners must have known, surely?" Mr Cragg declared, when Ruby told him. "And if they didn't know about that, they must have known about the ghost."

Mrs Cragg had nodded vigorously in agreement. "We've been deceived!"

"Not necessarily true,' Ness disagreed. "There are varying degrees of sensitivity. It's entirely possible the former residents weren't able to sense anything."

"They may have suffered a few more mood swings than normal," Theo added. "Headaches, irritability, that sort of thing. But, as people often do, they could have put it down to the everyday stresses of life." She'd inclined her head at that. "And in many cases, it *is* just the everyday stresses of life, so whoever lived here before, they can't be blamed."

They'd eventually been able to move the man on, but only because several guides came forward from the light to help him. Ruby marvelled at this. She'd seen one or two come forward before, but not a whole band of them. Were they former patients too – just as abused – waiting in the wings until he was finally ready? How the man cried when he saw them – a sound so despondent it was heart breaking to hear. After spending time with him, the spirits eased the man gently to his feet and walked with him to the light. No, they hadn't walked – they'd *carried* him.

Although the period following 'release' was normally a time of great joy for everyone, each and every one of the team had returned to Ruby's office in a contemplative mood.

"I know people aren't inherently evil," Corinna said, "but what that poor man must have suffered, how he'd been stripped of all his dignity – that seems pretty evil to me."

Theo agreed. "Sometimes what human beings are capable of confounds me."

Ruby hadn't said a word – evil was not a subject she wanted to dwell on.

After yet another busy day, Cash wandered into the office just as Ruby was mid-yawn.

"Hey," he said, walking up to where she was sitting and starting to massage her shoulders, "it's Friday. I hope you're not too tired to come out."

After a moment of savouring his touch, she asked him what he had in mind.

"Corinna and Presley are going to The Rights of Man for a drink. I said we'd join them."

"Sounds good. I could do with a rum and coke."

"Today been a bit of a trial?"

"The whole week has, to be honest, kick-starting with the Brookbridge case and just getting busier and busier." Tilting her head backwards so she could look up at him, she added, "I'll tell you what, though, something's going on up in Stornoway. I've had several emails now from people living there, complaining of psychic upheaval."

"You've got contacts in Scotland, haven't you? Haven't they been over to check what's going on?"

"Yeah, Lesley and Ronnie – both women, by the way, not men – but they've drawn a blank. They think there's more than one spirit involved, but they're having a hard time trying to connect with them. Lesley described them as 'fleeting'."

"Fleeting?" queried Cash.

"Hard to catch," Ruby explained further. "Theo's sent some long-distance healing to the trouble spots, but that doesn't seem to have had much impact either. I reckon we're going to have to head up there at some point if it can't be resolved. The team, I mean, not you."

"If you're going to Scotland, there's no way I'm missing out. I could do with a holiday."

Ruby laughed. "It's hardly going to be a holiday, Cash. It's work."

"Oh, come on, you guys are nothing if not efficient. There'll be plenty of time for sightseeing. Now, on to more

194

pressing matters – are we going to the pub or what?"

"We're going. You turn off the heater. I'll get my coat."

Corinna and Presley were already waiting.

"They look so loved up, don't they?" Ruby whispered to Cash, as they walked into the pub and went up to the bar.

"As loved up as us, do you think?"

"Just newer, that's all."

Glancing sideways at her, Cash winked in what he clearly hoped was a seductive manner. "It still feels like yesterday to me, babe."

Ruby almost choked on her drink. Despite the incessant rain, Cash lightened her mood. He was like her personal ray of sunshine. Without him, the forecast would be so much gloomier.

As they approached their friends, Corinna jumped up to greet them. More sedately, Presley raised his pint glass in salute.

"How's it going?" Cash asked his brother. Once again, Ruby was struck by their alikeness, how handsome they were. She smiled. She hadn't actually realised how low the cleansing at Brookbridge had brought her – the plight of that tormented spirit affecting her almost as much as Susan had. Briefly, she wondered if coming to the pub was a good idea; whether she should have gone straight home – got some much-needed rest. But no, it *was* a good idea. Being with Cash always was.

Presley and Cash immediately fell into talk about Presley's band and the role Cash was going to play in it. All band matters had been put on hold because of what had happened to Danny – both before and after his demise – but now it was time to move forward. Cash had agreed to stand in as drummer, but in a temporary capacity only. He hadn't yet committed to taking over permanently. Whilst they attempted, once again, to set dates for rehearsal, Corinna started talking to Ruby about books – she was as avid a reader as Ruby.

"Have you read any Anne Rice?" she asked.

Ruby thought for a moment. "Erm, yeah, yeah, I have. Not for a while, though. Didn't she write *Interview with the Vampire*?"

"Yes, she did. It's fantastic that book. Right now I'm reading *The Witching Hour*, which is also by her. It's set in New Orleans. You'd love it; it's so atmospheric." Her eyes grew more serious as she continued. "The story centres around the Mayfair Witches – Rowan Mayfair in particular – and the entity who attaches itself to them: Lasher. A chosen woman from each generation sort of inherits him for the duration of their life, and even though he's familiar to them, they don't know what he is, not really. He offers them great power, but he can also reduce them to madness. It's fascinating stuff and I thought—"

"It sounds great, Corinna, one to put on the reading list. But not right now, huh?"

Corinna was slightly taken aback. "Oh, it's just…"

Discreetly, Ruby nodded towards Cash's brother. "I'm sure Presley doesn't want to be talking about such things either, not after Danny."

Clearly, she hadn't been discreet. Immediately, Presley broke off his conversation with Cash. "Actually," he said, wading right in, "all this stuff around attachment, Corinna and I were talking about it just before you arrived – you know, what Danny might or might not have seen. I've been doing a bit of research of my own lately, trying to get to grips with it. Not in the realms of fiction – it's more factual stuff. Have you ever heard of the spiritualist Alexandra David-Néel?"

Ruby bristled slightly. Was she supposed to have heard of every spiritualist going? Before she could reply, however, Presley continued speaking.

"She was born in the late nineteen-hundreds and died in the nineteen-sixties. She wasn't just a spiritualist; she was an explorer, an opera singer and a writer. A bit of an anarchist too, by all accounts."

Cash looked intrigued. "Is she similar to Crowley?" he asked.

"No, I don't think so," Presley answered. "She was more into Eastern religion and philosophy than devil worship. I don't think she was into devil worship at all, in fact; I certainly found no mention of it. But she did like to push boundaries. It was actually Danny who first told me about her. He was interested in her as well as Crowley."

Ruby sighed – an indication that she didn't think it was a good idea they continued to discuss Crowley, David-Néel, or anyone else. If they heard her, however, they didn't let on. All eyes remained on Presley as he warmed to his subject.

"David-Néel experimented with thought forms – or tulpa, in other words."

"Tulpa?" Corinna queried.

Presley took a quick swig from his pint glass. "Yeah. According to Tibetan mysticism, a tulpa is an entity created by an act of imagination. Like fictional characters in a book, I suppose. But unlike book characters, they're not written down – they're created purely in the mind. For years, she lived in a cave near the Tibetan border, studying spirituality alongside a Tibetan monk. I forget his name, but he became her lifelong travelling companion. They travelled to Japan and a whole host of other places too. She wrote books on all sorts of things, including *Magic and Mystery in Tibet*. The point of the matter is she spent years studying thought forms, and eventually decided to create one."

"Wow!" Corinna was impressed. "That's some experiment."

Ruby let it be known by the look on her face that she thought the exact opposite. Again, no one noticed, her passive aggressive gestures falling woefully short.

"It was a monk or something she visualised; not an unpleasant character. On the contrary, she made him round and jolly – a bit like Friar Tuck in the Robin Hood stories, by the sounds of it. She imagined him flitting about in the real world, every detail of him: his clothes, the way he smiled, his quirks and mannerisms. Over time, the monk grew in clarity; in substance too. She actually started to see him."

"How very convenient," Ruby all but sneered.

Presley was undeterred. "Things got really interesting when he started to appear when she hadn't willed it, when she hadn't even been thinking about him. Also, he was getting less friendly. He'd started to slim down, taken on a more sinister aspect. People around her kept asking who this stranger was amongst them. The thought form had become reality. Others could see him, and they didn't like him. They found him… menacing."

Corinna's eyes were wide. "Sounds like all she'd created was a problem."

"She had," agreed Presley.

"So, what did she do about it?"

"She tried to reabsorb the creature back into her mind. But by then he wasn't willing to go. He'd developed a consciousness – a mind of his own. She did eventually succeed, but it took several weeks and left her exhausted. And a bit bloody surprised too, I should reckon."

Corinna giggled, but Ruby remained straight-faced.

"Okay, it is interesting," she conceded, "but what's it got to do with anything?"

Presley leaned forward, his face intent. "Do you think whatever it was that Danny kept seeing was something he created? Something he imagined at first, but then became real?"

"What I think," Ruby said, placing her empty glass back down on the table – the bang as it hit the table resounding – "is that Danny's at rest and whatever plagued him is gone. We shouldn't go over and over it; we shouldn't speculate. It's done with. It's finished."

"I'm just trying to understand," Presley explained.

"But you know what? Some things we can't understand."

"Hey, come on…" Cash's voice held a note of warning.

"No," Ruby continued. "You've got to know when to stop."

Cash raised an eyebrow. "Advice you should take regarding Susan, perhaps?"

Immediately Ruby saw red. "Susan is different!"

"How? She's gone to the light, just like Danny has. But you can't leave it alone. Every spare minute, you're on her case. Why get angry with Presley for doing the same?"

It was natural for Cash to stick up for his brother – deep down, Ruby knew that – but all this talk of thought forms, of attachments, was riling her.

Corinna also put her drink down. "Ruby, are you all right?" she asked.

Glancing up, Ruby noticed concern in her eyes; concern in Cash's too. The sight of it should have comforted her, but she felt picked-on suddenly – victimised.

Cash nudged her for an answer.

"I'm fine," she replied, making a point of shifting away from him. "I'm just sick of being asked if I'm all right, that's all."

Immediately, Cash held up his hands. "Look, if I've upset you, I'm sorry."

Liar!

The thought was in her mind before she could stop it. It startled her, perhaps obviously.

"Ruby…" Cash's voice was soft now. He was trying to cajole her, to lever her out of the black mood she'd slipped into.

As the awkward silence continued, Ruby tried to talk herself down. All too painfully she was aware of what was happening. She was ruining their meet-up. Ruining everything. Again.

"I need another drink." It wasn't what she'd intended to say. She'd intended to laugh, to say that yes, of course she was all right, change the subject and talk about something else, something trivial. But she couldn't. Standing up, her chair scraping against the floor, she made her way to the bar, not bothering to ask if anyone else wanted anything.

Before she had a chance to order, Cash was by her side. "We need to get out of here," he said, his face sterner than she was used to.

"I'll be fine in a minute. I just need another drink."

"You're not having another drink."

"What?" She was stunned. How dare he dictate to her!

"We're going."

"No," she started, but he took hold of her arm and steered her towards the exit.

Ruby considered making a fuss, shouting at him to let go, but decided against it. There were too many eyes on them. She'd wait until she was outside and give him what for then.

By the time they hit the pavement, her anger was ripe. "Let go, Cash. You're not the boss of me."

"I know I'm bloody not, but you changed in there. As soon as Presley started talking about that David-Néel woman, you went from happy to crappy in record speed. And I think I can safely say that process isn't about to reverse in our favour any time soon."

"All that talk of attachments – first Corinna and then Presley. I don't need it right now." Aware she was flouncing rather than walking, she started making her way back up the High Street, past her office and towards home. Cash had to hurry to keep up with her.

"What do you mean, you don't need it?"

Incensed, she came to a grinding halt. "Attachments," she all but screamed at him, "thought forms – I'm doing my best *not* to think about them. Surely you must know that!"

"Ruby, all that stuff that happened, that was weeks ago, months even. You've been fine for ages."

"I've been fine because I've worked at it!"

"But you said it was all over. You said your Gran had made you see sense."

"It *is* all over. It's… I… I don't know, okay? What I do know is I don't want to talk about attachments."

Cash dared to take a step closer. "You're not making sense. Are you still scared?"

"NO!" This time she did scream, her raised voice attracting the attention of several people passing by.

From the corner of her eye, she caught a flash of black.

"Oh great, just what I need," she said, rolling her eyes. "A full-on street party."

Cash followed her line of sight. Corinna and Presley had decided to follow them too. "Don't worry," he said. "I'll explain."

"You won't explain anything. *I* don't need explaining."

"That's not what I meant."

"Then what did you mean?"

"Not that."

"Liar!" The word materialised in all its dubious glory.

He was shocked, and so was she. Not just at what she'd said, but the way in which she'd said it: the rasping quality of her voice. It was so unlike her, so like… so like…

She brought both hands up to cover her face, closed her eyes, but only briefly. "Just… leave me alone, okay? All of you. I need to be on my own."

"Ruby, please…"

"Cash, I mean it. Give me some space."

Although he looked stricken by her request, he stepped back, realising she was in no mood to be remonstrated with. Turning again, she hurried away, wanting to escape before Presley and Corinna reached her too. Thankful that Cash was listening to her at last – that he was letting her go – Ruby deliberately let the tears that had started to fall from her eyes go unchecked. If she raised a hand to wipe them, Cash would realise she was crying. He wouldn't let her go then. But she'd meant it when she'd said she wanted to be alone. Truly meant it. The trouble was, she didn't think she was.

Chapter Eighteen

FEELING emotionally battered, Ruby showered when she got home, had a cup of tea – the decaffeinated variety – and went to bed. Seeing Jed occupying his usual space by her feet heartened her. He'd become her yardstick, and if he was laid-back, she could afford to be too. Not that she had been laid-back earlier. Not in any way, shape or form. She'd been bloody uptight. God knows what Presley must think of his brother's weirdo girlfriend.

You're not a weirdo! a voice snapped back at her – the part of her that wanted so desperately to be normal.

If you say so, the other part – the jaded part – replied.

In bed, Ruby tried not to think about what Cash thought of her too. She'd have to explain to him tomorrow in more detail, make a point of it. But what she was going to explain she didn't fully know right now. Her mind was too tired to even contemplate it.

Fitting her eye mask, she said goodnight to Jed and lay down. Sleep came quickly.

At first it was deep and energising – the type of sleep she needed. More than needed – *craved.* But dreams soon crept in and, even in sleep, Ruby was on guard. As usual, the dreams centred round her home in Hastings. Once again, she was a child. She'd been to school that day – she was aware of that – but now she was home, in the kitchen with her grandmother. Her mother, of course, was nowhere to be seen. She was out again – she was always out, especially lately. There'd been a time when Ruby had seen more of her, when Jessica used to take her to parks and the beach; to a zoo once upon a time, where she'd ridden on a train that encircled the animals – laughing at the monkeys and their playful antics. She'd have liked to go to the zoo again, but money was tight. She'd heard her mother and grandmother discussing financial worries on more than one occasion.

It was winter – the fire was burning in the grate. Once she'd helped Gran prepare dinner and they'd eaten, they'd go through to the living room and sit in front of it, Ruby edging closer and closer until Gran noticed and told her to back away.

She could see the flames – each and every one of them so graceful, like ballerinas. Elegant. The colours mesmerised her: orange, red, and yellow. Although she knew she shouldn't, because it would hurt, she wanted to reach out and touch them. It was a shame pretty things could hurt you.

Bedtime on a school night in her gran's house was strict – seven o' clock – and all too soon it came. Ruby could have sat in front of the fire for another hour. She wasn't tired in the least. There was one good thing about bedtime, however: Gran always read to her. A chapter from her favourite set of books, *The Chronicles of Narnia* – sometimes two. After that, she'd leave the lamp on, and Ruby was allowed to read a few more pages, before putting the book down and switching the lamp off.

"It's important to rest your brain," Gran would say, "to let it recover from the day."

Ruby thought 'recover' was a funny way to describe it,

as though her brain had been ill or something. But sometimes her mind did become overloaded, not just with what she was learning in school, but with the spirits she could see or, if not see, sense. There were just so many. Gran was teaching her to protect herself, to streamline her mind, to focus, but she was 'a work in progress' – another term Gran used that Ruby thought was funny.

She'd been asleep when she heard noises downstairs.

Mum's home, she thought, growing excited at the prospect. *I'll get a goodnight kiss.*

It soon became clear, however, that Mum was not dashing up the stairs to perform this often-yearned-for ritual. Instead, she remained downstairs, talking with Gran. No... not talking. Their voices were raised; they were arguing. Ruby tensed but only slightly. Often, Gran and Mum argued. It was nothing to worry about. It usually fizzled out. But as the voices grew louder and there was slamming and banging too, she realised this was out of the ordinary.

Stay in bed. Stay in bed. Stay in bed.

She should heed that voice, but she didn't. Instead, she climbed out of bed and ventured downstairs. Spying her, her Gran barked at her to go back to bed. Ruby was shocked. Gran *never* raised her voice, at least not to her, but it was her mother that stunned Ruby the most – she looked haggard, older than Gran even. Not young and vibrant – the mother Ruby was ordinarily so proud of.

The last thing she wanted was to go back upstairs. It didn't feel safe anymore – as though the moment she'd left, something had crept in.

Reluctantly, she did as she was told, avoiding the stairs that creaked the most. Especially the top step, which was the loudest of all. Treading on it might somehow alert it... whatever *it* was. At the top of the stairs, on the landing, she paused. Where could she go? To her gran's room? To her mother's? But they weren't safe either. Instinctively, she knew that. There was nowhere to hide.

The hallway light had been on, emitting a cosy yellow glow, but suddenly it switched off. Ruby didn't mind the darkness, but this was much denser than normal. Holding up a hand in front of her face, she couldn't see it. Disorientated, she reached out to locate the wall and, running her hand along it, started to inch her way forward, remembering where a narrow bookcase stood and managing to avoid it. She walked and continued walking, but something was wrong. Their house was small; it was just a few steps to her bedroom. Already, she'd taken too many. The path was twisting and turning, and the more she walked the less she could hear the voices from downstairs.

It's just a dream. It's just a dream. It's just a dream.

Why were her thoughts coming in threes? She had time to think this before a smell hit her – a smell that was pungent, rotten. She tried to think of another name for it... *rancid*.

The word brought her up short. She stopped walking and drew in a short, sharp breath. Yes, that was it – the smell was rancid, familiar too. But not familiar in a comforting sense – there was *nothing* comforting about it. She wanted to turn, run back, go downstairs again, and seek refuge in her grandmother's arms. But something was there in the dark with her, barring her way. She couldn't see it, not yet, but she could sense it well enough – she could *smell* it. Instead of turning round, she started to back up, inch by agonising inch. She'd find the stairway that way. When she slammed into a wall, she couldn't believe it. That wasn't what happened. There was no wall behind her.

What did happen? What did happen? What did happen?
"I don't know!"
Yes you do! Yes you do! Yes you do!
"I don't!"
Think, Ruby. Think, Ruby. Think, Ruby.
"No!"
Think. Think. Think.

"No," she cried again, but there was no force behind it this time – there was desperation only. She wanted to wake up, tried to open her eyes, but they wouldn't comply.

Eyes… that was it! She remembered eyes. A figure that had barred her way, stepping out of the shadows, yet at the same time a shadow itself. A figure that had stared at her with wry amusement and then with nothing like amusement, that had brought its finger up to its mouth and shaken its head. A figure that had frightened her into submission – eventually. The eyes – oh, the eyes – there'd been so much hatred in them.

I see you, Ruby. I see you.

The figure she'd forced herself to forget – it hadn't forgotten her. It had marked her, waited for her all these years – hovering at the fringes of memory, successfully suppressed, only to rise again, triumphantly, becoming vivid, too vivid. Not a dream at all, and not an imagining either.

'Define real,' Theo had said.
This was it.
I see you, Ruby. And you are mine.

Chapter Nineteen

RUBY woke drenched in sweat. Why was it so dark in here?

Your eye mask. Take off your eye mask!

That was why of, course. Manoeuvring herself into a seated position, she raised one hand to tug at it, flinging it to one side before staring around her. Normally, enough light filtered in from the windows to make out objects in the room clearly, but not tonight – the moon was in hiding. It was as dark as the dream had been.

Christ, the dream!

It came flooding back, images like snapshots crowding her mind – her gran, her mother, the darkness, and that smell, that awful, awful smell. She could still smell it, it was all pervading; making her feel as if she were about to be sick. She lifted her hand again, this time to cover her nose, but it didn't help. The smell was not only in the air around her; it was on her skin too.

Thoroughly confused, she swallowed hard. She'd woken up; the smell should be gone, the chest of drawers, and her wardrobe, easily discernible. Turning to the left, she reached for the lamp and that's when she heard it – Jed's low growl. Something was wrong, very wrong. She may have woken up, but it wasn't over. In many ways it was just beginning.

She snatched her hand back.

"Jed," she whispered. "Where are you? I can't see you."

At the bottom of her bed, there was movement.

"Jed!" This time her voice was urgent. "Is that you?"

Whatever it was, it started to come closer.

Please be you, Jed. Please be you.

The figure pounced, making her scream. She closed her eyes but then snapped them open again. Eyes were staring back at her, but not filthy, filmy, yellow eyes. They were brown. Up close, she could see the white surrounding them – the glorious, glorious white.

"Jed! Oh, Jed, thank God!"

Jed held her gaze, desperately trying to communicate.

"Don't worry," she said, throwing back the covers, "I hear you this time."

Hoping she'd got her bearings right, she made for the bedroom door, surprised in a way when her bare feet touched nothing more than carpet. She'd expected something akin to quicksand beneath her – something that would pull her down, as she'd been pulled down in the ocean, that wouldn't let go this time. Her hand reaching for the handle, she hesitated. What if it was there, on the other side? Should she run back to the bed, as she'd done as a child, and hide under the covers? Force it from her mind as well as her flat? Although she couldn't see her bed – the darkness had swallowed it – she looked behind her, almost longingly, but then shook her head. Jed had gone through; she had to follow him, get as far away as possible. If she stayed here – alone – she was vulnerable.

The hallway was equally black – no way to see if the coast was clear. Nonetheless, she sprinted down it, grabbing at her keys and mobile on a side table. She had pyjamas on, which offered no protection against the cold. Reaching the front door, she collapsed against it. Jed barked. He was right: there was no relief to be had just yet.

Reaching up to unbolt the door, she struggled. Again and again, she tried to find purchase. But it was as if her hands belonged to a puppet master, and he was overhead – jiggling the strings attached. She wanted to shout, tell him to *stop it!* She did shout, but it was no use. Her hands continued to shake violently. Jed, meanwhile, was becoming more agitated. As the stench grew ever pungent, he barked and bared his teeth simultaneously.

"I'm trying. I'm almost there."

At last the door flew open, and Ruby all but stumbled onto the porch outside, retching as she did. Bile had risen from her stomach and was also trying to find escape. Blinking back tears, Ruby reached behind her and pulled the door shut, hoping that whatever had invaded her flat couldn't simply pass through it like Jed could – that it would be contained. Thinking of Jed, where was he? Why wasn't he by her side? Surely that thing hadn't got hold of him and trapped him in there with it? Her heart plummeted. Going back in there – she couldn't bear it. She'd have to. Of course she would. She couldn't leave him. But, oh God, the mere thought…

He barked again and she looked up. He wasn't in the house – he was in her car already, sitting on the front passenger seat, jiggling about and fidgeting as he usually did. This time she allowed herself the luxury of relief – a giddy, lightheaded feeling; completely at odds with terror. He was safe, out of harm's way; he hadn't been captured at all. As she continued sprinting, the street around her was deathly quiet, as though no one really lived there. Instead, it was a stage set, caught in the midst of a twilight zone, waiting for the next ghastly events to unfold. Reaching the Ford, she threw herself into the driver's seat, slamming that door too – her aim to erect as many barriers between herself and the entity as possible. Jabbing at the ignition, she almost broke the key trying to force it in. Not once did she turn her head to look backwards. She had visions of darkness oozing out of the crevices around the doorframe and flooding towards her – a river of poison.

"Come on, come on," she urged.

Groggy from inaction, the car seemed to take an age to roar into life. When it did, she whooped loudly, swinging like some wild pendulum between emotions.

Pressing her foot down on the accelerator, Ruby only narrowly missed the car in front of her as she pulled out. Tyres screeching against tarmac, she continued to floor the pedal, barely lifting her foot – not even to brake at 'Give Way' signs and roundabouts – all the way to Hastings.

* * *

It was midnight when she reached the Old Town. Thankfully, there'd been hardly any traffic on the road – a blessing when you were exceeding every speed limit in the land. Parking the car as close to Gran's cottage as possible, Ruby ran along the pavement – the concrete unforgiving beneath bare feet. She was aware of how cold it was – goose bumps rising on both arms in protest. But it was nothing compared to the icy grip on her heart – squeezing tighter and tighter until she thought it might burst.

Racing up another path – the one that led to the door of her childhood home – she was about to lift her hand to bang the knocker when it opened wide.

"Ruby! What on earth is going on? What are you doing here at this hour? And look at you, you've hardly any clothes on!"

Not bothering to explain, Ruby hurled herself into her grandmother's arms instead. "I've got to come in. Please let me come in, please, please." Her teeth were chattering as she pleaded.

"Of course, of course you can come in." Sarah pulled her forwards. "But, Ruby, quieten down, your mother's asleep upstairs. I don't want her disturbed."

Still with her arms around her, Sarah steered her towards the kitchen.

Her voice taking on an authoritative air, she told Ruby to sit down. Ruby did, but immediately sprang up again, pacing back and forth, rubbing agitatedly at her scalp.

"Ruby! Sit down!"

Ruby whirled round. "Gran, I can't just... sit."

For a moment they stared at each other – *a standoff*, Ruby thought. She'd always obeyed her gran; she was a good kid. But therein lay the crux of the problem – she was no longer a kid, she was an adult. And the problem she had, it needed to be faced.

To Ruby's amazement, it was Sarah who backed down.

"At least let me get you some clothes. You're not much bigger than your mother; hers should fit you well enough. You must be freezing."

Ruby threw her arm out to make her stay. "Don't go," she pleaded, feeling as young as the child she kept dreaming about. "Please don't leave me. I don't care about clothes."

"But, Ruby, you've next to nothing on."

"GRAN!"

Sarah's eyes darted nervously upwards. Jessica was still her prime concern. *Always.* Ruby's new best friend – anger – flared.

"Why didn't you tell me, Gran?" Her voice sounded stark, even to her.

Any last vestige of colour in Sarah's face drained completely. "Tell you what?"

"You really want me to spell it out?"

"Ruby! You have got to keep your voice down!"

Ruby shook her head vehemently. "No, not anymore, I want answers. I *need* answers."

"Then you've come to the wrong place."

Ruby was momentarily shocked into silence.

"I've told you before," Sarah continued, her jaw set, her eyes blazing, "I will not entertain talk of evil in this house. I won't have Jessica upset again. She's beginning to improve… at last. And you…" Her disappointment was evident. "How can you fall victim to this after everything I've taught you – have spent my life teaching you!"

"I never invited evil in!"

"You've acknowledged it. That's enough."

"This is not my fault,' Ruby continued, but Sarah had turned her back on her, had put her hands on the kitchen sink, leaning forward slightly as though bracing herself.

Ruby took a step forward. "Gran, this is *not* my fault!" she repeated.

Sarah whirled around – such a youthful action. "Then whose fault is it?"

Ruby hesitated, but only for a moment. "Mum's! She's the one who brought this thing home with her, the night of her breakdown. She's the one who invited it in."

SHANI STRUTHERS

"Rubbish!" hissed Sarah. "Absolute rubbish!"

If Ruby was angry before, she was enraged now.

"It's not! All these years you've kept it from me – what happened to Mum. Both of you have. I've asked several times, but neither of you would tell me. You said it wouldn't do me any good to know, that I needed to believe only in the light, that the light would protect me."

"And that's right. The light *will* protect you."

"It hasn't! Darkness has found me, and I've been fighting it – subconsciously at first, but it's not that any more. It's conscious. It's real. And it won't leave me alone."

Sarah's hands flew to her head as if she too wanted to tear her hair out. "This is ever since Danny, isn't it?"

Ruby denied it. "It's always been there – since I was a little girl – lying in wait. All Danny did was remind me of it."

Lowering her hands, Sarah grabbed hold of Ruby's shoulders. "But you were fine. All the while you *weren't* thinking about it... whatever you think *it* is... you were fine."

Ruby gripped her grandmother right back. "I'm not fine now, though, am I?"

"Ruby," Sarah continued, "love is the most powerful force of all. You, me, every one of us, we come from source and we go back to it. The source is love – unconditional love. You've seen it, countless times, shining in the distance; how beautiful it is. All I wanted was for you to concentrate on that; to remain on a high vibration. If you do, nothing and no one can touch you. But somehow – and I don't know how – you've lowered your vibration. You've seen something, and you've allowed it to bring you

215

crashing down. And that's key here, Ruby. You've *allowed* it. Nothing can harm you – not unless you let it."

Ruby stared into Sarah's eyes, listened once more to the lessons of old, and then she found the courage to answer. "Liar!" she said.

Sarah's hands fell away.

First Cash and now Gran – *everybody* was lying to her.

"It is *not* here because I've allowed it. It is here because it's powerful too. Because it's equal in strength to the light – it's as relentless. Mum tried to tell me once, tried to warn me, but I insisted you were right and she wasn't. I took your side. I always did. But I was wrong. And you were wrong too. Naivety is *not* strength. I'm not equipped to fight what's out there. If I'd known... if you'd been straight with me, I would never have let my guard down. This is not my fault. And perhaps it isn't Mum's. It's yours. All yours!"

Sarah's voice had reduced to a whisper. "You don't understand."

"But I'm beginning to," Ruby continued without mercy. "And Rosamund – she knew too, didn't she? Your mother, my great-grandmother – she documented all her psychic experiences. Mum told me once she'd written about the dark side – reams and reams. She asked me if I'd read them. Of course, I hadn't, because you took those papers, didn't you? You hid them. Wanted me to continue in ignorance. Where are they, Gran? What did you do with them? Did you destroy them?"

"I... I haven't destroyed them. They're somewhere safe. You don't need to see them. Oh God, Ruby." There was abject despair in her voice. "I didn't want to pollute your mind."

"But that's just what it is. Polluted!"

"How, Ruby. How?"

"Because what Mum saw that night—"

"Ruby?"

It took a moment or two to register there was someone else in the room – another voice calling her name. A softer voice, she noted with relief – not one with a rasping quality to it.

She swung round. The door to the kitchen was open, and Jessica was standing in it.

"Mum!"

Sarah spoke before Jessica could. "Jessica," she pleaded, "go back upstairs."

They were the exact words she'd said eighteen years before, to Ruby, of course – not her own daughter.

Despite addressing Sarah, it was Ruby who answered. "You can't tell her what to do, Gran, like you did me. She's not a child – she's a grown woman."

If she had expected her mother to side with her, she was mistaken. Instead, Jessica stared beyond her – her eyes growing wider and wider, her mouth dropping open.

A crawling feeling started up in her belly again. What was her mother looking at? There was terror in her eyes, terror that infected Ruby like the most virulent of diseases.

"Oh no," she said, one hand flying up to her throat. "Is it here?"

As Jessica flew forwards, Ruby stood perfectly still, unable to move. What was her mother doing? Was she going to attack her? But it wasn't Ruby who was the target.

"Mum!' screamed Jessica, the word making Ruby turn on her heel. "Mum! Mum! Mum!"

"Gran…" Ruby's voice was a mere whisper in

comparison.

As though it were happening in slow motion, Ruby saw Jessica catch Sarah just before she hit the floor – the older woman's face a mask of pain, one hand clutching at her chest.

"Oh no, Gran!"

What was happening? Was it a heart attack? If so, it was one she'd very probably caused, turning up so late at night – on the attack herself. Overcome with panic, she was no use at all. She could only stand and stare – part of her unable to grasp the gravitas of what was unfolding. Gran was strong. Gran was their rock. Gran couldn't die – not now.

"Don't just stand there – call an ambulance!"

For a moment, Ruby wondered to whom Jessica was talking.

"Ruby," she screamed again, "call an ambulance."

It's me… she's talking to me.

Galvanised into action at last, Ruby ran into the living room, snatched at the phone in its cradle, and dialled the emergency services. All the while she was speaking, delivering details of what had happened and the address to come to, she was praying – harder than she'd ever prayed in her life. When the ambulance finally turned up and her grandmother was stretchered out of the house, Ruby continued praying, unable to stop.

Chapter Twenty

IT wasn't a heart attack Sarah had suffered, but an episode of angina – a bad one. In the starkly lit hospital corridor, the doctor informed both her daughter and granddaughter that she was, for now, stable, but that she was vulnerable too. The angina had caused some damage around the heart and a stent might be required. Further tests would confirm if this were the case. Ruby and Jessica were allowed to see her, but only for a few minutes. In the hospital bed, Sarah looked so small, so *unlike* Sarah.

I'm sorry, Gran, I'm so sorry. Ruby kept the words rolling in her mind, hoping they'd reach her somehow, and penetrate her psyche.

After a few moments, a nurse led them from the room.

"Why don't you go home and get some sleep?" she suggested. "Sarah's in the best possible place right now. There's really nothing more you can do – not tonight anyway."

Ruby had wanted to stay, but Jessica had insisted, surprising her with her conviction.

"Gran will be okay, Ruby. Let's go."

After a few moments of hesitation, Ruby allowed herself to be guided down several flights of stairs – there was no way she'd take the lift this time – to the hospital entrance.

"Look who's waiting for you," Jessica said, her voice not

unlike the nurse's.

It was Jed. He'd been sitting patiently in reception, but as soon as he saw them he jumped to his feet and started wagging his tail furiously.

"Hello, boy, glad to see you," said Jessica, smiling down at him. To Ruby, she said, "We need to call a cab."

"I… I haven't got any money on me."

"There's money at home. Do you have your phone?"

Ruby reached round to the back pocket of the jeans she'd borrowed from her mum to come to hospital, retrieved her mobile and handed it over.

Jessica pushed it back. "I'll tell you the number, you call. I don't know how to work that gadget of yours."

The taxi turned up less than five minutes later. Both women sat side by side in the back. Ruby stared blindly out of the window as scenery passed her – the despair she felt inside building with each mile the taxi travelled. Feeling her eyes water, she was glad – glad and surprised – when her mother reached for her hand and enclosed it in her own.

"She'll be all right," Jessica whispered.

After retrieving some money from inside the house and paying the driver, Jessica closed the door behind them. Ruby was standing in the hallway, not knowing which direction to turn. She wished Cash was here right now to put his arms around her, but she'd told him to leave her alone. It was best he continued to do that.

"Go through to the kitchen," Jessica said and, grateful for instruction, Ruby obeyed.

"I don't want tea," she said, sinking down onto one of the chairs. She couldn't face eating or drinking at all; she would gag if she did, she was sure.

"No tea," Jessica agreed, sitting down too.

Jed came and laid his head on her lap – surprising her as her mother had surprised her in the cab – staring up at her with sympathetic eyes before settling at her feet.

"He really loves you, doesn't he?" Jessica commented.

"Jed? He's a good dog."

"We need to get some sleep soon, so we can be at the hospital first thing."

"I know." But Ruby doubted she'd sleep a wink for what was left of the night.

Silence descended, but it felt too heavy.

"Mum, I…" Ruby began, but Jessica interrupted her.

"Not tonight, Ruby. I know we need to talk, but not now."

Ruby felt her vision blur again. *Don't cry. Don't let yourself down.*

Immediately, Jessica took hold of her hand again. "Cry if you want, it'll help."

Being given the go-ahead seemed to cause a dam to burst inside her, and water poured in torrents from her eyes and her nose. Her mother's arms came round her, held her – not with the timidity she expected, but with an impressive semblance of strength.

"There, there, that's it, darling, let it out. Let it all out. It's not good to keep it in."

Of all the things that had happened tonight, this was perhaps the most unexpected. Usually it was Gran who comforted her, who bolstered her. Jessica hadn't done so for years, since… since…

Although she was reluctant to, she pulled back. She had to ask. "Mum, are we safe?"

Jessica glanced at Jed. "I think so – for now."

Clearly, she was using him as a yardstick too.

"About Gran – I should never have said what I did."

"Ruby, it's fine…"

"How can you say it's fine? It's not! I attacked her. I don't mean physically, but with words. I… I blamed her for everything."

"Ruby, we *cannot* talk about this right now."

Ruby wiped roughly at her nose with the back of her hand. "Why can't we?"

"Because you're tired; I'm tired. You're also distraught; feeling all sorts of emotions. Negative emotions primarily – guilt and shame. You need to sleep, even if it's just for a couple of hours. It'll help put things back into perspective. We can talk tomorrow, when we're both feeling less shell-shocked. Tomorrow, I promise, I'll tell you what you want to know."

Ruby gasped. She couldn't help it. After refusing for years and years, her mother was finally promising to reveal what had happened the night of her breakdown. But did she want to know? Had Gran been right all along? Would it do more harm than good?

Jessica rose to her feet and pulled Ruby with her.

"Stop mulling it over. We're going to bed – my bed. Do you remember when you were young – you often used to sleep with me?"

Ruby did remember. That had all stopped when she was seven.

"I used to hold you close, didn't I?" Jessica continued.

Ruby nodded slowly, tears still wet on her cheeks. "Can Jed come?"

"Of course he can. In fact, I insist he does."

At the foot of the narrow staircase, Ruby hesitated. "We

need to protect ourselves," she said, glad she had Rosamund's necklace on at least.

"I've already done that, for both of us."

As her mother led the way, Ruby was amazed. Gran had insisted she was a little better lately – taking walks down to the beach, when previously she had shut herself away. But this could be described as more than just a little better – this was a transformation. Jessica was acting like a mother again, taking care of her child – just when her child needed her to.

Discarding her shoes and clothes, pulling on the pyjamas she'd arrived in, Ruby settled in the double bed, indicating for Jed to snuggle beside her.

"It's nice to have you home," Jessica said, pulling Ruby close and stroking her hair in rhythmic movements. "I've missed this."

"Me too," Ruby replied. More than her mother could know.

"You see – something good comes out of everything."

Although a part of her was still afraid to close her eyes, Ruby took that thought into dreams with her and, like Rosamund's necklace, clung to it as protection.

Chapter Twenty-One

THE sound of her mobile ringing woke Ruby just a few hours later. Although reluctant to remove her mother's arm, which was still around her shoulders, Ruby crept from bed. It was Cash. Apparently, he'd rung six times, but this was the first time she'd heard it.

He'd left messages too.

Where are you? Call me back as soon as you get this.

Are you okay? Call me, please.

If you don't call back, I'm coming round to your flat. You're starting to worry me now.

And the final one:

Right, that's it! I'm on my way to your flat. If you want to tell me to get lost when I get there, that's fine. I just need to know you're okay.

Ruby agitated the inside of her cheek. She didn't want him to worry, but she didn't want him to know where she was either – to involve him further in what was happening. But, as you couldn't trace a text, it was safe to send one, and so she did.

Hi, Cash, please don't worry about me. I'm fine, I promise. I've had to go away for a few days, but as soon as I get back I'll call you and explain.

Her hand slowed. She wondered if she should add *'I love you'* to the text? Eventually she decided she would. It was the truth. She did love him, and she wanted him to know it.

Switching off her mobile, she headed towards the shower, calling for Jed to accompany her. Afterwards, she'd raid her mother's wardrobe further. Thankfully, Jessica's taste wasn't too dissimilar to hers; she had plenty of jeans, jumpers and boots to choose from. There was no need to return to her flat, not yet. When she'd be able to, she didn't know. Work would have to wait too. This was more important.

Having dressed, Ruby rang the hospital on the house phone to enquire about Sarah.

"She's doing very well," the nurse called Jasmine said – the same one she and her mother had met the previous day. "She's had a good night and is now fully conscious. By all means, come in and see her, but you won't be able to stay long. We mustn't tire her out."

Assuring Jasmine she wouldn't, Ruby rushed back into the bedroom where her mother was also getting dressed, to tell her they could go and see Sarah.

In the throes of zipping up her trousers, Jessica paused. "How is she?"

"Fine, they said she was fine," Ruby replied, hope beginning to make a return.

They called another cab to take them to the hospital. Her mother used to drive. Ruby remembered the white VW Beetle she'd had – 'a rust bucket', her Gran affectionately called it. But she hadn't driven in years, not since the breakdown.

"My driving days are over," she'd said, when Ruby asked her once if she ever intended to get behind the wheel of a car again. She was only in her forties – perhaps there'd be time to contemplate that further if she continued to improve. Ruby hoped so.

At the hospital, they hurried back to Level Three. Sarah had been given her own room whilst they assessed her, but Ruby had been warned she'd be moved to a communal ward soon. For now, though, Ruby was grateful she had her privacy.

Eager to see her, Ruby was just opening the door when she was stopped in her tracks.

"Excuse me, could you please wait a few minutes before going in? The doctors are with her at the moment."

A nurse, not Jasmine – she was short and plump, as opposed to tall and willowy, and not gentle either, but all brisk efficiency – seemed to materialise from nowhere.

"Oh, erm... sure," Ruby replied.

The nurse pointed to a row of plastic chairs where several others were sitting.

Taking a seat too, Ruby placed the jacket she'd commandeered from her mother on her knees. The nurse, meanwhile, continued on her way. Her attention solely on the room where Gran lay, it took a while before Ruby noticed that her mother kept glancing to one side. Curiosity getting the better of her, she leaned forward. Sitting just a couple of seats down from her mother, in-between a bored-looking woman and an equally bored-looking man, was another man – probably no more than twenty and in a very sorry state. He looked as though he'd had a fight with a speeding car and lost.

"Poor lad," she heard her mother say.

"He's only recently passed, hasn't he?"

"Yes. He's very confused."

"Has he noticed us yet?" Ruby asked.

"Not yet – all he's trying to do is understand what's happened to him."

Ruby sighed. "He's so young."

"I know. The young ones always upset me. Such a glorious life cut short."

Ruby looked at her mother instead of the man, astonished she'd described life in that way. But then, Jessica's life *had* been glorious before the breakdown; she used to laugh so much before that thing... that beast, sucked the life from her, and from all of them. How she hated it! She hated it!

"Stop it!" Jessica said, her voice no longer soft but with a harsh edge to it.

Ruby recoiled. "What?" she asked but she knew full well.

"Your hatred will attract it. Stop it now."

"How... how did you know?"

"I can feel it rolling off you, I should think anyone can."

Ruby swallowed. "I'm sorry. I will."

Sitting back in her chair, Ruby took a few deep breaths. Jessica was right – of course she was. She just hadn't expected to be told by her, of all people.

There was movement at the door to Sarah's room. The doctors were coming out. Ruby stood, as did Jessica, and bolted forward.

"I'm Ruby, this is Jessica – Sarah's granddaughter and daughter. How is she?"

One of the doctors stepped forward, a reassuring smile on his face.

"Hello, Ruby and Jessica, I'm Greg. I'm pleased to say that Sarah should make a full recovery and, at this stage, no surgery is required."

The relief on her mother's face mirrored her own, she was sure.

"But we're not letting her go anywhere for a few days," Greg continued, "just as a precaution. By all means, go in and see her – she was asking for you both. But please don't stay too long. Sarah will make a full recovery, but only if she's allowed to rest."

Smiling again at them, the doctor then turned, and he and his colleagues drifted away, their gait not as hurried as the nurse's; it was much more leisurely in style, as though they were off to a barbeque or a drinks party, rather than to assess another patient.

"Come on, let's go in," Ruby said eagerly, one hand reaching out to grab hold of the door handle.

Her mother smiled too. "Ruby, you go in. Talk to Gran."

Some of Ruby's enthusiasm waned. "What about you?"

"I'll come in a while." Looking behind her, she added, "I'll deal with our friend first."

The man was still sitting forlornly, his head in his hands now.

"The live patients have gone," Jessica explained. "It's a good opportunity."

"Okay, I'll see you in a while."

"You will," Jessica said, taking the jacket from her and indicating for her to go ahead.

Turning to face the door once again, Ruby hesitated before pushing her way in – nerves overtaking enthusiasm. She was, after all, the reason Gran was in hospital.

The room was a large square box – stark in its symmetry. Bright sunlight filtered in through flimsy curtains, and in the centre was a grey metal bed, railings on either side pulled up to protect its occupant from falling. In that bed lay Sarah, exhausted. Ruby had often pored over pictures of Sarah as a young woman. She'd been beautiful – her shoulder-length hair immaculate, her dress sense elegant. She was still beautiful in Ruby's eyes, but she was careworn too – there was no denying it.

"Oh, Gran," Ruby said, tears overcoming her. "I'm so sorry."

Rushing forward, she pulled up a chair so she could sit close by her bedside. Threading her hands through the grey railings, she took Sarah's hands in hers. They felt so cold.

"Gran, it's me. It's Ruby."

Sarah opened her eyes. "Hello, darling. Your mother…"

"She's fine, she's outside. She said for me to come in first."

Sarah patted Ruby's hand. "Good, I'm glad." Trying to lean forward slightly, she instructed Ruby to lower the rail, removing the barrier between them.

When Ruby had done so she apologised again, but Sarah interrupted.

"I'm the one who's sorry. You were right. I've let you down."

"No!" Ruby almost shouted the word, before remembering it was imperative to stay calm – not just for her sake, but for Sarah's too. Lowering her voice, she continued, "You're my rock, Gran, and you've taught me well. You taught me what was right."

Sarah's head fell back slightly, and she closed her eyes again, but only briefly.

"Gran, do you want me to call someone?"

"No. I'm just sleepy, that's all."

"Of course you are, I'm sorry. I'm tiring you. The

229

doctor told me not to."

"Will you please stop apologising?"

There was a spark in Sarah's voice – a spark that both surprised Ruby and heartened her.

"Oh, Gran," she said again, leaning forward.

"Ruby, I *am* tired but we need to talk. I don't know how much time we have."

"Time? But, the doctor said you'd be fine. He's expecting you to make a full recovery."

"I'm not talking about me. I'm talking about you… and Jessica."

Ruby could feel herself pale. "Oh," was all she could say in response.

Sarah turned towards her, her eyes more silver than the green they used to be. "I told you once that what's a part of your mother's world does not have to be a part of yours. I was wrong. It seems to have been a part for many years. Ruby, when did you first see it?"

"When I was seven."

"The night your mother came home?"

"The night of her breakdown."

"And Danny… he brought it all back to you?"

"He did, but not intentionally."

Sarah sighed. "Ruby, I made a decision when I was very young, to walk in the light, to stay in the light, where I believe… where I *know* evil cannot thrive. People don't often realise it, but we define our world with our thoughts and beliefs, and I believed darkness was not going to be a part of mine. My mother was different. She explored the possibility of lower realms than ours, realms where bad things exist – dumping grounds. But she was an incredible woman. Throughout her research, she remained grounded, objective and, most importantly, unharmed. Even so, some of the things she documented…" Sarah exhaled. "But she felt for them rather than feared them."

Ruby remembered Gran talking about the level-headed Rosamund. She had mentioned the dumping grounds too, but only once. Nonetheless, it was an analogy she herself had used when talking to Danny, when trying to explain the unexplainable to him. Her great-grandmother had explored them and remained unscathed. Was she too emotional in comparison – not pragmatic enough? Her mother also, and that's why darkness had managed to infiltrate? Just as she couldn't hide her thoughts from Theo and, at times, Ness, she couldn't hide her thoughts from Gran either.

"Ruby, you *are* strong, please remember that. Your mother is also growing in strength. But what you don't understand, not fully, not yet, is that both darkness and the light live in you. People believe in an external god and that's fine, that's their prerogative. But, Ruby, my belief is God is within us and, if he is, then I suppose the devil must be too."

Ruby flinched at the suggestion. This was something Gran had never admitted before.

"The devil is real?" she asked, her eyes widening.

Sarah sighed again, as though in exasperation. "This is hard to explain, Ruby. I don't fully understand it. Rosamund didn't. We may be able to see beyond this realm, but we're only human and we suffer the limitations of the human brain. What truly exists beyond, we don't know, and nor are we meant to – not at this stage in our journey, I suspect it might just blow our minds. But, like my mother, I have studied. I have talked with supposedly enlightened people. I have done my utmost to educate myself so I can educate both you and Jessica. But there are so many theories to choose from. In the end, you have to pick the one that resonates with you the most – the one that you feel is instinctively right. The devil is real, but perhaps he's only real here. When we leave this plane behind, when we go to one that's higher – ascend, if you like – perhaps that's when we are truly safe."

Ruby marvelled, not only at what Sarah was saying, but also at the irony of it. "So, right now, in this realm that I'm living in, *whilst* I'm living, I'm not safe. But once I'm dead, I'm free?"

Sarah nodded slowly. "People think the devil waits for them on the other side. But from what I can make out, he doesn't – he waits for us here."

An image of the figure with the black and yellow eyes did its utmost to materialise in her mind, but she quashed it, replaced it with an image of Cash instead – that grin of his firmly in place. She also tried to imagine his smell – warm and masculine, with a slight hint of musk. Anything to stop the rancid smell of what had stalked her invading again.

"I don't want to die, Gran. Not yet. I've too much to live for."

Fire was back in Sarah's voice again. "And nor shall you, Ruby, nor shall you." It was a moment before she could continue speaking. "The Native Americans have their own take on this. They believe there are two wolves inside us; one is good, and one is evil. The evil wolf is anger, sorrow, regret, greed, and arrogance… I think you get the picture. The good wolf is joy, peace, love, hope, serenity, and kindness. Which wolf wins?"

Ruby thought for a moment. "The one you feed the most."

Sarah smiled, and it transformed her. Momentarily, she seemed young again, and strong. Seeing that, Ruby smiled too.

"You see, Gran, I have always listened."

"I know, darling, I know."

"But…" Ruby continued, "if evil is inside me—"

"Inside us all, Ruby."

"Inside us all," Ruby repeated. "How come I can see it?"

"Because it's broken off, like a shard or a splinter. It's become a thing apart."

Presley's mention of David-Néel came to mind – of the tulpa she'd created.

"A thing that has the power to destroy?"

"In Danny's case, yes. But I hope not in yours."

"And, like a shard or a splinter, it's a part of something much bigger?"

"We're all a part of something much bigger, darling."

Ruby was aware time was passing, that she was putting a strain on her grandmother, but Sarah, picking up on her thoughts again, simply said, "Ruby, this is important."

"How do I get rid of it?" she asked at last.

"Truly? I don't know. With your mother, I've always just managed it, and I did that by wrapping her in love, every day, from head to toe – unconditional and unstinting love. That's why I could no longer work. Looking after her was a full-time job, and only recently has she started to improve. It's been a long and weary process – for all of us. You know, Ruby, it would be easy for me to feel resentment towards this thing that has changed our lives so dramatically, and not for the better. But I don't. I monitor my feelings constantly – I keep them neutral. And I've insisted your mother do the same. I thought that might diminish it, make it lose interest, even – but seemingly not. It's found you instead." Her expression was more serious than Ruby had ever seen it before. "Quite simply, you need to go into battle. You need to fight it. And, my feeling is, sooner rather than later. Don't feed it anymore. Don't let it grow – or it *will* consume you. Not your soul, perhaps, but your heart and your mind. It will break you, like it broke your mother. It will snap you in half like a twig. Ruby, I wish I could help, but I'm so weak right now." Forcing a wry smile, she added, "My humanity is letting me down."

Before she could reply, the door to Sarah's room opened. Turning round, Ruby expected to see Jessica, but it was the nurse from earlier.

"What did I say about tiring your Gran? Come on, love, you know she needs her rest."

Leaving Sarah was the last thing she wanted to do, but Ruby acquiesced. As she bent over Sarah to kiss her cheek, the skin there as soft as petals, her grandmother found the strength to speak again.

"Find a way to send it back to where it came from, Ruby. Put away the frightened child you used to be and react as an adult. Have confidence in your ability, and your gift. Please, find a way, for all our sakes. This thing has been with us far too long."

Back in the corridor, Jessica came hurrying towards her. "How is she?"

"She's… she's fine," Ruby replied.

Over her shoulder, she noticed the spirit of the man was gone.

"You talked to him then? Got him to come to terms with his passing."

Jessica turned round to look at the row of seats also – now empty. "I did. He was a lovely chap – helped me as much as I helped him."

"Oh?" Ruby queried. "In what way?"

Jessica held up Ruby's mobile phone. It must have been in the jacket pocket. "He showed me how to work this," she explained.

"Why? Who did you want to call?"

"Cash."

"Cash? Mum, I don't want him involved!"

"But he wants to help, Ruby, and right now, we need all the help we can get."

Chapter Twenty-Two

RUBY fully realised anger was a negative feeling, but she couldn't help it. She was fuming. She tried to ring Cash back, tell him not to come over, but he was the one avoiding her calls now. On the way back home in the cab – the journey taking forever because of newly erected road works and heavy traffic combined – she could barely speak to her mother. Jessica, however, remained unrepentant, unperturbed, even, by her daughter's reaction.

Having made sure to bring money with them this time, Jessica once again paid the driver whilst Ruby climbed out of the cab. Still fuming, she walked up the path to Lazuli Cottage. Jed was waiting for her inside, and at least him she was pleased to see.

Going through to the kitchen, she threw her jacket on the table, Jessica a few paces behind her.

"Mum, what's happening to us… this… attack that we're under. The last thing I want is Cash here – he might get hurt."

"That's it, Ruby, that's better."

That wasn't the reply she'd expected.

"How is this better? I'm angry. Exactly what I'm not supposed to be."

"It's better because it's a healthy anger. It's spirited. Anger borne of fear is the kind we want to avoid. Fear altogether, if we can help it."

Ruby was aghast. "You've spent the last eighteen years living in fear. How can you avoid it now?"

"Because I have to," Jessica replied, her voice not quite as confident as it had been a few moments before. "Because Gran may recover this time. But next time, she may not. She's getting older, frailer. In contrast, I have to get stronger." She paused for a moment before continuing. "I've been an idiot in my lifetime. I've been stupid, vain, and arrogant. But one thing I won't be is a burden – not to you."

Ruby tried to reply but couldn't find the words. Jessica saved her the effort.

"Cash loves you. I've only met him a handful of times – perhaps not even as much as that – but it's plain to see. And you need all the people who love you to surround you right now. They're armour. I told Cash to contact the people you work with, and to bring them too."

"What? But, Mum, they've tried to banish it – they couldn't."

"Then they try again."

Before Ruby could argue further, Jed started barking. Immediately, Ruby's heart started to pound.

"Shit," she said, staring at her mother.

Jessica reached out a hand in comfort. "It's okay. He can hear people approaching. See? That's the bell. Your friends are here. They must have left straightaway."

Trying to regain control of her breathing, Ruby watched as Jessica walked towards the front door. Opening it, she saw Cash standing at the helm, his eyes searching. Behind him were Theo, Ness and Corinna. Wagging his tale at the sight of them, Jed rushed towards Cash – jumped up in greeting – although Cash remained oblivious.

"Ruby!" he said as Jessica stood aside to let him in.

"Cash," she whispered.

The sight of him wasn't just welcome, it was immense. All the horror, the fear, and the despair of the last twenty-four hours seemed to take flight – if only for a short while.

"Cash," she said again – not a whisper, more of a cry this time, as she rushed forward. Jessica was right. She needed him. She needed them all.

"I should never have let you go yesterday. I could kick myself for it." The words were tumbling from his mouth as he held her.

"It doesn't matter. You're here now – that's what counts."

"I love you, Ruby Davis," he said, a catch in his voice.

"I love you too, Cash Wilkins," she replied, holding him even tighter.

How long they stood like this, Ruby had no idea, but gradually she became aware of the others standing patiently by, looking everywhere, at pictures that hung on the wall, at dust on the skirting boards, at each other even, everywhere but them.

"Sorry," she said, breaking away.

Theo waved a hand in the air. "No, no, no, not at all. Displays of love and passion are most welcome in my eyes. Can't get enough of them."

Corinna started laughing at Theo's words. Incredibly, Ness did too, and Jessica. Ruby and Cash joined in, holding onto each other again as their bodies shook. It was a magical moment – such a contrast to the moments of late – a moment to treasure. Only Gran would have made it complete. The memory of her lying exhausted in a hospital bed sobered Ruby. There was a reason her friends were here, and it shouldn't be forgotten.

She ushered them into the kitchen, the room cramped with so many people filling it. Nonetheless, they each managed to find a seat around the dining table – all except Ruby, who perched on Cash's knee.

"Mum," Ruby began, "I've told you so much about these people, I'm sure you can work out who's who. But this is Theo. Next to her is Corinna. And Ness is on my right."

"Hello, Vanessa," said Jessica, fixating on her.

"Jessica, how are you?"

Ruby frowned. "Funny – you two sound as if you know each other."

There was a brief silence in which Theo looked at Ness curiously, and Corinna did too.

"Do you?" Theo prompted.

Finally, Ness answered. "We have met. Eighteen years ago, to be exact. Right here in Hastings – in this very house."

If Cash hadn't had his arms around her waist, Ruby would surely have slid from his lap and hit the floor. "You've met? Here, in this house? Why?"

As Jessica stared straight ahead, Ness examined her shoes – a pair of brown loafers.

"I can't wait to hear either," Theo remarked.

Ness lifted her head. "Tea? Can I make us all a cup?"

"I… well, yeah, if you want to. Or I can do it…"

"No, it's fine, Ruby, let me," Ness replied. To Jessica she said, "Is that okay?"

"Please, go ahead," said Jessica. "We may need two or three cups in all honesty, and some of Gran's homemade shortbread too. How we met, well… may I tell the story?"

239

Chapter Twenty-Three

HER audience rapt, Jessica started speaking.

"My story doesn't start eighteen years ago; it starts several years before that." Focussing on Ruby, she added, "Before you were born even." Despite herself, she laughed – a joyless sound, so different to how she'd laughed earlier in the hall. "God, but I was a trial to my mother as a teenager – headstrong and wilful. I thought I knew it all."

"You sound like a typical teenager to me," Theo offered.

Jessica denied it. "We both know there's nothing typical about me – about any of us."

Theo only shrugged in reply.

Jessica had been in her early twenties when she'd found herself pregnant. She'd had several lovers at the time – commitment not something she'd bought into. She preferred freedom, both spiritual and sexually. Being free made sense. Where was the harm in it? A few years after Ruby's birth she'd met a group of people who shared her ethos; who embraced it wholeheartedly, as they did her.

Sarah knew about the group. *Terra Stella,* they called themselves – an unashamedly romantic name.

"What does it mean?" Ruby asked.

"It's Latin; it means star dust."

"Star dust?" Ruby repeated. Her eyes widening slightly, she said, "The building Danny lived in, it was called *Seren*

– that's Welsh for star."

"A coincidence perhaps, or maybe, I don't know… all roads lead to where we are now."

"But why so romantic?" Corinna asked. "When romance wasn't encouraged."

"*'Every man and every woman is a star.'* That was our belief."

Theo raised an eyebrow. "Crowley was one of your interests?"

"He was one of them," Jessica admitted. "Our group was an offshoot of The Golden Dawn, which itself was an offshoot of the English Rosicrucian Society – formed for the practice of ceremonial magic and the acquisition of initiatory knowledge and powers. But," and here she paused, "as I was always at pains to point out to Mum, by the time I joined, it was more of a discussion group than anything else. That's all we tended to do – get together to discuss topics that interested us. Well… that and have fun."

Even so, Sarah still condemned it, warning Jessica to steer clear of occult matters. She wanted her to concentrate on her 'gift' instead, to help grounded spirits move towards the light. She also wanted her to focus on her daughter. Jessica wasn't averse to doing either but, as she explained to her mother, it wasn't *all* she wanted to do. And there was a part of her that just couldn't help it. The light fascinated her, but so did the dark – the flip side of the coin. And the people in the group, they weren't just friends; they were like family, sharing their time and their insights, as well as their bodies.

"So, it was a coven you belonged to?" Cash asked.

Jessica denied it. "We never called ourselves that. Never.

We were against categorising ourselves too. We didn't want to *belong* to anything."

Jessica knew Rosamund, her grandmother, had delved into darkness. She'd examined bad thoughts as energy: what happened to them, where they went, and whether such energy dissipated, or just the opposite. Rosamund Davis had died when Jessica was a baby. She'd had Sarah late in life, had several boys beforehand, none of whom were psychic. Jessica often studied photos of her grandmother, and 'esteemed' was always the word that sprang to mind whenever she thought of ways to describe her. She'd been held in high regard and Jessica could see why. She looked proud, capable of convincing even the most sceptical that there was more to this world than meets the eye.

Jessica had a desire to make people believe in her ability too, most notably the other members of *Terra Stella*. In school she'd been told by her mother not to talk about it; Ruby had been told the same. Both had heeded that warning, but in her late teens, just after college, she'd met a different set of people – people actively interested in what she could see, who encouraged her, who were stepping stones to the group she would eventually join. A group that hadn't believed she was psychic, not at first, Jessica remembered that.

"Prove it," one of them had said – Karl – older than Jessica by several years and Byronic with his dark hair and brown eyes. But it was Saul, a recent member like herself, whom she wanted to impress the most. Saul was the antithesis of Karl. He had Nordic looks: the blondest of hair and eyes that reminded her of cornflowers. It was Saul who mesmerised her, who looked at her with the same doubt as the others.

People came and people went, but by the mid-nineties, there were twelve of them in total – eight men, including Saul and Karl, and four women. Of the women, she liked Cally and Maria best, but one of them, Dervla, she couldn't bond with. She knew why. Saul adored her. The need to remind him that no one belonged to any other – the group's ethos – bordered on obsession. Dervla and he spent far too much time together.

Although they all liked to wax lyrical on theological and occult matters, including much talk of Crowley – a former Hastings resident and a personal hero of Saul's – regarding her psychic ability, they humoured her. She could sense it. And proving it to them was not easy. Ironically, for those deeply interested in the spiritual world, they were closed-off.

"Concentrate," she remembered saying to several of them on one occasion. She'd taken them to a site she'd previously visited, an abandoned house in which she knew a grounded spirit resided. Instead of helping her towards the light, she'd used her as bait.

"Cally, she's standing right beside you, staring at you. Don't tell me you can't feel her?"

As Cally shrugged her shoulders, Dervla sneered, her contempt plain to see. Jessica could just imagine the things she'd say to Saul afterwards, when they were alone together, how they'd laugh at her and her supposed 'gift'. If only the spirits would throw things, make audible noises, cause a light bulb to shatter – anything. But they never did.

"Those benign spirits I encountered, I cursed them. Can you believe it?" Jessica said, hardly able to believe it herself.

"I wanted them to perform. My arrogance astounds me!"

Returning to her story, Jessica told them how she continued to obsess about finding a way to convince the group she was genuine. Meanwhile, Saul and Dervla grew closer.

"They were practically monogamous," she said. "Why they bothered to stay in the group I don't know. One night, my mother was out. I stayed at home to look after Ruby. Whilst she was asleep in bed, I went to Mum's bedroom. I knew she'd kept all of Rosamund's papers and I began to scour through them. Every time Mum was busy, I took the opportunity to do that. There must be something of interest there, something I could use."

Pausing to take a sip of tea, Jessica looked at the faces around her once again, at Ruby in particular, the daughter she'd let down. Taking a deep breath, she continued. "This pit, where dark thoughts gathered—"

"Rosamund called it a dumping ground," Ruby interrupted.

It didn't surprise her that Ruby knew about it. "You're right, she did, and it's as good a description as any. This dumping ground – Rosamund was fascinated by it and what it contained. She felt it formed the basis for demonology, or at least the human take on it. I'm sure you all know Psalm 23. *Even though I walk through the valley of the shadow of death, I will fear no evil.* Rosamund's theory was that when we shed our physical bodies we pass through this dumping ground – home to our own negative thoughts as well as others – en route to the light. It's the tunnel, perhaps, that people who have near death experiences so often report – the darkness before the dazzle. We pass through it and we mustn't fear it; we have faith – in the light, in a Higher Power, in ourselves. In renouncing it, we *evolve*. But what about things confined to the dumping ground, some of which had taken on, if not human form, a recognisable form – at least to human eyes – were they damned forever?"

She noticed Cash nodding, his eyes wide. "It really does sound like hell," he said.

"The hell we know of," agreed Jessica, before continuing. "What if these beings weren't confined? What if they could manifest, if they could break free? Astaroth, Bael, Kali…"

"Aiwass," Ruby added.

Theo stiffened. "You mustn't let your thoughts linger on Aiwass, Ruby."

"But that's just it," Jessica replied. "People know about Aiwass; they know about the others too. Some worship them; some fear them. *Many* fear them – the majority of the human race. They're all part of our conditioning. Demons such as those are in books, and not forbidden books either, but children's stories and fairy tales. We're told certain beings are evil, over and over again, and how much they can harm us. Their image is all too clear, and once we've seen it, it becomes part of our consciousness. A mass image and a mass consciousness results in mass fear, and that's energy too."

Despite the seriousness of her words, Corinna scoffed. "What about the Tooth Fairy, Father Christmas, and the Easter Bunny for God's sake? Billions of kids around the world believe in them, but you don't see their likeness running amok on streets or in parks."

"But that's just it, you *do*, you see them everywhere. At Christmas, you can't go into a department store without encountering Santa Claus in his grotto. The difference is – with the exception of toddlers, perhaps – people don't fear those kinds of figures. And because they don't fear them, they don't give them energy. It's only when we fear something that we feed it. You see, it's not what makes us comfortable that captures the human imagination – it's what makes us uncomfortable."

"But there's Halloween?" Corinna continued. "People dress up as devils and demons then."

"They do," Jessica replied, "but in the spirit of fun. There's no fear invested."

"Mum," Ruby reminded her. "You were talking about the dumping grounds."

"Yes, of course, the dumping grounds. Remember, I wanted to prove that I was psychic to my friends? I wanted their respect."

"Saul's especially," Ruby pointed out.

"Saul's especially," Jessica conceded. "I took this idea of manifestation and I ran with it. We used to meet at Saul's house on the outskirts of Hastings, in St Leonards practically– a grand house it was, one of those big old Victorians. He came from well-to-do stock, his father often working abroad, and his mother usually accompanying him." Her eyes misted slightly at the memory. "It all seemed so glamorous to me at the time – his lineage, and how rich he was. Not so much now."

"You had your very own temple of worship." The disdain on Theo's face was clear.

"It's where we spent most of our time, where we practised our beliefs, where we were free."

"And where the trouble started," pointed out Ness.

"That too," Jessica said, bowing her head slightly. "Saul

was interested in manifestation, the possibility of it, and because I seemed to know more about it than the others, thanks to Rosamund, he began to spend more time with me. We'd talk for hours about the subject, about which demon we found the most terrifying, and what we would do if we could conjure it. More to the point, what it could do for us. Whether great power and wealth might be one of the rewards."

"Power and wealth gained dishonestly carries a heavy price," Theo said.

"I know that now. But don't forget, at that time, we were young, we were fanciful. Drugs were involved, and alcohol, as well as hormones. It's a potent mix. All of us were interested in the occult, in forces of good and evil. Some more than others, I have to admit. But come on, who doesn't question things? Who doesn't ask themselves if it's all a matter of perception? If Lucifer isn't bad, just misunderstood? If God is actually the great dictator?"

"This was the nineties, wasn't it?" Cash remarked. "You sound like a bunch of sixties hippies to me."

Jessica smiled, knowing the comment wasn't meant cruelly. "Even kids today question – more so than ever, I think." Not caring that it was lukewarm, Jessica finished her tea, staring for a moment at the empty mug. "Basically, Saul and I started to experiment, incorporating some of the elements from rituals Crowley had used, that Saul had read about. 'The Paris Incident' – have you heard of it?"

"Where Crowley and one of his disciples tried to raise Pan?" Theo said.

"Yes," replied Jessica, having to lower her eyes again. Could she continue? She had to try. "We tried to raise our own demon, calling on it to come forward, over and over again." She knew she shouldn't try to justify her actions, but she couldn't help it. "You have to realise, I'd have done anything to keep Saul happy, to keep him focussed on me."

"'The Paris Incident'," Ness interjected, "was a disaster, resulting only in madness and death."

"But Crowley died in Hastings not Paris," Cash pointed out.

"Crowley wasn't the one who died," Jessica explained. "That was his disciple. But when he was found the next morning, he was a gibbering, incoherent wreck – crouched in the corner of the room, his robes torn to shreds, and the furniture around him smashed to pieces. He disappeared off the scene for a while. Rumour has it he was committed to an asylum, where he stayed for several years. Eventually he was released, but he was never the same. He died at Netherwood, just up the road."

"And you knew all this before you started?" Cash looked astonished.

"I did."

"Yet you went ahead anyway? You tried to copy him?"

"It's the old saying, isn't it?" Jessica replied. "*It won't happen to me.*"

"The old saying?" queried Theo. "Well, if you're so keen on sayings, Jessica, here's another: *'If you play with fire, you're going to get burnt'.* Now please, get to the point about what happened. I don't want to linger on Crowley any more than we have to."

"Of course not. I can't repeat the incantations we used—"

Theo interrupted. "You certainly can't!"

Again, the rebuke was clear, and Jessica had to swallow

hard before continuing. "But in combining incantations with my psychic ability, we did it – we made a connection."

There. The words were out. The confession. Looking around, she could see how shocked they were, and shame – ever present – consumed her. Did they want more, a description perhaps? She'd spent so long blocking out what she'd seen, having to shut down her faculties one by one to do just that. What there'd been in the darkness – a light surrounding it, but a stark light, unclean, not the light of love, far from it – would her mind even *let* her recall it?

"I… I…"

Ness broke in. "Jessica, it's okay, we've got the gist."

Jessica felt almost faint with relief.

"Ness is quite right." Theo looked decidedly more sympathetic than she had previously. "Perhaps you can tell us about your involvement with Ness instead."

"Let me do that," Ness insisted and, again, Jessica was grateful. She needed time to collect herself.

"I was working for Sussex Police at the time – in a freelance capacity, of course, as a psychic – mainly involved in murder cases where the police were having a hard time finding clues. This case, I hesitate to add – the 'Hastings Incident', I suppose we can call it from here on in – wasn't a murder case. No one died. But it was clear it involved the paranormal, so I was called in anyway."

Ness turned towards Ruby. "Whether they did or not, that night your mother and Saul *believed* they invoked a demon. Visualising this dumping ground, focussing on what resided in it, they saw something – something that led to Jessica having a breakdown, and Saul… well, losing his mind, I think it's safe to say. Stark naked, he ran through the streets of Hastings, shattering car windows with a baseball bat – shop windows and house windows too. The police finally caught up with him but, like Crowley, he too was a gibbering wreck – kept reciting demonic names over and over again, insisting he was marked for death, and begging for mercy. The police, of course, didn't have a clue what to do with him, so they called me. I was living in Eastbourne then. It wasn't a long drive over; I was there when he was at his worst. I knew to protect myself as soon as I saw him. Unlike Ruby, I also knew *not* to tune into what he'd seen, not to even attempt it. To do that would make me vulnerable. Instead I talked to him, tried to calm him, to make him believe it was over, that he was safe."

"But if you help me, won't it make you vulnerable too?"

Jessica's heart went out to Ruby as she asked Ness the question. But Ness's answer, she could have predicted.

"We're a team. What affects you affects us all."

It wasn't just Ruby that grew misty-eyed at this display of loyalty – so did Jessica. Ness, meanwhile, continued speaking.

"After a few days, I managed to extract a name from Saul – Jessica Davis. He kept saying it was all her fault." Ness looked at Jessica. "Sorry, Jessica."

"Don't be. It's the truth. It was."

"There was nothing more I could do for him. We tracked down his family, informed them, and they flew back to England straight away. I believe they placed him under intensive psychiatric care. Meanwhile, I traced Jessica. I was curious about her; I wanted to know who this girl was who could supposedly conjure demons. I visited Lazuli Cottage and it was Sarah who opened the door to me. Immediately, I knew I was in the company of psychics. I introduced myself, and explained that I was a psychic too. She took me upstairs to meet Jessica." Looking solely at Jessica, she said, "You were in a fairly bad state, almost catatonic. I'm surprised you remember me."

"I remember you tried to help."

"I did. Sarah and I performed a cleansing. I advised Sarah what to do. Measures she could take to boost positivity – the same measures we employ today in Psychic Surveys."

"The measures Gran taught me." Ruby's eyes grew wide again. "Oh God, Ness, you taught her!"

"Maybe I did. But to be honest, what Sarah was doing, enfolding her daughter in love, *immersing* her in it, seemed to be working well enough. I've never met a person as capable of giving as Sarah. Although I recommended psychiatric care, she assured me she was the best person to care for her daughter. I couldn't have agreed more. Before I left, I felt a pair of eyes on me. I turned round and there you were. You were peeping out from behind the kitchen door. I remember thinking how pretty you were."

"You saw me? But… I thought the first time we met was at Harveys Brewery. We'd both been called in independently of each other to investigate that presence in the cellar."

"In effect, that *was* the first time we met," Ness answered. "When I came to your house, your gran didn't mention your first name – she hardly mentioned you at all. She wanted to keep you under the radar, I think, wary of social workers getting involved with her family, as well as the police. At the brewery, I suspected you were *that* Davis girl. Your surname, the fact you were psychic – it was too much of a coincidence. After a few meetings, my suspicions were confirmed, but I noticed something else. You only ever mentioned your grandmother, not your mother. From that, I guessed something was still amiss with her, and if you weren't talking about it, perhaps it was best I didn't talk about it either." Her voice more subdued, she added, "You see I understand when people want to keep things quiet. That need for privacy."

Ruby looked from Ness to her mother.

"Mum," she pleaded, "I know it's hard, but please, tell me what you saw that night. I have to know."

"Ruby..." Jessica began. She wanted to help, of course she did, but how could she even begin to explain? After a brief pause, she forced herself onwards. "Honestly? I think it was my own personal demon I saw." Again, she halted, trying to find the right words. "The sum of all the fears I've accumulated over the years, all the negativity I've built up in this body and soul of mine, the pettiness, the jealousy, the want, the need, the lust, the doubt, and the fury. It was like looking into a dark mirror and seeing the very worst of me glaring back."

Ruby leant forward, desperation making her eyes shine. "Mum, it followed you home."

"Home? What do you mean?"

"Because that night, whilst you were downstairs with Gran, it was upstairs with me."

"It was upstairs?" The thought was a sickening one.

Ness broke in. "Ruby, tell us what it is *you* saw."

As Ruby's hand went up towards her tourmaline necklace, Jessica could see how much it was shaking – almost as much as her own. She also noticed Cash's arms tighten around her daughter's waist – a gesture she found touching too.

"Erm… it was a figure. Male, I think, or predominantly so. He was clear, but he wasn't clear. Like Mum, I'm finding it hard to explain. But his eyes, I remember those. Even though the room was black, they were blacker by far, and surrounded by yellow – a horrid yellow, neon almost, lurid. I'd already been downstairs once to see what the noise was about, but I'd been sent back to my room. I couldn't stay there for long, though, not with everything that was happening. I was on my way back down again when this figure came out of nowhere and barred the way. It brought a finger up to its mouth, if you can call it a mouth – it was more like a gash. And it shook its head – a warning. It seemed amused… at first. I challenged it and any amusement faded. I ran back to bed and hid under the covers, convinced myself it was a dream, just a dream, and tried to forget it. I *did* forget it… until Danny. That's when I saw it again." Focussing on Jessica, she added, "The sum of all *my* fears I think, merged with yours, and with his too."

Everyone in the room tried to make sense of what they'd heard.

"What is it?" Corinna whispered at last. "I still don't understand."

"And that's a good thing, Corinna," Theo assured. "Honestly, it is. But my view is the same as it was. It's a thought form. It's got to be. One with a very bad attitude."

"That's become separate from the mass," Ruby added.

"That's been fed not wisely but too well," Theo continued. When the others looked at her quizzically, she explained, "It's a quote from Shakespeare's *Othello*."

"Is it?" Ness challenged. "I'm sure it's 'loved not wisely

but too well."

"It is but I adapted it. Clever of me, don't you think?"

As Ness shrugged, Jessica spoke again.

"But what if it isn't a thought form?" she asked, cursing the timidity in her voice.

"What if it's an alien?" In contrast, Cash looked almost excited at the prospect.

Theo laughed aloud – a sound that startled Jessica at first, but then warmed her. "I don't believe in aliens," the old lady replied, with a dismissive wave of her hand.

"But I do," he countered.

Theo laughed again. "Touché, young man, touché. And what are we always saying? Belief is everything. However, I still think we should roll with thought form rather than an entity from a dim and distant planet, and perform another cleansing."

"But it didn't work last time," Ruby fretted.

Jessica tried to convince Ruby too. "It can't do any harm."

"I suppose not," said Ruby, before adding pointedly, "All the harm's been done."

* * *

Before they started, Theo suggested they all relax in front of the TV for a bit, eating cheese or beans on toast – *'doing 'normal' things'*.

"All this talk of aliens has left me hot and bothered," she claimed dramatically.

"Whereas talk of demons hasn't bothered you one little bit?" Corinna teased.

"Don't get me wrong," Theo replied. "They're tricky

fellas to deal with – demons – but with aliens, it's that whole pointed ear thing that gets me. Oh, and tentacles – aliens usually have tentacles, don't they? With suckers on, lots and lots of suckers. Ugh, the mere thought!"

Ruby knew what Theo was doing; she was trying to lighten the atmosphere. But with her, at least, it wasn't working. She seemed to be carrying around a dead weight inside her. Switching on the TV for them, she hurried through to the kitchen to make preparations for supper. Cash had offered to help, but Jessica had told him to sit back down, that she'd do the honours. Cash agreed, and no one challenged them, leaving mother and daughter to it.

"Just take Jed with you," Theo called, still doing her utmost to feign nonchalance.

As Ruby was opening the fridge to find out what ingredients she could utilise, Jessica stopped her. To Ruby's surprise, she stepped forward and encircled her daughter in her arms. It took a moment or two before Ruby was able to return the gesture.

"I'm sorry," Jessica whispered.

Extricating herself after a few moments, Ruby replied, "It's okay, there's no need," but her voice was too high pitched to sound normal. She knew it, and Jessica did too.

"I don't deserve the gift we share, but you and Mum do. I don't deserve the pair of you either."

"Mum, what's done is done. What we need to do now is deal with the fallout. After that, we can move on – all of us."

Jessica only nodded in reply.

Ruby hesitated again. Should she ask her mother? Was this the time? She consoled herself that in many ways there'd never been a better time. Now was a time for truths.

"Mum, who's my dad?"

She must have asked this question a dozen times or more in her childhood, before deciding not to bother again. Her mother had one stock reply – "Ruby, I don't know." Would she say that again? Was it actually the truth? Ruby braced herself for the answer.

"It wasn't one of the members of *Terra Stella*, if that's what you're thinking. It wasn't Saul – I met him after I had you. Karl, too. No, Ruby, you don't have an Occultist for your father – nothing quite so grand. He's just an ordinary man: a policeman, and married."

A policeman? "He was married?"

"He was when I knew him. He was someone I had a brief affair with, before he and his wife moved away. I could tell you his name but there's very little point in contacting him. When I told him I was pregnant with you, he didn't want to know. He just walked away."

Despite his reaction, Ruby was awe-struck. "My father – he exists."

"Of course he exists, darling. I didn't conjure *you* up at least."

"No, I know that. He just seems so unreal to me somehow."

"He's real all right, and I *will* tell you his name. Whether you trace him or not is up to you. But right now, I think we've enough to occupy our minds, don't you agree?"

"Yes, you're right. Of course you are."

Even so, visions of an ordinary man – the policeman, her father – danced in her head. A man who'd been unimpressed she was coming into the world. Would he be unimpressed if he met her now? Or would he be proud? After all, he was a crusader too, someone who knew the difference between good and bad, who adhered to the former, just as she strived to do. They'd have that in common at least. And then another idea occurred.

"Is Saul still alive? Is Karl?"

Jessica looked slightly taken aback.

"I… I don't know what became of everyone in the group. After what happened, they may have disbanded. I'm really not sure."

"None of them ever checked up on you?"

Jessica hung her head. "No."

"Some friends," Ruby said.

"They're not like yours. But, Ruby, the friends I made back then suited the person I was. Like attracts like, remember? In the eighteen years following, I haven't made any friends. I've been a ghost, in hiding. I want things to be different now. I want to do the right thing, by you, by Mum, and yes, by me too."

"And what's that?" Ruby wanted to hear her say it, *needed* her too.

"Kick whatever it is that haunts us back into the abyss."

Chapter Twenty-Four

AFTER watching *Coronation Street* – Theo's choice, a double episode – Ness checked her watch. "I think we should get started, don't you?"

Theo wiped at imaginary crumbs by the side of her mouth. "It's as good a time as any."

"But my bag," Ruby said, referring to where she kept all her cleansing paraphernalia. "I didn't bring it with me."

"You didn't bring anything with you by the looks of things," Cash commented. "Those aren't really your clothes, are they?"

"They're Mum's," Ruby explained, smiling at the slightly baffled look on his face. "I only had time to grab my mobile and my keys. I haven't even got my purse."

"You don't need to worry about money; I've got some. But the bag – that's a problem."

"Nonsense," Theo cut in. "I've plenty of gear in the boot of my car – wouldn't dream of travelling without it." Grabbing at her handbag, which she'd put down by the side of her chair, she fished around in it for keys. "Be a love, Cash, and go and get what we need."

"I'll come with you," Ruby said, eager for the chance to be alone with him.

Night had fallen, and with it an autumn chill. She should really get the log fire going in the living room, warm the house up a bit, but the thought of naked flames dancing in the grate unsettled her. She'd considered them pretty as a child, like dancers. Now, they just seemed threatening. Everything did, but thankfully, not *everyone.*

Outside, the night air caused them both to shiver. Standing beside Theo's car, Cash pulled her to him once again.

"A word of warning," he said. "Don't ever tell me to stay away again."

"I was just worried about you, about myself too – the way I've been acting. How I've let everything get to me."

"We'll sort it out, you'll see. Everything will be back to normal soon."

"As normal as it gets with me, you mean?"

"Believe me, you're the most normal girl I know."

Ruby snorted. "God, you must have known some crackpots in your time!"

"Oh yeah, a fair few."

She nudged him in the ribs, but playfully. "Seriously, you don't know what we're dealing with here."

"And you do?"

"I know it's hazardous to health, and I don't want you to suffer."

"But you've suffered," he pointed out. Before she could answer, he spoke again. "Look, my ignorance on these matters–"

"You're not ignorant."

"Let me finish. My ignorance, take it as a positive, okay? I'm going in without fear, which I gather is exactly what we're supposed to do."

"Apparently so."

"One thing I do know – life's never boring when you're around."

"So you're an adrenaline junkie, is that it?" she teased.

"I'm a Ruby junkie."

As she started to shiver again, he held her close.

"Are you laughing or crying?" he asked.

"A bit of both, I think," Ruby confessed.

"I'm here for you, Rubes. I've told you that before and I meant it. All the way."

Ruby drew back. "Rubes? Since when have you started calling me that?"

"Since I decided it was better than babe." He inclined his head as though calculating. "Roughly about ten seconds ago."

Laughing outright now, she indicated for him to open the boot of Theo's car, which he did, grabbing what was needed before returning to the house.

* * *

Instructed by Theo, Cash brought two chairs from the kitchen into the living room and placed them back-to-back. Jessica and Ruby were asked to sit down. As they did, the others stood in a circle around them, Jed included.

"You all know the drill – the first step is white light," Theo began. "We need to visualise it surrounding each and every one of us: a shield that's impenetrable, that can withstand the strongest hurricane, weather the most violent of storms. We also need to breathe slowly and deeply. When you breathe in such a manner, it's nigh on impossible to feel panic."

As all eyes closed intently, Ruby could feel a cold sensation in her stomach, but she imagined the sun's rays warming her through.

After a few moments, Ness asked both mother and daughter how they were feeling.

"Okay," replied Jessica.

"Fine," said Ruby. *So far.*

"The next step is compassion," Theo continued. "We must banish all thoughts of anger, hate or fear – fear particularly because we know how dangerous it is. Whatever it is that afflicts us, send it love, light, and blessings in abundance. Remember it is wretched and its wretchedness is to be pitied. Shower the attacker with the pure white light of the universe. Imagine this light beaming down on it from all angles. Embracing it. Love is the strongest force in the universe. It heals all things – and if not heals, negates."

Again, Theo gave them time to imagine – *to feel* – before taking hold of Cash and Corinna's hands. Standing opposite her, Ness did the same thing, clasping them firmly.

Theo's voice took on an authoritative tone that Ruby found reassuring. Although she'd closed her eyes, she opened one slightly to peek at Jed; he looked relaxed, which settled her too. *This might work,* she thought – *this might actually work.*

"Whatever you are, wherever you've come from," Theo addressed the entity directly, "you are *not* welcome. You're a harmful being, intent on destruction, but even so, we wish *you* no harm. All we want is for you to leave Jessica and Ruby in the peace they deserve. We don't fear you and we don't blame you for being what you are. We send love and compassion to accompany you onwards. Within our hearts, you'll find love for *all* things the universe holds. Ruby, Jessica, isn't that correct?"

"That's correct," Jessica and Ruby said in unison.

Satisfied, Theo repeated her command, or at least the essence of it. "In the presence of love, you cannot harm. Leave." To Cash and Corinna, she nodded. They lit the smudge sticks retrieved earlier from the boot of Theo's car, and started fanning the smoke into each corner – the heady scent of white sage filling the air. Ness stepped forward and cupped some of the smoke in her hands, bringing it first towards Jessica and then Ruby, and rubbing it against the skin on their arms – a means of purifying them too. She then worked with crystals to cleanse the air further.

Theo, meanwhile, remained silent – communing, still, Ruby guessed, but via thoughts this time. Satisfied at last, Theo opened her eyes and smiled. "How do you feel?"

Ruby glanced at her mother before answering. "Okay, I think."

"Be more decisive, Ruby," Theo advised.

"Good. I feel good."

To Jessica, she said, "What about you?"

"I feel stronger."

"I know you do," said Theo.

"Is that it?" Ruby said, starting to rise.

"What did you expect?" Theo asked. "Hours and hours of bargaining? The process shouldn't take long – not if we believe in it. And, Ruby, you do believe in it, don't you?"

"I believe in you," Ruby replied. "All of you."

"Then what we've done is effective."

Cash came forward. "But when will we know for sure?"

Theo rolled her eyes. "It *has* worked."

To her mother, Ruby said, "Do you believe it?"

Jessica seemed too overcome to speak. She could only nod in reply.

* * *

More mundane matters began to occupy their minds – where everyone was going to sleep for a start. It was late, and Theo and Ness were reluctant to leave.

"We need to stay. We *should* stay," Ness had said.

But why, if you believe? The thought was in Ruby's mind before she could stop it. Immediately, she dismissed it. It felt traitorous somehow – ungrateful.

The fact that the cleansing hadn't provoked a reaction was both comforting and confusing. Could it really be that easy to get rid of something which had hung around, albeit peripherally, for eighteen years? But then again, why shouldn't it be? Too many times, people complicated things when complication wasn't necessary. And she knew already that time meant nothing in the spirit world. Susan, for example – dead for four decades – still thought it was 1966. *Poor Susan.* She had to remind herself that Susan was happy, that she was in the light. She herself had escorted her there.

"Ruby, did you hear what I said regarding sleeping arrangements?"

Ruby looked sheepishly at Theo. She hadn't. "Run it by me one more time."

Theo rolled her eyes, as well as sighed. "I said, you and Cash take your room, and Jessica will, of course, take hers. But might I have Sarah's room? My bones are too old to be lying on the sofa."

"Of course," Ruby replied. "I'll get some fresh bedding for you."

Theo nodded and asked Corinna if she'd like to bunk in with her.

Corinna shrugged. "If you don't mind."

"Not at all. Ness, are you sure you're okay with the sofa? I know you keep insisting it's fine, but nonetheless I'm worried."

"Please, Theo, don't worry. I think you've realised by now, I prefer to sleep alone."

Sometimes relations between Theo and Ness could be strained; in terms of personality, they were polar opposites. But both seemed amused by this comment. Ruby was encouraged. Things were going to be just fine. Correction – they *were* fine.

Turning to Cash, she said, "Bed sounds like a good idea to me."

Theo piped up again. "No sex, mind. Sex is energy, of the frenetic kind usually. Let's keep the atmosphere calm."

To Ruby's amusement, Cash's cheeks suffused with red. "It's the last thing on our minds," he assured Theo.

"Speak for yourself," said Ruby, but only so Cash could hear.

Struggling to keep a straight face, he ordered her to lead the way. Upstairs, Jessica was busy sorting out bedding; selecting sheets, blankets, and a pillow for Ness to make herself comfortable with. She looked really quite excited to have guests.

"Are you sure I can't help, Mum?" Ruby said, as she brushed past.

"I can manage," Jessica called back.

They were three simple words, but to Ruby there was a miracle in them.

In her bedroom, Cash closed the door before turning to survey his surrounds. "So, this is where you grew up."

"Well, I was allowed downstairs on occasion – birthdays

mainly. Occasionally Christmas."

Closing the gap between them, there was a grin on his face. "You know full well what I mean." Looking around, he added, "It's just… I don't know, this room represents a part of you I know so little about – Ruby the terrible teen." Turning his head to one side, he added, "I thought you would have had pop posters on the wall, stuff like that, but you've actually got some pretty tasteful art."

"I did have posters," Ruby informed, him, "but Gran took them down when I left. I don't think the good looks of the Gallagher brothers impressed her."

"You were an Oasis fan?"

"Yep. What about you?"

"I preferred Blur." His smile faded. "Are you really okay, Ruby? You're not nervous or anything?"

"I'm better with you by my side."

"And this no sex rule – I suppose we should observe it."

"The walls between these bedrooms are paper-thin – they'll know if we don't."

"Can you imagine it – Theo rushing in, catching us in flagrante? Her pink hair flying."

"Jeez, Cash – any thought of rebellion I might have had, you've just managed to kill stone dead."

Cash pulled her close. "It doesn't matter. We can cuddle instead. It's a single bed we're sleeping in – we'll be nice and cosy." Nuzzling her ear, he began to murmur. "Mmm, you still smell of sage. It's lovely. Beats that Chanel stuff anytime. This cleansing business – do you think it's worked?"

Ruby looked beyond him, to where she'd seen the entity in childhood.

"Let's just get through the night," she whispered back.

Chapter Twenty-Five

A raging thirst woke Ruby in the early hours. She cursed that she hadn't thought to bring a glass of water to bed with her. Trying to ignore it, she cuddled up beside Cash again. He was sleeping deeply – not snoring, but snuffling every now and then. At the foot of the bed, Jed was occasionally twitching, but he too was asleep. All was calm, she noted with relief. Cash moved slightly, and she had to follow suit. Although she welcomed his close proximity, she wished she had a bit more room to stretch out. Closing her eyes, she willed sleep to come again, but, as she suspected it would, it played hard to get.

"Damn!" she muttered under her breath.

Her throat felt so dry she was actually having trouble swallowing. The need for water – there was no way she could ignore it.

Moving with exaggerated care, Ruby swung her legs over the side and sat up. As careful as she'd been, Jed looked up, eyeing her curiously.

I'm going downstairs for a drink – stay put.

Jed seemed to understand her silent command and lowered his head again. Smiling at his obedience, Ruby stood. Unable to stop her eyes travelling to the spot where 'he' had stood all those years ago, she felt her breath catch. But Jed, asleep, assured her all was well. Nonetheless, it was little wonder she'd blocked the memory; if she hadn't, she doubted she'd ever have set foot in her bedroom again – in the house, even. She'd have had to live on the street or find a long-lost relative to move in with. A funny thing, she mused, as she pressed forwards – how people protect themselves by simply making 'disappear' what they can't cope with. The brain was an incredible organ: the keeper of memories – allowing some to resurface only when the bearer was deemed strong enough.

Am I strong enough? Gran thought so, her mother too. And before it had all kicked off again, she had certainly felt strong. But perhaps that was the prerogative of the young, the naïve; perhaps that's what enabled them to carry on – the *illusion* of strength.

For God's sake, Ruby, just get some water, will you!

As Ruby eased the door to her bedroom open, she smiled again, this time wryly. She'd do well to concentrate on the task at hand, and only that. From experience, Ruby knew where to step to avoid the floorboards creaking under her weight. Lazuli Cottage was over one hundred years old, and at times it could be noisy. Tiptoeing as lightly as she could on the landing, she couldn't avoid them all, however. Besides, there had been a few new additions since she'd lived there. Wincing at a particularly loud creak, Ruby stopped. Surely, it had disturbed someone? But as she strained her ears for telltale movement, she found there was none. Passing her mother's door, she stopped and put her ear to it. Absolute silence. She did the same at Sarah's door, listening to the occupants within. She could hear snoring, but it was slight. Who was the culprit? Corinna or Theo?

At the top of the stairs, she paused again. The stairs were

particularly choral. Should she just go to the bathroom for a glass of water? It would be so much easier. Then again, she was feeling peckish too. One of Gran's biscuits was as tempting a thought as the water. Deciding to risk it, she held onto the banister as she descended, trying to lean as much weight on it as possible in order to avoid waking the entire house. The stairwell was particularly dark, and she wished she could switch a light on, but that really would disturb someone. She had no choice but to feel her way.

In the hallway, she exhaled – her banister ploy had worked. She'd hardly made any noise at all. Snoring – much louder than she'd heard upstairs – was coming from the living room, revealing Ness's secret. No wonder she preferred to sleep alone!

Speeding up a bit now, she hurried towards the kitchen and pushed the door open. From the window, moonlight flooded in, eliminating the need for additional light. As she reached for the biscuit tin, her stomach growled, hunger nagging at her. Although a few of them had munched on biscuits with a cup of tea before bedtime, there were still plenty left. She took one out and rammed it in her mouth, ravenous all of a sudden, before remembering she was thirsty too. Grabbing at a glass that had been left on the drainer beside the sink, she turned the tap on, filled it to the brim, and drank greedily, the water dribbling out of her mouth and down her chin. Afterwards, taking another biscuit, she devoured that too. Unable to believe she was still hungry – Gran's shortbread was substantial stuff – she was about to take another, when she heard movement upstairs. Her bedroom was directly over the kitchen, and above her the floorboards creaked. Had Cash woken, discovered she wasn't there and panicked? She needed to get back upstairs and fast.

She turned around. Was it her imagination or was the kitchen darker than before? It had been a cloudy day, though, and there were probably still clouds in the sky, covering up the moon.

Leaving the kitchen, she retraced her footsteps. Ness was still snoring, a sound that broke the silence, but comfortingly so. Just as she'd paused at the top of the steps, she did the same at the foot. For years, she'd run up and down them without a care in the world. But now they looked different – eerie somehow. The top of the staircase seemed to stretch on forever. How was she going to manage it and where did it lead – to familiar surrounds or a location she didn't want to be?

Get a grip! If ever she needed to listen to that sentiment, it was now.

Utilising Theo's tip from earlier, Ruby kept her breathing nice and even. After a minute, maybe less, the technique seemed to work. The tight ball of fear in her chest began to dissipate. *Inhale for a count of four; exhale for a count of four.* Instructions she rigidly obeyed. She needed to get back to bed, to the safety of Cash's arms. One good thing – she couldn't hear Jed barking.

Ruby forced one foot in front of the other, grabbing onto the banister again; using it like a rope to haul herself up. First one step, then another. That's all she had to do – continue climbing. She'd managed to get halfway up when she heard growling. Her head jerking, she tried to kid herself it was just her mind playing tricks. Jed had been fine earlier. They all had. Why wasn't he fine now?

No longer was she able to keep her breath even. It was coming in short, sharp bursts instead. Her heart too was

like the beat of a drum, banging on and on and on. She
had to get off these stairs. She felt exposed on them. *Weak*
was another word that sprang to mind.

*You are not weak. You have never been weak. You are
strong!*

Keeping that thought present, she climbed another step,
and that's when she heard it. Cash was crying out, and Jed,
he wasn't growling – he was whining pitifully.

Her own safety forgotten, Ruby sprang forward.
Something was in her room, and Cash and Jed were at its
mercy.

Not caring about waking the others now – needing
them to wake up in fact – she continued to race down the
landing. Like the stairs, it seemed endless – the same as the
landing in her dream, with that thing, that monster,
waiting for her somewhere along the length of it. Reaching
the bedroom door, she expected to run straight in, but it
was closed. She frowned. That wasn't right. She'd left it
open. But then nothing was right. Everything was wrong,
and growing more so by the second. Grabbing at the
handle, she pushed, but it refused to budge. Banging on
the door instead, she screamed for Cash to open it. If he
heard, he gave no indication.

"Cash!" she screamed again, but only the sound of
crashing and banging came back at her. She imagined all
too vividly the bed being swung round like a child's toy.

The door before her might have remained steadfastly
shut, but beside her other doors flew open. Jessica came
rushing out. So did Theo and Corinna. Ness bolted up the
steps.

"What's going on?" Theo demanded.

Ruby swung round to face her, screwing up her nose as

she did. There was that smell again – that *rancidness*. Surely they could smell it too? Beside Theo stood Jessica – pale-faced and with one hand agitating the nape of her nightdress.

"In there," Ruby managed, her voice cracking with the effort. "It's in there with them."

"Them?" Ness pushed for clarification. "Cash and Jed, you mean?"

"Yes!" The frustration she felt was enormous. "I can't get the door open."

Theo bustled forward. "Cash, it's me. Don't be afraid – we're here."

Don't be afraid? She could hardly believe her ears. Of course he was bloody afraid!

As Ruby started to bang at the door again, Theo grabbed her by the shoulders. "Calm down, Ruby. Stop feeding this thing!"

"I… I can't help it."

"You have to help it, Ruby. You *have* to."

Frantically, Ruby looked from Theo to Jessica, hoping for more understanding. "Mum, what are we going to do?"

Jessica didn't answer straightaway. She seemed shell-shocked.

"Mum…" Ruby urged again.

"We listen to Theo," she replied at last. "We remain calm."

Frustration overflowing, she all but threw Theo off her and turned back to the door. Why wasn't Jed barking? Why wasn't he even whining? What was that thing doing to them?

"Cash!"

"Get her away from here," Ness commanded Corinna,

striding forward as she did so. "And for God's sake, somebody switch on the damned light."

Corinna did both, illuminating the landing before coming forward to place a hand on Ruby's arm.

"Get off me!" Ruby screamed.

Ness's voice was firm. "Ruby, you are making things worse."

Still Ruby refused to listen. "Corinna, just leave me alone!"

"Ruby." It was Jessica. "We don't have much time. Please come away."

Her words – perhaps because they were so softly spoken – managed to filter through Ruby's fevered brain. She *was* making it worse. Deep down, she knew that.

"Come on," Corinna said, just as gently.

From inside, there was another cry, but Ruby tried to ignore it. She had to stand down; let Theo, Ness, and maybe even Jessica, take over.

From further down the landing, Ruby watched as Theo and Ness stood outside the door. Jessica stood in-between them. All of them had their eyes closed, concentrating. She knew what they were doing. They were fighting what was in there with love – calling on the universe to help them too. But they had done that before, and it hadn't worked.

"Oh, Cash," she said, her voice as pitiful as Jed's whining.

"It's okay," Corinna whispered beside her. "You *have* to believe it will be okay."

Ruby tried, but if anything happened to Cash, anything bad, she'd never forgive herself. She'd put him in the line of fire. She'd welcomed his presence at her grandmother's house, when really she should have sent him away. She'd been selfish – completely and utterly selfish! The realisation of which caused even more tears to cascade.

As the moments passed, Ruby grew more impatient. She wanted to rush forward and hurl herself at the door again, but Corinna's grip was surprisingly firm. She'd have to fight against her if she wanted to extricate herself. Nonetheless, she was prepared to do that when the door to her bedroom suddenly sprang open.

Theo and Ness rushed forward, disappearing from sight as though they'd been swallowed. Only Jessica hung back – brave but not brave enough.

Corinna and Ruby also broke into a run – Ruby desperate and terrified in equal measure, to see what had happened inside her bedroom. She almost fainted with relief when she reached the threshold. Cash was sitting up in bed, the covers having fallen away, exposing his bare chest. Jed was sitting beside him, his entire body shaking.

"You're alive!" screamed Ruby, pushing past Ness and Theo and throwing herself on the bed.

He returned her hug, but she could feel him shaking too.

Drawing back, tears blinding her, she said, "You're okay, aren't you? Please be okay."

"I'm okay," he replied, his voice just as tremulous.

Behind her Theo was talking to Ness. "We need to cleanse this room," she said.

Immediately, Ruby whirled round. "It won't do any good. Nothing we've done so far has been any good. It's stronger than us."

"RUBY, WILL YOU PLEASE STOP SAYING THAT!"

The anger in Ness's voice stunned her into silence.

"Ruby…" It was Cash. "Can you help me to dress?"

Turning back to face him, all she could do was stare.

"Ruby, it's okay. I'm alive. Please, just get my clothes."

Corinna came forward with his jeans and tee shirt and handed them over. Forcing her limbs to work, Ruby began to help him – her movements as stiff and as awkward as his.

As he rose, Cash's legs buckled slightly. Immediately, Ruby put her arms around him, encouraging him to lean on her. Jed jumped off the bed to follow them – his body crouched lower than normal, his head swinging from side to side.

As she passed Ness, Ruby glanced at her. She looked angry, still, her lips pursed. Unable to hold her gaze, she limped with Cash towards the door instead. Jessica took Cash's other arm, and all three of them made their way along the landing. Before she was out of earshot, however, she heard more words exchanged between Theo and Ness.

"Have you ever dealt with anything like this before?" asked Theo. "Anything this… stubborn."

"Not this stubborn," was Ness's stark reply. "No."

Chapter Twenty-Six

JESSICA was doing her utmost to comfort Jed, whilst Ruby and Corinna tended to Cash.

"Do we need to call an ambulance?" Corinna asked.

"I don't want an ambulance," Cash protested. "What are they going to do anyway? I've no cuts or bruises on me."

Ruby could testify to that. She'd examined him thoroughly whilst dressing him. It wasn't, however, the state of his body she was worried about. It was the state of his mind.

Picking up a blanket that Ness had used when the sofa had been converted into a bed, she wrapped it round his shoulders. "I'm sorry," she whispered, as she did it.

"Ruby." His eyes sought hers and she was glad to see defiance in them rather than despair. "You've got nothing to be sorry for."

Jessica, who had seemed to retreat into herself again after what had happened to Cash, found her voice. "No, you haven't. But I have. I was such a fool."

Ruby tried to offer a kind reply; Jessica was suffering just as much as she was – had suffered far longer in fact. But she couldn't. There was a truth in her words that couldn't be denied. As Theo had said, Jessica had played with fire. But she hadn't been the only one to get burnt. The thing she'd brought home with her – it wanted to burn them all.

"I wish Gran was here," was all she could say.

"Me too," Jessica replied, turning her attention to Jed once more.

Behind them, the door opened, and Theo and Ness entered the living room. Approaching Cash, Ness knelt down in front of him and asked him, as Corinna had, whether he wanted them to call an ambulance. Again, he assured them he didn't.

"Hot sweet tea," Theo decided. "That's good for shock. Cash, would you like some?"

"I'd prefer whiskey," was his droll reply.

"Gran doesn't keep alcohol in the house," Ruby explained.

Cash sighed. "Hot sweet tea it is then."

Corinna volunteered to make it, rising from her seat beside Cash. Theo crossed over and occupied her spot instead.

"Cash," she said gently, reaching out to hold his hands. "Are you really okay?"

"I'm intact," he said, "if that counts for anything."

"Oh, it does, dear, it really does. But I think you know what I mean."

"If you're wondering whether I've been driven insane with fear, I haven't." Amazingly, he grinned as he said this.

"That's exactly what I was getting at," Theo confessed, smiling back at him. "Cash, I don't know if I've said this before, but you're a remarkable young man."

Corinna re-entered the room, a steaming mug of hot tea in her hands.

"Here, drink this," she said, handing it to him.

They all waited patiently as he took a few sips.

"Sweet," he said after a few moments, "as in, literally.

Thanks, Corinna."

Corinna smiled back, but Ness refused to. She pulled up a seat beside him also and, leaning forward, she asked him what he'd seen.

"That's just it," Cash replied. "I didn't see *anything*." He shook his head. "Actually, that isn't true – I *did* see something, but it wasn't solid, it was… I don't know, too much a part of the darkness to be clear. It was like a shadow but denser somehow."

"The eyes," Ruby asked. "Did you see the eyes?"

Cash shook his head. "No, I didn't. The eyes must be your spin on it. God, this is so frustrating – my first sight of something otherworldly and I've nothing much to report."

"What about the smell," Jessica asked. "Did you smell anything?"

Cash squinted as he tried to recall. "Vaguely, I suppose. Now you come to mention it."

"But you didn't notice it at the time?"

"Well, not really. I was too busy worrying I was going to be pinned to the ceiling and dragged across it, you know – like you see in all the best horror movies. And you know what? I'm a little disappointed I wasn't. I feel cheated somehow."

Behind her, Corinna snorted.

"It did sound as though the bed was spinning round and round," persisted Ruby.

"It was shaking from side to side, but it wasn't spinning. Bloody hell, can you imagine? That would have been impressive – second only to being pinned to the ceiling."

Ruby was incredulous. "Cash, are you really not scared?"

Cash took a few more sips of tea before replying. "Yes,"

he admitted finally. "I am scared. I know how serious this is. But I got the feeling that thing was toying with me, you know? That he... it... can do so much more. And there's a reason for that, I think."

"What?" Ruby steeled herself for his reply.

"Because it's not me he wants." Almost pushing his mug at Theo, he turned to Ruby and gripped her by the shoulders. "Ruby, I'm not leaving your side again, not until we've sorted this out. Do you understand? Even bathroom visits – I'm coming with you."

"You are not!"

"Well, all right, I suppose that is a step too far. But I'll wait outside or something. Honestly, Ruby, you can't be alone."

Ruby sank back on the sofa. "You said he doesn't want you. What you mean is he wants me. Just me."

Cash was the one who looked horrified now. "Christ, I'm a dickhead! I'm sorry, I shouldn't have said..." But his words died away as Ruby sprang to her feet.

As he began to follow suit, Theo stayed him with her arm. "Wait," she ordered.

Unable to stop herself, Ruby paced back and forth, occasionally glancing at Jed who was still crouched by her mother's side, still seeking comfort. Within her, all sorts of emotions were vying for attention – fear, anger, loathing – and, sick of quashing them, she let them fight each other for dominion. She was sick of this thing – sick of it!

"DAMN YOU!" she screamed at last. Turning on her heel to face Theo, to face Ness, she said, "We've *got* to find a way to beat this thing! I don't want it in my life anymore. I don't want it in my mother's life, or my grandmother's. I want our lives back!"

Overhead, the lights flickered, as they'd done on the landing upstairs. Ruby threw her head backwards. "JUST FUCK OFF! Don't even think about coming back tonight!"

It was Theo who rose to meet her. Facing Ruby, she looked determined.

"There *is* a way, Ruby. There's always a way. And together, we'll find it. We'll send it back to where it belongs and shut the lid on it, because believe me, I'm sick of it too."

Ruby threw herself into Theo's arms. After a moment, Ness stood up. So did Corinna, Cash and Jessica. Encircling Ruby and Theo, they put their arms around them also. She couldn't see what Jed was doing, but she felt a sensation of fur against her legs as though he'd thrown himself into the scrum. Ruby continued crying, trying to release emotions she'd carried for years, which she'd kept buried. She wanted to wash her soul clean – her heart and her mind too – build herself back up, ready for a confrontation. Because that's exactly what it was going to come to, once again: confrontation. They were going to have to face each other. She could get away with nothing less.

Chapter Twenty-Seven

AFTER bunking down in the living room for what was left of the night, morning arrived safely. Opening her eyes, Ruby looked at the bodies around her – some of them still sleeping, others beginning to stir. Instead of fear, the first thing she felt was love. Her heart swelled at the sight of everyone around her – particularly at Jed who'd noticed she'd surfaced and was busy trying to lick her face.

I don't know why you're still here, Jed, but, boy, am I glad you are.

By her side for nearly a year, he was a bona fide team member. She'd be heartbroken if he decided to take up permanent residence on the other side.

But I wouldn't stop you. You know that, don't you? If you want to go home – go.

Jed responded by licking her face some more.

By her side, Cash started to stretch. Switching her attention to him, she asked him how he was.

"Fine, babe, fine."

"So I'm not Rubes any longer?"

He smiled lazily at her. "Gotta ring the changes."

Leaning over to give him a quick peck, he caught the back of her neck, obvious intent in his eyes.

"Cash, don't!" she squealed. "I haven't brushed my teeth yet."

"Oh, Ruby, shut up," he said, lowering her mouth to his and kissing her anyway.

Finally extricating herself, she stared into his eyes. "You know he never left your side."

"Jed?"

She nodded. "Even though he was frightened, he stayed with you."

"I do know, yeah." Cash looked serious all of a sudden. "I felt him, Ruby. I felt him really strongly. If it wasn't for him... well, let's just say we're even better buddies than before."

Theo complaining about backache broke the intensity of their exchange.

"I really am getting too old for camping," she complained, but it was good-naturedly.

Ness also looked much brighter than she normally did, as did Jessica. Corinna was always bright-eyed but, having caught them kissing, she pulled a sad face.

"I miss Presley," she mouthed to Ruby by way of explanation.

As Ness bustled out of the living room to make tea, Ruby got to her feet.

"And where do you think you're going?" Cash asked.

"To the bathroom, to grab a shower."

"I'll come with you."

"No!" she protested. "I've told you before, some things are private – bathroom activities being one of them." Realising he only had her welfare at heart, she said, "I won't be long, I promise."

Although he looked far from convinced, he complied. After she'd finished in the bathroom, however, Cash, Corinna and Theo were standing outside the door.

"We're queuing," Cash attempted to explain, but as Corinna turned to accompany her downstairs without even going in, she knew it was a lie.

When they had all congregated in the living room again, having paid various trips to the kitchen to make toast and more tea, Ness stood up and asked everyone to listen.

"Yes, Ma'am!" Cash muttered, performing a mock salute and making Corinna giggle. A steely glare from Ness, however, soon silenced them.

"Theo and I have been talking and we've an idea we want to explore," she explained. "An idea that might help us. We need to do some research, which means we have to leave you, but only for a couple of hours or so, and then we'll be back."

"Does this mean we're staying here?" Corinna asked. "In Hastings, I mean, rather than returning to Lewes?"

"I think we do need to stay here, yes," Theo answered. "For one thing, Sarah's here, in hospital, and I should imagine Ruby and Jessica want to stay close."

Both mother and daughter agreed.

"We need to go and see her," Ruby pointed out.

"Actually," Theo interjected, "can you stay in touch with Sarah via phone? I realise she's adept at protecting herself, but I think at the moment it's wise if you *don't* visit."

Ruby looked at her mother to see what she thought about that.

"I agree," said Jessica. "I'll call her when we've finished talking."

Ness took back the reins. "In our absence, do go out and get some fresh air. In fact, it will do you good to do that. But please, stay together. It's very important that you do."

All four nodded in compliance.

"Jed, I mean you as well," Ness said.

Jed wagged his tail avidly.

"Can I ask what it is you're researching?" Ruby said, as Ness turned to fold up bedding on the sofa.

"World War II."

"World War II?" Ruby cried. "What's that got to do with our situation?"

"That's what we're going to find out," was her enigmatic reply.

* * *

In Theo and Ness's absence, the others sat around the kitchen table, Ruby unable to stop glancing nervously up at the ceiling what felt like every few seconds. Jessica had phoned the hospital and Sarah had improved further, Jasmine assuring her she'd only need to be kept in for a couple more days – a time span that seemed more like a deadline than anything else. They had to get this situation sorted before she came home.

"Shall we go for a walk then?" Cash asked. "Do as Ness says."

"I don't mind," Corinna said. "It looks like a nice day outside."

"Fine by me," Ruby added. "It's not raining at least."

"Where shall we go?" Cash continued. "Down to the seafront? Or for a stroll around the Old Town? They've got some cool shops there and the cafes are good as well. Ruby, what was that one we went to a couple of months ago – the one that does really pukka coffee?"

"Hanushka," Ruby answered. "They do nice cake too. You ate about a ton of it."

283

Noticing that her mother hadn't said anything, Ruby said, "Mum, is that okay with you?"

Jessica, however, looked lost in thought.

'Mum…" Ruby prompted.

"World War II," Jessica said at last.

"Erm… yeah, that's what Ness and Theo have gone to research."

Cash rolled his eyes. "God knows why. This is hardly the time for a history lesson."

Jessica turned to face him. "Oh, but it is," she said, holding his gaze. "This is very much the time for a history lesson. We need to get to a computer too. We need to research."

"Damn! I knew I should have brought my laptop," Cash muttered. "Normally I never go anywhere without it. But we've got our phones – we can research on them."

"We can't," Ruby interjected. "We've no broadband connection."

"No, we haven't," Jessica agreed, "but there is an Internet café in George Street. I've passed it a few times recently." More shyly, she added, "I've even been in once or twice."

Cash stood up. "Fair enough, let's get going. Jessica, you can tell us why on the way."

* * *

Hurrying along the street, Jessica was animated again.

"As well as more conventional methods of fighting during World War II, there was also what was known as 'The Magical Battle of Britain', undertaken by a band of people who got together to fight Hitler's Nazis with occult

284

ritual."

Ruby looked at Corinna as Jessica said this, but Corinna just shrugged her shoulders. 'The Magical Battle of Britain' clearly wasn't something she had studied either.

"Magic has been used throughout history when it comes to war," Jessica continued. "It's nothing new. Doctor John Dee, Queen Elizabeth I's adviser, is alleged to have conjured a massive gale to blow the retreating Spanish Armada into disarray."

Cash raised an eyebrow. "Well, well, well. You learn something new every day."

"And the threat of Napoleon's invasion in 1807," she enlightened them further, "was turned back, at least in part, by British witches performing rituals to psychologically deter the French from thinking they could cross the sea in safety. During World War I itself, the Angels of Mons supposedly protected members of the British Army in the Battle of Mons."

"Angels." Cash fell into footstep beside her. "And people believed that?"

Jessica glanced sideways at him. "They did. In fact, it became unpatriotic, even treasonable, to doubt that those particular claims were based on anything other than fact. There are various versions of the story, but some hold that St George and a gang of phantom bowmen stopped the Kaiser's troops in their tracks. Others claimed angels had thrown a protective curtain around the British, saving them from disaster. In that early skirmish, we were heavily outnumbered, but we won… with a little help from the divine."

"How do you know all this?" Ruby was curious.

"It's the sort of stuff *Terra Stella* were interested in – it's what we used to discuss."

"So, World War II," Cash interjected. "What happened there?"

"We'll find out in a minute," Jessica replied.

Moments later, the four stopped outside Loose Connection.

"I do hope not," Cash remarked, noting the name.

"Me too," Ruby said, pushing past him and opening the door. "We need everything firing on all cylinders today."

Painted lime green, the café walls could only be described as lurid, with the colour peeling in several places – although a variety of posters had been strategically placed to hide this fact. Floorboards beneath their feet had been stained the darkest shade of brown and, like the walls, were decidedly grubby, even sticky in places. Unsurprisingly, except for the barista – a young man, in his late teens, Ruby guessed, who looked bored out of his skull – the café was empty. Cash went up to him and took drink orders, whilst Ruby, Corinna, and Jessica selected a computer to huddle round.

Coming back with the drinks, he divulged the password so that Ruby could log on.

When the Google bar appeared, Jessica told her to type in 'The Magical Battle of Britain', and immediately the screen filled with pages and pages of information.

"Dion Fortune," Cash noted, "Oh, and surprise, surprise, look – there's mention of our old friend, Aleister Crowley. No getting away from him, is there?"

"Or what he spawned," Ruby added, referring to Aiwass.

"Ruby, don't mention its name," Jessica implored.

"He-Who-Must-Not-Be-Named," Cash muttered. "How very Harry Potter."

Jessica shot him a look. "By naming a thing, you give it substance," she replied, somewhat tersely.

Sipping on either coffee or tea, they selected a page and started to read.

"This is fascinating," said Cash, after a few minutes. "Dennis Wheatley and Ian Fleming were part of British Intelligence." To Ruby, he said, "You know who I mean, don't you? Ian Fleming, the guy who wrote James Bond." After she'd nodded, he continued. "Staff duties included feeding disinformation about astrological predictions regarding Hitler directly to the German high command."

"That was one of the reasons given behind Rudolph Hess's flight to England in 1941," Jessica informed them. "He wanted to forge peace between the English and the Germans, because he believed this was Hitler's secret desire. It was said mystics, astrologers and healers manipulated Hess to undertake the journey, knowing that the flight would end badly for him."

"And did it?" asked Corinna.

"It did. His plane crashed; he was captured and later tried at Nuremberg. He was sentenced to life imprisonment but later hung himself at Spandau Prison."

"Was there ever any proof mystics and the like were involved?" Cash asked.

"Not concrete proof, but they were working behind the scenes, don't doubt that."

"Mum," Ruby said, worried now, "I agree with Cash, this is fascinating. But time's running out and, Gran, she'll be home soon…"

"Ruby, continue reading please. It's Dion Fortune I want you to focus on."

"Dion Fortune," Corinna repeated. "A one-time

member of the Golden Dawn, it says. Hang on, wasn't that the same order as Crowley?"

"Yes, but she left it," Jessica said. "To set up a group of her own. They may have had a few interests that overlapped, but in reality she was considered the antithesis of Crowley."

Her eyes scanning the text also, Ruby said, "It says here she often perceived herself to be under some kind of magical attack. She... she had a breakdown too."

"A woman after my own heart," Jessica replied, but not without wit.

"She also considered occultism to be a true crusade against the Powers of Darkness," Ruby pointed out. "A woman after my own heart as well, it seems."

"Sorry?" Cash said, slightly confused by their exchange.

"The crusade bit, I mean," Ruby explained. "I often think of what I'm doing – encouraging grounded spirits to go towards the light – as a bit of a crusade. I've told you that before."

"Yeah, yeah, you have," he acknowledged.

"Here, this is it." Jessica re-captured their attention. "This is what's important."

All three looked to where Jessica was pointing on-screen.

"Fortune organised a magical 'call-up'," Ruby said, after a few minutes.

"She did," Jessica agreed. "And that's what I think Ness and Theo have gone off to research. Fortune's followers throughout Britain and even those who didn't follow her particularly, but who were psychics of some sort, or healers, or naturopaths, or Reiki practitioners – you get the gist – visualised protection techniques around Britain. They did this at prescribed times every week. Her intention was to build up a vortex of powerful psychic imagery – a 'national spirit'. She believed this national spirit resided in Glastonbury, personified by an Excalibur-wielding King Arthur; according to legend, he's buried beneath Glastonbury Tor. They would focus on this supposedly hollow space, visualising Jesus, the Rosicrucian Cross, Merlin, the Holy Grail and the Archangel Michael too – all of them standing firm in a bid to protect Britain."

"That's a powerful image." Cash was still awe-struck.

"Very. They all meditated at the same time of day, adhering to a strict set of instructions, for fifteen minutes or so, no more. These instructions got more complex as time went on. As well as Arthur and his army, they were to imagine angelic presences – red-robed and armed – patrolling the length and breadth of the land. They imagined them as a vast shadowy form along the coasts, moving from north to south and east to west, keeping watch, and forming a shield, a barrier. Using remote viewing, Fortune pushed these forces across the waters and into the Baltic, towards Germany – entering the headquarters, the bedrooms even, of leading Nazis, and performing magical attacks on them in an attempt to incline their behaviour towards good rather than evil."

"Do you want more coffees?" The barista interrupted their musings. Ruby couldn't help but laugh at the looks on their faces as opposed to his. He really could do with livening up.

Perhaps we should ask him to sit in on this. That might do the trick.

Ruby, can we please get on. Her mother's own thought invaded her mind directly.

"Mum! I didn't know you could do that!"

"Oh, I can do a lot of things. But after what happened, I choose not to."

After taking their orders for the second time, the barista disappeared. Cash asked if the Germans had any idea they were under magical attack.

"I think so," Jessica answered. "There are many who believe Hitler was a natural Occultist too, and that the Nazis had their own esoteric interests. As Fortune and her followers were sending out telepathic messages to interfere with the Nazi war machine, the Germans were also busy broadcasting their ideology through magical means. She believed a battle was being waged on inner, invisible planes, as well as on earthly planes."

The barista returned.

"Thank you, erm…" Ruby said, taking her mug from him.

"My name's Gary."

"Thanks, Gary." Turning her attention back to her mother, she continued. "Were Fortune and her cohorts successful? Did they have an impact on the outcome of the war, do you think?"

"Fortune? As in Dion Fortune?" Gary asked.

Ruby hadn't realised he was still hovering. "That's right. You know about her, do you?"

"The guy who owns this café – he's into stuff like that. You know, arcane stuff. A lot of people in Hastings are. It's a bit of a hotbed."

"What about you, Gary?" Jessica asked. "Are you into it?"

Gary shrugged. "Don't know really. I could be. He brings books in for me to read sometimes. They're interesting enough."

Before he could elaborate further, Gary's mobile rang. Retrieving it from his pocket, he walked away as he answered it. Jessica, meanwhile, placed her full cup of coffee down on the table beside the computer, her expression contemplative.

"The war," she began after a brief silence, "was won by the incredibly brave soldiers who fought on land, sea and air, but, in my opinion, Fortune's magical war cannot be dismissed. She harnessed the power of the universe, and called on all the good that exists within it to fight the bad. Essentially – and I've always believed this – World War II came down to a battle between good and evil. It really was as fundamental as that. People chose their sides and they saw it through to the bitter end. And it *was* a bitter end, whichever way you look at it. There were no winners – not ultimately. Everybody suffered in some way. All Fortune tried to do was up the ante – on behalf of the light, of course – and she got many, many people to do the same. To send love and light through in tidal waves – to drown out the dark. She put a whole new spin on the term 'Blitz spirit'."

Cash burst out laughing, "Blitz spirit – I like it."

Jessica laughed too – a sound that Ruby used to love as a child and which she had missed so much. "Whether it was psychological or not, what she tried to do was a good thing. In a world where so much bad was happening, we needed all the good intent we could muster. Many believe her work had an impact. After all, we won the war, didn't we? Against such shocking odds. So, yes, I believe her work was essential."

Staring at the screen again, Corinna leant forward. "It says here she died after the war – that it took its toll on her.

She never fully recovered from the effort she put in."

"She did die soon after," Jessica confirmed. "In many ways, she sacrificed herself too."

"Amazing woman," Cash said, his voice solemn.

"I think so," Jessica replied, equally sombre.

Draining her second cup, Ruby spoke next. "Okay, okay, as incredible as all this is, and as much as a trip to Glastonbury is now very much on the cards – in fact, I can't think why I haven't gone there before – what has this got to do with our situation? How can it help us?"

"Just as we're being assaulted, we need to organise an assault," Jessica explained. "But of the good kind."

Gary, who had returned to collect their cups, started hovering again. Jessica let him.

"Ruby, I've heard you tell Gran how much your business is expanding. That you're now in contact with psychics up and down the country. Well, you need to get in touch with them – ask them to get in touch with people they know. Cash, Corinna and… Gary, isn't it?"

Gary nodded.

"You too, if you like – contact anybody that follows a more spiritual path. As I said before, naturopaths, Reiki practitioners, homeopaths, psychics, of course – anyone and everyone of that ilk. And at a time we've yet to appoint, get them to send love to our house in Hastings – as much love as they can muster. We need to describe the house to them, and get them to pinpoint it on Google maps or on an ordinary map. Expect some people to slam down the phone on you. But others… well, others, and a good proportion of them, I think, will take up arms and fight. Wherever they are, whatever they're doing, they've got to drop everything, find a quiet area, sit down and concentrate on sending love to Lazuli Cottage. To us and the area that surrounds us. Pure love – unconditional – the kind this thing, this creature, abhors."

Gary's jaw had dropped open. The look of boredom he'd worn when they first walked in had vanished completely. "I'm not psychic or anything, but count me in," he said. "I'll do my best and, like I said, I know plenty of people who are into all this – I'll ask them too."

"You do that, Gary. We need to give everyone some sort of time frame. Ruby, what are your thoughts on that?"

Although the thing had struck in broad daylight on occasion, it was night that agitated Ruby more. All that darkness – it seemed complicit somehow. "We need to get a build-up in place by evening. Fortune had years to do this in. I think for us, everything's going to hit the fan a lot sooner than that."

"I agree. Time isn't something we've got on our side." Turning to Gary, Jessica said, "Do you know East Street in the Old Town?"

"Yes," Gary replied enthusiastically.

"We live there. Number 16 – Lazuli Cottage. Try and get as many people involved as you can."

"I won't let you down." Holding up his mobile, he added, "I'll get started straight away."

Jessica smiled as she watched him retreat. "Now *that's* what I call the Blitz Spirit!"

Chapter Twenty-Eight

RUBY, Jessica, Cash, and Corinna arrived back at Lazuli Cottage the same time as Theo and Ness.

"We've got an idea to put forward," Theo said, on seeing them.

"Funnily enough," Ruby replied, "so have we."

"Oh? What is it?"

Ruby opened the front door. "We'll tell you when we get inside."

Seating themselves around the kitchen table – or their 'headquarters', as Ruby was now beginning to think of it – she and Jessica explained their plan.

"Well, blow me down," Theo said. "That's our idea exactly."

Ness, meanwhile, looked impressed. "Great minds think alike," she said.

"Ah, but fools never differ," Cash pointed out.

They all turned to him.

"Thanks for that," said Ruby, rolling her eyes.

Cash had the good grace to look sheepish.

"When were you thinking of getting started?" Theo asked.

"Straightaway," Ruby replied. "It'll take time to filter through, I should imagine."

"It may well do," Theo conceded.

"We've got the whole night to get through."

"Get through *together*," Theo reminded her.

"Yeah," declared Cash boldly, "I ain't afraid of no ghost."

"Cash!" Ruby admonished him more sternly this time. "What's got into you?"

"Nothing. I'm just trying to jolly things along a bit, that's all."

"And jollying us along is a good thing," Theo assured him, smiling indulgently. "But, remember, this isn't a ghost we're dealing with. If only it were that simple…"

"It's the monster from the deep," Cash said, raising his hands and wriggling his fingers.

"No, don't stop him," Theo said, before Ruby had a chance to. "Humour is a weapon too."

Ruby sat back in her chair. Despite Cash's humour, despite Theo's reassurances, the thought of enduring another night in Lazuli Cottage was getting to her – badly.

Clearly sensing this, Theo clapped her hands together, startling just about everyone. "Right, let's get cracking. We need to contact everyone we can think of, starting right now, and ask him or her to contact everyone they can think of too – spreading the net far and wide. Ask them to visualise this dear little cottage, and us in it. Once we're firmly ensconced in their heads, they need to send love and light – waves and waves of it – the intent, as you all know, to obliterate the darkness attached to us. And yes, it's no mistake I use the word *us*. As Ness said, we're connected. An attack on Ruby, and for that matter, Cash, is an attack on everyone." Pausing briefly to look at each of them in turn, she added, "It's one for all and all for one at the moment. The Six Musketeers!"

Cash raised a hand. "Erm… sorry to have to rain on your parade, but there's one problem with this plan: we need a laptop and a broadband connection in order to log onto Ruby's Cloud backup and download her database. Unfortunately, we have neither."

Immediately, Theo was crestfallen. "Ah, that's something I didn't think of."

"Me neither," admitted Ruby, before giving in and smiling at Cash. "But you're an IT guy – you've got the solution, right? You could always go back to Lewes and get your laptop."

"I've told you, I'm not leaving you – not for one minute."

"But in this instance…" Ruby protested.

"No. The laptop will have to come to me."

"How?" Ruby quizzed.

"Via Presley, of course. I'll phone him – tell him to drop whatever he's doing, and bring his over. I can access the Cloud from it easily enough. Regarding the problem of broadband, Jessica, I noticed on my mobile earlier that there's Wi-Fi next door, but we're going to need a password in order to access it. How well do you know your neighbours?"

"Mum knows them well enough," she answered. "They're nice people, apparently; I'm sure they won't mind. I'll go round and ask them. Make up some sort of excuse."

"Yeah, best not tell them about the demon stand-off just yet."

This time Ruby did laugh, Cash looking triumphant she'd done so.

Delaying no more, Cash called Presley, and Jessica went

next door. The others, meanwhile, busied themselves listing people whose numbers could be accessed from their individual mobile phones. Just over an hour later, Presley arrived.

Opening the front door, Cash took the proffered laptop. "Thanks, bro, I'll keep it safe."

"I know you will," Presley replied. "I'll be here to check."

"You can't stay…" Cash began, as Corinna and Ruby came up behind him.

Corinna flashed one of her megawatt smiles, before adding, "He's right. You can't. It's not safe."

Presley was bemused more than anything. "I don't know what you lot are up to. And I don't know what use I can be. But I do know, from what I could wrestle out of Cash, all this started with Danny, and Danny was *my* friend – my best friend. Whatever trouble you're in, I feel responsible. If I hadn't got you involved, perhaps none of this would have happened."

"Oh, it would have happened." Ruby's reply was grim. "It was always going to happen."

"Even so, I'd like to stay."

Cash turned to look at Ruby and Corinna. "The thing is, we've got a lot of work to do. We could use his help." To Ruby, specifically, he said, "What do you think?"

She was uncertain, still, and she knew from Corinna's face, she felt the same. Theo, who had entered the hallway en route to the kitchen, must have sensed their dilemma.

"If Presley's offering to be another deck hand, snap him up – that's what I say."

Corinna smiled even wider. "Come on in and stay close to me. I'll keep you safe."

"I don't doubt it," Presley replied, hurrying in before anyone could change their mind.

* * *

In the living room, Ness and Jessica only glanced up as Ruby, Corinna and Cash walked in with Presley – as if they'd been expecting him to insist on joining them. Nonetheless, Ruby made introductions, after which Theo advised them all to get started.

"The days fade quickly in winter," she pointed out.

Everyone busied themselves, disappearing into corners of rooms so they could hear themselves speak. Jessica, who had been virtually housebound for the last eighteen years, didn't have anyone to call, so she was given a list of names, and worked her way diligently through them.

About an hour into it, Cash walked over to Ruby. "I've just spoken to Mum. She's on board and is busy phoning round everyone she knows."

Ruby groaned. "Your mum? Oh no, she'll think I'm even more of a head-case now!"

Cash gave a dismissive wave of his hand. "Of course she won't. She loves you, does my mum. Besides which, she's very open-minded. Where do you think I get it from?"

"And me," Presley piped up from his corner.

In-between phone calls, someone mentioned food and the provision of it. Luckily, Ruby had suggested they stop in the local mini mart en route home from Loose Connection, to stock up on provisions – Gran's larders were running perilously low. Ruby suspected they were going to eat a lot of cheese on toast over the next 24 hours, as the mini mart was not exactly well stocked with exotica.

Aside from cheese, they'd also brought plenty of pasta, and they'd eat that tonight with a tomato sauce Cash had promised to rig up. Meanwhile, to fortify them during their phone calls and emailing, Presley offered to switch phone duty for kitchen duty, making round after round of toast with either peanut butter or marmite.

The afternoon flew by. It was ten past five in the evening, the skies becoming darker, when Jessica looked up and said, "This isn't going to work."

Ruby was not the only one astounded.

"What can you possibly mean?" asked Theo. "This is our best shot."

Jessica stood firm. "It is but it's not enough."

Ness too looked stricken. "Well, what else do you suggest?"

As she stared at her mother's face, Ruby's heart sank. Speaking to people all afternoon, garnering such a positive response from them – friends and contacts promising to speak to other friends and contacts – she had felt like the whole world, let alone Britain, was on her side. To be fair, some of the people she and others in the team had contacted did live abroad, so the worldly aspect had some oomph behind it. So many had agreed to get involved. Hardly any had dismissed their cry for help. It said a lot about the calibre of the people she was contacting.

Sighing, Ruby let her head fall forward. If this was not enough, then they were done for. What else was there? With something akin to despair, she said, "So what do we do? Call everyone back? Tell them they're wasting their time? That it's no use?" Certainly, if anyone had got started on sending love and light in their direction, she couldn't feel it – not yet.

"No, of course not," Jessica said, reaching out to touch her daughter's arm. "But, Ruby, eighteen years this thing has been in my life and, unbeknown to me, in yours too. It's fixated on us. It's *part* of us. It isn't going to go as lightly as we think."

"You know what, Mum?" Ruby said, her voice louder than it should be, she knew. "You've got to stop creating more problems!"

"Ruby!" It was Theo this time. "Have some respect."

"Respect?" Ruby almost spat the word back at her, preparing herself to challenge further, but her mother reached across again, started speaking before she could.

"It's true. I don't deserve your respect, Ruby. Even before the breakdown, I wasn't there for you – I left Gran to bring you up. I'm selfish, I'm vain, and I'm weak. I'm the opposite of you. I invited something in, wantonly so, that should never have seen the light. And for many years, I couldn't face that truth – what I'd done, the lives I'd destroyed in the process. I've been living in hell. But I'm back, Ruby. When I came to visit you in December, you were working on that Highdown Hall case. Something waited for Cynthia in the shadows; you didn't know what it was. You *feared* what it was. That was when something in me started to change. For the first time in ages, I had someone else to think about. I feared for *you*. But not only that, I saw you. I actually *saw* you. And you know what? You dazzled me. Despite my advice, despite being scared, you went in anyway – you and the rest of the team. You didn't desert your post; you didn't even contemplate doing that. I know I don't deserve your respect. But you have mine. I'm proud of you."

For a moment, Ruby was stunned – speechless, in fact.

Everyone around her appeared to be the same – they were all staring at Jessica with eyes or mouths wide open. Ruby tried to process what she'd just heard, to take it on board. The beast had seen her; her mother had seen her. Perhaps the old adage was true – every cloud has a silver lining.

"Thank you," she said, the anger that had flared up in retreat.

Jessica looked away, but only briefly, before speaking again. "I *am* trying to rectify what I've done, Ruby, but I didn't just hurt myself, or you and Gran. I hurt someone else too."

"Who?" Ruby asked, bracing herself.

"Saul," Jessica replied, lowering her eyes slightly as she spoke his name. "What we're involved in needs to come full circle. We can hurl love and light at it all we like, but if there's someone out there who's still feeding it, still giving it energy, it's going nowhere."

Ruby looked at Theo, who was nodding in agreement.

"But that's not the only reason I have to see him," Jessica continued.

"There's another reason?" What other reason could there possibly be?

"That little word 'sorry'?" Jessica continued.

"Yes?"

"I have to say it to him too."

Chapter Twenty-Nine

LOOKING at the clock on the kitchen wall, at the minutes, the seconds counting down, time slipping precariously away, Ruby tried to come to terms with this latest piece in the jigsaw.

"We have to go and see Saul?"

"*I* have to go and see him," Jessica replied.

"Mum, we're supposed to stick together. Besides, do you even know where he is?"

Jessica sat back in her chair, brushing aside some strands of hair that had fallen into her eyes. Despite being in her mid-forties, she had so much grey.

"I haven't just been going to the beach," Jessica started. "Your gran thinks I have but I haven't." She paused for a moment. "Actually, that's not true. At first, I did. I spent a lot of time there, just thinking. Inevitably, my thoughts led to Saul. He was with me that night eighteen years ago, as you all know – the two of us conjuring demons together. As you also know, that was the night he went mad, breaking away from me and running riot through the town, as though not just one demon was after him, but entire legions. Again, as you're aware, I somehow managed to find my way home, alive – although in what sense, I'm not really sure. Inside, I've felt dead for years." Jessica had to swallow hard before continuing. "I had no more contact with Saul after that, but I often wondered what it was that he saw. He wasn't psychic– far from it. Even so, he'd seen something."

Her words impacted on them all, but none more so than Corinna.

Turning to Presley, she said, "I think you should go."

Like Cash, however, he was not easily swayed. "I'm going nowhere," was his staunch reply.

Ness spoke next. "You know, Jessica, it's entirely possible Saul didn't actually see anything. He could simply have fed off you."

"An imagining, you mean? If so, it was of the very worst kind."

Ruby was eager to get the conversation back on track. "Mum, you said you haven't just been going to the beach..."

"That's right. I've also been trying to find out where Saul lives. I've already told you I don't know what happened to the others; whether *Terra Stella* still exists or not. But I don't care about them either. It's Saul I care about – he suffered because of my vanity."

Theo looked worried. "I hope you're not going to tell us he's living on the far shores of Scotland or anything. We haven't got time to go travelling."

"No, he's not. He's not very far away at all – just down the road, in Bexhill. His parents must have sold the Hastings house and swapped it for an equally grand one, overlooking the sea. The genteel atmosphere of the place, and how quiet it is – I should think that appealed."

Ruby was curious. "How did you manage to find out?"

"I asked around. Hastings is a small town; it's a close-knit community. The people here, they remember things.

Certainly, there are those who remember Saul and the night he went wild. His talk of demons and how they were after him. It was big news at the time."

"Like Crowley, his reputation went before him," Corinna noted wryly.

"Mine too, I should imagine," Jessica replied. "It was no secret I was involved with him."

Cash was getting impatient. "If we're going to visit him, we need to go now. It's getting late."

"Fair point," said Theo. To Jessica, she said, "I gather Saul's not expecting us?"

"No, he's not," confirmed Jessica.

"And his current mental health – did you find out about that too?"

"He's a recluse, or so the rumour goes. Just like me."

Theo seemed to consider Jessica's plan. "The driving worries me," she said, after a while.

"Why?" Cash asked. "We've both got our cars – there's room for all of us."

"I don't mean that," replied Theo. "What worries me is the possibility of coming under attack whilst we're at the wheel of a car. With Ruby and Jessica travelling with us, we're vulnerable."

"I can get a cab," Jessica offered, "and go on my own. I *should* go on my own. It's going to be enough of a shock just me turning up. En masse, we'll probably tip him over the edge."

Upstairs, they heard a scrape, as though a chair were moving across the floor.

Jessica paled visibly.

"No," said Theo hurriedly. "We all go. As I said before, we stick together."

"But what if he refuses to see us? What then?" Corinna asked.

"We *have* to see him," Jessica insisted.

"I agree." It was Ness. "As you said, there's a need to come full circle here."

Theo stood up, brusque and business-like again. To Ruby and Jessica, she said, "You can't travel in the same car, you'll need to split up. And pop music, pure pap – One Direction or something – we need to blast it out of the speakers as we drive."

Both Cash and Presley looked aghast.

"One Direction?" Cash said, "Are you serious?"

"What I mean is," Theo explained further, "we need music of that type – light and ineffectual – nothing deep about it at all. And we need to sing along to it at the tops of our voices. Doesn't matter if you don't know the words – you can just... tra la la, or something."

"Can I ask why we have to do this?" Cash said, still unimpressed.

"Because it's hard to be frightened when you're engaged in a jolly old sing song. You're too busy enjoying yourself."

"Not to One Direction I won't be."

"Cash!" Theo admonished.

"Okay, okay," he all but grunted. "But I haven't got any of their CDs."

"What CDs do you have?"

"Well, just ambient stuff at the moment."

"Ambient?" Theo queried.

"Music without lyrics," Cash explained.

"One Direction it is then."

"I haven't got any of their CDs. I've just told you."

The smile on Theo's face was smug. "But I have. You

can borrow mine."

"So what music will we play in our car?" Jessica asked, looking confused.

"I've got pap galore, don't you worry," Theo replied. To Cash, she explained, "My granddaughter insists I keep up to date. Those teen CDs – I've quite the collection."

Before anyone could complain further, Theo issued more instructions. "Grab what you need and let's go. The love light is coming in, but it takes time to build. When it reaches maximum level, we need to be back here to make the most of it. Jessica, you're in with Corinna and me. The rest of you, go with Cash."

"What about Jed?" Cash asked, frowning slightly.

"If I know Jed, he'll be in the car already," Ruby informed him.

* * *

"Thank God it's only fifteen minutes to Bexhill," Cash said, parking behind Theo's car and switching the CD player off. "Honestly, I cannot take any more of this rubbish."

"It's not all rubbish," Ruby retorted. "I quite like some of the more ballad-type stuff."

"You *like* it?" Cash was so appalled he was spluttering. "Ruby, don't be so soft."

"And don't you be such a music snob!" she retaliated.

Incensed, Cash looked at his brother for support.

"I'm saying nothing," Presley said, holding up his hands.

Ness too was deliberately non-committal as she exited the car.

Following her lead, they all congregated on the pavement. Evening had fallen and fallen hard. The moon was barely visible, and a sharp breeze was blowing in across the ocean. Looking to where dark tides lapped the shore, Ruby could easily imagine Fortune's angels, clothed in red robes and clutching spears, patrolling this very coast during the 1940s; doing their utmost to keep the evil that would rock the very foundations of humanity, at bay. She shivered and turned her mind to more practical matters.

"Which house is it?" she asked.

"Number forty-three," Jessica replied, pointing to a four-storey house, from which lights shone.

"All of it?" Cash asked.

"I told you they were rich."

"You weren't kidding."

As all seven and Jed reached the pathway, Jessica came to a halt.

Turning to face the others, she said, "As I said before, we can't all go in. It'll be too much for him to cope with."

"Mum, it might not be safe for you to go in there alone."

"I'll protect myself, Ruby, don't worry."

"But there'll be so much fear involved – bad memories. It could make you vulnerable."

Theo stepped forward. "Even so, I agree with your mother – we can't all go in. But what we *can* do is protect you, surrounding you in light." To Jessica, she said, "You're doing the right thing, making amends. That will work in your favour."

Realising it would do her little good to argue further, Ruby reached up to her neck and undid the clasp of her tourmaline necklace.

Immediately, Jessica started to protest. "Ruby, no, that's yours…"

"I'll have it back when you come out. Just wear it in there, please, for me."

Yielding, Jessica took it from her and fastened it around her own neck. "Rosamund's necklace," she said, stroking it reverentially. "I've always loved it."

As she turned to go, Ruby called out again.

"Mum, take the dog."

"Are you sure?"

"Sure I'm sure – he's insisting. He's by your side already."

"So he is," she said, smiling. "What a brave dog." She paused slightly before continuing onwards. "Wish me luck," Ruby heard her say.

"Luck *and* love," Ruby shouted back, hoping she heard her too.

Chapter Thirty

SAUL – how she'd adored him. Every time he'd made love to her, she'd wanted it to last forever. The group's ethos – never belong to anyone – she had agreed with it wholeheartedly, but not once she met Saul. She *wanted* to belong to him. Dreamed of it. But he, it seemed, dreamed only of Dervla, with her Amazonian-figure and long, flaxen hair. He'd described her as a warrior queen – breath-taking. But one thing she wasn't was psychic. She couldn't compete with Jessica on that score. And although Saul might not be able to see spirits – the trip to the abandoned house had proved that much – she could perhaps make him see other things, things more *willing* to be seen.

Lifting her hand to ring the doorbell, Jessica shivered, as Ruby had earlier. What had she been thinking, exploiting Saul's interest in Crowley, summoning, *antagonising*, foreign entities? Not of him, that was for sure. Only of herself and her desires, to the exclusion of everything, *everyone* else – even her own daughter. She had so much to be sorry for, so much to put right. But would Saul be as forgiving as Ruby? She'd find out soon enough.

Her finger making contact with the coldness of brass, she rang the bell, not once but twice, standing back afterwards to wait patiently. Briefly, she looked behind her. The team had moved across the road, just out of sight.

Looking down, she was glad of Jed at least.

Every second she waited seemed to last an indefinable age. When, at last, the door drew inwards, she felt her breath catch in her throat. Who had come to answer it?

A man as tall as Saul stood before her – as tall, but much older, his back slightly stooped. Even so, she could see the dignified figure he'd been – where Saul had inherited his looks.

"Can I help you?" the man asked, eyeing her with naked suspicion.

"Good evening, Mr Bauer, I'm… I'm here to see Saul." God, she felt as nervous as a teenager on her first date. Fervently, she hoped her trembling was only visible to her.

Surprised that she knew his name, he asked her who she was.

"A friend," Jessica replied.

"He has no friends." The man lifted his hand as though preparing to close the door. Before he could, Jessica stepped forward.

"I'm Jessica… Jessica Davis."

He looked confused. "I don't know any Jessica…" And then he did. His eyes widened and his mouth fell open. "*You're* Jessica? The woman who destroyed him?"

"No, I—"

Fury marked him now. "How dare you? How dare you show your face around here, after what you did to my son?" He threw his arms out to banish her, as though she too were something spawned from hell. "Go on. Get away with you. We don't want you here."

It was nothing less than Jessica had expected.

"Please listen to me. Saul's in danger – more so than ever. We all are."

"I won't hear this nonsense. Leave now or I'll call the police."

Refusing to go anywhere, Jessica could only continue to plead. "Mr Bauer, it's imperative you listen to me. I mean it when I say he's in danger, still, after all these years. And... you might be too. I need to see him. I started this whole sorry train of events – I know that, and I'm sorry for it. So very sorry. But I'm trying to put an end to it, once and for all, to rectify matters. And to do that, I have to see Saul. There's no other way. I can't stop it without him."

"It? What exactly do you mean by it?" Mr Bauer started, but a voice from behind him interrupted – a voice Jessica instantly recognised, despite its frailty.

"Dad? What's going on? Who's at the door?"

As his father whipped round, Jessica held her breath.

"Stay back, son. Don't come out here."

"Please," she entreated, "I'm not the one you need to fear."

The old man looked far from convinced. Nonetheless, he was focussed solely on his son.

"Saul, stay back. I've told you!"

The man who came into view bore no resemblance whatsoever to the demi-god she'd once worshipped, and yet, at the same time, he was unmistakable.

Jessica couldn't help herself – she took another step forward. "Saul?" she whispered, her eyes brimming with tears.

Saul too was astounded. "You're alive?" Whether he was glad about that or not, Jessica couldn't tell.

Breaking rank, the tears flowed. He seemed older than his father, even, his blonde hair – once so thick – now wispy, and his body with the same painful stoop in it. He was an old, old man, despite not being much older than her. What had she done to him? Why had she destroyed him? And destroyed herself in the process?

As if reading her thoughts, his father started speaking again. "See what you've done? You and that group you belonged to. Mad, the lot of you. Demon worshippers."

Dragging her eyes from Saul, she couldn't help but retaliate. "We did *not* worship demons!"

"Then how do you explain this?" he said, gesticulating wildly towards his son. "Because he saw something that night; something conjured by you. And he's seen it every night since in his dreams. He's like a child; he can't be left alone, not for one minute. What you did to him, the stress of it, it killed his mother. Yes, that's right, it killed her. She died just a few months ago. And it will kill me too. And then what? Who will help him then?"

During this tirade, Saul had come closer. Jessica looked beyond his father as he did so. There was wonder and horror in his eyes – in equal measure. A good sign, perhaps?

"Jessica," he whispered, and she chanced a smile at him. He was still Saul. He was still the man she'd loved to distraction. "Let her in," he instructed his father.

"What? Don't be so ridiculous. She's dangerous, Saul – dangerous."

"Not anymore."

"But—"

"Please, Dad, I can't go on anymore, and you can't. You've as good as said so. Let her in."

For a tense few moments, his father stood his ground – a barrier between them – and then he moved aside. As Jessica edged past him, Jed only slightly in front, the look in his eyes made her recoil. If he could get away with putting his hands around her throat and squeezing the life out of her, she'd bet he'd do it. And she didn't blame him. Not one bit.

The door slammed shut behind her, closing her in.

Be strong. Be brave. Be… like Ruby.

Thinking of her daughter emboldened her.

"I'm not leaving you alone…" Mr Bauer began.

"You are, Dad," Saul replied, his voice firmer than before. "The time has come. I need answers."

The old man's shoulders slumped visibly. He was so very tired, Jessica realised. They all were – either tired or dead.

Saul indicated for her to go into the lounge – the light in there so bright it caused her to squint.

"I like the light," he explained, noticing.

At last, she thought, remembering his fascination with things not-so-bright.

Part of her had been expecting him to live in chaotic surrounds – a reflection of his mind, perhaps. But nothing could have been further from the truth. The room was neat, minimalist. It held just a sofa, two armchairs, a table, and a lamp. There was nowhere for anyone – *anything* – to hide.

"Take a seat," Saul said, closing the door on his hovering father before shuffling over to the armchair.

She did, perching on the end of the sofa rather than sinking back into voluptuous comfort. Jed remained at her heel.

A clock chimed on the mantelpiece, startling her.

"It startles me too sometimes," Saul said.

All at once, words seemed to rise up from the pit of her

stomach, rushing forth in a torrent. "What I did, I'm sorry, I didn't mean to, it was wrong of me, I was jealous – Dervla."

He stopped her senseless babble. "All that matters is we stop it. It's killing me too."

At his words, despair threatened to overwhelm her. They had opened the gates – let something out that should have stayed hidden. Correction – *she* had let it out. Had encouraged it to rise. Coaxed it forwards, every step of the way. Not just a threat – despair *did* overwhelm her. The figure – a memory of how it had moved. Jerky, stiff, like something new born. Although it wasn't new at all; it was ancient – as ancient as man himself. At first, they'd been delighted with their achievement – had whooped and cheered – but then delight had swiftly fled. As it drew nearer, *they* had fled. Saul first, scrambling over her, pushing her to the floor, her head banging against hard wooden boards, almost knocking her out. For a moment, she'd lain there, had thought she'd be captured, but then she'd managed to drag herself along the floor – away, further away, until she could get to her feet. Once on them, she had run, like Saul had run, all the way home – banging on the door of Lazuli Cottage, almost breaking it down. Her mother's face when she had seen her, her daughter's…

Remembering, she felt hopeless again, as hopeless as she'd been these past eighteen years – caught like a fly in a web of misery. Imprisoned, having set the prisoner free.

Something nudged at her ankle. It was Jed. Barely, she acknowledged him, but he wouldn't give up.

What is it? What do you want?

The dog was looking up at her; she couldn't avoid his

314

gaze. Those eyes of his, round and brown, held nothing but love; the purest kind she'd ever encountered. They looked at Ruby with love, and now they looked at her in the same way. As she continued to stare, she began to change further. The despair she felt, so much a part of her, went careering in the opposite direction. This animal, this strange but delightful creature, this sentinel – if he could love her, did that mean she was loveable? Still? Despite everything she'd done? And the havoc she'd wrought? He came from somewhere good, somewhere light – unquestionably. Somewhere the exact opposite of where the thing that hated her – hated *them* – came from. And he loved her. It was plain to see. He truly, truly loved her.

Who are you, Jed? Who are you really?

She asked in amazement, but if she wanted a reply, it was not forthcoming.

Exhaling, she wiped at her cheeks. Got on with the job at hand. Saul was right. Answers were needed. They could run no more, none of them.

As Ruby had asked her, Jessica now asked Saul. "What did you see?"

Had it been an imagining, as Ness suggested, or something more?

In response to her question, a tremor ran through him, swift and violent.

"Saul," she prompted.

"Something no man should ever see. I know that now."

"The devil?"

"Hell," he replied, the tremors overwhelming him this time.

Chapter Thirty-One

RUBY couldn't believe it when the door opened and both Jessica *and* Saul came out. From her position across the road, she darted forwards, the team following close behind her. Jed met her halfway across the road. He looked happy, she noted – smug. What had happened in there? Before she had time to wonder further, Ruby started. She recognised the man beside her mother. How? She'd never seen him before, hadn't even known about him until very recently. But he was familiar – there was no doubt about it.

"Mum, what's happening? Is he coming with us?"

"Yes, he is," confirmed Jessica.

Someone else came hurrying out of the house. By the look of him, Ruby guessed it was Saul's father. He was shrugging on a three-quarter-length coat.

Jessica spun round. "What are you doing?" she asked him.

"You think I'm going to stand by and let you take my son?"

"You can't come…" she replied.

"You can't stop me."

"No," she continued, but again he cut across her.

"I've been living with this thing for as long as you have. I want an end to it too."

The rest of the team, as well as Ruby, had reached

Jessica by this time, had heard the exchange between her and Saul's father.

"Ness, what do you think?" Theo asked.

Ness pondered for a moment. "I think he has a point."

So did Ruby.

Still, Jessica continued to protest. "There's too many of us for the cars."

"Then Corinna had better sit on Presley's lap," Ruby advised, grabbing hold of Cash's hand and returning to where his car was parked.

* * *

Less than twenty minutes later, they were back outside Lazuli Cottage. The house stood in darkness, and looked all the more foreboding because of it. Everybody piled from cars onto the pavement yet again, Cash shaking his head at another enforced listen to One Direction.

"Now, that's what I call an assault," he said, coming to stand beside Ruby.

Presley joined them. "The same could be said of your singing, Cash."

"My singing? What's wrong with it?"

"Let's just say, thank God you're a drummer."

Whilst Cash continued to contest this slur on his vocal abilities, Ruby noticed the lights were on in the houses either side of the cottage, their occupants no doubt busy bustling about inside, oblivious to what had taken place just feet away from them last night, and what was still to come. A demon standoff, as Cash had described it. Rather, they were living normal, everyday lives – concerned about their children, the bills, what was on TV tonight. Thinking this, she had a sudden desire to be normal too – a *yearning*

317

for it.

Theo was by her side. 'Normal is overrated," she said, reading her mind again. And Ruby had to smile. Perhaps it was, perhaps it wasn't. She guessed she'd never know.

"Why are we standing on the pavement?" Saul's father asked, his voice indignant.

"Sorry, I didn't catch your name," Theo turned her attention to him instead.

"Ronald. My name is Ronald," he said.

"Follow me, Ronnie," she continued, stepping forward.

"I said, my name's Ronald." But if Theo heard him correct her, she gave no indication.

As Ruby opened the door, she reached inside to find the hall light. A soft, reassuring glow immediately hugged the narrow walls. They all filed in, one by one, turning left into the living room, Jessica insisting that Saul occupy the armchair she usually did, and plumping up cushions behind him. As everyone stared at each other, there was an initial awkwardness, but then people started chatting or offering to make tea, and it soon passed.

"I can still do pasta," Cash offered, "if anyone's hungry."

It seemed no one was. Various cries of 'a piece of toast will do' had Cash shrugging his shoulders in disappointment.

"Well, I'm bloody hungry," he said, to no one but himself.

Jessica finally stopped fussing over Saul. Straightening up and looking at Ruby, she said, "It's our house; we should do the honours."

"Good idea," said Theo. "I'll help."

"Me too," Ness added.

Ruby recognised a call to conference when she heard

one, and led the way into the kitchen. After a few minutes, Cash joined them.

"Is everyone okay in there?" Ruby asked him, thinking it was an odd assortment left behind – Corinna, Presley, Saul, and Ronald.

"They're fine," Cash assured her. "Corinna's holding court, explaining procedure to them. Presley's not the only one who seems taken with her. I think Ronald is too. All this stuff about the light and protecting yourself with it, he's growing more fascinated by the minute."

It was still bugging Ruby where she knew Saul from, and then it hit her. "My dream – I saw him in my dream!" she cried.

Jessica, Theo, and Ness looked confused by her sudden outburst. Cash, meanwhile, appeared to be put out. "Ruby! You've been dreaming about someone other than me?"

"Cash, be serious for one minute," Ruby admonished him. But, actually, she was glad of the way he was. If what had happened to him earlier – his third attack since knowing her; the first by Susan, the second by her – had affected him deeply, he was showing no sign of it. That's not to say it hadn't. He might be putting on a brave façade. But somehow she didn't think so. Reminding herself that people were waiting for an answer, she enlightened them.

"Not long ago, I dreamt of Saul. In the dream, I was a child again, in this very cottage, and Mum had come home with someone. It was obvious Gran didn't like him. We all sat down for dinner, but the table started to spin. Mum and Gran did too. Only Saul and I were static, and he was looking at me, staring at me, like, well... like the devil himself, I suppose."

Immediately, Jessica rushed to his defence. "What we did was wrong, but Saul is no devil."

"No, I know that. Maybe it's just another memory resurfacing – the picture completing."

Jessica nodded. "I did bring him back for dinner once, and you're right, Gran didn't like him. But he's not evil. If you say he is, then you'll have to say that about me; after all we shared the same beliefs, the same arrogance. Do you think I'm evil?"

It sounded like a challenge. Ruby tried not to show how taken aback she was.

"No, of course not."

"No one is beyond redemption – that's what Gran thinks. One time, I would have disagreed. One time, I thought *I* was beyond redemption—"

"Mum, no—"

"It's okay. I don't think I am – not anymore. I…" Faltering, she glanced at Jed, who'd settled himself under the kitchen table. "Perhaps no *soul* is beyond redemption, but I still believe there are plenty of things out there that are. Things born from human minds, without a doubt, but that don't grow in the light – that grow in the dark. Deformed things, which become more and more depraved."

Theo looked tired all of a sudden. "Where are we going with this, Jessica?" she asked.

"I asked Saul what he saw," she replied.

"And?"

"His reply was 'hell'."

Cash gasped. "Hell? Woah!"

Ruby could see Theo bristle slightly. "If hell does exist, it's in this realm only," she said.

320

"Theo, I understand that, but right now this is the realm we inhabit – it's our reality," Jessica countered. "We live in a world of balance, of duality. Where there is day, there is night. Where there is right, there is wrong. Where there is hope, there is despair…"

"And where there's God, there's the devil," Ruby finished for her.

"Yes," Jessica said, "because we've created him. We *perpetuate* him."

"We?" asked Ruby.

"The human race," she clarified.

"What about indigenous races? Races that have no concept of God or of Satan?"

In answer to Ruby's question, Jessica shrugged. "Simple. They invent their own deities to worship and to fear."

Ness was also trying to make sense of it. "So, we're fighting the devil of popular western culture. Not just a thought form made manifest, but a common image made manifest too?"

"We're fighting what we *expect* to see," Jessica replied. "We may feed the image, but long before that it was fed to us."

Cash was still awe-struck. "Blimey, I'm going to meet Lucifer!"

"Lucifer?" Jessica smiled, but wryly so. "If that's what you want to call him. But, as you know, he goes by many names."

Cash seemed to contemplate this. "Okay, okay, what you're saying, it makes sense – albeit in a totally-out-there kind of way. But what about Danny? Did he see the devil too?"

"Danny was an alcoholic, wasn't he?" Jessica asked.

"And a drug user?'

"Yeah, yeah, I suppose he was."

"Then he had more than one demon to fight."

Cash lowered his eyes. "Poor Danny."

Ruby too was thoughtful. The devil of popular culture… Was that what she'd seen that night so long ago with its yellow eyes? Eyes similar to the black shuck, but with the vague body of a man – a man she'd found disturbing in her youth. Saul, perhaps? An image she'd pieced together like some sort of gruesome photo-fit – different to what Jessica had seen, to what Saul had seen, to what Cash had seen, but fundamentally the same. And if not the devil, then something from 'hell', as Gran had intimated. Something that had splintered off, which had enough energy invested in it that it was able to take shape, smash through the barriers and develop consciousness. Something that had been *desired,* wantonly. Another thought occurred, one that caused panic to gallop through her.

"What if he doesn't show up tonight? What if everything we've done is for nothing? What if he comes back again when we least expect it? When we're unprepared, vulnerable."

"What if he hides again, you mean?" asked Jessica.

Ruby nodded her head vigorously.

"As a child, you were able to use your mind's defences to block him out. Kids are incredible like that. But, Ruby, would you be able to block him out now?"

"No." There's no way she could forget him now.

"And," Jessica continued, "are you frightened?"

She was, despite trying so hard not to be.

"Then he'll show. But there's one thing you need to

remember."

"What's that?" asked Ruby.

"In a world of balance, if you're frightened, he's frightened too."

"*He's* frightened? Of love, you mean?"

"Of course, and we've got it coming in by the truckload. Already it's starting to build."

Was it? She still couldn't feel it. Not yet.

"Ruby, he's not invincible. No one ever is."

Trying to share her mother's conviction, she found she couldn't do that either.

* * *

The evening that passed was actually a pleasant one, considering the circumstances. The sense of camaraderie amongst them was strong. Although Ronald never left his son's side, he visibly relaxed, listening to Corinna as she continued to talk about Psychic Surveys – his attention held particularly rapt by the Highdown Hall case.

"Cynthia Hart," he said, referring to the movie star who had resided at the hall long after her demise. "I remember her in a Hitchcock movie. She was terrific – a real stunner."

Saul listened with interest, but his eyes rarely left Jessica. She too seemed unable to look away from him. They'd found each other again, and both seemed to be in thrall to this fact. He was far from the sinister man of her dreams, but then she supposed fear had dissolved whatever arrogance he may have once courted. In-between eating toast and drinking tea, Presley and Cash were chatting about a forthcoming gig, Cash really excited about it. Ruby was sitting on the floor with her back resting against Cash's legs as they spoke – Jed beside her. As for Theo and Ness, they were deep in conversation too, but not about anything paranormal – seemingly more light-hearted subjects. Occasionally, great gusts of laughter bellowed from Theo, and Ness even chuckled too. Previously, the pair had explained to Saul and Ronald the importance of visualising white light at all times, reinforcing what Corinna had already said. They'd also assured them they would be visualising white light, surrounding not only them, but also everyone in the room, and even those who lived in the houses either side – adding to the abundance. Ruby had never seen the two women so united. Although the living room was cramped with so many people in it, it was also cosy. Gran would have loved the atmosphere, but Gran was safely out of it. Jessica had already rung the hospital to ask for a progress report, and had been told she'd be out tomorrow, during the afternoon. She had asked Jasmine to stress to her daughter and granddaughter that she was looking forward to being home again. On some level, Ruby wondered if Gran was passing on her vote of confidence? Very quickly, she decided she was.

It was just after eleven when people started to stretch and yawn. Jessica and Corinna stood up to go and find bedding. The plan was to sleep in the living room, all together. Ruby stood too, thinking it entirely possible they'd pass a peaceful night, not least because the fear she'd felt earlier seemed to have subsided – an effect of all that positivity being sent their way, perhaps? She felt happy, hopeful, even – emotions that had been strangers to her for quite some time. She was just about to rope Cash in to help make beds, had bent down to haul him to his feet, her hands in his, when there came a loud bang from upstairs – a furious crash – followed by another, and another. People stopped talking in mid-sentence, stopped laughing, stopped breathing, even. Instead, all eyes flew upwards as though they were a single unit and, just as they did, the lights went out.

Whether it was frightened or not, the darkness was back.

Chapter Thirty-Two

THEO'S voice rang out, loud and clear.

"Remember there's a lot of love in this room. We're surrounded by it, and love is the strongest protection of all. Please – the last thing we should do is panic."

Striving to follow her command, Ruby focussed her mind on more practical matters. Torches – they needed torches. Why the heck hadn't anyone thought to bring torches?

A light started shining. Cash had hold of his mobile and had utilised the torch on it. Spurred on by his example, Ruby reached into her back pocket, retrieved her phone, and did the same. A third and a fourth light joined them – Corinna's and Presley's.

God bless the iPhone, thought Ruby.

"I'd say round one to us," Theo commented. "Used to call them the devil's own implements, those phones. Oh, the irony of it!"

The crashing above had stopped. What state her bedroom would be in, Ruby dreaded to think. Instead, footsteps started up, hurtling backwards and forwards at high speed.

"There's someone up there, there has to be!" Ruby heard Ronald exclaim.

"Not someone – *something*," Cash informed him.

Reaching for her hand, he held it tightly – the warmth of him on this occasion barely combating the spread of ice within her.

She couldn't see Jed; it was so dark. But she could feel him rub up against her legs. He hadn't hightailed it, even though he could. He hadn't left Cash, and he wouldn't leave her.

As quickly as it had started, the noise stopped. Silence ensued, much worse somehow. Everybody stood still, heads to one side, listening. The creature... Where had it gone?

"It's playing with us," Ness explained. "Trying to frighten us further."

"Don't give it the satisfaction," Theo warned. "Saul, Ronald, remember what I said earlier. We must not feed it anymore."

But it was easier said than done. They were human. That's *all* they were. And this thing that stalked them, that stalked her in particular – *I see you, Ruby, I see you* – was not. It was soulless. It wanted her, but it would use the others to get at her. It would try to hurt her in any way it could, because that's what something soulless would do.

Frantically, she turned round and stared at shapes in the dark. "Get out," she cried. "All of you. You can't stay here." Despite her words, how she beseeched them, no one moved. "Please, I'm better off facing this on my own."

Theo gripped her arm. "We're not going anywhere, and you have to remain calm."

Calm? It seemed like such an impossible 'ask'. Mr and Mrs Ledbetter's poltergeist came to mind – a phenomenon fuelled entirely by their angst-ridden teenage daughter. When she wasn't around, all *was* calm. The same applied to her. She was the common denominator in this situation, the one fuelling the entity upstairs – the star attraction.

She shook Theo off, took a step back from her, from Cash too. Instead, her eyes sought out Jessica. Still by Saul's side, Ruby shone the light on her.

"Mum," she said. "What you saw – has it ever called you by your name?"

As if sensing the urgency of her question, Jessica took only a moment to respond. "I… erm… no, no it hasn't."

Next, Ruby pointed her torch at Saul. "What about you?"

"No," he said, not hesitating at all.

"And did you ever see it again after the night you supposedly conjured it, either of you? I'm not talking about in dreams. I mean when you were awake. Did you see it? Did you *smell* it?"

Jessica looked at Saul quickly and then back at Ruby. "No," she said, speaking for them both.

"So, all these years, it was the fear of the memory that crippled you?"

Jessica seemed appalled. "Ruby, it was much more than that!"

"But it wasn't, Mum, it really wasn't. What you saw, I don't doubt it was real. But it didn't see you. You looked into the abyss – then what did you do?"

"I… I fled."

"Saul did too?"

"Yes, I've told you that before. We both did."

Ruby swallowed. "But, you see, I didn't. I stood my ground."

"Ruby, I don't understand," Jessica responded, such confusion in her voice.

"Mum, I asked who it was. I dared to challenge it and I didn't flee – not at first." She recalled who she had tried to be like – Lucy from *The Lion, the Witch and the Wardrobe* – and almost laughed. Almost. "And with Danny, too, after I'd seen it, I went back – I threw down the gauntlet. And because I did, it marked me."

Jessica was shaking her head vehemently. "No, no, no. That can't be true. People challenge the devil all the time in their own ways. Why would it mark you in particular?"

"I don't know why," replied Ruby, the desolation in her voice painful even to her own ears. "All I know is, it's not your demon anymore, Mum. It's mine."

"Don't do that," Theo warned. "Don't own it."

Cash spoke next. "I know why."

She turned to him. "What do you mean?"

"I know why it marked you in particular. It's obvious."

"Cash…" He was babbling, surely? How could he know?

"Remember when we first met," he hurried on, "back in December? We'd just been to visit Mr Rawlings, the man who duped Cynthia. I loathed him; he was no better than a rapist. But you – whilst you didn't condone what he did, you didn't condemn him either. You tried to look beneath the surface, to understand the fear that had prompted his actions. I said I wished I could see what you saw. I didn't mean the spirits – I meant the good in everyone. I told you – your compassion, it shone. Do you remember that, Ruby?"

She did remember it, as well as the way he'd looked at her when he'd said those words. His eyes had been shining too – with the beginnings of love, she now realised.

"What's that got to do with this?"

329

His hands came up to grab her by the shoulders.

"That's why it's marked you, that thing upstairs. Because you shine."

"Cash... what are you trying to say?"

He started grinning again.

"I don't doubt it's afraid of love – that makes sense. But more than that, it's afraid of you."

"Me?"

"Yes," Cash confirmed. "If it's a world of balance we're talking about, then guess what? I reckon the scales just tipped in your favour."

Cash's words – his *conviction* – hung in the air between them.

It's afraid of you.

Could it be true? Is that why it had hidden for so long? Growing bigger and stronger. Maybe. But she'd grown bigger too.

"And stronger," Theo broke into her thoughts. "Don't forget that part."

Jessica stepped forward. "You've also got Jed."

If Cash had surprised her, so did her mother. "What do you mean, I've also got Jed?"

"Your guardian angel," she replied.

She shook her head. "Mum, he's just a dog. A dog Ness and I tried to send to the light. But, for some reason, he didn't go – he attached himself to me instead."

"Another attachment," she heard Ness muse. But before Ruby could question her further, Ness started speaking again. "That animal spirit we went to investigate, just before Highdown Hall – we watched him go towards the light. He disappeared."

"I know he did, but he came back, when I was driving

to meet Theo. He materialised in the footwell of my car."

"The same dog? Or something clothed in what you'd just seen? A safe image – one your conscious would accept without question."

"Something I conjured, you mean?"

"Or something that was waiting for you in the wings," Ness replied. "Until you needed him."

Ruby looked down to where the dog was standing. She could barely see his black shadow, the night too great a camouflage. But his eyes – she could see them and they were shining, even though her torch wasn't aimed at him. She marvelled at what Ness was saying. He was no accident, no coincidence – he was an attachment?

"You knew this battle was coming," Jessica said. "On some level, you've always known it." She looked pointedly at Cash. "You've been putting measures in place all your life."

Ruby was nothing less than thunderstruck. She could see spirits, had always been able to, but Ruby the Demon-Slayer? That was the stuff of fiction.

"Ruby," Ness explained gently, "if you can see the light, you can see the darkness too."

"And, Ruby," Theo reminded her, "you can see the light better than anyone I know."

Trying to take on board all that was being said – to minimise the magnitude of it, to break it down into bite-sized chunks so she'd have half a chance of understanding it – she heard the top board of the stairs creak. The board she normally tried so hard to avoid.

"It's coming," she whispered.

There was another creak – the floorboard below it. Whatever *it* was, it was descending.

As it did, every image she'd ever seen of the devil flew at her, stuck to the front wall of her mind, and melded into one. She could feel herself shaking at the horror of it all.

"I'm not strong enough. I'm not Lucy."

In contrast to hers, Cash's voice was unwavering. "I don't know who this Lucy girl is, but I'm telling you, she can't compare to you. No one can. You're incomparable."

"Cash—"

"More than that, you're invincible."

"No one's invincible," she countered, echoing her mother.

"But you're not just anyone. You're Ruby Davis – the one who's going to rid us of this thing."

"Amen to that," Jessica whispered from behind.

As fast as it had run overhead, it was now approaching them slowly – deliberately slowly. Ramping up the tension in the room, building their fear, as Ness had said. Revelling in it, feeding on it – *gorging* itself. That crash of love – the tidal wave that would blast this thing back to where it had come from, that would close the portal, that would seal it up forever – hadn't reached its full momentum, not yet. How long before it did?

We can't fight this on our own.

"We're not on our own," Cash said.

What…? He could read minds now?

"Don't doubt yourself, Ruby," he continued. "You're more than capable."

I can save us all?

"You can save us all," Ness confirmed.

All I have to do is believe?

"That's all you have to do." Again, Ness answered aloud.

Ruby looked at Jed.

Are you really my guardian angel?

Dogs couldn't shrug; she knew that. Even so, she'd bet that's what he'd just done.

It was on the bottom stair now, edging closer. Ruby could feel that amusement again – cold, hard and cutting. It had them cornered, trapped.

I wish you'd gone when you had the chance. I told you to.

"We're going nowhere," Cash said.

But it just wants me.

"We're all throwing down the gauntlet this time."

That did it. "Cash!"

"What?"

"Are you reading my mind?"

"No, of course not." There was genuine surprise in his voice.

"But you keep answering my thoughts."

"Really? I don't mean to. I'm just saying, that's all…"

"You're just saying." She repeated his words whilst nodding her head. "Well… listen up, because I'm just saying something too. I love you, Cash Wilkins, I bloody love you."

Before he had a chance to answer, she turned to the others. "I love you all. I love your bravery, your loyalty, and your faith. In fact, your faith astounds me. I'm blessed to know you and to be loved by you also. Saul, Ronald, I'm including you in this. I know I *don't* know you, but you're a part of my history – you always have been, and always will be. We've been in this together for a long time. And if Cash is right, if I shine, it's only because of you. You all *make* me shine."

As the group stared back at her there was silence – a perfect moment of silence, with nothing ominous about it at all. Afterwards, Ruby darted forward, Jed falling into step beside her.

"What you doing?" Cash asked, panic in his voice.

"I'm doing what I do best," she replied, yanking the door open. "I'm shining."

Chapter Thirty-Three

THE first thing that hit Ruby was the smell. She didn't know if she'd be able to stand it, let alone anything else. Worse than ever, the stench, its fetidness, made her eyes water, effectively blinding her and putting her at an immediate disadvantage. Inciting nausea, it choked her, and this time it choked the others too. Behind her she could hear coughing and spluttering. If she'd rushed headlong into a charnel house where bodies had festered for centuries, she couldn't imagine the smell to be worse.

Reaching a hand up, she wiped roughly at both eyes. Still she was blind. It was black on the other side – of course it was – but in the darkness something writhed. Gradually, her sight adjusted. She could just make out a shape – formless at first, fluid – but quickly moulding itself into a man. Not a mere man – a man mountain. It was gigantic, much bigger than she'd remembered – swamping her. As her jaw dropped at the sight of it, she heard Jed whimper. There were gasps also. What were the rest of the team seeing? The same as her, this time, or something different but equally as dreadful?

Jed, be strong.

She aimed that thought at him, but whether it penetrated, she didn't know. She wouldn't be surprised if it hadn't. Be strong, she'd told him. But upon seeing what was in front of her, the strength she'd gathered left her. She'd never felt so afraid, so weak. How could she compete with this thing? Even think she could? There was no way her best was good enough. It had fought its way out of the charnel house – the dumping ground – and it wasn't going back. Not unless it dragged her with it.

As the creature moved towards her – she wouldn't refer to it as a man any longer; it was far from that – Ruby tried to take a step back. Her feet, however, remained rooted.

"Ruby!"

Someone was calling her name? A female, but who? The voice sounded far away, smothered, as though the door behind her had slammed shut. Isolating her further.

"Ruby," the voice continued. "The tidal wave – can you feel it? It's coming at last." And then, "It's not just a tidal wave, Ruby – it's a tsunami! Everyone's pulling out the stops!"

Tidal wave? Tsunami? What was she talking about? Her mind felt shrouded.

Something brushed against her leg and she started. That thing – it wasn't touching her, was it? If it did, she wouldn't be able to survive it, she was sure.

DON'T TOUCH ME!

Again, something did, but with overwhelming relief she realised it wasn't the something in front of her. It was the something beside her. Jed. Doing his utmost to bring her back from the farthest reaches of her mind, to which she'd so readily flown.

"Ruby." The voice was clearer now – a male voice this time – strident. "You're actually shining. Look at you. Your hands. It's like they're firing sparks!"

She didn't want to take her eyes off the creature, not

336

even for a second, but she had to. She had to see what he was talking about. She was actually shining – what did he mean?

"The light, it's gone straight to you. You're the conduit, Ruby. Hold your hands up!"

Even though they felt like concrete was pouring into them, she managed to obey the instruction. What she saw startled her almost as much as the creature had. The voice was right. She was shining, and not just her hands, but also her entire body. Jed was no longer nudging her, or whimpering – he was barking, shifting from paw to paw, excited suddenly.

Ruby lifted her hands higher and some of the darkness receded. Perhaps the creature would too. Love. It was the strongest force of all. It had the power to obliterate. Quickly, she thrust her hands out, desperate to see the effect such an action would have. The heaving, writhing thing stilled. Success! Surely it was a success. Ruby was just allowing herself to think so when the creature's eyes snapped open. Those black, black eyes with their neon yellow surround. Eyes that greedily hugged all the pain and all the misery in the world to them. All the envy, the hatred, the anger and the intolerance. All the things that lowered the human soul, but which sent this thing soaring. And she could see it all perfectly because of the light shining from her hands – the light that, in this moment, was being used against her. Gasping, Ruby snatched her hands back. She didn't want to see such things! She didn't! It was more than the parameters of her mind could cope with.

"Oh God!" She screamed aloud this time. "I can't do this. I can't!"

She yearned for blindness again.

The creature appeared to laugh at her despair.

I see you, Ruby. And you are mine.

Was it true? Was it really true? Had she been earmarked from such an early age?

"Oh no!" Someone behind her was screaming. "No, no, no!"

It was a female voice again, younger than the first had been.

"Cash, Cash. Are you all right?"

What did she mean, was Cash all right? Cash was her boyfriend, wasn't he? Yes, yes, of course he was. Why did she keep forgetting who these people were? The shutters in her mind that had closed as a child – that had only recently sprung back open – were doing their best to shut again. An attempt at protecting her. But it was too late for that; she had to keep them open, stay firmly in the present. There was no protection in amnesia – not anymore. The voice: it belonged to Corinna, her friend and colleague – slim and tall with long red hair. And the voice joining hers was Presley's, Cash's brother – just as panicked.

"Come on, bro. Breathe. Just breathe."

Breathe? Why wasn't Cash breathing?

Ruby tried to turn her head, but found she couldn't. It wasn't a case of not daring to this time; she'd dare anything for Cash. It was more that she was caught in an invisible grip. Her eyes, too, refused to break the creature's gaze. She was quite literally held captive.

Jed, go back. See what's happening.

She could sense the dog start to obey at first, but then he stopped.

Jed, go back!

Instead, he started snarling and crept closer to the mass.

What are you doing?

Buying her time – that's what he was doing. Just as he'd done with Susan. Standing in-between them both, the dog appeared to have taken on a different guise. No longer a Labrador, he was the shuck from the storybook of old. But as magnificent as he looked – as fearsome – he was not in the same league as what threatened them.

Jed, please, you have to go back!

Looking from her to the demon, the dog – the shuck – faltered.

Whatever you're going to do, don't! Whatever you're thinking, stop!

But her thoughts had no impact. Instead, he turned from her. Faced the abomination squarely and threw himself at it.

As Corinna had done earlier, she found herself screaming. "NO! NO! NO!"

Jed had gone – disappeared. No, not disappeared, he'd been *absorbed*.

A sob caught in her throat. She thought it would stay there – be the thing to choke her and mercifully put an end to this nightmare – but it didn't. It came bursting out, followed by more sobs – so many of them, building one on top of the other.

"Ruby, you have to do something!".

It was Corinna again, beseeching her. But what could she do? The creature had hurt those dearest to her, and soon it would destroy the others – just as she'd warned it would.

Another voice tried to get through to her – Theo's.

"Ruby, we will lose if you don't banish your fear. Cash

339

is hurt. Control your fear."

Reiterating those words, the voice came closer.

"Stay back, Theo," Ruby warned. "Stay back or it will see you."

"Ruby, Cash is hurt. Don't you care?"

The fact that Theo could ask such a question pierced her.

"OF COURSE I BLOODY CARE!"

"THEN CONTROL YOUR FEAR!"

Before she could answer, the old lady screamed. Something had happened to her too.

"THEO!" Ruby yelled. They were being picked off, one by one, like apples from a tree. Being bitten into and then spat out, as if they too were rotten at the core.

"What do I do?" She was the one whimpering now. "I don't know what to do."

She had expected Ness to answer her cry, but it was someone else. It was Saul. Although his voice was quiet, barely above a whisper, she heard him perfectly.

"Rise to it. That's what you have to do. You have to rise to it."

Rise to it? What did he mean?

"If you can't control your fear, control the light."

Now Ness did speak.

"Yes, yes, of course, that's it. Saul's right! Control the light. The light is in you, Ruby, but it's also coming out of you. It's becoming weak, chaotic. You need to contain it."

Her mother spoke next, as urgent as Ness. "Ruby, claw back the light. Gather it to you and then shoot it out, in one concentrated beam. It has to come from the heart!"

What Ness was saying – Jessica too – made sense. One intense, focused ray of light. Made up of love, faith and, most importantly, good intent. It had to work. It had to!

Before she could do anything, though, she needed to know.

"What about Cash? Theo?"

"Ruby, we haven't got time…" Ness replied.

"Are they still alive?"

"They're still alive."

The words *for now* seemed to hang provocatively in the air.

"And Jed?"

"Jed knows what he's doing."

"He rushed at the thing – he tried to fight it. He's gone."

"I know," was Ness's reply.

Before she could falter again, Ruby did as she'd been asked. If those closest to her had died, she'd grieve later. She'd never stop grieving. Souls may go home, but she was selfish; she wanted them with her – always. Right now, however, there were others to think of: Ness, Saul, Corinna, Ronald, and Jessica. She had to stop them from being harmed too.

Still staring at the creature, Ruby began to visualise the light within her, to do as her mother had said – claw it back from each extremity, her hands and her feet, and centralise it. As she did, her opponent stopped laughing. The game – *its* game – was over.

As she continued to draw the light to her – encasing it, *entombing* it – the mass stepped forward. Took another step. Came closer still.

Behind her, all was silent, but for a muffled cry. Jessica? Corinna? She couldn't tell.

When it had stepped closer before, when she was seven,

she'd stepped back. This time, she stepped forward – no longer rooted to the spot.

"Damn you," she said, her voice shaking with the effort. Struggling to control that, too, she repeated the words, much louder this time, and with more conviction. "DAMN YOU!"

I see you, Ruby.

"I know you do. You've told me often enough."

And you are mine.

"Oh yeah? We'll see about that."

Some of her fear dissolved. The creature had made its first mistake. If Cash and Jed were gone, it had already done its worst. In this moment, nothing could hurt her more. As she grew bolder still, she also grew taller. How could that be? Was it some sort of psychic illusion? '*The glamour*' as Theo had once described it? It had to be, although it felt real enough. The light within, that she was now harnessing – it was expanding. And, in turn, so was she. She was rising, as Saul had told her to do – meeting the darkness head on. The creature's eyes – so full of all things foul, so conceited and cock-sure, so *unconquered* – blinked. Not once, but twice. Was that surprise in them?

"If you've hurt my friends," Ruby spat the words out, "I will hurt you."

You are mine!

"Is that it? Is that the only thing you're able to say? I am *not* yours."

She was taller than the creature now. She was sure of it. Impossibly tall. Lazuli Cottage was tiny. There was no way it could hold such huge beings. No way. The walls around them – where were they? They seemed to have gone. It was just the two of them – again.

Ruby... the creature began, but she refused to let it speak.

"All you are is fear. That's what you're made of – fear and loathing."

They were so close, barely any division between them.

Ruby...

"And if fear is what you are, then you fear too. You fear *me*."

Its face, for want of a better word, twisted and turned.

"I'm right, aren't I?" she declared. "You're afraid!"

It was! She could see it. Not only was it blinking, it had turned its head to the side slightly. She was the one blinding it. The realisation thrilled her.

"Bloody hell! You're not invincible!"

She felt herself grow taller still – swamping it, as it had swamped her.

"What you are is nothing, do you hear me? Nothing!"

Ruby... the creature called again.

She felt like throwing her hands over her ears; only just stopped herself from doing so.

"Stop saying my name. Stop it! You have no right to say it!"

Eighteen years, this being had tormented her family, had ripped them apart – fractured them – and now all she wanted was to rip *it* apart. Rush into it, as Jed had. Tear it from limb to limb – *devour* it. She imagined doing just that, the satisfaction she would feel – how *happy* it would make her. And its eyes – those horrid, horrid eyes. The stuff of nightmares. She would save them for last, in a sense she would savour them. With her fingertips, she would pluck them from its head and hold them in her hands. She would squeeze until each one exploded.

Elated at the prospect, her teeth grinding against each other as she bared them, Ruby prepared to shoot, and then stopped, horrified at herself. She was mirroring it, becoming feral, wanting nothing more than to destroy it. As Gran had said, good wolf, bad wolf – they were both inside her, merging. She had to tear them apart; side with one, absolutely and irrevocably. They both wanted her, in equal measure. But right now, which one did she want? For a fraction of a second, perhaps even more, the darkness seemed so inviting, so pleasing – so damned easy to align with. She could surrender to it; give up the fight, relinquish her self-appointed crusade. Relax. And that was how it would win. Not by physically attacking her – this wasn't the set of a teen scream movie. It would win by *altering* her, by staining her soul, by making her someone she wasn't. The darkness had never seemed so inviting – like a soft woollen blanket on a cold, cold night. It had reached out, and she had wanted to reach back, and be absorbed too. But also in that moment, she had felt herself lessen, shrink. Because that's what darkness truly did – it made you small.

Taking a deep breath, ignoring how ragged it was, she had to decide. What was she? Good or evil? She couldn't afford to be at war with herself. The first step in the right direction was to banish all images of Cash from her mind – that cheeky grin of his. Of Jed and his unstinting devotion. Of Theo and her booming laugh. Such visions, ironically, would fuel the part of her that wanted vengeance, and vengeance only. Her grandmother, her mother too – she wouldn't think of them. She'd think solely of the light. Welcome it; encourage it. Let it fill every vein, every sinew, every cell; lift her when she had fallen so low – when she had not only been touched by hell, she'd become it. Actually *become* it.

'*Rise to it*', she'd been advised. No. That was wrong.

"*You* rise to me," she declared, inhaling the light, keeping it focussed – feeling it.

Everyone who had sent the light her way, who'd stopped what they were doing, taken time out from demanding lives, who'd stood united – she could imagine each and every one of them. The looks on their faces – their eyes closed, their expressions intent. Gary from the Internet café, Cash's mum, Theo's friends, Ness's friends, Corinna's, Presley's. People at once ordinary and extraordinary, who were ready to defend her, to aid and abet her. She wasn't alone; she'd never been alone. She was, as Gran had said, a part of something much, much bigger. She added the light of the multitude to her own. She let it buoy her, fuel her; let it cement her belief. Belief was everything. She could do this.

When she was able to, when she could trust herself enough, she spoke again

"You poor thing," she said. "You poor, poor thing."

Nothing should have to hurt that much – not even the devil.

As though the light had purified her vision as well as her mind, she could see the mass for what it really was: wretched. She really had no other word in her vocabulary to describe it. It had no glory, no power – except the power invested in it by proxy. Beneath that, it was hollow.

Realising its grip had loosened, the creature howled – a sound that served only to stir further sympathy. She had to shoot, still. She knew that. The battle had to end. But she had to aim with love. Whatever it had done – to her, to her family, her friends, her lover – it had done because it didn't know any better. It was the antithesis of all things good. In a world of balance, that was the role it played.

"Go back to where you came from, and go with love."

Words that weren't quite enough.

"Mum, Saul," she called.

From behind her, she heard them answer.

"Come and stand with me," she instructed.

To their credit, they didn't hesitate.

"Yes, Ruby?" Jessica sounded so young – the child rather than her.

"Another apology is needed."

There was silence, initially, and then Jessica spoke.

"I'm… I'm sorry, for what I did. I'm so sorry. I should never have brought you here."

"I'm sorry too," Saul echoed, his words ending in a sob.

As they stepped back, Ruby inhaled deeply once again – slowly, purposefully, leisurely, almost. With one almighty breath outwards, she released the light – an intense beam that flowed uninterrupted from her very core. So many times, she'd seen the light, helped countless spirits towards it, but always it had been in the distance. Now, she was its source, and it was everything she thought it to be – bright, beautiful and so very, very forgiving.

"Go back with love," she said again. "*All* our love." Against which, it could not stand.

The creature thrashed and squirmed – protested – even though defeat was now inevitable. Was it really beyond redemption, she wondered? It had never been human, but the human race had created it. Did that count for something? Was it possible it could evolve, as souls could evolve? Reach a higher plain? One that wasn't full of torment?

As it shrank to nothing, keening now instead of howling, she could only hope so.

* * *

When the lights came back on, Ruby was still standing. But she was no longer statuesque in size. And the light within her – the *psychic* light – had gone. She was normal, or as normal as she'd ever be. The first thing she did was look for Jed. As the creature diminished, she expected the dog to somehow be expunged from it. But that was not the case.

"It's over. At last, it's over!"

It was Jessica – a look of abject wonder on her face.

In reply, Ruby could only utter two words. "Cash! Theo!" She had to see how they were.

She threw herself forward, past her mother, past Saul, and into the living room.

Two bodies lay on the ground – the rest of the group huddled around them.

"It's okay," Ronald said, on seeing her. "They're coming round. Nasty bumps to the head, the pair of them, though. They were quite literally picked up and hurled backwards."

"Should I call an ambulance?" Ruby all but squealed the words.

"Oh, please, not this ambulance business again."

The protest belonged to Cash. He was rubbing at his head as he sat up, his rather stunned-looking brother helping him. Theo was also stirring.

"And I might have mentioned this before," she said, her words slightly slurred, "but I think it's worth mentioning again. I'm getting too old to be thrown around like this."

Ruby didn't know who to jump on first.

"Cash," said Theo, realising her intent. "I'd really rather you jumped on Cash."

Ruby didn't hesitate.

"Hello, babe," he said, as she threw her arms around him. Burying his face in her hair, he added, "You were magnificent by the way."

Magnificent? Perhaps she was, in the end. But for a moment... She shook her head. That moment was over – best not to think of it anymore.

"*We* were magnificent," she countered. "Everyone who got involved." Before adding, "But hang on – how do you know what I was? You were out for most of it, weren't you?"

"Erm... yeah, I meant before I was knocked out. Anyway, the point is, you were the front man, Ruby. You put yourself out there – you smashed it."

"I did, didn't I?" Frankly, she was amazed too.

"You faced your fear."

Ruby exhaled. "And what a fear it was."

"Jed," Cash said next. "Where is he?"

Immediately, Ruby's face clouded. "He's..." That was just it. She didn't know.

Concern clouded Cash's face too, but then he relaxed. "Oh, he's there, he's fine."

Confused, Ruby followed his gaze.

Sure enough, Jed was running through the doorway and heading straight for her. He looked unharmed, despite the horrors he must have witnessed. He'd actually gone *inside* that thing – fought his own war. As he settled beside her, his usual self, a sneaking suspicion formed. Had he gone

348

inside knowing it would provoke her; would make her fight back? If so, how had he been so sure he'd escape? Cash and Theo looked surprisingly well too. Had they really been hurled backwards? Or had they done it for effect, a bid to get her to stand her ground? And then, another thought occurred.

"Cash, you said Jed was fine. Did you see him? Actually *see* him?"

Cash was impressively nonchalant. "I might have caught a glimpse," he teased. "All this hanging around with psychics, it's clearly rubbing off on me."

Ruby laughed then. They all did. Whatever tactics had been employed, it didn't matter. Only the end result mattered.

As she returned to Cash, Corinna grabbed Presley. Theo and Ness also exchanged a rare embrace, before turning their attentions towards Ronald, who looked startled at such a prospect. As for Jessica and Saul, their bodies heaved slightly as they held each other. They were relieved – it was obvious – but they were grieving too. Eighteen years they'd lost – a long time for anyone. And they mustn't forget Danny; he had lost his life.

Cash interrupted her reverie. "Can you feel it? How different the atmosphere is?"

Ruby could. It was ordinary – something that couldn't be beaten.

"You did that," Cash continued. "The beast is gone."

When she asked Cash later if he'd seen 'the beast', as he called it, he said no. As before, he couldn't quite make out what it was – the darkness had been too complete.

"Then why call it a beast?"

"Well, I thought we were all agreed. You know, it's the

devil, the beast – a monster with cloven feet and horns."

"The devil we're brought up to believe in?"

Cash pulled a face. "I've got this wrong again, haven't I?"

"It was unpleasant; I'm not going to lie. But cloven feet and horns – I didn't see them."

"I've bought into the myth. I've been conditioned. How do I get round it?"

"You know the answer. Don't feed the myth anymore; don't give it life. If we ever have kids, Sunday mornings are strictly for lie-ins."

Cash had laughed outright then. "If we have a kid, and it's a girl, she'll be like you – psychic."

"And if it's a boy, it'll be like you – a geek."

"A geek? Hey! I'm way cooler than that."

"If you say so," she said, leaning in to kiss him.

As everyone suddenly discovered an appetite, Cash and Presley got on with dinner – the pasta and tomato sauce that Cash had promised earlier – and to hell with the fact it was well past two in the morning. They ate, and then they bedded down in the living room, all still feeling the need to be together – not through fear this time, through friendship.

Only Ness and Ruby rose early. They tiptoed out of the room and went into the kitchen, careful not to disturb the others.

As Ruby filled the kettle and switched it on, she turned to Ness.

"Is that it? Will we see the darkness again?"

"In this world, the darkness is always waiting. We mustn't get complacent."

As the kettle boiled, Ruby found two mugs, popped a

teabag in each, and filled them with water. "So, what we've done, *all* we've done, is hold it at bay."

"Don't get complacent, and don't belittle it either. What we've done is quite something."

Ruby considered this. It *was* quite something – there was no denying it.

"But, Ness," she said, still desperate for answers, "what was it really? A thought form? The devil incarnate? Cash's alien? Was it even real? Because, right now, standing here in Gran's kitchen, in the cold light of day – what happened, it seems so… *fantastical.*"

"In the cold light of day, even the fact that *we* exist – human beings, more complex than a jet plane, more sophisticated than even the best computer – is fantastical."

"You know what I mean."

"I do," Ness granted, "and in truth, I don't know."

"But did you see it? Did you see how *big* it was?"

"I was focussed on you, Ruby, and your brilliance."

Ruby sighed. She supposed she'd have to get used to it. Not every question had an answer. Instead, she thought of more pressing matters.

"I'd better phone the hospital, see what time Gran's coming home. And then, you know what else we have to do, don't you?"

"What?" Ness asked. The smile on her face was unusually indulgent.

"Start ringing round again. All those who rallied – they'll want to know the outcome."

"They will indeed," Ness agreed. "And hang the expense."

Chapter Thirty-Four

EXAMINING her reflection in the bathroom mirror, Ruby wondered if she'd aged. She looked different somehow, as though the first bloom of youth had suddenly disappeared – the innocence. She looked, not old exactly, but more mature. Definitely more mature – her green-flecked eyes worldlier. Or perhaps otherworldly might be more apt.

Returning to her office along the narrow corridor, she shivered as she went. It was cold outside and, as usual, it had found its way into the attic that she occupied during working hours – she, Jed, and even Cash, on occasion. Jed and Cash were in situ today – Jed in front of the Calor Gas heater, and Cash leaning over his laptop at a second, much smaller meeting desk. Her desk, mammoth though it was, was not big enough for two – covered, as it was, in reports, notebooks and papers, as well as her computer, printer and phone. In the doorway, she stood and stared at her companions – guardian angels, both of them, in their own way.

Entering at last, and closing the door behind her in order to retain as much heat as possible, she pulled out her captain's chair and took a seat opposite Cash.

"Do you think I've aged?" she asked him, clicking her mouse to wake her computer up.

Cash glanced up. "Uh oh, is this one of those trick questions that women ask?"

"Another example being?"

"The size of your bum."

Ruby looked horrified. "My bum? What do you mean? It's not big, is it?"

Cash sighed. "No, your bum's not big and you're still young and gorgeous. Why do you ask?"

"I just… I think I look different. I *am* different, I suppose, after what happened."

"Of course you are. I am too." Cash sounded uncharacteristically solemn. "It's quite something to realise life isn't so petty after all."

"Petty?" Ruby quizzed.

"You know – it's rich, it's complex. It's a layer cake."

"A layer cake?" Ruby mused. "Trust you to use a food analogy. But, yeah, it is. Spiritualists tend to describe those layers as planes, but they're one and the same, I suppose."

Turning back to her computer, Ruby started to sift through various emails and phone messages. Having been absent from work for a few days, they'd mounted up. She was relieved to find she still had the office in Burgess Hill to cleanse – it had taken Mrs Woods months to get clearance from Head Office – and replied straight away with a suggested appointment. Also, a mother whose son had thrown himself off Beachy Head – a well-known East Sussex beauty spot and, unfortunately, death spot – had called. Distraught, she begged Psychic Surveys to patrol the spot where his body had lain.

"I need to know he's gone," her recorded voice said, "properly gone. I'm sure I don't have to explain – you people know what I mean. I want to make sure he's at peace – at last."

Ruby noted down her name and number, resolving to call her back that very day. For her, there'd be no charge.

The last message was one that stopped her in her tracks.

"Oh… erm… hello, my name's Annie. I've… well… I've got a strange situation going on really. It's not a haunting, as such. Oh, sorry, it's probably a bit rude to call it a haunting – a problem of a spiritual kind, I mean. It's to do with my little girl… my little girl and a bridge. I've got a friend, Lisa Cragg – you carried out a cleansing on her house recently. She lives where that asylum used to be. She suggested I call you. She said you'd know what to do."

Ruby twisted round in her chair. "Cash, did you hear that? She mentioned a bridge."

Cash had heard it and was staring back at Ruby. "But there are lots of bridges in Sussex. Do you know which one she meant?"

Ruby shook her head. "I'll call her back; ask her. Hang on."

After a few minutes of speaking and taking notes, Ruby ended the call.

"Is it the same bridge?" Cash said, his eyes hopeful.

"It is. The daughter's fixated on it. Let's go."

* * *

Ruby and Cash were at the bridge near Uckfield within the hour. Ruby had asked Jed if he wanted to come, but the dog had remained curled up in a ball – his way of declining.

They had arrived there slightly before Annie and her daughter – seven-year old Sadie – and en route, Ruby had filled Cash in on what had been happening.

"The little girl talks incessantly about the bridge; she says she's been there before, that she died there."

"Died there? In another lifetime, you mean?"

"Obviously."

Cash ignored Ruby's sarcasm. "Wow, reincarnation. Now there's a subject to get your teeth into."

"Makes a change from dealing with the devil, huh?" she said, grinning at him.

Annie and Sadie had been on a family walk, one that had taken them under the bridge. The path leading up to it and beyond was flat, and so ideal for Sadie to scoot along.

"Apparently, she stopped her scooter just before the bridge and pointed to the place where she was pushed," Ruby continued to explain. "She hasn't stopped talking about it since. Has insisted her mother bring her back on several occasions too. Throws tantrums to make sure she does, which is completely out of character for her. She's a good kid normally."

Cash nodded in understanding. "Even so, if we're talking about reincarnation, she can't be Susan."

"Why not?"

"Because Sadie's seven and you only moved Susan into the light a few months ago."

"I get the impression time isn't linear in the spirit world, but even so, it's a fair point."

"Did Annie actually mention Susan?" Cash asked.

"No, she didn't."

"And I never heard you mention her whilst you were speaking on the phone."

"No, I thought I'd do that face-to-face," Ruby

explained. "Oh look, here they are now."

Annie was young, not much older than Ruby. Mother and daughter shared the same dark hair and large, expressive eyes. Noting that Annie looked nervous, Ruby adopted what she hoped was a reassuring smile as she introduced herself and Cash.

"Thanks for meeting me," Annie said. "My partner knows about Sadie's fascination, but he doesn't know I've contacted you. He'll think I'm mad getting other people involved."

"It's not madness," Ruby assured her. "It's…" What was it? "Concern," she decided.

"It's just…" Annie inclined her head towards the little girl, who was busy staring at the bridge – one spot in particular. "She talks about it all the time, you know. And when she does, it's not like Sadie talking. It's like someone else completely."

Whilst she spoke, Cash knelt down so his eyes were level with the child's. "It's a great bridge, isn't it?" he said to Sadie, smiling at her.

"It's where I died," Sadie promptly replied.

"See?" Annie said. "What's wrong with her? Is she possessed or something?"

Possession. It was hardly Ruby's favourite subject – not after what she'd been through. Nonetheless, this might be a good possession. If it was Susan, how could it be less?

Gesturing for Annie to step slightly away from Sadie, and glad that Cash was still occupying the child, she said, "I don't know if it's possession as such. We shouldn't get too carried away at this stage." Again, remembering her own experience – what had happened at the end of it – she added, "What's more likely is Sadie is being used as a conduit."

Annie's already-wide eyes widened further. "A conduit? What do you mean?"

Ruby tried to explain. "It's possible that Sadie has a psychic ability; that she's able, even if she's not actually aware of it yet, to tune into someone previously passed. Someone might be using her as a form of communication, to get some kind of message across."

"Passed?" Annie asked.

"Died," Ruby clarified.

"Oh God. Who?"

Before Annie could panic, Ruby told her what she knew. "Locally, this bridge is known as Emily's Bridge, referring to a suicide that was allegedly committed here in the late nineteenth century by a distraught bride to be. Are you familiar with that story at all?"

Annie shrugged. "Never heard of Emily. Never even been to the bridge until recently."

"Teenagers hang out by this bridge quite a bit," Ruby continued, "drawn by Emily. They think she haunts here still, and they're after a thrill. Basically, they come to taunt her."

"Taunt her?" Annie looked astonished. "How cruel!"

"My thoughts exactly. Worried in case her spirit was grounded, that she was in distress, I also came here to check the story out, but instead of Emily, I found Susan."

"Susan?"

"Yes, Susan," Ruby repeated. "Whether Emily died here or not – if it's true or just an urban myth – I don't know. If she did, her spirit isn't grounded. Susan's, however, was. I performed a spiritual cleansing and sent her where she belongs – to the light."

"The light?" Annie queried again. All this spiritual-speak was clearly confusing her.

"It's where we come from. It's home."

"Heaven, you mean?"

"That's what some people call it," Ruby replied.

"Do you think it is Susan that's using her?"

"Considering Sadie's fixation with this particular bridge, it might well be." Ruby could feel herself frown. "You see, I may have sent Susan to the light, but whether she stayed there or not, I don't know. She left behind... how can I put it? Some unfinished business."

Annie's back straightened. "Tell me more about Susan – I want to know."

"She died in 1966. Unlike Emily, it wasn't suicide. She was pushed – murdered, in other words – by her lover. Her much older, married lover." Briefly, Ruby wondered whether to mention that Susan had Down's syndrome; then decided against it. That was something that had concerned her physical body, not her spirit. It was no longer relevant. "The unfinished business I'm referring to is the name of her murderer. Susan wouldn't reveal it to me. I'm not sure the world knows it either."

"He went unpunished?"

"That's my feeling."

"And you think she's come back to reveal it? Via Sadie?"

Ruby nodded. "Perhaps she's reconsidered. She wants justice done after all."

Annie looked fed-up suddenly. "You know, I'd really rather my daughter wasn't being used as a conduit."

"If your daughter is able to tune into someone this way... that's special."

"Even if that someone was murdered?"

Ruby sighed. "Well, that is rather unfortunate."

Annie was silent for a moment, contemplative. "So what do we do about it?" she asked at last.

"We find out if it is Susan using Sadie and, if so, what it is she wants to say."

Annie grew silent again, chewing at the inside of her mouth – something Ruby did too when she was nervous.

"Annie…" Ruby prompted.

"Okay, okay, I've got no choice, I suppose. Go ahead and talk to her. But… be gentle with her, okay? Go easy."

"Of course," promised Ruby.

Cash and Sadie were laughing conspiratorially together when she approached them.

"Hey, Rubes, Sadie can do a magic trick – look."

Raising her eyebrow at the re-emergence of her nickname, Ruby stood by expectantly. Clasping her hands together, Sadie folded her middle fingers over each other and twisted her hand round, sticking her middle fingers out either side and wiggling them.

"I see you," she trilled happily.

At such familiar words, Ruby felt herself start to tremble, but quickly she checked it. The voice that spoke them – the voice just underneath Sadie's own – was not deep and rasping. It was distinctly female – gentle, even. It was the voice of Susan.

Susan, I'm here. Speak to me!

Sadie took her hand, and Ruby stared at her, the eyes staring back more knowing than they should be.

"Come with me." It was the child's voice, but Susan who said it.

They walked towards the bridge and stood beneath it. Ruby could hardly believe it. Sadie *was* Susan, or, at least, a channel for her. She had come back to give her answers, to reveal the name of the man who'd killed her – the man who'd left her grounded, cold and alone, to be taunted so mercilessly. Ruby would avenge her; she could be sure of that. She felt almost breathless at the prospect.

Susan, give me his name and I'll find him. I'll expose him, I promise. Even if he isn't alive, I'll do it. I'll destroy his reputation. I'll ruin him.

The little girl looked up. "Let it go," she said. "Let *me* go."

Ruby's mouth fell open. That was the last thing she'd expected to hear.

Let you go? What do you mean?

Sadie laughed. "I just felt a funny tickling inside my head," she declared.

Ruby flinched. The child seemed totally unaware of what was happening.

"Sadie," she asked, "do you know who Susan is?"

"Susan?" Sadie replied, her smooth features creasing.

She's not aware. It was Susan again, communicating in thought this time. *She has a rare talent, but one that's not realised, and probably never will be.*

Just as Ruby suspected. But was that such a shame? She couldn't decide. Instead she pleaded again. *Your murderer, tell me who he is.*

A rabbit darted out of the bushes and ran alongside the bridge.

"Oh, look!" Sadie said.

Whilst the child stared delightedly at it, Susan again took over.

It doesn't matter who he is. That life is over.

But if you help me, I can find him. His name, that's all I need.

Ruby... please. You have to let me rest.

The appeal in her voice, so plaintive, shocked Ruby, causing tears to prick at her eyes. Susan didn't want vengeance – only she did. Still. The bad wolf was rearing its head again... the all-too-human side of her soul. She was not only contrite, she was ashamed.

I'm sorry. I didn't mean to keep you from going fully into the light.

I know you didn't.

It was never my intention to ground you.

There was a brief silence before Susan spoke again.

Can we make a pact?

Of course we can, Susan. Anything you want.

Don't worry about me anymore. Promise?

Ruby had to swallow hard. Had to be sure she meant what she was going to say.

I promise.

And I won't worry about you.

Again, shame swamped her.

You're a good person, Ruby – the only one who cared.

The only one? So, she'd been right on that score.

Never forget how good you are and how bright you shine. Hold onto that.

Now, Ruby was taken aback. Of course she'd hold onto that. Why the warning?

Susan, wait...

"You're crying!"

It took a moment to realise it was Sadie who was speaking.

"Am I? Oh..." Ruby wiped at her eyes. "It's because of Susan," she explained.

"Is she your imaginary friend?" Sadie asked. "I know someone who has one of those. She calls her Darcy, talks to her all the time. I do too, sometimes, but only to please my friend. I think it's all a bit silly really."

Before Ruby could reply, the little girl let go of her hand and ran back to Cash, excited about showing him another magic trick. Susan was gone. Entirely.

Praying her eyes weren't red-rimmed, Ruby returned as well.

To Annie, she said, "We've had a chat, Sadie and I. Her obsession – it's over."

Annie was visibly relieved. "Oh, that's great. I'm not even going to ask you how you did it. I know you people have your ways. I don't think I'd understand, even if you did explain."

You people – Annie had said it and the mother of the Beachy Head suicide had said it. So many people said it. As though she were a breed apart. But did she realise her daughter was part of that breed also? Maybe even Annie herself. Psychic abilities were often inherited. Ruby consoled herself that deep down a part of them would know what they were capable of. And whether they chose to exploit or suppress their gift was up to them. It was none of her business.

With a start, she realised Annie was talking again. "I just want us to be us, you know?"

Yes, she did know.

After stringently refusing any offer of payment, Ruby and Cash bid Annie and Sadie goodbye.

"That little girl's good at magic tricks," Cash said, beside her. "She can teach me a thing or two, I'm telling you."

"Me too," Ruby all but whispered.

Cash turned to face her. "Everything okay?" he asked.

"Everything's okay," she replied.

But Cash looked far from convinced. "Honestly?"

Ruby smiled. "You know what, you worry too much."

"It's because I care," Cash protested.

She linked arms with him. "That's all right then. Go ahead and care. In fact, don't stop, ever."

Cash looked a bit bemused by her comment, but assured her he wasn't planning on stopping any time soon.

Slowly they walked back to her car. The rabbit from earlier appeared again and eyed them curiously, before darting back into the bushes.

Cash selected a CD for the journey home. One of his favourites – The Decemberists.

"I'm trying to steer Presley's band in this direction," he said, his hands banging at some imaginary drum kit once he had settled himself in the passenger seat. "They're brilliant, don't you think? That rock/folk thing, with a bit of prog thrown in – they've really nailed it."

Whilst he lost himself in rhythm, Ruby lost herself too – in thought.

There is more between heaven and earth than you can possibly know.

Her mother had said that once.

More good things, Ruby had insisted.

That was something else to hold onto in the weeks, months and years to come.

Whatever else there was, she'd try to leave well alone.

THE END

A note from the author

As much as I love writing, building a relationship with readers is even more exciting! I occasionally send newsletters with details on new releases, special offers and other bits of news relating to the Psychic Surveys series as well as all my other books. If you'd like to subscribe, sign up here!

www.shanistruthers.com

Printed in Great Britain
by Amazon